Unicorn For Sale

Cheryl Terra

Bang It Out Writing

Content Warnings

Please note this book is written in Canadian English, which has aspects of spelling from both American and UK English.
This is book 2 of a 3 book series. For the best reading experience, begin with The Unicorn Confessions.
I have tried to address potential triggers here without spoiling the story, however if you have concerns about any of the items listed and wish to know more, please reach out to me via email at info@cherylterra.com
This book ends on a slight cliffhanger. Book 3 in the series will be released September 6, 2023.

This book is intended for mature adults. There are multiple explicit scenes and profanity. This book is categorized as "why choose" and discusses non-traditional relationship structures, including discussions of "unicorn hunting," polyamory, ethical non-monogamy, unethical non-monogamy, and casual sex.

Themes + Plot Points: cheating (not by the main characters and not presented in a positive light), age gap relationships, toxic family situations, lying/deception, and divorces/breakups. Brief mentions of implied slut-shaming, queerphobia, and racial stereotyping also occur. Body image and fat positivity are main themes of this book. There are brief mentions of fatphobic situations or comments, but that is not a primary focus of the series and is not internalized by the main character.

SA + Consent: An in-depth discussion of a situation where dubious consent/revoking of consent during sex is not respected occurs. This is relived in detail but the situation does not occur "on page."

Mental Health: A supporting character discusses depression, mental illness treatments and stigmas, and alludes to prior and "off page" self harm behaviours.

Spice Variety: Characters in this book enjoy casual hook-ups, "breeding," using the endearment Daddy, and public hook-ups. Pairings include MFF, MF, and FF.

Other: There are moderate mentions of alcohol use, anxiety, pressure to have children, and misogynistic opinions.

Part 1

Confession: Friends come
first. If you're doing it right.

One

It was the first of May and while hell may not have frozen over, there was a significant chance of frost covering the brimstone mountains located a reasonable distance from the nearest lake of fire.

There may not have been any pigs flying across the sky, but somewhere, a large sow may have taken an abnormally long leap that left her hanging in the air over a puddle of slop longer than usual.

And the moon might not have quite been blue, but at a fleeting glance, there was probably a cerulean tint to that lifeless hunk of rock above us.

That was because, on that unreal Monday morning of the first of May, Dinah Sullivan—anxiety-ridden she-devil and overreacting nasty boss babe—had accomplished what I had deemed impossible.

I felt a little bad for her.

Just a little. A very small amount. The itsy bitsy teeny weeniest tiny bit sorry for her. Anyone would have broken down after that fateful staff meeting when Loni Less, certified rich bitch and airhead extraordinaire, had decided she wanted to add a team of artists to handcraft designer lingerie live at the Recycl-Ball using upcycled and reclaimed materials. I couldn't blame Dinah for having her third mental breakdown of the week, even though it was only Monday morning. Having to arrange something like that just four days before our biggest fundraising event of the year was going to take a miracle.

So yes, I had the most miniscule iota of sympathy for Dinah when Loni finally left and she started hyperventilating.

But that didn't change the fact that Dinah was an asshole.

Because sure, *technically* it was my fault that we had no designers available to handcraft said garbage lingerie. But I didn't think it was fair to blame me for firing all the artists we'd hired back when we'd abandoned the original masquerade theme.

"I was trying to save us money!" I said as Dinah made a noise only the neighbourhood dogs could hear. "We hired them to make the upcycled masks for the guests. Why would we have kept them when we changed the theme to something that didn't involve masks?"

"We could have used them to create this trashy fucking lingerie!" she shrieked back.

"How was I supposed to know Loni would decide she'd want us to make sexy lingerie out of literal garbage?" I asked.

"Will you ever stop making my life difficult?"

I shrugged. "Probably not."

Dinah opened her mouth, but instead of saying anything, she slouched forward so quickly that Chuck almost lurched across the room to keep her from faceplanting on the board room table. He didn't have to, though; Dinah slammed her forearms on her knees and put her head of white-blonde hair between her hands.

"Time for a Code Oh Shit?" I asked Chuck.

He sighed. "We don't have time for a Code Oh Shit. How about a code Get Back To Our Office And Get Started On Hiring New Artists For Thursday?"

And if Chuck was telling me to get some work done instead of handling it all himself while I went to Starbucks until it was safe for me to return to the office, well.

That's how I knew shit was serious.

Leaving him in the room with the flushed, watery-eyed mess that was the director of Vancouver's second-best recycling-through-the-power-of-art charity, I made my way back to the office Chuck and I shared.

"Did you get fired this time?" asked Jia, who, despite being nineteen, had been working for CARE longer than I had after joining as a student-intern-slash-receptionist when she was in high school.

"Nope," I said as I walked through the lobby. "Still gainfully employed."

"Darn. I'm going to have to start a new betting pool with Austin. Can you try to get fired by the end of August? He said he'd take me out for dinner if Dinah finally snapped by then."

"Wouldn't it just be easier to tell him you like him?" I asked.

"Tessa!" she said, then let out one of those giggles only nineteen-year-old girls seem to be capable of as her cheeks turned pink. "I do not."

"Mm. Right. Well, I'll do my best to get canned so he's forced to take you on a date."

"It's not a date!" she said, but she was still giggling as I walked away.

By the time Chuck finished calming Dinah down in the boardroom and returned to our office, I'd managed to re-hire a handful of artists to attend the Recycl-Ball and do Loni's ridiculous commission, albeit at a much higher rate than they'd originally agreed to. Not that I was particularly efficient or anything. I mean, all I did was email the people I'd originally talked to asking if they were still available and offering more money than we'd originally offered.

It just took Chuck longer than usual to get Dinah's blood pressure within the normal range.

Which was fair. Working at CARE was never what anyone would have called smooth. Or efficient. Or beneficial to anyone except Loni and her rich-person pissing contest against Paige Martelle of the Martelle Makeup Group, which was the only reason CARE had been started in the first place. But planning this year's gala had gone beyond Loni's typical brand of quirky air headedness and into legitimately worrisome.

There was the theme, of course: a year of planning a masquerade-themed gala only for Loni to deem the new theme to be Trashy Love after somehow discovering and falling in love with a bin of discount Valentine's Day decorations. Which would have been fine on its own. Redo a colour scheme here, talk Loni out of hiring six different string quartets and keeping the original stand-up comedian we'd hired on the guise of laughter being the language of love there… it wasn't ideal to change a gala theme six weeks before the event. But it was doable.

And then Paige Martelle happened.

"Loni, we can't just fire the venue a month before the event," Dinah had said approximately one month earlier.

"I very much doubt they did it on purpose, Loni," Chuck had added. "It's not like they knew—"

"Everyone knows!" Loni had screeched. "Those twats *betrayed* me. Honestly, how could they do this to me? And who hosts a golf tournament at a country club?"

"Well, it *is* a golf club," I said.

"Shut up, Tessa," Dinah said through clenched teeth, but it didn't matter anyway because Loni hadn't heard me as she ranted around the boardroom, swinging her purse in arbitrary directions as Chuck, Dinah, and I all ducked to avoid getting smacked in the face.

"Years of loyalty," Loni was lamenting. "Years, and they let Paige Fucking Martelle waltz in there with her—" She pitched her voice up into a nasally mockery. "—'*charity golf tournament for the benefit of young inner city artists*' like those years meant nothing. Nothing!"

"It doesn't mean we can't have the gala there," Chuck said. "Lots of venues host different groups for—"

But Loni turned on a heel, pressing an offended hand to her chest as laser-beam levels of disgust emanated from her eyes.

"Ab-so-lute-ly. Not," she said, enunciating each syllable carefully. "Absolutely not. Paige is doing this on purpose and I will not let her win. She wants me to look like the fool who hosted my gala at the same venue a month later? Not a chance. I want that club *shut down*. I want it blacklisted. I will not have my charity associated with that traitorous company."

"But it's a month away and—"

"*FIGURE IT OUT!*" Loni shouted, then she picked up the horrendous blue faux-fur stole she'd thrown across the room in a fit of dramatic anger and stormed out.

After spending a good chunk of the morning trying to calm Dinah down, Chuck had gone into focus mode. By four o'clock, he had a list of alternative venues for us to check.

And by list, I mean there were two, and Dinah vetoed one of them immediately since it was a high school gymnasium.

Which left us to convince Loni that there was nothing that said "trashy romance" like an evening under the stars. Not the real stars, of course. The only thing that would have been more impossible than booking a gala venue a month before said gala would be planning an entire outdoor gala, what with having to rent everything from chairs to tents to God knows what else.

No, we had to convince Loni that some private local rundown planetarium was a great investment.

"There's so much trash in space," Chuck had said to her. "And also like... you know. Love? To the moon and back?"

And somehow that had worked, so despite now having to figure out a way to decorate an entire planetarium after the last children's program ended at five-thirty and the doors to the gala opening at six-thirty, we all breathed a sigh of relief.

Except then Loni had become insistent that absolutely nothing was to be the same as what Paige Martelle had done for the ArtCycle golf tournament.

Bartenders? No. We needed mixologists that served drinks based on the emotions someone was projecting. Not, you know, what they *wanted* to drink.

Invitations? Email was nowhere near good enough. No, now she wanted to send personalized handwritten notes on recycled paper to each and every guest, even though they'd already all bought their tickets.

And then there was today's meeting.

"Designer lingerie," Loni declared, pushing her signature black hair with its single platinum blonde streak off her face.

"W-What?" Dinah had asked, frantically taking notes.

"At the Recycl-Ball. They can use reclaimed materials to create the sexiest skivvies imaginable. Live, while the guests watch. It will be perfect. So few people will relate to the experience of performing that kind of labour. It will be sending a *message*."

Chuck and I had exchanged looks.

"I think, um, a few more people at the event than you realize will relate to... performing labour," Chuck said.

"It's a gala, Chuck. Like the working class is going to take a night off of... of... you know." Loni waved her hand with a pointless flourish. "And then once the designers are done creating their works, they get modelled."

"We can use the artists we hired to create the masks for this, but who's going to model them?" Dinah asked with an expression of horrified intrigue on her face.

"Whoever," Loni said. "Just make it happen!"

And that was when I had my fleeting moment of sympathy for Dinah. I mean, we were four days out from the event and I hadn't even told her I'd fired all those artists we'd hired to create the masks.

"Please tell me you've got at least one designer hired," Chuck said when he finally returned to our office to see me sitting with my feet up on my desk and my phone in my hand. There was a ragged look on his usually unbothered face as he closed the door behind him.

"Better." I took my feet down and spun my chair to face him. "I have three."

"Oh, thank God," he breathed, then slumped into his chair and put his head in his hands. "How illegal would it be for me to fake an anxiety disorder, go to the doctor, get a prescription for Valium, and start sneaking them into Dinah's morning coffee?"

"I'm pretty sure that's about eight different levels of illegal before you even consider the implications of literally drugging a woman," I said.

"But who would judge me?" he asked. "Really. Who would take one look at this situation and judge me, even for a second, for doing what needed to be done?"

"A judge, probably."

He let out a tired groan before sitting up and grabbing his mug, taking the final swig of his coffee that was ninety percent over-sweetened creamer with two extra sugars added. "At this point, I wouldn't even have to fake the anxiety disorder. If I make it to Thursday night without developing a stress-induced breakout, it will be a fucking miracle."

"I think you're more likely to develop a sugar-induced breakout."

He snorted. "Sugar is what gives me my youthful glow, Tessa Andrea Lane."

"And your myriad of intestinal issues."

"A healthy bowel is not an intestinal issue." He sighed and leaned back in his chair. "I'm going to leave early this afternoon so I can raid the recycle depot for supplies for the trashy lingerie."

"Can I pretend to help you so I can leave early?"

"Why do you need to leave early?" he asked, then held up a hand. "Let me guess. You have a date."

I glared at him. "It's not a date."

The stress on Chuck's face began to fade as an anticipatory smile spread across his lips. "So you *are* going to see Finn and Julie?"

"Well, no," I said. "Just Julie. She just messaged me to say she's got the day off because she had to deliver a baby while she was on call on Saturday. So if I finish work early, I can go hook up with her."

He blinked at me. "But... Finn?"

"He's working until six. He's on four ten-hour days again. Fridays off."

Three distinct lines wrinkled Chuck's forehead as he raised his eyebrows. "So the two of you would mess around without him?"

"Yeah. Wouldn't be the first time."

"He doesn't mind?"

I shook my head. "He wants us to be happy, and it's not like he doesn't know we're doing it. Julie texts him as soon as I get there. He's one of those weird people who thinks delaying gratification is enjoyable or something."

Chuck nodded slowly. "Do you ever get to be with him alone?"

I shrugged. "I'm sure if it came up, I would. But it hasn't yet."

I should have picked my words more carefully. Chuck pressed his lips together as if he was trying not to laugh.

"*Yet*, you say?"

"Don't. It's not serious."

He heaved a huge sigh, tilting his head back and looking up at the ceiling in exasperation. "Tessa Brianna Lane, you have got to be kidding me."

"It's *not*," I repeated. "I'm still messaging them on MatchMi."

Chuck groaned. "Still? Tessa, it's been ages. Get off the dating app and text each other like normal people."

"No," I said stubbornly. "It's casual. We don't need each other's phone numbers."

"You've been with them for a month."

"Yeah," I said. "A month of casual, mind-blowing sex and nothing else."

"Mm, right." Chuck folded his arms and crossed one leg over the other. "And you've slept over how many times, again?"

"Staying at their place after sex doesn't mean it's serious. It means I was fucked so hard that it would be irresponsible of me to try to walk down a flight of stairs to catch an Uber."

"Oh, right. How silly of me." He unfolded his arms and held up his hand, counting off his fingers. "First, it was 'one-and-done.' Then it was '*two*-and-done.' Then it was 'no more staying the night'... then—"

"Then nothing," I said. "It's not serious. I'm still refusing to meet their dog. Everyone knows it's not serious if you haven't met their dog."

"Tessa, the goalpost has moved so many times it might as well be on wheels."

"Goalpost? Did you learn a sports word from Charles?"

It almost made him laugh, but he managed to hold it back. "Not the point, Tessa Connor McDavid Lane. You know it's not a bad thing for you to admit you're into Finn and Julie, right?"

"I am into Finn and Julie," I said.

His eyes went wide. "Wait, what—"

"To be fair, most of the time I'm *in* Julie," I continued. "But Finn's getting really interested in exploring some buttstuff, so sooner or later I'm sure I'll be in there, too."

He twisted his mouth to the side in amused annoyance. "I expect details when you finally introduce him to the joys of buttstuff. But I still think you need to admit you actually like them as people."

"I do like them as people," I said. "As *friends*. We're three friends who just happen to have amazing sex once in a while and that's it."

"Oh, of course." He folded his arms again and tilted his head to the side. "So are they coming to the Recycl-Ball, then?"

I looked at him warily. "I just said it's not serious. Why would I invite them to attend a work event with me?"

He shrugged nonchalantly. "Well, all your other friends are going to be there. So why wouldn't you invite those friends, too? Unless you're not really *friends* and you secretly have feelings for them that would make you not want to invite them to the Recycl-Ball because it might *seem* too serious."

I rolled my eyes. "Not *all* of my other friends will be there."

"I mean, I'll be there. And then... well."

"Shut up," I scoffed. "I have friends other than you."

"Oh, did you invite Millie and Dottie?"

I glared at him. "Dogs aren't allowed and Dottie has bingo that night. And *no*. I invited some friends from university and a couple of artists I know. I do community outreach, Chuck. All the people attending are my friends."

You would've thought I'd fallen perfectly into his trap with the twisted, knowing smirk that crossed his face.

Which I kind of had, I guess.

"So you *are* saying you've invited all your friends," he said. "Except Finn and Julie."

"Shut up," I grumbled. "It's different. They have no connection to the art community. And anyway, what about you?"

"What about me what?" he asked.

"Are you inviting Charles?"

One of these days, I was going to buy Charles a drink. Well, not a drink. Charles didn't drink. But maybe a bouquet of flowers or something. Whatever I had to in order to thank him for becoming my new secret weapon. Because all I had to do was *allude* to the man and Chuck's brain switched into the half-exasperated, half-infatuated state that I liked to call The Charles Zone.

The Charles Zone started with a huff and a derisive sniff, sometimes accompanied by an eyeroll like the one Chuck gave just then.

"Are you kidding?" he scoffed. "He invited himself. I couldn't stop him from coming if I tried."

Then, as soon as he finished with whatever bitchy complaint he came up with, a small smile started to spread across his lips. It was never intentional, that smile. I doubted he even knew he was doing it. His lips would get a little thin as he pressed them together, the corners just barely turning up, but even from across the room, I could see the sparkle already beginning to flicker in his eyes.

"Did you try to stop him?" I asked.

"Of course not," Chuck said. "I couldn't crush his poor little heart like that. He's so excited to go to our first 'big public event.'" Another huff and eyeroll. "It's almost exhausting, honestly. He made me go shopping with him for ties. *Matching* ties."

"And you loved it," I said.

That kicked Chuck fully into The Charles Zone. The unintended smile became not-so-little and the sparkle in his eyes went from flickering to full-on glee.

"I did," Chuck said in a hushed voice. "I really, really did." Then, reigning it in a bit, he sat up straight. "And if you ever tell him that, I'll deny it. And you and I will never speak again."

"Don't threaten me with a good time," I said.

I turned to my desk, but Chuck pushed his chair across the office so it was right beside me.

"I'm serious, Tessa," he said. "He's already moving so fast that I can barely keep up. There is *no* telling how much faster he'd go if he found out I actually like him back as much as he wants me to."

I stared at him incredulously. "Oh, so it's okay for you to get on *my* case about things not being serious, but with Charles, it would be bad for things to move faster?"

"It would." A protective look settled onto Chuck's face. "I'm his first actual boyfriend. He's got no experience with this type of thing and after what happened with *Fletcher*—" He spat the name like it was a particularly bitter piece of licorice. "—I want to make sure his feelings are real and that he's feeling secure before we go further."

Asshole that I was, I hadn't thought of that, but it made sense.

Charles had told both me and Chuck about Fletcher, his former best friend and the whole reason he'd realized he was gay. It had started like a bad porno: two roommates, both single, both having dating trouble, who decided to make a "deal" to help each other "release some tension." It was just some utilitarian stroking at first, but then it morphed, and changed, until one day they kissed and Charles fell *hard*.

And, from the sounds of it, so had Fletcher. But when Charles wanted more—to go out together, to tell people, to hold hands and meet each other's parents and all that—Fletcher panicked and responded by outing Charles to everyone they knew.

I guess that meant I could count Charles as a friend now. Not just because he'd felt comfortable enough to tell me that, but because when he had, I'd wanted to track Fletcher down and lose my shit on him for what he did to Charles.

I mean, I firmly believed that outing someone was one of the worst things you could do to a person. It was a betrayal in one of the worst ways, stealing their security and putting them in awkward situations at best and dangerous ones at worst. It changed their lives without their consent and tore away the opportunity to choose how they shared that vital bit of themselves with the world.

Not to mention that hurting Charles was like kicking a baby duck or something.

"That makes sense," I admitted to Chuck. "But... did you just say..."

"What?" he asked.

I raised my eyebrows at him. "Did you just say you're his boyfriend?"

Chuck opened his mouth, a stunned expression crossing his face as he realized he'd let that word slip out without even noticing.

"I did," he finally said. "I... am."

"That's so sweet," I said. "It's disgusting."

Chuck snorted with laughter. "I know, right? But I want this to be right. I don't want him to fall for me so fast that he crashes. I want... I want him to float down gently so I can catch him in my arms and he can see it's real."

I stared at him. "That was fucking poetic."

"Yeah." He shrugged, then pushed his chair back to his side of the office. "I've been thinking of writing some poetry again."

"You write poetry?!"

"I used to." He looked at his laptop. "My mom thought it was weird and eventually I just kind of stopped writing."

"And now Charles is making you want to write poems again."

"Tessa," he said in a warning tone.

"Just because you *like* him so much," I teased.

Chuck huffed. "Yes. He does, okay? And maybe if you'd just admit you have fucking feelings for Finn and Julie, you'd be able to—I mean, you'd want to write poetry, too."

His words caught, just enough that I knew "write poetry" was what he'd said instead of "be able to paint something other than mountain landscapes that compliment the colour of the curtains in some rich person's house, like the painting for the Clarkdales Kira commissioned from you and that almost caused your eyes to bleed with how boring and generic it was."

And yeah, that stung, even though he hadn't actually said it. But in fairness, I kind of deserved it. I *was* being a bit of an asshole. So I shoved that sharp little stab of pain in my chest down and shrugged.

"Maybe you're right," I said.

"Really?" Chuck replied.

"Mm-hmm. But there'd have to be feelings there for me to admit to in the first place."

Chuck studied me for a moment, then shook his head and turned back to his laptop.

"Come on. Let's get to work so we can leave early."

Two

Despite my eagerness to get to Finn and Julie's so Julie could have her regular session of pussy-eating practice, I didn't end up being able to leave work early. After the third or fourth Loni-induced emergency, I messaged Julie on MatchMi to let her know I couldn't sneak out.

TessTheUnicorn

Loni wants to give away garbage. Literal garbage. As swag bags.

Finn&Julie

And her oh-so-logical reason for that is…?

TessTheUnicorn

To quote, "Swag bags are full of garbage no one wants anyway, so why not use it to make a STATEMENT?" So now Chuck is going to the boardroom to try convincing her that the companies who donated the items for the actual swag bags may not appreciate having their products compared to… you know. LITERAL garbage.

Finn&Julie

> Fingers crossed it works. You'll still come over to see me after?

> Yes please. I'm going to need a beer and like, three orgasms to get over this day.

> I'll put a couple of bottles in the fridge for you and start doing some tongue exercises.

"Tessa, I swear, do you do *anything* around here besides smirk at your phone all day?" Dinah snapped, startling me as she poked her head into the office.

"I'm working," I said. "I'm coming up with new ways to—"

"Ugh," she interrupted, turning on her heel. "I don't even care. Just do some actual work for once and don't cause any more problems."

"You're gonna have to pick one or the other," I called after her, smirking at the aggravated growling sound she made before taking pity and actually getting back to work.

Not because she told me to. But because Chuck had to spend a good chunk of the afternoon convincing Loni that giving bags of garbage to gala attendees was a bad idea without actually telling her it was a bad idea. That meant he wasn't going to be able to finish the last-minute paperwork he was supposed to do for the venue *and* dumpster dive for lingerie supplies.

So I did the paperwork for him. Because I wasn't about to make like a raccoon and fall into a garbage bin as I searched for whatever random things I could find that might make a decently sexy babydoll chemise.

Or whatever it is raccoons do in their spare time.

But of course, after Chuck left, Loni had yet another brilliant idea. I tried to help Dinah talk her out of calling the charity beneficiaries that

would be attending the gala "Loni's Lovers," but I wasn't Chuck. Also, it was kind of hilarious, especially when she insisted she wanted them to wear sashes emblazoned with the term in big red letters.

"I don't even know if we can get sashes made in less than three days," Dinah protested.

"Dinah, darling, all I'm hearing is 'blahblahblah *excuses*.'" Loni flapped her hand in the air as if it was talking. "And now all you're going to hear is 'blahblahblah *just get it done!*'"

"But—"

"What part of *'blahblahblah get it done'* are you not understanding?"

"I'll go see if I can find someone who can make custom sashes before Thursday," I said helpfully.

"Thank you, Tessa," Loni said. "See, Dinah? Look at what can be done when you don't waste so much time making excuses."

And while I didn't *think* Dinah could set people on fire with her mind, I wasn't entirely sure that I imagined the smell of burning just then.

Armed with Loni's credit card and the insatiable desire to see people walking around unironically labelled as Loni's Lovers, I found a company that could make a bunch of satin sashes with sparkly sequin trim and embroidered text by Thursday at noon. Rush fee aside, they were surprisingly inexpensive.

It was past my usual quitting time when the proof for the sashes was finally sent back. Dinah noticed but promptly ignored my obvious dedication to CARE, so I loudly told Jia that I'd approved the final design and finished up a few more of Chuck's other tasks before heading out nearly half an hour later than usual. By the time my Uber dropped me off at Finn and Julie's building, it was just after five-thirty.

Which was fine. Finn would be off work soon, too, so it all worked out.

"You made it!" Julie said from the living room as I let myself into their apartment after she buzzed me in.

"I did," I replied. "I couldn't sneak out early."

"It's okay. You're here now."

She didn't get up to greet me as I kicked off my shoes, which was unusual for Julie. Frowning slightly, I put my purse down, then wandered into the living room and had to immediately bite back a smile.

Finn and Julie had a huge couch, probably because Finn was a huge guy. It was deeper than most, with a chaise on one side and a number of large, cushy pillows on it. Julie was lying on her side, looking like an adorably fuckable burrito wrapped in a large grey plaid blanket. It was bunched up where she clasped it under her chin and I could see the enticing outline of her curves beneath the plush fabric. Her blondish-brown hair was piled on top of her head in a loose, messy ponytail, strands of hair framing the side of her face that wasn't pressed into a pillow. She had no makeup on, but her cheeks had a healthy pink glow on her warm white skin.

"Hey," she said, not looking up at me. "This episode is just about done. Help yourself to one of those beers you wanted."

"One for you, too?" I asked as I walked into the kitchen.

"Yes, please."

"Sorry I'm late." I opened the fridge to grab a beer for each of us. "Hope it wasn't an issue."

"Nope," came the response. "All I had to do today was go get Alfie."

"From where?"

"Finn dropped him off at doggie daycare this morning so I could chill today. I had to go get him before it closed, but I brought him straight over to the neighbour's so we could hang out."

See? Not serious. I wasn't meeting their dog. And even in Julie's words, we were just hanging out.

"So you had a day completely to yourself. Sounds like a dream."

"Mm-hmm. I love that dog, but it's nice to have a break. He's so needy sometimes."

"Dogs generally are." I twisted the caps off two of the beer bottles and took a sip from one before closing the fridge. "You're more of a cat person?"

"Yeah," Julie said. "Cats are the best."

"Agree to disagree," I said, walking back into the living room.

She finally glanced over at me, the corners of her eyes crinkling. "I thought you loved pussy."

I laughed. "Pussy, yes. Felines, no. They make me sneeze." I took another sip of beer before setting both on the coffee table. "Is there room for me on the couch?"

"Uh-huh." She wriggled forward as I returned to the room, creating a space between her body and the back of the couch that I would be able to just slide into, so long as I didn't mind having her entire body pressed against mine.

Which I did not.

"Aren't you cold?" she asked once I'd awkwardly crawled over her and nestled into the gap she'd left with a hand resting on her hip overtop of the blanket.

"Uh... not really," I said.

"Oh," she said, her voice almost sweetly sad. "I was going to share my blanket."

"Oh, well in that case..." I inched my fingers towards the edge of the blanket. "Did I mention I'm freezing?"

She laughed and I leaned forward a little, pressing a kiss to the back of her neck.

It took me a regretful amount of time to realize that the only thing Julie was wearing was that grey plaid blanket. I mean, I figured it out the moment I slipped my hand beneath the fabric, but every second I didn't have access to Julie's naked body was a tragedy. I made a noise of appreciation as my fingertips grazed across bare skin, which drew another giggle from Julie, although this one was far more mischievous.

"Surprise," she said.

I chuckled, running my palm down her bicep, then letting it jump to her ribcage and caressing the dip of her waist as I pressed my lips to her shoulder.

"It's almost six," I said. "You didn't want to wait for Finn?"

"He'll still be a bit. But he's okay with joining later."

I half-shrugged, then nibbled on the spot between her shoulder and neck. "If you say so."

Taking that as me agreeing, Julie started to twist, but I threw a leg over hers and tightened my grip on her. "No. Stay like this."

"But you—"

"*Stay*, Julie." I nipped at that tender spot on her neck again. "You said you wanted to watch the rest of your episode."

"Yeah, but—*oh*."

Her final word came out in a soft puff of breath as I moved my hand up to her breast, pinching her nipple as I nuzzled against her shoulder.

"Don't move," I said.

Her throat flexed as she swallowed. "Okay."

And she didn't.

Mostly.

I mean, she squirmed a bit as I felt her up, cupping and caressing a heavy breast in one hand as I rested the other against her shoulder. I kept kissing her, kept tasting the faint saltiness of her skin and finding all those delicate little spots on her neck and shoulder and collarbone that made her quiver in my arms. Her ribs rose and fell, nudging my arm up and down with her breath.

"You taste so good," I murmured, licking a spot on her shoulder and making her giggle.

"If you think that's good, you should taste my pussy."

That wasn't a bad idea. I slid my hand down her belly, skimming my fingertips along the softness there before walking them down to her mound.

"Are you wet for me already?" I whispered in her ear.

"I think you know the answer to that," she replied. "I think you're hoping I've been wet and waiting for you since you said you were going to come over tonight."

Those words sent a shock of something through me.

Something good.

Something warm.

Something I didn't even know I'd been craving until she said it.

I slipped my fingers between her thighs. She moaned softly as I dragged my middle finger along her slit, which was just as wet as I'd hoped, and again when I pushed it between her folds and played with the dripping entrance to her pussy.

"You're soaked," I said. "You *have* been waiting for this."

"Mm-hmm," she said, her voice high-pitched.

I made lazy circles around her entrance with the tip of my finger, collecting as much of her wetness as I could. Once I was satisfied that my fingers were coated, I pulled my hand away. Ignoring her whimper, I brought my hand back up, carefully avoiding dragging it along her skin so that when it reached my mouth, I could suck the taste of her off my fingers.

"What does it say about me that I think it's so hot when you do that?" she asked, trying to turn her head to watch.

"I think it says you know just how delicious your pussy is." I finished licking my fingers, then moved my hand back down. "Now, quiet. Watch your show like you wanted."

"But—"

I sank my teeth into her shoulder. "Watch it, Jules. I'll amuse myself in the meantime."

If she caught a single second of what she was watching, I would have been surprised. Especially considering that I saw the credits roll before the next episode started up and Julie didn't even seem to notice. Her breathing was coming in quick gasps as I caressed and stroked every inch of her, occasionally pushing my fingers inside her slick pussy and painting her clit and her skin and her nipples with her own wetness. She shifted in my arms, rubbing her gorgeous ass against my thighs and stomach, and I knew my pussy was just as wet and needy as hers was.

But it could wait until I was done playing with Julie.

When her squirming got to be too much, I moved my other arm over her shoulder, grabbing one of her tits and pinning her back against me before pushing my hand between her legs. It was a move Finn used on both of us often, though he usually did it when he was fucking one of us from behind, yanking her body back so he could shove that big cock of his inside as hard as he could. I was nowhere near as strong as Finn, so I couldn't hold her in place quite the same way, but that was okay. Julie seemed content not to move a single muscle.

Probably because I shoved my hand back between her legs and started stroking her swollen clit with firm, steady fingers.

"Don't stop," she gasped.

I pinched her nipple. "You're not the boss of me. Watch your show."

She made a strangled noise, but didn't say anything as I played with her pussy and rolled her pebbled nipple between my fingertips.

And she didn't need to say anything when I held her against me tighter so I could push my middle finger inside of her while using the base of my thumb against her clit.

She didn't need to say anything for me to know when she was about to come. I knew what she sounded like in those moments just prior to shattering. How her pussy felt when it started to contract, the way her head would tilt back and her whimpers would turn to wails. She didn't need to say anything as I held her in my arms and fingered her pussy until she exploded all over me.

She didn't need to say a single fucking word, but she did.

"Tessa," she gasped, and a hand clamped down on my wrist. "T... Tessa... *Tessa*."

And oh my God, I loved how she moaned my name.

I held her as she came, smiling into her shoulder as she shook in my arms, struggling to writhe against me. And when she finished, when every one of her tensed muscles relaxed and she slumped back against me, I pressed a gentle kiss on her shoulder again.

"So what was this episode about? I missed some of it," I said.

She let out a tired laugh. "I don't even know what show I put on."

Three

It was almost crazy how good Julie had gotten at eating pussy.

I mean, it was only a month earlier that she'd done it for the first time. Now, it was like she couldn't live without it. I doubted there was a single time we'd hooked up when she hadn't eaten me out in some capacity and if Finn was taking his turn, she'd do everything she could to join him so they could spoil me with their tongues together.

Part of me was starting to think she was doing it for her pleasure more than mine. Not that I didn't get any pleasure out of it—Julie made it her personal mission to make me come on her face every single time she was down there—but I'd never seen someone so enthralled by the act itself. She luxuriated in my body, touching and kissing and caressing me like it was a relief to finally give in. When she was licking me, she lapped and lingered, diving in and savouring each moment like she was indulging in the freshest, sweetest piece of fruit she'd ever tasted.

After I'd made her come in my arms, she got up and, still blissfully naked, pulled me off the couch. Once she'd stripped my jeans off, she urged me to sit down again.

"You don't want my shirt off?" I asked, amused as she dropped to her knees in front of me.

"You said you needed a beer and at least three orgasms." She twisted, reaching for the bottle of beer I'd left on the coffee table and passing it to me. "So as much as I'd love for you to be completely naked every time I see you, I have a job to focus on."

Then she put a hand on each of my knees, wrenched my legs open, and buried her face between my thighs.

And let me say, getting my pussy eaten out while I relaxed against a plush, cozy couch with a beer in one hand and some random show on in the background was just... just fucking phenomenal.

I would have never guessed how enjoyable it was to just sit there, to just watch as Julie sucked on my clit and slipped her fingers inside me. To glance up and see—oh, a cooking show, apparently, except the chef was standing in a children's ball pit for some reason as a maniacal looking host watched in the background—then look down and see Julie's tits jiggle as she licked my entire slit from bottom to top with a flat, wide tongue.

Most of the time while I was getting eaten out, there was something else going on. A cock in my throat or a pussy suffocating me as its owner rode my tongue. Even when it was just me and Julie, I was focused on her, pulling her hair or licking her pussy back after she discovered she had a particular penchant for sixty-nining. So this... this moment of sitting back, of just existing and not *doing*...

It was amazing.

Especially when she made me come, then brought her hands up to my hips and pushed me back as I moved to stand.

"Is your beer done?" she asked thickly, looking up at me with hooded eyes.

"Huh?" I asked.

"If your beer isn't done, then neither am I," she said, and dove right back in.

That was the position we were in when Finn got home not too long after she went in for that second round: Julie naked and on her knees, her hands on my thighs and her face buried in my pussy. Then me, sitting on their couch, half-dressed, head tilted back with a hand resting on her head and my eyes closed in tranquil ecstasy until I heard the door open.

"Hey babe!" called a familiarly cheerful voice.

There was a pause, but before Julie could respond, he spoke again. "Wait... where's Alfie? Babe, did you get Alfie from daycare?"

Julie sighed as she pulled away, running the back of her hand across her mouth. "Yes, I got him. Just come here."

There was the sound of someone kicking their shoes off and a voice doing its best to mask the panic in it, which made me frown in concern.

"But he didn't come to the door," he said. "The daycare's closed now, but if I rush I can probably—"

"Finn!" Julie said, exasperated. "Just come over here."

She'd barely finished speaking when Finn entered the room looking every bit as delicious as he always did. More delicious, even. I don't know what it was about that fucking courier uniform, but *damn* did he wear it well, and even better when it was a little mussed up like it was just then. The top button of his greyish blue polo shirt was undone, but it was still tucked into the dark blue shorts that showed off his toned legs. And for some reason, the fact that he'd taken his shoes off and was padding around in just his tube socks was equal parts hilarious and attractive. His blonde hair was tousled, flattened slightly where it had been under his baseball cap all day.

What was missing, though, and quite conspicuously, was Finn's usual bright, panty-dropping smile.

Instead, there was an expression on his face I hadn't seen before. His eyebrows were furrowed and those big, blue puppy-dog eyes of his were full of unmistakable worry as they met mine. My heart didn't quite jump into my throat, but it jolted a bit, guilt mixing with confusion mixing with realization.

Finn hadn't known I was there.

Before I could panic, the worry faded off his face and was replaced by a look of absolute delight that was so warm and genuine it was like being wrapped in the telepathic version of one of Finn's all-encompassing hugs.

"Surprise," Julie said. "I brought Alfie downstairs to Ionna's."

"Tessa!" Finn exclaimed. "Hey!"

"Hi," I said. "Um... sorry. I didn't know you... didn't know."

"Oh, that's okay," he said.

I raised my eyebrows. "You're sure?"

His trademark grin spread across his face. "Well, yeah. Otherwise you wouldn't have been surprised."

I had to laugh. "That's not what I meant, but... okay. As long as you're okay with this."

The tip of his tongue poked out, wetting his lips as his eyes flicked to Julie and then back to me.

"Are you kidding?" he asked, his voice lowering to something husky and hoarse. "I walked in to see one of the hottest woman on the planet kneeling naked on the floor eating out the other hottest woman on the planet. Yeah, Tess. That's—" He inhaled sharply, his chest rising and falling as he shook his head with his eyes trained to the two of us. "That's so okay."

Well, that was about as best as I could hope for. Julie looked up at me, her eyes round and her forehead creased with concern. There were so many thoughts flying through my head—the need to better communicate, the scenario I'd never shared with them where I'd walked into something like this in a totally different way, the fact that assuming it was okay for us to hook up without Finn knowing wasn't okay because respect of their relationship aside, that had *implications*—but I was sure she had been trying to do something sweet.

I was sure she hadn't meant anything by it.

Finn was okay. She was okay. I was okay. So I reached down, brushed a loose piece of hair off her face, then lifted my beer bottle and tilted it playfully.

"I'm not done yet," I said, and the concern on her face broke into a wide grin.

"Well then, where were we?" she asked.

I think it was a rhetorical question. She didn't wait for an answer before putting her hands on my thighs and burying her tongue between my pussy lips again. I took a breath and let it out before looking at Finn and beckoning him forward.

"How was your day?"

"Better now," he said, leaning in and pressing a warm kiss to my mouth. "Yours?"

"Best Monday of my life. I can't remember a single thing that happened before I walked into this apartment."

Between my legs, I felt Julie chuckle, the sensation matching Finn's quiet laugh.

"Me neither," he said. "Is there room for me over here?"

"There is," I said. "But unfortunately there isn't room for your clothes, so you'll have to strip for me first."

He grinned and brought his hands to his belt buckle. "Yes, ma'am."

Watching Finn undress was a guilty pleasure of mine. Seeing anyone get naked was thrilling, but the way Finn moved, looking at each inch of skin as he revealed it while simultaneously *knowing* that he didn't realize how fucking erotic he was... I didn't think I'd ever get tired of that. And watching it happen while Julie put her eager and talented tongue to good use on my clit...

I couldn't think of a better sensation.

By the time Finn was naked, his cock was so hard that it jutted straight out from the light curls of hair around the base. I stared at it unabashedly, sipping my beer and basking in the sight of his body and the memory of how good every part of him felt.

Once his clothes were discarded on the floor, he stepped forward again.

"How's it going?" he asked casually.

"Let's see. I'm drinking beer and getting eaten out at the same time." I paused to take a sip. "I'm in fucking heaven."

"I've never tried drinking during sex." He moved onto the couch, kneeling beside me so he didn't accidentally kick Julie as he leaned in to kiss me. "It sounds relaxing."

I kissed him back, slipping my tongue into his mouth so he could taste the lingering hint of beer. "You should try it."

"Mmm. I couldn't take your beer," he said, bringing a hand to my cheek and cupping it. "Besides, when you're with us, I want to make *you* feel good."

"I always feel good when I'm with you."

The words slipped out without my permission. I don't know if they shocked Finn or Julie as much as they shocked me. If they did, neither of them reacted, and I forced a laugh against Finn's lips.

"I mean, you both make me come almost constantly, so of course I do," I added, then nipped at Finn's lip. "And there's another open beer on the table that Julie's been ignoring."

He glanced at the table, the corners of his lips turning down with an amused frown of consideration. "Well, maybe..."

"Finn," I said in the authoritative tone that I knew he liked. "Pick up that beer and let Julie suck your cock."

He groaned. "Yes, ma'am."

While he grabbed the beer off the coffee table, I leaned down, brushing Julie's hair off her forehead.

"Is that okay?" I asked her.

She lingered a bit, sucking on my clit before reluctantly pulling away.

"I guess," she said, her voice teasingly sad. "If you don't want me to eat you out anymore."

"Don't put those fucking words in my mouth," I said with a laugh. "I'm feeling generous and want Finn to see how great it is to have a beer and get oral after a long day at work."

She traced a random pattern on my inner thigh with the tip of her finger. "Do you think he'd like it more if we both sucked his cock?"

"I have no idea," I said. "I guess we could test that hypothesis if Finn feels like being our guinea pig."

"I've always wanted to be a guinea pig," Finn said.

"Have you? I thought you wanted to be an otter."

He shrugged. "Whatever animal I have to be to get you to do this experiment of yours, that's the animal I want to be."

I'm sure there was some sort of scientific protocol we were supposed to do that we didn't, like comparing a two-person blowjob to a regular one-person blowjob. Or not switching partway through said blowjob when Julie decided she wanted to stop sucking on Finn's balls and start sucking on my tits. Or Julie not making me come with her fingers while Finn's cock was still in my mouth. Or Finn not actually coming from the blowjob and us stopping because he wanted to fuck someone.

But whatever. I was an artist-slash-community-outreach-assistant. Not a scientist.

Either way, we agreed the experiment was a resounding success. The impromptu after-work threesome finished with me kneeling on the floor, Finn fucking me from behind while Julie lounged on the chaise section of the couch, taking her turn to experience drinking a beer while getting her pussy eaten. The last of the three orgasms I'd told Julie I needed happened while she had my face pinned against her pussy, grinding against me as an orgasm ripped through me and her at the same time. Finn wasn't far behind, gasping and hunching over my body so he could grip one of my breasts as he finished.

"Are you hungry?" Finn asked after we'd flopped onto the couch, tangled together and catching our breaths while the cooking show Julie had put on played in the background.

"I am," Julie said.

That was my cue, so I sat up. "I can get out of your hair."

"Or you could stay for dinner," Julie said.

"I… I probably shouldn't," I replied.

"You can, though. Finn was going to make something. And he's a really good cook."

"Yeah!" Finn said enthusiastically. "Do you like pasta?"

"I mean, I'm not a monster."

He grinned, the corners of his eyes crinkling. "Okay, so tonight I was gonna do skillet gnocchi stuffed with cheese and BBB mushrooms."

"What's a BBB mushroom?"

"A thing I invented," he said. "Brown butter button mushrooms. They're little and bite sized so I just leave them whole and then I fry them so they get all crispy on the outside, and there's this kind of like nutty-sweet flavour from the butter. Oh, and I put some spinach in with it too."

"As good as that sounds, I—" I started, then my stomach finished the sentence by betraying me and growling louder than I'd ever heard it growl before.

Finn grinned, tilting his head as he looked at me with a knowing expression as Julie giggled. "So that's a yes?"

I should have said no. I *knew* I should have said no.

But I said yes.

Four

"Which bread do you think you could throw the farthest?"

I looked up from my plate of gnocchi at Finn, who was contemplating a perfectly fried mushroom on his fork. We were all sitting on the couch, Julie and I both still naked, though Finn had pulled on a pair of boxers and an apron while he was cooking. He'd shed the apron when he brought three plates of mouth-watering gnocchi to the couch where Julie and I were cuddling lazily, though he'd kept his boxers on.

"Which *bread*?" Julie repeated, sounding exasperated.

"Yeah." He popped the mushroom in his mouth. "Like if there was a bread-throwing contest and you got to pick the bread you threw, which would you pick?"

"Hmm." I chewed on a piece of gnocchi thoughtfully. "Probably a baguette."

"Yeah?"

"Like one of those really hard, skinny ones they sell at the grocery store and always seem a little stale. You could probably throw it like a javelin."

"Oh, good call," Finn said, eating another mushroom. "I was thinking a pita. Or maybe naan. 'Cause you could, like, Frisbee it."

I tilted my head thoughtfully as I speared another piece of gnocchi. "That could work. But would they be too light?"

"Depends on how you throw it. I mean, Frisbees are pretty light. They're plastic."

"Good point." I put the fork in my mouth and looked at Julie. "What about you?"

"Um..." she said. "I guess, like... a bun?"

"Like a hamburger bun?" Finn asked, frowning.

"No, like a... a round one." She sighed. "Like similar to a ball. I used to play softball so I feel like I could throw that pretty far."

We all nodded, then ate silently for a few moments.

"Okay," Finn said. "A hippo is chasing you. What do you do?"

Julie sighed. "Finn—"

"Climb a tree," I said. "Hippos can't climb, right?"

"I don't think so," Finn said. "But I mean, hippos are terrifying, so who knows."

"Hippos are not terrifying," Julie said.

"They are!" Finn insisted, his eyes wide and earnest. "Like, hippos kill so many people every year, and they don't even eat them. They're vegetarians. They just kill because they're *mean*."

"Yeah, but on what planet would answering this question be useful?" she asked.

Finn's lips parted, but he looked to the side. I could almost see the gears turning in his head as he processed Julie's question.

"Well," I said. "I think it's prudent to have an emergency hippo plan. Or a... a hippo emergency plan. You just never know."

The deer-in-headlights look on Finn's face faded as he smiled. "Exactly. And like, it's just fun to think about. *And* you never know when you might end up with a house hippo infestation."

Julie looked at him incredulously. "A house hippo?"

"Yeah. They might be tiny, but they can seriously mess things up. Didn't you ever see the commercial?"

"They aren't real, Finn. The commercial was to teach you not to believe everything you see on TV," Julie said, her voice flat.

"Oh." A frown clouded Finn's face. "That's too bad. I always thought Alfie might like a house hippo buddy."

"You could get a skinny pig," I suggested, trying to lighten the oddly tense mood.

Finn blinked. "I think a regular sized pig would be more like a hippo than a skinny one."

I laughed and shook my head. "No, a 'skinny pig.' It's a guinea pig, but it's hairless. They kind of look like hippos when they have no fur."

"Oh," Finn said.

It was quiet for a few moments again, forks scraping against our plates as we ate.

"Okay," he said. "If a skinny pig—not a naked guinea pig, a pig that's skinny—was chasing you, what would you do?"

The very serious discussion between me and Finn of what constituted a "skinny" pig and eventual reasoning that a skinny pig would be more dangerous than a hippo due to the pig being extra hungry and *not* a vegetarian took us through the rest of dinner. When we finished, there was that awkward moment of trying to follow social etiquette where I offered to take their dishes, but Finn waved it off with a smile and took the plates.

While he returned, I'd already ordered an Uber and was pulling my jeans on as Julie pulled up a pair of sweatpants.

"Heading out?" Finn asked.

"Yeah," I said. "I have to work tomorrow and I should walk Millie tonight. Dottie's knee has been acting up again."

"Will I get to see you again soon?" Julie asked, her voice almost sad.

And I just should've said something like "Yeah, for sure, maybe this weekend?" and then "Wait, no, not this weekend, I have this event to go to where I'm going to be pretending to be my brother's best friend's girlfriend because of this whole thing where I need him to keep a massive secret from my family for me. You know how it is. Sometime next week?"

But the slight gloom in her voice, the feeling that she didn't *want* me to leave...

Fuck.

"Well, I was actually wondering if you wanted to, uh... come to this work thing I have," I said, not looking at either of them as I buttoned my jeans. "It's the gala I've been telling you about. On Thursday night. And we could hang out after, maybe."

"A work thing?" Julie asked.

I swallowed back the nerves in my throat, trying to sound casual. "Yeah. It's called the Recycl-Ball."

"It sounds fun," Finn said.

"Oh, it's a total shit show," I said. "I mean, it's a real dumpster fire. But it's an entertaining dumpster fire. The theme is Trashy Love and we're having it at a planetarium because rich people have mortal enemies that they battle by way of ostentatious charity events, apparently."

"And you want us to go to a gala... with you?" Julie said.

"I mean, yeah," I said. "A bunch of my friends are coming."

I finally finished fiddling with my jeans and risked a glance up. Finn looked thrilled and Julie was nodding, even though I hadn't really said anything for her to agree to.

"Do we get to dress up and stuff?" Finn asked. "Like in a suit?"

"Yeah, it's semi-formal," I said.

"Hell yeah!" He looked at Julie and grinned. "What do you think, babe? Get dressed up, watch a dumpster fire, and support our friend and also, uh... a charity?"

Julie smiled, though it was a little off. "Yes, yeah. Of course. We can... we can totally make it. Where do I get tickets?"

"I'll put a couple aside for you at the door," I said, but something worried was prickling under my skin.

I didn't bring it up then. I didn't say a word as Finn asked Julie if she'd go get Alfie from the downstairs neighbour's so he didn't have to put his pants back on. And I smiled and kissed him back when he kissed me goodbye.

It wasn't until Julie and I had left the apartment and were almost at the front door that I stopped her.

"Are you okay?" I asked.

She smiled, though she wasn't quite looking me in the eyes. "I mean, I just had the hottest girl in the world come over, make me come a bunch of times, then got to eat some delicious gnocchi with her and my boyfriend before getting invited to a cool gala. Of course I'm okay. Are you okay?"

"Do you remember the zombie rule?"

She blinked at me. "Um... yes?"

"The one where if anyone started developing feelings, they had to tell everyone else right away?" I continued. "Same as how if you ever get bit by a zombie, you have to tell everyone in your party about it so they can escape before you turn?"

There was a slight hitch in her chest as she took a breath. "Yeah. Yes, I remember."

"So... is everything okay, Jules?"

Another beat passed before the frown on her face morphed into a look of understanding.

"Oh, of course," she said, and a smile spread across her face. "Thank you for checking in. I'm so okay. I'm completely awesome. And like, super happy that we're friends."

She enunciated the final word clearly, enough that a sense of relief immediately washed over me.

"Okay," I said. "Good. Me too."

"Good."

I nodded. "So, I'll see you Thursday, then?"

She stepped forward and reached up, putting her hand on my cheek and pulling me in close.

"Of course," she said.

Then she kissed me, soft and sweet and deep, and when we parted I walked away to catch my Uber with the faint taste of brown butter still lingering on my lips.

Five

ONE REASON I LIKED to walk Millie was because of the peace and quiet.

Like sure, she was a cute dog. And yeah, it was a nice thing to do for an elderly neighbour. Even when said elderly neighbour threatened to dig out her biggest cast iron pan that she never used anymore because it was just her and whack me upside the head with it for calling her an "elderly neighbour."

"You can call me Dottie or you can call yourself an ambulance, ya damn taint licker," she'd said as I leashed Millie up for her walk.

"I don't usually lick the taint," I said. "Though, for the right person, I'd consider it. And damn, Dottie. You've gotten vulgar in your old age. Where'd you come up with 'taint licker'?"

Dottie had pounded her cane against the floor as she let out a vibrant howl of laughter. "I've been reading these new books. They get a little naughty, you know."

I raised my eyebrows. "You're reading dirty books?"

"I said *naughty* books."

"So smut. That features the licking of the taint."

She snorted and waved a hand at me. "I'm too old to put up with you judgemental taint lickers. Let Millie in when you come back. I'm gonna crawl my ass into bed with my smutty little book. Don't get murdered, dear."

So yes, me walking Millie could be a nice thing to do for an elderly neighbour with a bad knee like Dottie Price. But that assumed that I had a modicum of altruism in my body and wasn't doing it for selfish reasons like the taint licker I was.

It gave me a chance to be alone. To decompress. To just be with my thoughts. Which, to be fair, was not always a good thing. Yes, it had taken a walk over the weekend for me to get the inspiration I needed to finish my latest commission for Kira, but today? When my mind was racing, trying to find meaning in something that was obviously meaningless?

Not as good a thing.

Luckily, I had the luck of a herd of black cats brawling beneath a ladder in an overcrowded mirror shop on Friday the thirteenth. So instead of the lonely, quiet walk I was craving so I could overthink whatever was going on with Finn and Julie in peace, I was distracted by multiple people deciding that approximately eight p.m. on a Monday was the perfect time to contact me.

"What does this asshole want?" I muttered just after Millie and I reached the park next to the beach.

She responded by ignoring me and sniffing a yellow patch of grass.

Sighing, I hooked her leash around my wrist and unlocked my phone screen so I could see what *Z Biggest Asshole*—a.k.a. Zain Hameed, a.k.a. my brother Josh's best friend, a.k.a. a total prick who was making me go to a work event with him as his fake girlfriend in exchange for not telling my entire family I'd been faking a marriage for the past five years—had texted me.

Z Biggest Asshole

Good news, Teacup. There's a couch here for you.

I wrinkled my nose at the childhood nickname as a second text followed his first—a photo message showing a decently nice hotel room. The carpet was grey and there looked to be a balcony of some kind just past the king bed, which was neatly made with a pristine white duvet beneath an unreasonable amount of throw pillows. Beside the bed was a nightstand and a few feet away from that was a couch that looked slightly more padded than your average bus bench.

I knew we were sharing a room. We had to if anyone was going to believe that I was his actual girlfriend so he could get a promotion at his clearly misogynistic company. He'd told me that back when I'd been standing in a hotel room in a terrycloth robe after he'd discovered my fake-husband-slash-real-ex-husband "cheating" on me. But he'd also told me that if there wasn't a couch, he'd get a spare cot brought up for me.

Which was the least he could do.

Especially after my parents' anniversary party. After he'd told me the only reason he *hadn't* asked me to do something far dirtier than just go to a work event with him was because he didn't want to feel like it was me paying him back for something.

After he'd said he would want *it*, whatever *it* happened to be, in the most disrespectful way.

Because even though I knew he was just teasing me and trying to get under my skin, I let him do it. Despite being an almost thirty-one-year-old divorced woman with a job and all those other grownup problems no one tells you about when you're a kid, Zain somehow made me revert into a nervous tween with an embarrassing crush on her older brother's best friend.

While I was overthinking that, a third message came in from Zain.

Z Biggest Asshole

> Lucky you. I won't have to tell the whole hotel about your horrific digestive issues when requesting a cot.

"Such a fucking asshole," I told Millie, who continued to ignore me.

I'd barely sent that text when my phone buzzed again. For a moment, I thought Zain had superhuman fingers, but my screen lit up and I audibly groaned when I saw the name on it. I considered ignoring the call or declining it, like I did every time she called, but that pervasive familial guilt always forced me to answer.

"Hi, Mom," I said.

"Teacup!" Mom replied excitedly. "Good, we caught you!"

"Hi, Tessa," said another woman.

"Um... hi?" I said, frowning at the familiar-but-not-quite-familiar voice.

"It's Audrey," she said, her voice amused. "Remember me? Your brother's fiancée? You're one of my bridesmaids? That Audrey?"

"Oh!" I forced a laugh. "Sorry. I don't think we've ever talked on the phone before."

"We haven't, but that's okay," Audrey said good-naturedly. "I'm sure we'll have plenty more phone chats between now and the wedding. And after, since you'll be my new sister-in-law!"

"Right, of course," I said. "So, um, what are you both up to?"

"Auds and I are having some Monday night margaritas," Mom said, and I clocked the familiar slur of tequila that time. "Mother-in-law-daughter-in-law time. You know."

I wasn't sure if she thought I knew about mother-in-law-daughter-in-law time or about mother-daughter time in general, but I didn't know a fucking thing about either.

"Yeah, sure," I said.

"Sure?" Mom repeated. "You… I mean, you must with Brad's mom sometimes. Don't you?"

"Uh, once in a while," I said lightly. "They travel a lot now, though. We don't see them often."

Surprisingly, that was true. Even when Brad and I had actually been married, we'd rarely seen his parents. It wasn't that they disliked me. I'd gotten along with both of them well enough, but they seemed to have the same amount of regard for me as they did for their son.

As in, not a lot.

There weren't a lot of families as cold and disconnected as the Schuberts were. And considering how dysfunctional I felt about my family, that was saying something. So if mother-in-law-daughter-in-law time was something people did, I sure as hell didn't know much about it. And it wasn't like Brad had any other siblings that I could've studied for the answer.

"Well, that won't be the case for us," Mom said firmly. "Audrey is part of my family now, and we're going to see each other as often as possible."

Poor Audrey, I thought, even as my future sister-in-law laughed.

"So speaking of mother-daughter time, Teacup," Mom said. "We've been drink-thinking, and we had a *brilliant* idea!"

"Did you?" I asked.

"We were talking about the wedding and I mentioned we had to figure out your dress," Audrey said. "Since we need to order it as soon as possible so it's here in time for the wedding."

"And I thought, you know what we could use?" Mom said. "A *girls' weekend*! Just the three of us!"

"Oh," I said. "Wow. That is… an idea."

"Right?" Mom said. "And now, I know you have that little charity job and all, but we thought you could take Friday off and fly in so we could get your bridesmaid dress ordered."

I frowned. "Uh... sure. You bought the dress in Burnsley?"

"No," Audrey said. "We got them in Kelowna. But you could fly into Kelowna and we could go shopping, then get a hotel and do a spa day or something on Saturday."

I had to hand it to them. There weren't many things out there that would make going to Zain's work dinner as his fake girlfriend the more preferable option, but suddenly, I was incredibly thankful for that.

"Oh, that sounds... amazing," I said. "But I... I can't this weekend."

"What?" Mom said, sounding drunkenly devastated. "Why not, Teacup?"

"I have a... work... thing," I said.

"I thought that was on Thursday?"

I blinked. "What?"

"The... the thingie," Mom said. "I wrote it down in my calendar. Auds, what was the thing Brad told Josh about? The..."

"The Recycl-Ball!" Audrey said. "Yeah, Josh had asked him how work was going for you, Tess, and Brad was talking about how proud he was of you for all your work for this gala."

"So sweet," Mom said mistily.

Ugh. It took everything in me not to gag.

"Right," I said. "Well, yeah, I do have that, but I have a different work thing on Saturday. A... dinner. With some of the donors. I can't miss it."

"Damn," Audrey said. "That's too bad."

"Me too," Mom said. "I was so excited about this."

And *fuck*.

Because of course they both sounded disappointed. And that same familial guilt that made me answer the phone even when I didn't want to rushed through me.

"We could do it next weekend," I said.

"Next weekend?" Mom said.

"I can make next weekend work," Audrey said slowly. "Maybe not overnight in Kelowna or anything and I can't do anything Sunday night since we're taking my mom out for dinner—"

"Oh my *God*!" Mom gasped. "Teacup, you could be here for Mother's Day?"

I almost screamed as the horrible realization that I'd just suggested getting together on Mother's Day weekend dawned on me.

"It sure seems that way," I forced myself to say.

"Oh my God," she repeated. "*Oh my God*. I wonder if... I bet you, I just *bet* you I could get Dylan to come in from Kamloops and—" Her voice caught and there was silence, then a loud sniffle.

"Aw, it's okay, Lorelei," Audrey said, so softly I barely heard it.

"It would be the first time in *years* I have everyone here for Mother's Day," Mom said, her voice thick.

"It would be perfect," Audrey said. "We could do brunch so Josh and I can be there, and that way Tessa can still get a flight back to Vancouver on Sunday night."

"And Brad, right?" Mom asked.

Fuck.

Fuck.

Fuck.

I swallowed hard and took a deep breath. "Mom, I'm sorry, but he—"

"Don't you dare say he's on a business trip, Tessa. I will cry," Mom said.

"I thought you were already crying," I said.

"I will cry harder." Her voice wavered. "So let's try this again. And Brad, right?"

I pressed my lips together and didn't say anything.

"Teacup?" Mom asked after a moment. "Are you there?"

"You told me not to dare say it," I said.

"*Tessa*—"

"Mom—" I said, trying to cut her off before the histrionics started.

"You *said* he was travelling less now!" she said as I completely failed to stop the histrionics. "You said he got a promotion and now he doesn't need to travel and—"

"*Less* travelling," I said. "Not never. And it's not... it's not like we knew you wanted to do something that weekend."

"I swear, he is *never* around," she said. "Do you even see him yourself half the time? Is he even going to be at your big work event this week?"

"...yes," I said carefully, trying to think of any way she might find out I was lying. "Yes, of course. Brad will be at the Recycl-Ball. He wouldn't miss it."

"He damn well better not," Mom said. "I expect a photo of you two all dressed up."

"You deserve a man who's going to be there for you and support you, no matter what," Audrey said. "Don't let him forget that, Tess."

My throat was dry enough that I coughed, making Millie look up and tilt her head. "I won't."

"And what about the baby?" Mom continued.

"The baby?" I repeated, confused.

"How can you be trying for a baby if he's still gone all the time?" she asked. "I thought you were trying for a baby now that he wasn't travelling so much."

Fuck. I'd almost forgotten about the whole fake-baby lie.

"We are," I said. "He's... he's very cognizant of my, uh, cycle. So he's not travelling when I... when it's a good day to try. Which is why, um, he had to go that weekend. Because he couldn't go... earlier."

"Well, at least there's that," Mom said. "And he's making sure not to use hot tubs while he's away?"

"What?"

"Hot tubs are terrible for sperm count," Audrey said. "Also, he might want to consider maca root or zinc supplements. Not that he's, you know, *old* or anything, but it can't hurt, you know?"

"That is an excellent idea, Audrey," Mom said. "And lots of leafy greens and water so he stays hydrated. And make sure he's wearing nice, loose boxers so his testic—"

"Okay, I promise you, we know how to make a baby," I said quickly. "You do not need to be this invested in my sex life."

"You know we just want the best for you, Tessa," Mom said.

Which was hilarious, all things considered.

I had been half-hoping the two of them would be too drunk to remember the entire call the next morning. Of course, there was that whole thing with all the luck I had being bad, so Mom booked me plane tickets while we were on the phone. Which was a good thing, I guess, since I also made a mental note to increase my line of credit temporarily. All these trips back to Burnsley for Audrey's wedding stuff were going to eat into the meager savings I'd built up. And I'd rather declare bankruptcy than ask Brad for money.

Technically, he *was* supposed to pay me alimony. But in what should not come as a surprise to anyone, I had stubbornly refused to accept it when we got divorced, thinking things like "my pride" were more important than paying my rent. Brad, of course, tried to give me money anyway. But after a year of me rejecting every single money transfer he sent, he'd stopped, telling me the moment I needed cash to let him know.

Which I would definitely do. Probably around the same time the Toronto Maple Leafs won a Stanley Cup on a hockey rink in hell.

When I finally hung up from Mom and Audrey, the world seemed exceptionally quiet. I could hear the waves on the beach not too far from me and the hush of traffic on streets beyond the little park where Millie and I sat. She was sniffing something on the ground, but stopped when I hung up and looked over, her head tilted to the side.

"Why can't I just say no, Mills?" I asked the little white dog.

She huffed in offense.

"Not to you." I sighed and reached down to scratch her ears. "There's something seriously wrong with me. You'd think knowing that would make it easier to fix, but here we are."

She snorted again, but nudged her head harder against my hand.

"How many times do you think I can lie my ass off and hope for the best before it catches up with me?"

She licked my hand, which didn't answer my question at all and was frankly kind of disgusting given that I knew where her mouth had been, but it made me feel better all the same.

At least, until my phone buzzed.

Again.

Unluckily, it was still just Z Biggest Asshole. Who was, apparently, a triple texter if you ignored him long enough.

Z Biggest Asshole

> Buy something? Don't feel like you need to get a new outfit. It can be something you already have.

The second message was sent just a few moments after that, a short enough gap that it was clear he hadn't been waiting for a response.

Z Biggest Asshole

> Or are you saying you don't have anything that works? If that's the problem, let me know. I can send you some money or something.

And then the third text, which he'd just sent after I'd apparently been on the phone too long:

Z Biggest Asshole

> The silent treatment, Teacup? Really? Don't get pissy with me for trying to help. Just didn't want

> to make you spend money on this if you don't want to.

How he managed to be condescending, insulting, and kind of thoughtful all in one text, I didn't know.

Me

> Wasn't the silent treatment, asshole. My mom called and now I have to go to fucking Burnsley for Mother's Day. And I don't need your help. I can buy my own clothes.

Z Biggest Asshole

> Calm yourself. I was just offering.

"Oh, that one was just condescending and insulting," I said to Millie. "He's starting to slip."

Millie wagged her tail because she had no idea what I was talking about.

Z Biggest Asshole

> Sorry you have to go back to Burnsley. Is your "husband" going with?

I frowned at the screen. There was that sort-of-thoughtfulness again.

Me

> He's not.

Z Biggest Asshole

> Good.

"The fuck is that supposed to mean?" I muttered.

It was almost... well.

I needed to shut that shit down right away.

Why are you still texting me? Don't you have anything better to do than sit around your hotel room texting the girl you're blackmailing into going to your work event?

Blackmailing? I seem to remember this favour being pushed upon me by someone who thought I was the kind of asshole who would blackmail her.

I started to reply, but before I could get more than the first three letters of "Fuck you" typed out, another picture message came through.

And fuck.

It was a selfie. Zain Hameed sent me a selfie. And it was a *good* selfie. He was in what looked like a club, richly saturated light splashing bold shades of pink and green across his dark hair, which was shiny and styled to allow a few pieces to flop over his forehead. There was a smirk on his stupid face, the corner of his mouth curling up enticingly and a knowing sparkle in his eye that was just not.

Fucking.

Fair.

And I'm not sitting around my hotel room. Or should I say OUR hotel room?

I glared at him. Even though he couldn't see me. And as I was glaring, I caught sight of something in the background that made the glare fade as curiosity took over.

Are you at a drag show?

Z Biggest Asshole

Maybe.

Me

Tell that queen I like her dress. What are you doing at a drag show? I thought you were at a work conference.

His next reply took a little longer than his previous ones. Long enough that I almost double-texted him before the message came through.

Z Biggest Asshole

Always gotta hustle, Teacup. This is where the prospective clients are hanging out tonight, so this is where I am tonight.

Me

And yet you're still texting me. Loser.

Z Biggest Asshole

Just making sure you don't forget. My coworkers are looking forward to meeting you and I'm looking forward to getting this promotion so I can get the fuck out of Vernon and move here. I got a lot riding on this, Tessa.

Me

Enough to never tell anyone about what happened last month?

Z Biggest Asshole

Which part?

Me

What do you mean, which part?

Z Biggest Asshole

The part where I discovered your and Brad's naughty little secret? Or that other part, where you got on your knees for me?

I couldn't be sure, since it was dark and I wasn't looking in a mirror, but I was fairly certain my face went completely red just then. Partly from what he said, yeah, but also partly because...

Well.

My stubbornness had brought me to a lot of places, but to my knees in front of Zain as I called his bluff about asking me to suck his dick should *not* have been one of them. I wasn't supposed to know what my brother's best friend looked like from that angle. What the shocked expression on his face would look like as he stared down at me, holding my gaze with my head just inches away from his body, the hint of desire in his eyes that I was certain I'd been imagining.

Except maybe I hadn't been.

Me

Both.

I could almost hear his voice when his reply came through. The low, husky smoothness of his tone, the hint of amusement, the constant coolness that was wrapped in heat.

Z Biggest Asshole

> My lips are sealed, Teacup. I'll even give you the metaphorical key after Saturday. As long as your tits look reasonably good in whatever you end up buying.

Me

> Fuck you.

Zain wasn't much of an emoji person, but he sent a laughing one.

Z Biggest Asshole

> Now come on. Fair's fair.

Me

> What?

Z Biggest Asshole

> Fair's fair. Show me what you're doing right now.

Me

> What??????

Z Biggest Asshole

> Send me a pic. Something I can use to show off my "girlfriend" to the assholes I work with.

I doubt he was expecting a photo of me cradling an alarmed Millie while flipping off the camera, but that was what he got.

Part 2

Confession: Men don't like
it when you call them
caterpillars.

Six

My tits looked fantastic.

Not in the outfit I was wearing to Zain's work dinner. I didn't have that outfit yet because it wasn't Saturday morning and I wasn't panicking as I tried to find the least frumpy last-minute plus-size dress I could afford before getting on the ferry to Victoria.

No, it was Thursday night and I was in my trademark fancy event wear, which *always* made my tits look good.

Zain might have insisted that his work dinner was formal, but I had no such qualms about the Recycl-Ball. Frankly, my black leather pants and satin top were almost *too* nice for what was about to be the biggest dumpster fire of the year. I was sure Dinah would have some complaints that I wasn't "dressed to theme," but seeing as no one could tell what the theme was anymore, she would complain about that even if I showed up clad in the trashiest lingerie I could find.

Because that was what the theme seemed to have morphed to. Loni had stormed into the office late on Wednesday to inform everyone she would be wearing a—in her words—"subversive Avant Garde look celebrating the female body."

Then she'd thrown open her floor-length pink faux-fur coat, Chuck managed to turn his shocked scream into something that represented an impressed gasp, and Dinah had gone so pale that I was sure she was going to pass out.

Which was fair. I mean, it's not every day you see your boss's nipples on full display.

Loni may have been a total airhead, but she was also gorgeous. She was thin, because of course she was, because she was a fucking billionaire heiress. Instead of gorging herself exclusively on expensive cheeses like I would if I had a billion dollars, she ate healthy food and had time to go to the gym to maintain her slim, toned body.

And standing in the middle of our boardroom, she was showing off most of that body in a thong-style bodysuit made of mesh and lace that was held up by hopes and dreams. Her nipples were almost completely visible, not because the material was see-through, but because there were holes there.

Like, purposeful holes cut right over her nipples and trimmed with circles of rhinestones.

"Well?" she'd said as we all stared at her, speechless. "Thoughts?" When no one spoke, she started snapping her fingers. "Hello? I'm *speaking*."

"You are an absolute fashion icon, Loni Versace Less," Chuck said.

"You're so unique," Dinah said.

"It's so differently... different," I said.

Loni set her lips into a pleased smirk. "Excellent. Just what I'd hoped."

"And you're sure—" Dinah started, but her voice cracked.

"Sure what?" Loni asked, the smirk fading as she turned to her.

"That... that's going to be... okay to wear in public?" Dinah finished.

"What are you trying to say here?" Loni asked. "Do you have a *problem* with the female form, Dinah?"

"No!" Dinah said, horrified. "No, I just—"

"I think what Dinah is trying to say is that you could make this even *more* of a statement," I said.

Dinah's head snapped towards me. I was sure she was attempting to throttle me with her eyes, but I didn't look at her, instead holding Loni's gaze as she switched her attention to me.

"Explain," Loni said.

I cleared my throat and stepped forward. "Well, as CARE's resident artist, I think it would be *extra* subversive to pair this with a full-length bodysuit underneath. It would, um, speak to the layers of censorship placed on the female form, even when we as women—or men, or nonbinary folks... anyone, really—try to celebrate the natural state of our bodies."

"Hmm," Loni said.

Taking her lack of immediate anger at my suggestion as a good sign, I continued. "What you have here says so much, that's true. It's an incredible outfit. But I think going a step further would really stick it to Paige Martelle and—"

I'd said the magic words.

Loni immediately told Dinah and Chuck to get out so I could help her plan the "next level" of her outfit. By the time she left, I'd managed to bullshit my way into getting Loni to wear not only a full bodysuit, but also a traditional gala-style gown overtop so she could do a dramatic reveal partway through the night, hopefully after all the donors were too drunk to realize she was prancing around half-naked.

Which was kind of sad, honestly. I mean, yeah, Loni could be a handful, but I respected her reasoning for wanting to censor every part of her body *except* her nipples. It was clever, in a way. And subversive.

And likely to get us kicked out of the planetarium.

So despite the fact that Loni was going to be wearing something that may have been more appropriate for the Met Gala over the Recycl-Ball, I was wearing my go-to leather pants and black top instead of justifying the cost of a new dress by wearing it to two events. Besides being comfortable, the general busyness of the week and Loni's last-minute demands and mood swings meant I'd barely had time to do the things I enjoyed doing, let alone buying a new outfit.

But I took the time to make sure I looked *extra* good. I rubbed all the scuffs out of my favourite black peep-toe pumps and made sure to paint my toenails red for where they peeked out of the shoe. I spent a bit more time than usual doing my makeup—not much more, since my everyday makeup routine and my fancy event makeup routine were the same. But I used lip liner before applying my trademark red lipstick, which was an extra step. I even styled my hair so I could turn my waves into curls and steamed the wrinkles out of the low-cut black satin top that made my tits look amazing.

In short, I looked fucking phenomenal that Thursday night when I walked into the planetarium. Because I was a dedicated and helpful CARE employee who cared about making a good impression. It had nothing to do with the fact that Finn and Julie were going to be attending.

I didn't expect them to be there when I got there, and they weren't. That was totally normal, since I got there about fifteen minutes after the doors opened and the actual programming didn't start until seven-thirty. Hardly anyone ever showed up that early.

But since I'd invited them, it was only polite to check to see if they were there so I could say hello, obviously. And when they weren't there, it was definitely just a nice thing to do to open up MatchMi and send them a quick message to let them know I was already there so they could watch for me when they arrived.

Will you be here soon?

I cringed at how needy it sounded before deleting it.

I'm here! Where are you?

Nope.

No fucking way.

"Who are you texting?"

I jumped as Chuck walked up behind me, throwing an arm around my shoulder and peering down at my phone. Yanking it out of his line of sight, I hit send and then locked the screen.

"No one," I said, and before he could call me out on my bullshit: "You look nice. Where's Charles?"

"Where *isn't* Charles," Chuck muttered, but he was trying not to smile as he said it. "He's getting me a much-needed drink. We've been here supervising the decorating since the little gremlins finished their astrology program."

Despite only having an hour before doors opened, Chuck had done an amazing job with the decor. It was unclear what the theme was, but he'd made it look like high art instead of something from a discount bin. The actual planetarium dome was dimly lit, showcasing the twinkling fake sky. Strips of jewel-toned lights ran along the aisles and down the stage in the center of the room, where the entertainment would be taking place. There was a hall outside where hors d'oeuvres were being served, guests were mingling, and—most importantly—the bar was located.

He'd managed to do all that while also taking the time to dress in a sharp-looking suit with a subtle textured tie. His black hair was neatly styled, pushed off his forehead and highlighting the strong structure of his face.

And, unfortunately, the semi-stressed grimace that was on it.

"Is everything okay?" I asked.

"Oh, of course," he said breezily. "Loni is just already on my last nerve and we haven't even officially started the event."

"Loni's already here?"

"Mm-hmm. She brought a gaggle of her rich friends with her."

"Isn't that... good?" I asked. "I mean, her rich friends have money, and we're trying to raise money, so..."

"Mmm, but that would require them to *spend* their money," Chuck said. "And currently they're wandering around treating the other attendees like animals in a zoo. You know. 'Look at the *poors* in their natural habitat.'" He took a deep, calming breath and let it out. "I've yet to figure out why they seem to think poor people live in planetariums, but here we are."

"Oh," I said, trying not to laugh. "That's shitty."

"So far, no one's been mortally offended. Except Dinah, who is probably hyperventilating in the bathroom for the eighth time already."

"Well, it ended up looking pretty good," I said. "All things considered."

Chuck smiled. "It did come together into... well, *something*." He looked away from me for a moment and sighed in relief. "Oh, thank God."

I turned to see Charles striding up, a glass of water in one hand and something neon green in a martini glass in the other. I couldn't help but smile as I saw him; the man was glowing brighter than the lights in the room.

Which wasn't saying much since the lights were pretty dim.

But he still looked radiant. Charles often had a bit of scruff on his cheeks, but he'd shaved and was wearing a light grey suit. And despite Chuck's complaints about wearing matching ties, it was actually just a similar tie in a complimentary colour.

"What... is that?" Chuck asked, looking at the drink Charles was holding as he walked up.

Charles shrugged. "They asked how I was feeling and I said it was for my boyfriend, not for me, and they asked how *you* were feeling and I said 'Well, he's usually grumpy and right now he's quite stressed' and they made you this."

He handed the martini glass to Chuck, who eyed it suspiciously before taking a very careful sip. As he did, his eyes widened almost comically.

"Holy shit," he said. "This is... amazing. Good job, darling."

Charles looked like he could have melted into the floor, but managed to remain corporeal as he turned to me.

"Hey, Tessa," he said. "You look awesome."

"Thanks," I said. "You look awesome by default, but I like your tie. It compliments Chuck's really well."

And like, cynical and sarcastic as I could be, the way that made Charles smile gave me a warm, fuzzy feeling. He extended his arm towards me for a hug and I took it, of course, because who *wouldn't* accept a hug from a guy as gorgeous and sweet as Charles?

"It's so good to see you," he said, then lowered his voice. "Sorry he's so stressed. I've been trying to keep him calm, but I know he's on edge right now. But like, I think things are going good. For... for him and me, I mean."

"They're totally going good. He might be a drama queen, but I know for a fact he's head over heels for you."

Charles's shoulders shook as he laughed. "Oh, thank God. 'Cause I am, too."

He pulled back, still smiling, and glanced at Chuck in a way that made me think Chuck had completely failed at the whole "not letting Charles fall too fast" thing. Chuck, thankfully, had an expression on his face like he didn't regret that at all, which he hid the second he saw me looking at him.

"So, Tessa Germaine Lane," he said in a snappy voice. "Where are *your* friends?"

"What friends?" Charles asked.

Chuck let out a delighted laugh and put his hand on Charles's shoulder. "That was so shady. I love it."

Charles looked at me, his eyes wide. "No, I meant... um... *which* friends? Oh, God. I'm sorry, Tessa."

"It's okay," I said.

"She said she invited her 'friends' that she 'totally doesn't have feelings for' even though she 'hasn't seen any couples other than them for over a month,'" Chuck said.

A knowing look spread across Charles's face. "Was it that last couple I saw you with? I was wondering why I haven't seen you around Bar One for ages."

I sighed. "Yes." Then I glared at Chuck. "And *no*. I don't have feelings for them. We have an arrangement."

"Mmm, yes," Chuck said. "An *arrangement*."

"Oh, shut up," I grumbled. "And they're on their way. There are two tickets for them at the front doors."

"Sure. I'll believe it when I see it."

"Go see it, then. They're on the list. They just aren't... here yet." I rolled my eyes. "It's not even close to seven-thirty."

"Mr. David!" interrupted a familiar voice before Chuck could respond. "And Ms. Lane! And... Mr. Grey?"

We turned to see none other than Brenda McClane waltzing up to us. She had her grey hair slicked back in a neat bun and wore a black turtleneck reminiscent of the ones she used to wear when she was doing gallery showings across the country. It was a good look on her; most of the time these days, she was in a canvas apron and paint-stained shirt as she taught art classes out of her studio in downtown Vancouver.

Which, of course, was where Charles and Chuck had met after Chuck accidentally signed me and him up to nude model for a beginner's class that Charles attended.

"Ms. McClane," Chuck said, his voice smooth as he extended a hand to her. "It's so lovely to see you! Thank you for coming to this year's Recycl-Ball."

"Of course, of course," she said, her eyes still on Charles. "Mr. Grey, what a surprise. I didn't know you were so involved in the art community! Most of my beginners aren't invested enough to attend semi-obscure events like this." She glanced at me. "No offense."

"Hi, Brenda," Charles said, his voice somewhat nervous. "I, um, don't usually. I'm here with... with Chuck."

Brenda looked from him to Chuck and back to him. "I see. You two are...?"

Charles nodded.

Brenda fixed her unblinking gaze on him. "And did that happen because of my class?"

Charles's throat flexed as he nodded again. "Is that, um, an issue?"

There was a long moment of tension as Brenda stared at him.

"An issue?" she repeated, then we all jumped as she let out a high-pitched cackle. "My dear, of *course* not! I just expect a wedding invitation when you get there. It's only proper to invite the person who matched you up. I knew the two of you would—"

Biting back a laugh, I excused myself as Brenda insisted she simply *knew* Charles and Chuck would be perfect for each other, despite not knowing either of them all that well. Glancing around, I tried to pinpoint other people I should greet or talk to.

I saw Loni, who was indeed strutting around with a group of people who looked as obscurely out of place as she did. She was still wearing the floor-length gown I'd suggested and the rest of them were dressed similarly, clad in outfits that cost more than my year's salary.

Just a few feet behind her was Dinah, who I begrudgingly admitted looked lovely in a blue cocktail dress with her white-blonde hair curled into a half-up, half-down style. She was tailing Loni in what appeared to be an attempt to wrangle her while trying to greet donors and attendees at the same time.

There were various other donors, some who I knew and some who I didn't, most who were already absorbed in conversation with other people. Jia, the receptionist, was standing near the bar in a low-cut dress showing off her thin frame, talking to a group of donors who seemed very interested in whatever her breasts were saying. At the bar, Austin from accounting was watching her miserably, ignoring the two men standing with him who were chatting animatedly.

And then there was *her*.

Seated beside Austin was a thin white woman who looked entirely out of place in the best way. She had long brown hair showing off a delicate, impish face and was dressed in a full three-piece navy blue suit. Her eyes seemed to be just a touch too big for her face and she had a smile that made her look like a particularly tricky faerie.

And she was shooting it straight at me.

I had no idea who she was. I'd never seen her before in my life. And yet somehow, I was certain that she was just the person I was looking to talk to.

Seven

"CAN I JUST SAY that your body looks phenomenal in that outfit?"

I hadn't noticed the man when I first walked up to the bar. I was too busy trying to act cool and casual so the woman in the blue suit would think I was chic and mysterious or something. But after I'd gotten there and attempted to flag the mixologist down so I could find out how much I had to bribe him to get a rum and coke instead of whatever concoction he thought I'd feel like, someone else slid in beside me.

While he was attractive enough, he had the air of someone who thought that he was destined to finish last—a.k.a. he couldn't get a girlfriend, which was obviously everyone else's fault because he was *such* a nice guy. In reality, he was just an asshole like the rest of us, except he was too busy idealizing himself to recognize it.

What a guy like that was doing at an event like this was beyond me. The whole point of it was for CARE to dig into the donor's pockets and snatch whatever they could out of there. This guy didn't look like the kind of person who gave money to charity. Not when he was wearing an ill-fitting suit and nursing what seemed to be a glass of water.

All that was to say I didn't feel the need to be overly nice to him in the hopes he'd donate a chunk of change to CARE.

"Thanks," I said as impersonally as I could.

The Nice Guy leaned against the bar, eyes flicking down and then back up.

"No, seriously," he said. "You are just—" He stopped and brought his hand up to his mouth, making a loud smacking sound as he literally did a chef's kiss. "—so beautiful. I had to come over and say hello."

"Well, hello," I said, still keeping my voice flat.

Cursed with the inability to take a hint, The Nice Guy raked his teeth along his lower lip in the least sexy way I'd ever seen. "I'm Riley. Riley Jordan."

"And I'm not interested." I leaned forward, looking pointedly at the mixologist in the hopes he'd feel my gaze on him. He, however, was in what seemed like minute three of explaining the concoction he'd created for Austin, who looked like he didn't give a shit so long as there was alcohol in it.

Riley let out an incredulous sound that was half-scoff, half-chuckle. "Jesus, that escalated quickly. I was just trying to be nice."

"And I'm just trying to tell you I'm not interested in getting hit on." I blinked hard, but the mixologist still didn't notice.

Riley The Nice Guy snorted. "Bold of you to assume I was hitting on you."

"Trust me, I've been hit on enough times to know when someone's trying to shoot their shot."

"You sure about that?" he asked. "Because I definitely wasn't. Just thought I'd try to be nice since I figured a female with a belly like that would be grateful for the attention."

Instead of tearing up and rushing from the room like Riley seemed to expect or suddenly deciding my love language was being insulted by a guy who had no real-life experience with a vagina and falling hopelessly in love with him, I burst out laughing.

"Honey, if being fat stops me from having to deal with prickly little caterpillars like you, then hal-le-fucking-lujah, bring on another cheeseburger."

Riley's mouth dropped open for a moment before his lip curled into a snarl. But before he could find some other whiny bullshit to slur at me, my ears were relieved of having to listen to him by one of the worst laughs I'd ever heard in my life.

It was horrible. *Horrible.* A nasally sort of bark that resembled a honk from a Canadian goose with a bad case of strep throat more than it did a laugh. And it was coming from the woman in the blue suit, who was still perched on her stool behind Riley.

I fucking loved it.

"I would be *delighted* to bring you a cheeseburger, gorgeous," she said. "Name the time and place."

I looked past Riley, exaggerating the way I flicked my eyes up and down so there was no chance he could miss it. "Anytime and anywhere, as long as it's with you."

Riley made a disgusted noise. The sexy stranger's alluring smirk faded instantly and she leaned forward so her face was just above his shoulder.

"Got something to say?" she snapped in a brusquely commanding voice.

Riley jumped and turned, stammering for a moment. "What? No, I... I didn't. Don't. I have nothing to say."

"Because I will fight you," the stranger said matter-of-factly. "And I will win."

"Jesus Christ," Riley muttered, shoving himself away from the bar. "Fuck this. I'm leaving."

"Bye, little caterpillar!" called the sexy stranger, waving at Riley's back before turning to me with a wide grin on her face. "Excellent insult, by the way. Ten out of ten. I will absolutely use that in the future."

"Use it as often as you like," I said. "There simply aren't enough caterpillar-related insults being used these days."

She grinned and stuck her hand out. "I'm Claire. I know you said no to him, but would you be willing to give me your name?"

"Oh, no way am I falling for that faerie shit," I said. "If you're actually a fae, you can fuck right off, too."

That earned me another barking laugh, which made me grin. "Oh, I like you. Let me buy you a drink. What name should I give for the order?"

"Nice try. Too soon. I'll take the drink, though."

"Foiled again!" She clenched a fist and waved it in the air playfully, then leaned forward and flagged the mixologist down. "What are you drinking?"

"Isn't he supposed to make me a drink based on my aura or something?"

Claire shrugged. "If you want. But I found the key to get him to make what I want instead."

"And what would that be?"

She looked at me out of the corner of her eye and winked, but said nothing until the mixologist walked up.

"Another double scotch on the rocks for me," she said, pulling out a red fifty-dollar bill seemingly from nowhere and sliding it discreetly across the bar. "And whatever my friend here is drinking."

The mixologist looked at me expectantly.

"Uh... make it two," I said.

"Coming right up," the mixologist said, but he leaned towards Claire before turning around. "But this time I'm gonna have to stand here and make some shit up, okay? My boss is getting on my case."

Claire didn't even hesitate, just pulled a second fifty-dollar bill from wherever she'd got the first and handed it to him. "Tell him he'll get the same as what I'm giving you for every drink I *don't* have to listen to you ramble about my scotch."

Damn.

Despite looking like she was maybe in her late twenties, *this* was a donor. A big donor. The kind of donor Dinah and Loni would probably make a point of talking to. The kind of donor that would allow Dinah to win her battle of getting me fired if I fucked things up. Frantically, I thought back to the list of major donors Dinah had passed out last week and told us to memorize, trying to picture it.

And I did picture it. I could distinctly remember using it as a coaster for the iced flat white I'd gotten on Wednesday morning. That didn't do me a lot of good, however. I probably should have at least glanced at the names at some point.

"So," Claire said, resting an elbow on the bar as she leaned towards me. "What's a gorgeous girl like you doing at a trash heap of an event like this?"

"Would you believe me if I said I work for CARE?" I asked.

She pursed her lips, her large eyes widening even further until she looked almost cartoon-like. "Oof. I should've at least washed the caterpillar guts off my shoe before putting my foot in my mouth."

"You can take it back out," I said. "I've been petitioning to rename this the Dumpster Fire Gala since back when it had an actual theme that didn't involve lingerie made of plastic pop can rings."

She snickered, which was a less hideous sound than her laugh, though I still liked it very much. "I guess it's always those closest to a thing that hate it the most."

"What about you?" I asked. "What brings you here?"

Claire's tongue poked out, wetting her full, pink bottom lip. "I guess you could say I *care* about both art and the environment."

"You are incredibly cheesy," I said, then almost winced as I reminded myself this was a fucking *donor* and I wasn't supposed to fuck it up.

Thankfully, Claire was hilarious.

"Actually, I'm lactose intolerant," she said. "But I do eat a lot of corn, so..."

I chuckled. "So, um, I obviously work at CARE. What do you do?"

Claire shrugged as the mixologist returned with our scotches and set them in front of us. "Oh, you know. A little of this. A bit of that. I'm one of those family disappointments who's more about having a good time than doing anything useful with my life."

"Oof. Tell me about it," I said, reaching for my glass.

"I'd love to," Claire said, then leaned in as the tone of her voice dropped a bit. "Maybe over dinner or a drink sometime?"

I liked her. There was no question about that. It was one of those instant clicks, those moments where you just *knew* that person was supposed to be in your life. Those moments that triggered a huge wave of bisexual panic because I couldn't figure out if I wanted to be her, befriend her, or be fucked by her.

Probably all three.

Every instinct in me was screaming to agree. To go for a drink with this woman. To at least become acquaintances with her since if I had an in with a major donor, Dinah might calm the fuck down about firing me for a couple of weeks. Or at least until Monday.

So yeah, I wanted to go for a drink with her. But before I could say yes, Finn and Julie appeared.

Not in person. Just in my mind.

And I hated that. I shouldn't have been thinking of them at that moment. I shouldn't have been feeling guilty about wanting to go for a drink with Claire because of them.

Because we weren't anything more than friends. And they weren't even here.

"Or not," Claire said gently when I took too long to reply. "That's okay, too."

"No!" I said. "I mean, not no. But yes."

"No but yes?" she repeated, amused.

I opened my mouth to respond, but before I could speak, a loud voice called my name.

"Tessa!"

I turned to see Loni fucking Less snap her fingers before striding across the room in a lunging powerwalk.

"Just the person I was looking for," she declared as soon as she was close enough.

"Oh," I said. "Really?"

"Well, no. I just needed one of you." She stopped short in front of me and struck a Loni pose, showing off the bodysuit-under-bodysuit outfit she had already changed into. "I need you to tell me when the date auction is beginning. My friends are intrigued by what bidding on people for dates entails."

I blinked at her. "The... what?"

"The date auction," she said, enunciating each word.

I stared back at her. The date auction? The...

Oh, *fuck*.

I'd brought up doing a date auction during a brainstorming session a month and a half earlier when Loni decided to change the theme. My thinking had been that it went along with the whole Trashy Love concept, but it was apparently such a bad idea that Loni thought she was having a stroke.

No one had spoken of it since.

"Loni, you said you didn't want us to do that," I said.

"I said no such thing," she said. "This was *always* the plan. And I have informed several esteemed donors that there will be a very lucrative date auction. Do you mean to tell me everyone single one of you was too incompetent to—"

And I admit it.

I panicked.

Because dealing with Loni's freakouts wasn't a *me* job. It was a Chuck job. And Chuck was probably making out with Charles beneath the thousands of fake stars in the planetarium dome. But as much as I hated this stupid job, I needed it, and there was no way this would be pinned on anyone but me since the suggestion was mine in the first place.

So I did the only thing I could think of.

I lied.

"*Oh!*" I said, then let out a bright, fake laugh. "The *date* auction. I thought you said the *plate* auction."

Loni looked bewildered. "Why would I say a... What even *is* a plate—"

"Not to worry, Loni," I said in my best happy-go-lucky employee voice. "The date auction is happening very soon. Or... in a little while. I have to double check with Chuck and Dinah because I said we should do it before the comedian but they said after the comedian and I can't remember off the top of my head when we decided to. But I'll go check with them and get back to you, okay?"

She stared at me for a moment, then a placated look spread across her face.

"Good," she said, then looked at the bar. "Oh, perfect. You got me a beverage. Excellent work, Tessa."

With that, she picked up my scotch, took a sip, then turned and flitted across the hall. I watched, mouth half open, until she was gone.

"What the fuck," I whispered as I turned back to Claire to apologize, but the barstool beside me was empty.

Eight

"I CANNOT BELIEVE YOU did this to me," Dinah said as she hyperventilated into her own hands.

"Me?" I didn't even need to fake the offense on my face. "Loni's the one who was about to go nuclear. I *saved* the day."

Dinah glared at me, her pinched face more pinchy than usual. "You wouldn't have needed to *save* the day if you'd never brought up this stupid suggestion in the first place!"

I flipped my palms up. "Loni said no and no one has said a single word about a date auction since. It was over a month ago. Like, I didn't even know her memory went back that far."

"Take this as a lesson to keep your mouth shut next time."

"Okay, first of all—"

"Both of you need to calm down," Chuck said, rubbing the bridge of his nose between his fingers.

The three of us were standing in what seemed to be an empty classroom we'd been using for storage. It was down a small service hallway outside the planetarium, close enough that we could still hear the chatter of people at the gala.

I'd been wrong about what Chuck was up to when I rushed to find him after Loni walked away. He wasn't exploring Charles's tonsils with his tongue, instead using his typical charm to sweet talk a couple of potential donors while Charles looked on proudly. When I'd walked up to him, he glanced at me out of the side of his eye, but continued talking.

"Chuck," I whispered. "I need your help."

"It can wait, Tessa," he said before turning back to the donors.

I looked at Charles desperately. "It can't wait, actually."

Charles, taking pity on me, stepped forward and put a gentle hand on Chuck's arm. "I think it's urgent."

Chuck looked at me, then sighed and excused himself from the donors.

"This better be—"

"Loni thinks we're doing a date auction and I told her we were and that I had to go check with you to find out what time it was starting because she was about to throw a tantrum in the middle of the hall and now we have to plan a date auction," I said.

He blinked at me. "What?"

I took a deep breath. "Loni thinks we're doing a date auction and I—"

"We have to do *what*?!" he repeated. "Jesus, Tessa. Why didn't you say it was urgent! Oh my God, we need to go find Dinah."

"I did say it was urgent," I said, but Chuck had already turned around and started power walking across the planetarium to track Dinah down. Sighing, I told Charles to hang out for a minute, then hurried after Chuck found Dinah, looped his arm through hers, and began leading her towards the exit.

"What are you *doing*, Chuck?" I heard Dinah ask as I caught up with them.

"I'll tell you in a moment," Chuck replied. "As soon as we're out of earshot of—"

"Dinah!"

I winced as Loni came out of nowhere and marched up to them, her shoulders square and her nose stuck up like she was trying to sniff something on the breeze.

"Yes, Loni?" Dinah asked.

"Did Tessa find you? I want to know when the date auction is."

Even from behind, I could see Dinah's face go pale. "The *date—*"

"After the comedian," Chuck said. "We're actually just on our way to get the final details prepared."

"Perfect," Loni said, hitting the final *T* hard before turning and waltzing away without another word.

"The *what*?!" Dinah repeated, her voice so high-pitched a couple of the light bulbs in the projector probably cracked.

Chuck managed to get her into the empty classroom before her full meltdown started, which was good. He made me come with him into said classroom, which was less good, although justified since I was the one who... I don't know. Had the details or something.

"Alright," he said after Dinah had finished tearing me a proverbial new one and her breath stopped coming in deep, wheezing gasps. "We can figure this out. All we need is... well, everything."

"Oh, is that it?" Dinah asked dryly.

"We could just call a Code Oh Shit," I suggested.

It wasn't a serious suggestion. It was clearly a joke, because things were tense and uncomfortable and for some reason, I thought trying to lighten the mood was a good idea. As one of my closest friends, Chuck should have realized that, but instead of laughing, he shot me an exasperated look.

"You are not allowed to leave and go to Starbucks right now," he said.

Dinah stared at him. "Is that what a Code Oh Shit is?"

"It was just a joke," I said.

Chuck sighed. "No, Dinah. I was just saying there's no need for a Code Oh Shit and *also* that Tessa can't leave and go to Starbucks for unrelated reasons." He closed his eyes and bowed his head, then took a deep breath through his nose and let out a long exhale through his mouth. Once it was out, he rolled his shoulders back, puffed out his chest, and lifted his chin.

"Okay," he said. "Here's the plan."

As certain as I was that Chuck wanted to kill me just then, he wouldn't have been able to deny that he was in his element. He was organized and efficient and diligent, not to mention brilliant enough to execute anything he set his mind to. And I wasn't just saying that because he was saving my ass. Everyone knew Chuck was incredible at his job, which made it all the more surprising that he didn't care that I wasn't good at mine.

Well, most of the time, he didn't care.

"We have until the stand-up comedian is done," Chuck said. "Then add fifteen minutes for a break so people can get drinks. We should be able to pull something together that will at least fool Loni. Everyone else, well… that's what thoughts and prayers are for." He turned to Dinah, whose lip was trembling with a nervous quiver. "You'll be the auctioneer."

"What?"

"You're the only one who can talk fast enough," he said. "Channel your anxiety into that speed-talky thing auction people do. Your sole focus from now until go-time is to learn everything you can about doing an auction."

Dinah frowned. "But what about—"

"We will deal with everything else." Chuck pointed at an empty table. "If you need a charger for your phone or something, come find me, otherwise you will stay there until you know how to run an auction. I'll work in the hallway so you have a quiet space."

Without waiting for her to respond, Chuck turned to me.

"You need to find people to auction. Do whatever you have to do to get them to agree."

"*Whatever* I have to do?" I repeated.

He looked at me, unimpressed. "You don't have enough time to give blowjobs to everyone before the auction starts."

Well, at least he got the joke, even if he didn't think it was funny.

"When you get someone to agree, ask them for some basic cheesy information Dinah can use to intro them. Like 'I like long walks on the beach and having wrenches thrown into all my plans.' And if there's anything they *don't* want to do for their dates."

"What kind of dates are we thinking of?" Dinah asked.

"That's what I'll be doing," Chuck said. "I'll come up with a list and try to think of some that relate to the person who might be auctioned off. So, like when you bid on Tessa, you get a personalized art lesson and enough drinks to become an alcoholic in a single night."

"Wait, what?" I said. "Why am I being auctioned off?"

"And who would buy her?" Dinah muttered, but I ignored her.

Chuck raised his eyebrows and closed his mouth into an inverted pucker, jutting his chin forward and saying everything with a single look. Like "You're being auctioned off because you fucked up" and "I'm disappointed in you."

You know. All that positive stuff that made me feel super good about myself.

"I will get things started by being the first person available," Chuck said. "So we have at least two. Everyone understands what they're doing?"

I didn't make a joke that time, just nodded.

"Good. Let's go."

We all moved at once, Dinah towards the table and Chuck and I towards the door. Once we were in the hallway, I took two steps, then stopped and turned back around as the door closed behind Dinah.

"Wait, how many people should I try to find?" I asked.

Chuck heaved another heavy sigh as he moved further down the hallway. "As many as possible, Tessa. I need you to take charge of this part of it."

"I know, I just—"

"Look," he said, holding his hands up. "Just do it. Please don't fuck this up, okay?"

Alright, so he was *super* pissed at me.

I didn't say anything as he put his back on the wall and slid to the floor. Instead, I took a deep breath and pushed the lump of emotion out of my throat. I had work to do, and even if Chuck was being kind of an asshole, I didn't want to disappoint my friend. So I turned around and started walking back to the hall, trying to figure out who would help.

My first thought was Finn.

He would be thrilled to do it. And he would pull in a *ton* of donations. Plus, I was pretty sure Julie wouldn't mind as long as I promised to come over and eat her out while he was on his auctioned-off date.

But I hadn't seen them when I was rushing around looking for Chuck and Dinah and they hadn't sent me a message yet. I thought for a moment, then pulled out my phone and opened MatchMi.

TessTheUnicorn

Hey, I've got a work emergency happening. Not sure if you're here yet or not but if you are, let me know? Or come find me. I'll be the one running around frantically.

"Tessa, I'm not joking," Chuck said from behind me. "You need to take this seriously otherwise—"

"I am," I snapped, turning back around. "I was messaging someone who might be able to help."

He looked exasperated. "Just, go find... Go talk to... I don't know. I need your help for once, okay? I can't deal with that and planning the dates and Charles is off by himself and—"

"I am dealing with it," I said, and my voice cracked. Heat rushed up my cheeks and I cleared my throat before glaring at him. "I am trying, okay? Be pissed at me all you want but I'm *trying*, Chuck."

The annoyed look on Chuck's face morphed and he blinked at me. "Wait, I—"

"Shut up," I muttered. "I'll go tell Charles what's going on. And don't worry, I wasn't going to ask your precious boyfriend to be auctioned off or anything."

Before Chuck could respond, I'd turned back around and walked away, my heels clicking on the tile.

Despite being upset and hurt and angry, I managed to collect a decent number of people to auction off. After tracking down Charles, who was in the same area we'd left him looking like a lost puppy without Chuck there, I found my first victim: Jia.

"A date auction?" she repeated when I explained the concept after pulling her away from the group of people she was talking to.

"Yeah," I said. "If you're interested. You'd just have to stand up there and people would bid, then you get to go on a date that CARE will pay for with whoever wins and—"

"Absolutely," she said, clapping her hands together and bending her knees in an excited bounce. "Oh, this sounds *amazing*."

I blinked, surprised at how easy it had been to convince her. "Okay, cool. What can I write down for your intro?"

She gave me a few details, then gasped.

"Oh!" she said. "Can I like, request the date?"

"What do you mean?"

She brought her clasped hands up to her chin in a pleading motion. "My parents own a tea shop in Chinatown and they do these tastings there. It's *so* much fun and I could, like, teach whoever wins about the different teas and everything."

I shrugged. "I don't see why not. I'll tell Chuck that's what you want to do."

Clapping, she grinned before turning back to the group I'd found her with.

"You guys, we're doing a *date* auction!" she said, and for some reason, that group of people seemed thrilled to hear that cute little Jia was going to be up there.

Except Austin, who looked even more miserable than he had before.

I doubt he realized it, but Chuck gave me the easiest job. Like, I still worked my ass off, but it was *shocking* how many people were excited to be involved. I'd had to pull myself away from Brenda McClane, who was especially eager after I proposed Chuck's painting lesson date idea to her and wouldn't stop talking about it. A few other CARE employees here, a couple of artists and acquaintances I knew from university there, and the mixologist at the bar later, and I was feeling pretty good about things.

By the time the comedian was nearly done his set, I was sweaty from scurrying around the hall and planetarium. Circling back to the empty classroom, I found Chuck still sitting on the floor outside the door with Charles beside him. Their heads were nearly pressed together as Chuck jotted notes frantically on the back of a receipt, but he looked up when he heard my heels clicking on the floor.

"Alright, Tessa," he said. "I know my expectations weren't high, but please tell me you've exceeded them."

He meant it as a joke. I knew that. Chuck and I had that kind of friendship. Our love language was insults and mockery, and normally, that wasn't an issue.

But I'd also thought Chuck and I had the kind of friendship where he wouldn't be an asshole about me panicking when trying to appease Loni.

"If you expected more than ten, then no, I didn't," I said, then held up my phone. "Do you want all the cheesy information about the people being auctioned off or should I go piss off Dinah by interrupting her training session?"

"*Ten*?!" he repeated, his voice going high.

"I did as many as I could," I said defensively. "If that's not good enough, then too fucking bad."

He frowned. "I meant that as a good thing. I expected maybe five. What is going on with you?"

"Do you want the info or not, Chuck? Or do you just want to know what dates I promised people?"

"The... dates?" he asked. "I was coming up with the dates."

"Yeah, but some of the people would only agree if they got to do specific things." I looked down at my phone. "Brenda McClane wants to do your painting lesson idea. Jia wants to do a tea tasting at her parents' shop in Chinatown. Uh... who else... Freesia said they wanted to bring the person who won to the opening of their next show, which I'm not sure if that's... like, it might not be a good enough date? I don't know. I have a bunch here."

Chuck stood as I was speaking, taking my phone without asking. "Does *anyone* need the dates I came up with?"

I shrugged. "Me, I guess. I didn't have time to think of anything. And I'm assuming you came up with one for yourself. Everyone else was excited to come up with their own ideas. Oh, and I told them CARE was paying for it all, so I hope that's true. If not... surprise. Anyway, if that's all, I'll go talk to Dinah and—"

"Wait a second," he said, pulling my phone out of my reach as I tried to take it back. "What is going on?"

"What do you mean, what's going on?" I asked.

"You're being kind of snappy."

I looked at him, unimpressed and suddenly very tired. "I'm being snappy? You and Dinah are both blaming me for Loni being unreasonable and pissed that I did the best I could at calming her down."

Chuck pressed his lips together for a moment before he sighed.

"Tessa Violetta Lane, I am very sorry," he said.

I blinked at him. "What?"

"I am very sorry," he repeated. "I was anxious and frustrated earlier. I took that out on you and that was entirely uncalled for."

"Oh."

He tried to smile. "I know this is Loni being Loni. You're right. I was not a very good friend to you just now. I just heard 'Hey Chuck, we have to do this absolutely insane thing with no preparation and no time' and I panicked."

"It's fine," I said gruffly. "It'll be fine. Thanks. I'm sorry, too."

"Don't be." He handed me my phone. "Do you super-hate me now?"

"A little."

"But like, in a good way, right?"

I rolled my eyes. "In the best way. I forgive you."

Chuck smiled and put his arm around my shoulder. "Alright. So we have the people. We have the dates. We have the auctioneer... you know, I think we just might have pulled this off."

Nine

DINAH, OVERACHIEVING PERFECTIONIST THAT she was, actually seemed to know what she was doing up there.

"Alright, let's get ready to bid!" she declared from the platform in the center of the auditorium, where she'd just finished explaining how the auction would work. The people in the planetarium cheered loudly. Chuck and I clapped along from where we were sitting in the front row with the other people who had volunteered to be auctioned off.

"First up," Dinah said into the microphone as she turned towards us. "Folks, you may know him as the pride and joy of the CARE offices. That's right, it's Mr. Chuck David!"

"Oh my God," Chuck muttered, his face flushing as Dinah beckoned him up.

"Go get 'em, tiger," I replied.

"Many of you already know Chuck," Dinah continued as he walked up onto the platform to join her. "He's our office administrator and everyone knows CARE wouldn't be able to run without him, unlike some people!"

She meant me. I rolled my eyes.

"Chuck here loves travelling and speaks nearly fluent Japanese from his many trips to visit his extended family in Osaka. He also—" She looked at her phone, which had the notes I'd sent her on each person, and frowned. "—likes to take long walks to, um, nowhere."

Chuck shrugged. "I'm kinda lazy," he said, loud enough that most people could hear him without the mic. Dinah laughed along with the audience.

"Alright," she said. "And Chuck's favourite candy is... well, there's a list here, but let's just assume it says everything." She paused for more laughter. "So, do you think you're sugary enough to satisfy Chuck's sweet tooth? You can find out when Chuck takes you on a date to his favourite candy store so you can stock up on treats before a private picnic in Stanley Park. We'll go ahead and get the bidding started at—"

And then she froze.

"Dinah?" Chuck whispered.

She looked at him, her eyes wide with panic. "What do we start the bidding at?"

Unfortunately, she had forgotten to move the microphone away from her face, so her voice echoed around the semi-quiet room. An awkward chuckle rippled through the audience and Chuck shrugged uncomfortably.

"Well," he said. "We all know I'm priceless."

The audience laughed again and Chuck looked at me desperately.

"It was a hundred dollars, Dinah," I called. "You wanted to start at one hundred, remember?"

I thought it was a nice way of making it seem like she'd forgotten rather than us not having our shit together. And Dinah shot me a less nasty look than usual, so I figured she agreed, then turned back to the audience.

"Alright," she said. "Bidding starts at a steal of a deal for this one-of-a-kind date: one hundred dollars! Do I have a bid for a hundred dollars?"

I couldn't say how Chuck felt as the room went quiet, but I knew how I felt.

Terrified. Nervous. Horrified at the prospect of my best friend standing up there in a room full of people with no one bidding on him.

I hadn't even *thought* of that prospect, but now that I was sitting there, I couldn't stop. What if no one bid? What if all the people I asked to do this had to stand up there, taking hit after hit to their self-esteem? And some of the people were donors or stakeholders or other people who could get offended and—

And then six hands went up in the air.

"Alright!" Dinah said. "I've got a hundred dollars, do I have one fifty? Oh, we've got one fifty, thank you. Two hundred? Two… yep, you have it! Two hundred dollars is the current bid, can we get three? Three hundred dollars—"

"Three-fifty," someone called.

"Thank you, four hundred, do we have—perfect, we're at four-hundred."

"Four-fifty," said another voice.

That voice made Chuck whirl around, so of course, I had to, too. Charles was standing there, his hand in the air.

"Babe," Chuck said, half-laughing. "No. You don't have to pay for a date with me."

"I want to," Charles said.

I don't know if Chuck's eyes were sparkling or glistening, but light seemed to reflect off them as he blinked rapidly.

"You can have me for free anytime, Charles," he said.

"Yeah, but that doesn't mean you're not worth everything I can afford," Charles replied, then glanced nervously at the other person who had been bidding on Chuck. "Which is, um, not much more, and I'm really sorry."

Dinah looked from Chuck to Charles to the other person. "So, we're at four-fifty… Do I have five hundred for Chuck here?"

"Like I'm *gonna* bid after that sweet little exchange," the person said, laughing. "I'm out."

"Alright," Dinah said. "Four-fifty going once, going twice... sold to Chuck's boyfriend."

She'd barely finished speaking when Chuck jumped off the platform and beelined for Charles. As he kissed him, the audience let out one of those collective "awws." When they parted, they should've put Charles up on the ceiling of the planetarium dome, because that man was *definitely* over the moon.

The auction was riveting, honestly. It was exciting. The audience laughed and chattered, heckling each other as Dinah bounced back and forth between bidders. There was a relaxed sort of electricity in the room, something joyful and fun and completely unexpected. Even the people who didn't bid were having a good time, waiting to see who won each date.

Brenda McClane went for six hundred dollars. Unsurprisingly, Jia went for the most—a cool eleven hundred, though it was to a group of three guys who seemed to have pooled their money together. Even more unsurprisingly, Austin was one of those three guys, and he looked a lot more cheerful after Dinah declared them the winners of the auction. And Freesia, whose art show date went back and forth until it sold for nine hundred dollars, so I guess it was a good date after all.

And then, last and least, it was my turn.

"Now, if you've spent all your money tonight, not to worry," Dinah said after waving me onto the platform. I blinked, not realizing how bright the lights were, and glanced around. "We have a very special deal for our last date of the night."

I raised my eyebrows. I hadn't known I was going to be a sale item. Trying to look amused, I looked over at Chuck, who was sitting with Charles in the front row. He was watching Dinah, a deliberately blank expression on his face.

"Meet Tessa," Dinah continued. "She's CARE's community outreach coordinator. No one's exactly sure what she does around the office, but she enjoys short walks to Starbucks and painting. Oh, because she's an artist. So, since everyone's spent out, let's start bidding for an evening out for drinks with Tessa at a reasonable twenty-five dollars."

I think she regretted that.

Part of it likely had to do with the awkward silence in the audience while everyone tried to figure out if it was a joke or not.

And she was probably at least a little embarrassed at the semi-disgusted look Chuck and a few others shot her way, if the sudden redness of her cheeks was any indication.

And maybe part of it had to do with the fact that I laughed, which meant she knew right away that it hadn't gotten to me in the way she'd hoped, especially once the audience started to chuckle along.

But mostly, I think she regretted it when the first hand went up and shot down her little insult.

Because that's when I regretted it, too.

"Five hundred," a familiar voice said, and I felt like the world had slammed on its brakes and lurched to a stop, sending my insides spinning and whirling through my body.

I would have taken almost anyone else. I knew better than to hope for Finn and Julie because they weren't there, but still. A complete stranger could have bid. Riley "The Nice Guy" Jordan would have been preferable.

But no. It had to be my fucking caterpillar of an ex-husband.

Ten

BRAD WAS STANDING AT the back of the planetarium.

Between the lights and the distance, if I hadn't known who it was, I would've glanced right past him. Someone who walked in late and stayed near the back instead of interrupting people to get into a seat.

But once he bid, well.

His hand went up and Dinah's eyes snapped towards him. While my stomach felt like it was going to fall out of my ass, I looked at Chuck, who had a satisfied smirk on his face because he had no idea who was bidding and probably thought someone was just sticking it to Dinah.

At least, until he saw the look of horror on my face and realized something was very, very wrong.

I don't know why I looked at him. It wasn't like there was anything he could do. I mean, if I couldn't spare the five hundred dollars to bid on myself, there was no way Chuck could, either.

Besides, it wasn't going to stop at five hundred dollars.

I knew the kind of money Brad made.

"Five hundred," Dinah said, trying not to sound as incredulous as she looked. "Alright. I have five hundred. Do we have, um, five-fifty? Or maybe five-twenty-five if—"

"Five-fifty," called out a loud, clear voice from the other side of the room.

I didn't recognize the voice and wasn't entirely sure where it came from. I looked at Dinah, trying not to squint as I watched where she was turning to, but she'd barely moved when Brad's hand shot up again.

"Six hundred," he said.

"Six-fifty," the mystery person replied.

"A thousand," Brad snapped, and a ripple of chatter spread throughout the room.

"A thousand," Dinah repeated, her voice high-pitched. "We have a one-thousand dollar bid folks, now just... just wait one second here, please, while we see who the other bidder is and make sure these are real, legitimate bids. I mean, as much as we all... *adore* Tessa, this person has to be at least a little crazy..."

I figured it out long before Dinah trekked across the room to see who it was. All it took was that horrendous, cackling honk of a laugh echoing through the auditorium.

Claire.

My eyes finally focused on her sitting in a section to my left, one leg folded over the other and her scotch glass in one hand. She was looking at me, a roguish look on her face, then lifted her glass to her lips and took a casual sip as Dinah walked up to her.

"Well, there you are," Dinah said. "You seem... real. So, bidding is currently at one-thousand, can we go up to eleven-hundred or—"

"Fifteen hundred," Claire said, her voice ringing through the planetarium.

"Two grand," Brad said immediately.

"Twenty-five hundred," Claire said, lifting her drink again.

"Thirty-five hundred," said Brad.

Dinah's head was swivelling back and forth, looking like a wide-eyed bobble head. She didn't speak, even as Claire paused to sip her scotch before bidding again.

"Four thousand dollars," she said.

My stomach rolled with nausea as I looked over at Brad. There was a pinched look on his face. It wasn't a look I knew well, but I did know it.

He didn't wear that expression often because it meant he was losing. And Brad did *not* like to lose. When we were going through the divorce, he'd been certain I would change my mind. Completely certain. But after every meeting, every round of paperwork, every single time I insisted things were irreconcilable and that I would never, ever, *ever* love him again, it was only on the day everything was completely finalized that I saw him make that face.

Because he'd lost.

And he couldn't *believe* he'd lost.

God, I loved seeing him look like that. That grouchy, poor sportsmanlike sneer that twisted his lips was just phenomenal. Honestly, seeing him miserable like that almost turned me on a little.

Not for him, obviously. Just in general.

"I've got four thousand," Dinah said in disbelief. "Four thousand for Tessa, the community outreach coordinator, to take you out for *drinks*. At a normal bar. Do we have another bid?" She waited, then raised her eyebrows. "Alright, four thousand, going once, twice—"

"Five grand," Brad said, and a cheer went through the audience.

I couldn't blame them. We were raising money for charity. It probably looked amazing from the outside. No one else there knew I was being bid on by an eccentric stranger who was apparently dropping mad amounts of money just to annoy someone she couldn't even see on the other side of the room. And also by my ex-husband, who was a complete fuckwit of a caterpillar.

They just knew that someone said they'd pay five thousand dollars for me, and five thousand was a big number.

Not the biggest, though.

"Ten thousand," Claire said as though it was pocket change.

Dinah's mouth dropped. "Are... are you sure?"

The casual expression on Claire's face disappeared and she regarded Dinah with a stony expression.

"Ten. Thousand," she repeated.

Dinah looked back at me like I knew what the fuck was going on, then over to where Brad was standing.

"Alright, ten thousand," she said. "Ten thousand is the current bid for... for Tessa. Do we have another bid? Eleven thousand? Eleven freaking thousand dollars?"

She was gazing at Brad, but Brad wasn't looking at her. He was too busy staring at me, and I was watching that pinched look on his face as I held my breath, throwing as many telepathic signals at him to just fucking *stop*. That even if he won the bid, I wasn't going to go on a date with him. That I would refuse and I didn't care if he threw a fit or if it cost me my job or *what*.

He looked at me, then tore his eyes away to look at Dinah. I watched his throat flex as he swallowed, as he considered it, as he opened his mouth...

And then shook his head.

"Alright," Dinah said, turning back to Claire. "Tessa goes to the lady in the suit for ten thousand dollars." It was almost like she was going to choke on the amount as she looked back at me. "Wonder what kind of date it's gonna be for that amount of money."

It was meant to be another dig, but no one seemed to hear her over the excited cheering and applause in the room.

Eleven

"Who is she?" Brad demanded.

"What are you doing here?" I shot back.

He ignored me. "Who is she and why is she paying so much for you?"

I ignored him. "What the fuck are you doing here?"

"Who *is* she, Tessa?"

This conversation was going nowhere.

I should have known it wouldn't. As soon as Dinah told all the winning bidders where they could make their payments and declared the auction over, Chuck had jumped out of his seat and rushed towards me. But I'd blown past him, my eyes focused on one thing and one thing only.

"Why are you here?" I'd hissed as soon as I reached Brad.

"Hey, beauti—*oof*," he'd said, mainly because I'd grabbed his arm and started half frog-marching, half pushing him out of the planetarium, not letting go until we'd reached the hallway near the empty classroom.

Which is where the cyclical conversation had started.

"Who is she?"

"Why are you here?"

"How do you know her?"

"What the fuck were you thinking, showing up like this?"

"Tell me who that woman was."

"I'm not saying a fucking word about anything until you tell me what the actual fuckity fuck you're doing at my event!" I snapped.

Brad opened his mouth, probably to ask me yet again who Claire was, but finally seemed to realize he was a goddamn moron and I was more stubborn than he was. Drawing in a deep breath, he let it out, clenching then loosening his jaw as he tried to regain some semblance of restraint.

"I am here to support you," he said calmly.

"Support me," I repeated. "*Support* me?!"

"Of course. This is your biggest work event of the year and you're my—"

"Nothing."

He sighed. "Tessa, to me, you'll always be—"

"Nothing," I said. "I am your nothing. I am nothing to you. And you? You are even less than that to me."

Maybe I was too vitriolic towards Brad.

Not that I thought I should be nicer to him or something. But because he was so used to it that the insult didn't phase him. He just put on that practiced expression of slight sadness mixed with pity blended with martyred longing in his green eyes.

"You will never be nothing to me," he said. "I will always care about you."

He was so full of shit.

"If that were true, you'd leave me the fuck alone," I said.

"I want to be part of your life."

"And I don't want that." I folded my arms. "I don't want you. I won't ever want you. Accept it or don't, but stay the fuck out of my life, Brad."

He took another steadying breath, ignoring my anger yet again. "Regardless, I also came because we need to talk after what happened in Burnsley."

"And you thought you should come here instead of, I don't know, calling me? Emailing me? Sending a goddamn telegram?"

"You've been ignoring my calls for over a month, Tess."

"Don't be stupid. I've been ignoring your calls a lot longer than that."

He almost laughed. I saw the hint of it, the way his mouth twitched, and that familiar warm feeling at making someone laugh threatened to flare up in my chest. As soon as it did, I suppressed it, reminding the parts of my body that didn't seem to have any fucking brainpower that we *hated* Brad.

We didn't want to make him laugh.

"Right," he said. "But it doesn't leave me a lot of options to reach you when we need to talk about something."

I stared at him. "What do you think we need to talk about?"

"All of it." His eyebrows crinkled into a pained expression. "I know you hate me, Tessa, but if that asshole Zain tells people—"

"He won't."

"You don't know that."

He was trying to manipulate doubt into me. I knew that. But the joke was on him, since I'd already put something in place to take care of that doubt, and it was costing me my entire weekend.

"I have the situation handled," I said. "Which you damn well know, because if I didn't, I would have picked up one of your calls to tell you what to do. So why are you really here, Brad?"

"I told you, I—"

"I know when you're lying. You spent our entire marriage doing it, remember? So tell me why you're here when I don't recall inviting you."

"You didn't. But your mom called a few days ago."

Yet again, my mom was behind all of this. I was going to lose it on her. Not in real life, of course. The in-my-head version of me was a lot braver and more outspoken than the real-life version of me, who was definitely a coward who caved to the particular brand of familial guilt my mom used each and every time.

But in my head, I was screaming at my mom.

"Why the hell did she call you?" I asked. "And more importantly, why did you pick up?"

"Because she thinks I'm being a terrible husband."

I wasn't sure which question that was the answer to, but it didn't matter, since it sort of answered both. "Well, that's not true. You *were* a terrible husband. But now you're a terrible ex-husband."

Hurt flashed across Brad's face. "I was a good husband."

The statement was so hilarious I couldn't even laugh. "You think so?"

"I was," he said. "Except for, you know…"

"All the cheating and lying and manipulation?"

"I didn't manipulate you. But I was good in other ways, Tess. Don't pretend like I had no good qualities at all."

"I'm not pretending," I said. "Every time I see you, I forget another one of your good qualities. It's not my fault you're such an asshole."

"Yeah, well, that doesn't matter, does it?" he said irritably. "Because your family thinks I'm good. And they think I'm your husband. And that means when your mom gets concerned that I'm not around enough after we said I wouldn't be travelling as much, she calls me because she thinks I'm going to let you down by not showing up at your event."

"I mean, technically, she's right," I said. "Your existence in general is a giant let down, so by association, you'd let me down whether you showed up or not."

He ignored me. "I had to tell her I'd be here. She went on and on about how you were worried and upset that I wasn't going to make it."

"You know as well as I do she made that up."

"Come on, Tess." Brad ran a hand through his hair. "Look at this logically. We've got your brother's wedding in a few months, right? Not to mention, like, his bachelor party and stuff. He already said he wants me there and unless we come up with a *really* good excuse, I'm gonna have to go. So we should probably do some stuff together. Keep in touch. Make sure we can be more convincing about—"

"You're using my brother's wedding as an excuse to harass me," I said.

"No, I'm trying to help you. What's gonna happen if someone asks me how this event was and I can't even tell them the theme?"

"You wouldn't be alone," I muttered. "None of us know what the theme is anymore."

"Okay, the location," he said. "The activities that happened. I didn't know there was going to be a date auction. That wasn't on the ads or anything. So I'm being—"

"Pushy. You're being pushy," I said. "You're inserting yourself into my life and making me despise you even more, which is honestly impressive. Impressive, but not surprising. You know why? Because every time I think it's not possible to hate you any more than I already do, you prove me wrong."

He lifted his hands in exasperation. "How am I supposed to prove I've changed when you won't give me a chance?"

I laughed. I couldn't help it. The fucking nerve of the man was equal parts hilarious and horrifying.

"I don't want you to prove you've changed," I said. "And you're delusional for thinking you have. You literally fucked another woman while you were pretending to be my husband a month ago and ruined everything. You couldn't keep it in your pants for *three fucking days*. You don't deserve a chance. You never *have*. I don't want you and I don't need you."

He stared at me, then nodded slowly. "So you are seeing someone else, then."

"What?"

"Is it the woman? The one who bid on you?"

"That's none of your—"

"Who is she, Tessa?" he demanded. "Just *tell* me if you're seeing someone."

And sure, I could've just answered. I wasn't seeing anyone. But he wouldn't have believed that. And he wouldn't have believed me if I said I didn't know Claire, either.

Which was fair. I doubt anyone would have believed that.

"I'm going to say this one more time," I said. "Slowly, so you can process it in that itsy bitsy little brain of yours, okay? It is. None. Of. Your. Business."

"It *is* my business. Especially when I was putting my money on the line."

"You shouldn't have been doing that in the first place!" I snapped. "You should've known I didn't want that. Why in the fuck would I *want* to go on a date with you? What makes you think I'd *ever* agree to that?"

He stared at me, then chuckled as something dark crossed his face. "So it was rigged."

"*What*?!"

"It was rigged. She's not gonna pay, is she? You got her to bid on you so you didn't have to give me *one* date. You hate me that much?"

"Are you... are you for real?" I asked. "I didn't even know you were *here*. The first time I saw you was when you put your fucking hand up during the auction. I was standing on a stage in front of a ton of people. How the fuck could I have arranged that?"

"Yes, and who said I wasn't going to pay?"

The voice made both of us jump. In unison, we turned our heads as Claire wandered nonchalantly towards us like my knight in a shining navy-blue suit for the second time that day.

Seriously. She looked like a fucking superhero to me just then. I hadn't realized earlier how tall she was, but she was practically the same height as Brad. While her face had delicate features and she had a slim, willowy frame, the way she held her shoulders back and her chin up made her look like she could take on the world and win without even breaking a sweat.

Shooting a casual smile at Brad, she extended her hand.

"Hi," she said. "I'm Claire. And you're the guy who lost the bid."

Brad didn't shake her hand because he was an unsportsmanlike loser. "I didn't lose if you're not paying. You cheated."

Somehow, the irony of Brad being upset that someone else might be cheating was lost on him, as was the fact that he sounded like a whiny twelve-year-old instead of a man of forty. I raised my eyebrows at him, but he didn't notice, too busy glowering at Claire.

Claire, on the other hand, simply smiled. "Well, you're technically right about part of that."

Brad made a scoffing, offended noise. "See? I fucking knew it. This whole goddamn thing was rigged."

Claire ignored him as she dug into that mysterious pocket of hers and withdrew a slip of paper, then held it out to him.

"I said *technically*," she said. "I'm not paying at the moment. Because I've already paid for it."

Brad's eyes flicked down to the piece of paper, then back up to her. After a moment, he grabbed the receipt and studied it, his jaw clenched so tightly that his cheek was twitching.

"Does it meet your scrutiny, Mr...?"

"Schubert," I said.

"Mr. Schubert?" she finished.

"It doesn't even have your name on it," he said. "How—"

"I submit my charitable donations through my business accounts," she said, then plucked the paper out of Brad's hands. "Which means I need that back, please. Gotta keep the paper trail for tax purposes. You know how it is." Then, she turned to me and extended her elbow to me. "And I'd like to cash in on my date now, Tessa darling. Let's blow this banana stand, yeah?"

For as hyena-like as her cackling bark of a laugh was, the way Claire said my name had an almost lyrical roundness to it. I smiled and took her arm, not even looking at Brad as we turned to walk back to the hall.

"Thank you," I whispered when the din of voices from the people at the gala could cover my words.

"It was nothing," she said. "I had a feeling you didn't like that guy."

I suppressed a laugh. "That's putting it lightly."

She tightened her grip on my arm. "So, for real. Can we go get that drink now?"

I nodded. "Just let me go tell my coworker I'm leaving and get my jacket."

"I'll be waiting."

I left her near the exit, walking briskly into the planetarium to find Chuck, who was standing with a group of donors. The moment he saw me, he turned and rushed away from them without even saying a word.

"It was him, wasn't it?" he asked as soon as he reached me. "It was Brad."

I nodded.

"The *fucker*," he spat. "And the... the woman?"

"I... it's a long story. I swear to God, I'll tell you everything at work tomorrow, but she wants me to go on the date with her now." I glanced around the room, but Dinah wasn't there anymore. "I figured that'd be okay with how much she donated."

"Yeah, for sure," Chuck said. "I'll tell Dinah where to stick it if she has a problem. But Tess..." He took my hand intently. "I would have bid twenty thousand on you if I could have, okay? It was *killing* me that I couldn't do anything to help."

I didn't deserve Chuck. Sure, we might have fought sometimes, but an asshole like me didn't deserve a friend as amazing as him. I twisted my wrist, squeezing his hand three times.

"Don't let it bother you," I said. "Really. I would've survived."

"You're sure you're okay?"

"I am. I really have to go, though." I let go of his hand, then glanced at the group of donors Chuck had left, where Charles was still standing somewhat awkwardly. "You go have a fun romantic night with that guy who bought a date with you. He seemed pretty cute."

The apples of Chuck's cheeks rounded and stained red as he fought back a smile. "When I tell you that man is getting the most premium fellatio tonight... Like, the most intense, elite, in-depth, and thorough blowjob I've *ever* given..."

After saying goodbye to Chuck and promising him one more time that I'd be okay, I backtracked to the empty classroom to get my jacket. I grabbed it and turned to leave, then hesitated.

There was no chance Finn and Julie were going to show up at that point. I knew that. But I just...

I don't know.

I don't know what I thought I was going to send them. Maybe a worried message asking if they were okay. Or an angry one, asking why they didn't show up when they said they would. Or a bitchy one, telling them I was going to "hang out" with someone else that night because they hadn't bothered coming.

It could have been anything. Or it could have been nothing. I had no answer for what I was thinking when I pulled out my phone, opened MatchMi, and clicked on the message thread I had with them.

But as it turned out, it didn't matter.

The most recent message was mine:

TessTheUnicorn

> Hey, I've got a work emergency happening. Not sure if you're here yet or not but if you are, let me know? Or come find me. I'll be the one running around frantically.

Below that, the text box was greyed out and a system message was typed in bold over it:

> ***User account does not exist. You can no longer reply to this thread.***

Which was fine.

It wasn't like we were serious.

It didn't matter.

I repeated that as many times as I needed to for the stinging sensation in my eyes to go away, then took a deep breath, shrugged my jacket on, and went to meet the woman who thought I was worth something.

Part 3

Confession: You can't rebound if there was nothing to rebound from in the first place.

Twelve

"So you're loaded, eh?" I asked.

Claire let out one of her hair-raising laughs. "I get by."

It took everything in me not to gape at her. "You call *this* getting by?"

We were at The Place. I'd never heard of The Place. The only people who seemed to know about The Place were people who had been to The Place before, because The Place didn't have a sign. Or a street front. And it was located in a building that looked more like a warehouse than any sort of nightclub.

But that's what The Place was. It was the swankiest, most expensive, most exclusive bar I'd ever seen in my entire life. When we pulled up, there was a lineup on the street, but I couldn't have said where the entrance was. It was only when Claire saw me staring at the people with a bewildered expression that she pointed it out: a black door on the black wall, tucked behind some trailing ivy and barely visible except for when a bouncer occasionally opened it and selected someone to invite in.

"It's not first-come, first-served," Claire explained.

"How long do you think we'll be waiting?" I asked.

She just smiled.

Because we didn't wait in line. Oh, no. Claire's driver—because of course this mystery woman had a fucking *driver*—pulled into the alley in the back and up to an entrance that was even more VIP than the front entrance. It was VVIP. Or maybe VVVVVIP. Or I guess it could be VIF, as in Very Important Fae. She was so unlike anyone I'd met before that I still wasn't entirely sure Claire and I were the same species.

The VIF door opened as Claire and I walked up. A short woman dressed in a white halter-top jumpsuit with bright red hair stood there, smiling politely.

"Hello, ladies," she said in a soft, smooth voice. "Welcome to The Place. It's so good to see you again, Claire."

"And you," Claire said. "The usual, please?"

The short woman inhaled just sharply enough that I noticed.

"Well, as it stands, the suite is booked tonight," she said. "I am so incredibly sorry for the inconvenience."

The look on her face remained professional, but her shoulders tensed as she braced herself to be yelled at. But Claire smiled.

"Not a problem," she said. "It's going to be two of us. If you've got a private table, that will be perfectly fine."

The short woman nodded, her shoulders relaxing. "Please, follow me."

I should have probably expected something other than what I pictured. Because what I pictured was something like my usual booth at Bar One, which wasn't exactly a *private* table but was kind of tucked out of the way. What I hadn't pictured was a small room raised above the main bar area and filled mostly by a u-shaped booth with a table in the middle. On one side of the booth was a wall with an abstract colour-block painting, and on the other was a curtain where the servers came and went to get our orders of drinks that didn't have prices next to them on the menu.

Which didn't end up being an issue, because Claire didn't look at the menu. Nor did she place an order. Immediately after we sat down and the hostess left, a server came in with a bottle of scotch and a bucket of ice.

"The usual, Claire?" he asked. She nodded and he turned to me. "Would you like something different, miss?"

I shook my head and he conjured up two glasses, added a crystal-clear ice cube from the bucket to each of them, then poured us each a drink and left. He took the bottle with him, which was unfortunate because oh *hell* could I have used more than one drink.

But I guess they'd come back for that.

The reason the area was called a private table rather than a private room was because the area across from us wasn't a wall. There was a railing there, but it looked out over the rest of the bar where the peasants who couldn't get a private table were drinking, dancing, and lounging around. Black lights lit most of the space, adding to the exclusive, private vibe. Music throbbed through the darkness, beams of light flashing and flaring in time to it, shooting splashes of green and blue and purple across the bar. Everything dripped with luxury and every person who worked there seemed to know Claire and exactly what she'd want at any given moment.

So yeah, I figured she was doing a touch more than "getting by."

"Well, *I* get by," Claire said in response to my incredulous remark. "My parents, on the other hand, may have legitimate cannibalism insurance in case anyone decides to follow through on that whole 'eat the rich' thing."

"And what do your parents do?" I asked.

"They get by."

I couldn't help but laugh, which made Claire smile as she lifted her scotch to her lips and sipped it. I mirrored her action, then put my glass down firmly.

"Look, you just took me out to a hidden nightclub after dropping ten grand to go on a date with a woman whose name you didn't even know," I said. "So I think it's fair for me to be curious why."

She brushed her long brown hair back, hooking it over one shoulder. "You just kinda looked like you'd rather drink paint than go on a date with whoever that guy was."

I twisted my glass of scotch on the table before lifting it to take a sip. "I mean… as long as it wasn't lead paint, probably, yeah."

"Don't feel like you owe me an answer or anything just because I paid for the date, but if you're willing to tell me… who was he?" she asked.

It was sweet of her to make sure I was comfortable, but seeing as she wasn't part of my family, I had no reason to keep it a secret from her. "My ex-husband."

"Blegh," she said, her tongue sticking out as she fake-gagged. "Dodged a bullet with that one?"

"I mean, sure," I said. "If by 'dodged' you mean I got hit with the bullet, then clung to life because I'm a stubborn asshole."

"Mmm," she said. "I love a good stubborn asshole. Makes it worth it when they relax and open up so you can get your fingers all up in there."

I laughed. "You're dirty."

"You like it."

I couldn't argue that, so I didn't.

"So," she said after a moment. "He's an ex because…?"

"Oh, you know. The usual reasons." I sipped my scotch. "He's a liar. A cheater. And he was too old for me at the time."

Claire frowned, tilting her head to the side. "He didn't seem… I mean, how old is he?"

"Forty," I said.

She curled her lips in, pressing them together. "Mmm. I might be too old for you, then."

"I mean, I doubt it. I'm thirty. We got married when I was twenty-two. You do the math."

She let out a low whistle. "Oh. Yes, that is very different. And I'm only thirty-five, so… bonus."

"Really?" I raised an eyebrow. "I wouldn't have guessed that."

"I know. I pass for at least fifty."

"No, I mean—"

But she started laughing and shook her head. "It's okay. I've gotten that my whole life. I still get ID'ed every now and then, actually."

"Really?"

She nodded. "But enough about me. What about—"

"Oh, hell no," I said, laughing. "You gave me *one* tidbit of information."

She tried to look innocent, which succeeded because she had big doe-eyes and long eyelashes, and also failed because she had a devilishly wicked smile. "I mean, that's one more tidbit than you originally had."

"Come on," I said. "Give me something here, Claire. At least try to convince me you're not a faerie princess trying to trick me into the faerie realm. Or hunt me for sport in a rich person tournament or something."

She contemplated me before glancing towards the railing and out over the bar. For a moment, she was quiet, but when she looked back at me, she leaned in and wetted her lips.

"Okay," she said, her voice just loud enough to hear over the thumping music. "Real talk?"

"Yeah," I said. "Of course."

Her eyebrows pinched together. "Promise not to freak out first."

She was so serious that I had to chuckle, albeit awkwardly. "Jesus. This got intense. Are you a secret agent or an assassin or something?"

"Oh," she said, sitting back a bit. "No. Is that disappointing?"

I shrugged. "I mean, a little. You're hot enough to be a sexy assassin, but then you've got the secret agent suit going on, so..."

The corners of her eyes crinkled. "Sorry. It's nowhere near as cool as that. Want another guess?"

"Hmm." I stared into her eyes, thinking. "Are you a politician's kid?"

"Slightly better than that."

"Oh," I said. "You're the child of an oil tycoon who rebels by supporting environmental charities."

She surprised both of us with one of her cackles. "You're close, actually."

"Really?"

She nodded. "Want another guess?"

I thought for a moment, then shook my head. "I don't know."

"Okay." She took a breath, then let it out. "Have you ever heard of Paige Martelle?"

It was my turn to surprise us with a laugh. "Of *course*. That's Loni's nemesis. Like, legitimately the whole reason Loni started CARE was because Paige Martelle started ArtCycle and this is apparently how rich people fight or something? She's completely convinced that Paige tried to sabotage the Recycl-Ball by booking the same venue for a golf tournament thing last month."

"Well, that's true, actually," Claire said.

My laugh faded. "How do you know?"

"She's my sister."

"Oh," I said. Then, as the words sank in: "Wait, she's—"

"You said you wouldn't freak out," Claire said.

"I said no such thing," I replied. "You're... you're Claire *Martelle*? Like, Martelle-Martelle? Like the makeup brand Martelle?"

Claire's nose scrunched as she grimaced and nodded.

Fuck. Loni was going to fire my ass so fast. I let out a huge huff of breath and took a long sip of my scotch.

"So... you're trying to sabotage CARE?" I asked.

She gave me a half-amused, half-exasperated look. "Darling. Since you haven't mentioned it enough times, remind me *how* much I just donated to CARE?"

Which was a good point.

"Why, then?" I asked.

She shrugged. "You got the whole 'nemesis' thing right about Loni and Paige. Literally the only person in the world Paige hates more than me is Loni."

I looked at her suspiciously. "Paige doesn't like you?"

"Have you seen Paige? She's a princess. I'm the lesbian little sister who embarrasses the shit out of her." She smirked and sipped her scotch. "She's been talking about the CARE gala for ages. Honestly, Tessa, she was trying *so* hard to fuck it up. Bribed this country club to let her host an event there and everything, just because she knew it would annoy Loni. So knowing the Recycl-Ball was a success anyway? It'll drive her fucking *nuts*."

"You're diabolical," I said.

"My parents decided to have a second kid so their first one would have someone to keep her busy. I'm just doing what I was born to do."

There was something sad in her tone and in the way her jaw set as she looked out over The Place, splashes of light crossing her pale white skin. I waited for a moment, but she didn't seem to want to talk about whatever it was.

"Is that why you took off when Loni came up to me at the bar?" I asked.

Claire blinked and turned to me, the gloom disappearing in an instant as she slipped back into the mischievous happiness that seemed to be her signature. "Yeah. Trust me, it almost physically pained me to walk away from you, but I couldn't risk it. I don't think I've ever met Loni in person before, but I didn't want to risk getting kicked out on the off-chance she's got files of all Paige's known contacts."

"I doubt it," I said. "That would require Loni knowing how to use a computer, so you're safe."

She tapped a finger against her cheek. "Can never be too careful. But I am sorry for ditching you like that."

Nodding, I processed what she said as I took my turn looking over the club. I couldn't see much detail, just the abstraction of bodies swaying and morphing, flashes of glowing white under the black lights shifting like ghosts to the beat of the music. At the bar, there were people who deemed themselves too cool for The Place, slumping and leaning and scoffing at the sight of people daring to enjoy themselves in a place they were meant to enjoy themselves.

"You don't think because you spent ten grand on me for my boss's shitty charity that I'm going to hook up with you, do you?" I asked bluntly.

The spark of laughter flared in Claire's eye seconds before she let out a soft chuckle, which was much more sensual than her boisterous cackle-bark. "At the risk of sounding like someone you would guillotine in eighteenth century France, ten grand isn't *that* much to me."

"Oof. You're right. Off with your head. More for the insult than anything."

Claire's lips twisted in amusement. "Insult? We both know I would've kept bidding until that asshole ex of yours gave up. Just like we both know you were going to hook up with me for free."

I might not have actually known the first part of that, but she was right about the second part. Not that I was going to admit it. I mean, I had to at least *try* to play hard to get. "You seem pretty confident about that."

"I am. Wanna know why?"

"Why?"

"Well—" Claire took a lingering sip of scotch, then put the glass on the table before shifting so she could put her arm up on the back of the booth bench and lean in closer to me. "Remember how you keep thinking I'm some kind of faerie?"

"Are you saying you are?"

She shook her head. "But I do have magical powers."

"Do you now?" I asked, amused.

"Yep. And one of them is that I can always tell when a woman's been thinking about getting in my pants."

"And how can you tell that?"

"It's a neat little trick," she said, her voice just quiet enough that it pulled me forward so I could better hear her. As I did, she slipped the hand that wasn't around my shoulder onto my knee, then began dragging it up the top of my thigh. "See, it starts with me putting my hand down her pants."

I fought back a laugh. "Oh, how clever. And then what?"

She met my gaze, her face about eight inches from mine and her eyes wide with a playful wickedness as her fingers moved higher up my leg. "And then I put my fingers in her panties."

"And after that?"

Eight inches became six and Claire's tongue poked out, wetting her lips. "I push them down further and further until I can play with her—"

She lifted her hand slightly, then tapped her finger against my leg with each word

"—wet—"

Tap.

"—little—"

Tap.

"—pussy."

And then her entire hand slipped back onto my thigh, nearly at my groin. I glanced down at it and when I looked up, her face was just four inches from mine.

"Ah," I said, struggling to keep my voice steady. "So if she's wet, you know she's been thinking about fucking you?"

Claire raked her teeth along her lip. "Oh, not at all. I already knew she was."

"How?"

"Well, she let me stick my hand down her pants, so..."

I couldn't stop myself from laughing. She grinned and those four inches between our faces became three.

"So what do you think?" she asked. "Can I put my hand down your pants, Tessa?"

I glanced toward the railing that was the only thing separating us from the rest of the club. "You mean... here?"

"No one can see us," she said, her voice like water. "The front of the table is solid. But—" She took her hand off my thigh, the spot she'd been touching suddenly chilled as she moved her fingertips to my arm and began tracing up there instead. "—we don't have to. We could... you know."

"Know what?" I breathed.

Her eyes flicked down to my mouth. "We could just... kiss a little. If you want to."

And I wanted to.

I did.

I wanted nothing more than to feel her full pink lips against mine and let her put her hand down my pants with nothing but a booth and a railing and a dark club between us and the world. I wanted to fool around as neon lights flashed around us and the music thumped and the abstract construct of other people danced and partied and lived somewhere beyond our little world. I wanted to kiss her, to indulge, to forget about the stress of the evening seeing Brad and—

Well.

And that the couple who definitely weren't anything more than friends were assholes who had proved why I didn't ever let people get to the point of being my friend.

I wanted to kiss her. But I didn't want to be thinking about Finn and Julie while I did it.

So I hesitated.

Thirteen

CLAIRE MAY HAVE BEEN the kind of person who could spend more money in a year than I'd ever see in my life.

But she was also kind and decent and observant. So when I hesitated, she noticed immediately.

"Alternatively," she said, unwrapping her arm from around my shoulder. "You can tell me to back off and I will. I don't want to pressure you, Tessa."

"You aren't," I said quickly, all but reaching for her hand so I could put it back on my body. "I'm not. I just…" I stopped, then sighed and picked up my scotch. "I have these friends. They were supposed to come to the gala tonight. And instead, they ghosted me."

She wrinkled her nose. "You have shitty friends."

"Had," I said. "I know I'm worth more than being treated like that. It's just that they were, uh… well. They were a couple. That I was kind of… sleeping with."

Claire stared at me, her face blank as she processed what I said. Then slowly—incredibly slowly—she drew in a breath, her big eyes starting to go even rounder.

"Oh my God," she said.

Fuck. Of course she was going to be judgemental about it. "I'm not going to justify why I—"

"Are you my dream girl?"

I stopped short. "What?"

"Are you poly?" she asked, excitement threaded through her voice. "Or into, like, ethical non-monogamy in general?"

"I... I'm a unicorn?" I said, though it came out like a question.

"So... yes?" she asked, a grin spreading across her face.

"I guess so?" I replied. "I mean, sort of? I like... I like being with more than one person at a time. But I don't see people more than once. I just hook up with couples because they don't want anything else from me." I cleared my throat, almost apologetically. "I'm not looking for anything serious. At all."

Whatever I'd expected her response to be, it wasn't for her to moan.

But she moaned.

Like, actually moaned as though I'd put my fingers inside of her instead of telling her I wanted to fuck around.

And when she did, I finally understood why she had such a terrible bray of a laugh.

Because the universe had known that if it gave this woman too many sexy characteristics, the rest of us would implode. Her moan was as sensual as her laugh was horrid. It travelled through my body the same way, but with far different results; instead of giving me goosebumps, it gave me a warm, needy sensation somewhere in the pit of my stomach. Instead of making my hair raise, my nipples started to harden.

Instead of making me want to laugh, it made me want to drop to my knees in front of her.

"Jesus, Tessa," she said. "I can't tell you how much I want to fucking *kiss* you right now."

"What?" I asked, because what the fuck else was I supposed to say?

Claire's head snapped back down. There was so much excitement on her face that I could've sworn she was vibrating, but that could've just been the way the lights were flashing.

"I don't do monogamy," she said. "At all. And like, I'm not saying I'd never be with anyone long-term or seriously or whatever, but it's just so not a priority for me. I'd rather fuck around and have fun, which most people get very offended by."

"So if I tell you this is, like, a one-time thing...?"

She shrugged. "If that's what you want, darling. I'm into it. But we can still be friends after."

"That's what the couple said, too. I'd say it doesn't work out so well. I like being a unicorn. One-and-done. It's easier."

"Okay," she said. "I'm into being your rebound."

"I'm not rebounding. They were just friends. And now they're just a couple of assholes that I hooked up with a few times too many."

She lifted her hands defensively. "There's nothing wrong with rebounding, Tessa."

"That would imply there's something for me to rebound from." I grabbed my scotch and took a healthy sip. "And there wasn't. It was a dick move on their part, but I'm *not* rebounding."

She nodded and then, wisely or unwisely, chose not to press the issue. "Fair. But counterpoint: I am way cooler than your 'friends' are. This isn't my first time at the non-serious, non-exclusive rodeo. Also, I'm not a couple. Also-also, this is my preferred way of doing things."

"To just... fuck."

She nodded. "Look, you're everything I want in one perfect little package. I want to be your friend, but I don't *need* that. All I need right now is a sexy, curvy babe in leather pants and killer red lipstick to come all over my fingers. The rest can be figured out later. I've always said you think more clearly after getting fingerbanged in a nightclub."

I burst out laughing. "Is that so?"

"Maybe. Maybe not." Her eyes flicked down, focusing on my lips. "You might have to see for yourself."

And that was as good a reason as any.

So I kissed her. I leaned forward and I pressed my mouth to hers and I let the taste of scotch and lipstick and chaos on her breath push out any lingering thoughts I had of whoever those two assholes that ghosted me were.

"*Yesss*," Claire hissed in a warm exhale, then pulled me in closer.

It was one of the most delicious kisses I'd ever experienced. Her lips were soft and smooth and full, molding against mine like they were made to be there. Maybe I was imagining it or maybe not, but the slight burn of alcohol flavoured our kiss, a familiar hint of sweet smokiness and malt that tasted far better on her tongue than it did coming from my glass of scotch.

For a while, we explored each other's mouths, tasting and sucking and nipping at each other's lips. Claire lifted the hand that wasn't around my shoulder to my face, pushing my hair back before cupping my cheek and teasing her fingertips along my cheekbone. In return, I rested my hand on her thigh, feeling the warmth of her skin through the smooth texture of her suit pants as we made out in an unhurried feverishness, lingering in a timeless moment that existed just between us.

But that couldn't last forever. Not when she tasted so fucking good.

"Tessa," she murmured against my mouth.

"Mmm," I replied dreamily.

"Is it okay if I touch you?"

"Yes."

I felt her smile. "I don't have to if you don't want me to."

"Don't be stupid," I said, and her laugh vibrated against me. "I want you to."

"Good." She took her hand from my cheek and brought it down to my thigh, but immediately started sliding it up towards my stomach. "Tell me if there's anything you don't want me to do to you."

"I will." I shivered as her fingers started walking up the swell of my belly. "Is there anything you don't want?"

She moved her mouth from my lips to my jaw and began kissing my neck. "As much as I'd love to lay you out on this table and eat your pussy until you're adding a new set of vocals to this music, I'll probably limit us to the stuff that won't cost me a fortune to have expunged from our records."

I snorted. "That was such a rich person thing to say."

"Mmm. Gotta save up for the next time I need to drop ten grand on you."

"There doesn't need to be a next time. There didn't even need to be a this time."

A sudden jolt of pain surprised me. Well, not pain. Not really. But I wasn't expecting the feel of her teeth sinking into the tender skin at the base of my neck.

Not expecting, but also not complaining.

"It was a joke, darling," she said. "Now, can I touch your tits or not?"

"Only if I can touch yours back," I said, then laughed as she grabbed my hand and unceremoniously plunked it on her left breast before setting to work on my breasts.

We kept our hands over our clothes at first. Like, for the first eighteen seconds, maybe. I don't know what it was—the music, maybe, the way it thundered around us, or the darkness that wasn't really darkness, or the lights, or the intoxicating taste of her lips—but it was like something tipped. Suddenly kisses weren't enough; suddenly fingertips being feathered along skin were insufficient.

I needed more, and so did she.

She had the advantage. A quick tug of my shirt loosened it from where it was tucked in, and then her hand was leaving a trail of heat and need along my skin as she moved it up to my tits. I, on the other hand, needed to unbutton her suit vest, then start to work the buttons of her dress shirt loose.

So yeah, I had to put in a bit more effort, but my reward was *more* than worth it.

"Shit," I gasped, pulling away from her mouth once I slipped my hand into her unbuttoned shirt. "I didn't know—"

"It's okay," she said. "No one can see us."

"You're not wearing a bra."

She smirked. "Generally not. I have, like, zero tits."

I tilted my head as I stared down, biting my lip gently before reaching back up.

"I wouldn't say that," I said. "I would say you have—" I cupped my hand around her breast, feeling her already-hard nipple press into my palm "—*exactly* the right amount of tits."

Because sure, they were small. But they fit perfectly into my hand. Her nipples were dark and wonderfully perky, and it was only the fact that we were trapped in a somewhat small booth that stopped me from dipping my head to suck on them. Instead, I settled for rolling them between my thumb and forefinger, teasing the little nubs until Claire leaned forward, buried her head against my neck, and moaned.

Her hand was still under my shirt. It was over my bra because I *was* wearing a bra, since I had a non-zero amount of tits and wasn't quite brave enough to go out on a day-to-day basis without one. There was no convenient way for me to take my bra off, so Claire worked around it. She tugged the cups down and lifted my breasts over them, tracing her fingers back and forth along the underside of them before tweaking my nipples, then using her elbow to nudge my hand away from her breasts so she could better access mine.

"You can touch me later," she said.

"But—" I started.

She shut me up with a heated kiss. "You look so damn good in this top that I haven't been able to stop thinking about your tits since the second I saw you. Relax and let me *touch* you, Tessa."

So I did.

I closed my eyes, listening to the music surrounding us as she felt me up, squeezing and cupping and sending delightful shivers through my body as she teased my nipples. The bass pumping through the bar thrummed through my body until I couldn't tell the difference between it and my heartbeat and the surges of arousal Claire was drawing from me. She kissed my neck, her tongue flicking out to taste me, licking and devouring the salt off my skin.

The way she touched me was unreal. She could have touched me like she owned me. Like I owed her, like she'd spent money on me and expected something in return.

But that wasn't who Claire was. She touched me like I was valued. Desired. Wanted.

Like I mattered.

And God, that was exactly what I needed.

I couldn't quite figure out why. Partly because I was trying to think about it while someone was playing with my nipples, but mostly because it didn't make sense. I mean, maybe if I'd been rebounding from the hit that was Finn and Julie ghosting me, I could have understood why I was craving that feeling.

But I wasn't rebounding.

They thought they didn't need me, and maybe they didn't.

But I'd never needed them, either.

So I focused on the woman with the long fingers and warm lips who was now nibbling on my collarbone as she indulged in my tits. I gave in to the way she made my body sing, drawing out a melody only she and I could hear from the rhythm of the club. And when I couldn't take it anymore, when my pussy was soaked and aching and so needy I couldn't keep myself from squirming under her touch, I felt her smile before she kissed her way up to my ear.

"I think it's time for me to find out if you've been thinking about getting into my pants," she said.

"I think you're right," I replied, and half a second later her hand had disappeared from under my shirt and moved to the waistband of my pants.

Now, had I known my night was going to end with me getting fingered in a private booth at an exclusive club, I would have likely chosen to wear something other than leather pants. They were not the most convenient things to wear when someone was trying to get her hand between your legs and her fingers in your pussy.

Luckily, Claire was very talented.

I don't know how she did it, but she made it work. A shift here, a nudge there, and suddenly my pants were down enough that she could maneuver her wrist around and thrust her hand between my thighs. One of my legs was hooked over hers and her arm was still around my shoulder so she could kiss me as she traced her fingers along my slit.

"Hmm," she said as she pushed a finger between my folds. "My magical faerie powers are telling me you've been thinking about getting into my pants for *ages*."

"Your magical faerie powers could have just asked," I replied. "I would've said yes."

"Where's the fun in that?" she asked.

I opened my mouth to answer, but all that came out was a moan. A loud one, too, but the music covered the noise. I couldn't help it; Claire picked that moment to slide two fingers into my dripping entrance, finally satisfying my aching need. A moment after that, her thumb pressed on my clit and I clutched at her, squeezing my eyes shut.

"You like that?" she asked.

I tried to say yes, but all that came out was a word that sounded sort of like "Ungh." Mainly because she took her fingers out of my pussy and started focusing her attention on my clit.

"Do you like it fast—" She started rubbing my clit faster, making me tremble in her arms. "—or slow?" Her movements slowed, but she kept the same deep intensity that made me dig my fingers into her arm.

"Yes," I gasped.

She laughed. The soft chuckle kind of laugh, not the hyena one.

"And do you like it when I put my fingers inside you?" she asked, moving the tip of her finger to my entrance and slipping it in.

"*Yes*," I moaned. "I love all of it, Claire."

"Of course you do," she murmured. "You're a fucking dream come true. God, I wish we were in the suite right now."

"The suite?" I managed to ask.

"The VIP suite." She sucked on my neck, then moved her fingers back to my clit and began rubbing it again. "It's in the corner over there. I'd lock the door and strip you naked so I could kiss every inch of you and eat your pussy until you were dripping down my chin. And I'd play with your cute little asshole because you're the kind of girl who *loves* that, aren't you, darling? You love having your ass touched and fingered and fucked, too. Don't you?"

"Yes," I breathed.

She moaned, her fingers moving faster. "And here I didn't even *think* of bringing my strap-on tonight. I was just going to piss off my sister. I didn't think I'd find you at that dumpster fire gala."

"Well, you know what they say," I gasped. "One man's trash..."

That earned me one of her horribly wonderful cackles. "You are a treasure, Tessa. Don't ever forget it."

I wasn't going to. I wasn't going to forget any of this. It was seared into my memory, the flashing lights in the darkness, the music, her words, the way her fingers felt on my clit... And there was no way I would ever forget how hard I was going to come.

Because I was going to. I was close, so fucking close, and Claire's breath was heavy against me and her fingers were *so* good on my clit and—

And then the curtain blocking the entrance moved.

Claire reacted instantly. She shifted back far enough that it hopefully looked like I'd cuddled up to her while we flirted. You know, instead of like I was being fingered in a fucking nightclub like I was a particularly adventurous twenty-something instead of a thirty-year-old divorcee.

Even though I was definitely still getting fingered in a nightclub when the server walked in, because there wasn't enough time for Claire to get her hand out of my pants before he came in with his bottle of scotch and bucket of ice.

"How is everything?" he asked.

"Wonderful," Claire said, her voice smooth and easy. "Thank you."

The server motioned to her glass. "Would you like me to pour another for you?"

"Please," she said.

I watched as he poured what was apparently the slowest-flowing scotch in existence into Claire's glass, trying not to move even when Claire's fingers accidentally twitched and brushed against my clit.

Until they twitched again and when I glanced at her, I realized it was no accident.

"And for you, miss?" the server asked, turning to me. "Would you like more?"

"Y-Yes," I said. "That would be—"

"Actually, didn't you say you wanted to try something else?" Claire asked, then slipped a finger inside of me.

"Ah—no," I said. "I changed my mind."

"Are you sure?" she asked. "They make a wonderful old fashioned here. He'll even smoke it right at the table for you."

"Yes, miss," the server said. "It's not a problem at all, if that's what you'd prefer."

Claire shifted her wrist and I laughed. I had to, otherwise I would have whimpered and the server would have probably thought I was insane.

"No," I said again. "Just scotch, please."

I punctuated it by clenching my pussy as tightly as I could around Claire's finger, hoping she took the hint.

She did, finally taking pity on me and smiling innocently. "You heard the lady. One more scotch, please."

Her finger stayed inside me as we watched him refill my glass before sliding it across the table.

"Anything else for either of you?" the server asked.

I shook my head.

"Are you sure?" Claire asked. "You don't want a snack or—"

I squeezed my pussy around her finger again and she burst out laughing.

"Never mind," she said to the server. "We're good, thanks."

The moment he walked past the curtain, her hand started moving at the same speed it had before we got interrupted.

"You are the *worst*," I gasped. "He was standing right there!"

"It was so funny, though," she giggled.

"He probably knew what we were doing."

"Oh, there's no 'probably' about it," she said. "He did. And he saw my tits."

I glanced down, remembering I'd unbuttoned her shirt. Sure enough, the swell of her breasts was visible, along with her dark, hard nipples.

"Fuck," I whispered, and Claire laughed again.

"It's okay, darling," she said, then leaned in and kissed me. "They expect it here. The Place is... unusual like that. It's part of its charm. I promise, it's okay."

I should have had more questions about what that meant, but she started rubbing my clit again and I couldn't focus on anything else. My breath hitched and Claire captured it as she kissed me.

"Don't stop," I whispered. "Please don't stop."

"I won't, darling," she murmured. "I can't. I *need* to feel you come on my fingers."

I clung to her, digging my fingers into her upper arm as she brought me closer and closer to the edge. It took everything in me not to cry out, to not shriek with pleasure. Because even though the music was loud and we were apparently in a place that condoned and expected semi-public sex, I knew the way she was making me feel would definitely drown out the music.

Moments later, I was burying my head against her shoulder and shuddering, my pussy clenching around her fingers as my vision flashed white, then dark, then full of the colours of the bar. Claire held me, kissing me as I gasped and quivered, not stopping her movements on my clit until I was finished. Then she kept them there, soothing my overwhelmed pussy with little motions until I caught my breath.

When I finally did, she pulled her fingers out of my pants and brought them to her mouth. I watched as she licked them clean, then took a casual sip of her scotch.

"Mmm," she said. "You pair very well with this."

I laughed. I couldn't help it. It was fucking absurd, but wonderful, and Claire smiled as I tried to straighten my shirt.

"Maybe I should find out how you pair with it now," I said.

Claire bit her lip, then shook her head. "You can get me next time."

Fuck.

"I don't do next-times," I said. "I told you that."

"Then call it a gift."

"But—"

"Shh." She leaned in and kissed me, nipping at my lips.

"Claire—"

"Tessa, I promise it's okay." She lifted her hand to my face, stroking my cheek. "It takes a *lot* to make me come. In public, it's nearly impossible."

"Maybe I'm up for the challenge."

She smiled, but there was something sad behind it. "I know you are. But it's... it's just going to frustrate us both."

There was a reason for this. I knew there was. But whatever it was, Claire wasn't willing to share, and it wasn't my business to pressure her to answer.

"Okay," I said.

She brushed my hair off my cheek. "Just kiss me, okay? Kiss me hard enough that when I go home and get myself off after this, I can still taste you."

So that was what I did.

Fourteen

"Oh good, you didn't get murdered," Chuck said when I walked into our office the next morning with an iced flat white in one hand and a caramel macchiato with extra caramel, extra whip, and a chocolate drizzle in the other. "That means I win."

"Was that an actual concern?" I asked, putting the caramel abomination on his desk before crossing to mine and putting my purse down.

"Charles thought so."

"And you... bet on it? Is that why you win?"

"Absolutely not," Chuck said. "Charles refused to bet on something as macabre as your potential murder. But while he was recovering after the first round of me sucking his cock, I made a bet in my head. And since you're here and not murdered, I won, so I think that means I get to pick who's bottoming tonight." He lifted his no-longer-actually-a-coffee to his lips and sipped it thoughtfully. "Who am I kidding? We're both going to. Again. But I get to go first."

"So that premium fellatio he earned after spending way too much money to date a guy he's already dating went well, then?" I asked, settling in my chair.

"So well," Chuck said dreamily. "My throat may never be the same."

"Damn. Guess that means I lost the bet I made in my head."

He frowned. "What was your bet?"

"That you'd end up drowning in cum."

Chuck let out a loud bark of laughter, tilting his head back as it morphed into a giggle. "You're so lewd."

"Us being lewd is eighty-four percent of our friendship." I finally took a sip of my coffee. "I know way more about your sex life than I should."

"Me too," he said. "But for the record, you *were* close to winning that bet."

It was my turn to laugh. "Was I?"

"Mm-hmm." He pressed his lips together puckishly. "*Three* times."

"Damn," I said. "Good for... well, both of you, I guess."

"Thank you," Chuck said, then yawned and took another sip of coffee. "But it did take most of the night after we got back from the gala. So I'm going to be useless today because I am *exhausted*."

"Don't let Dinah hear you say that. She's probably already freaking out about starting to plan next year's Recycl-Ball."

"Oh, she won't. She's not in today."

A loud, offended scoff slipped out of my mouth before I could stop it. "Seriously? She said we had to come in today after having a work event all night and *she* didn't?!"

"I know you think she's literally the Antichrist—"

"I do not. I've always said she's more of a demon lackey type."

"—but I don't think she *intended* to not come in today," he finished, ignoring me as he tapped his phone screen and scrolled for a moment. "The exact words she used were that she's taking an 'unplanned out-of-office day but may be available for minor questions and uncomplicated issues via email later this afternoon.'"

"What the fuck is that supposed to mean?"

"She's hungover."

I laughed. "Yeah, right. Dinah hungover? Did they accidentally give her one of those dealcoholized wine spritzers instead of grape juice or something?"

"Perhaps, but I think it may have been all the drinks Loni bought her after the auction," Chuck said. "I mean, there's a chance that she's not even hungover yet. Unless she puked most of it out after she got home, it's possible that she was still drunk when she emailed me."

"You're joking."

"Not even a little. She was dancing, Tessa Margarita Lane. *Dancing*."

I almost cried. "I missed her *dancing*?! Oh God, please tell me she's horrible at it."

He tilted his head from side to side. "An odd mix of terrible and excellent. Like a taxidermied chicken that took ballet lessons."

"Wow," I said, taking another sip of coffee. "That sounds epic. I'm kinda sad I missed Drunk Dinah."

"Ah," he said. "So your date didn't go well?"

I gave him an unimpressed look. "I said *kinda* sad. Not actually sad."

Chuck set his sugar-laden coffee concoction on his desk and leaned forward with a hungry look on his face. "I want *all* the details. From the very start."

"Well," I said, then took a deep breath. "In the beginning, when God created—"

"Tessa!" he said, offended, and I dissolved into laughter. "Come on. I have been waiting all *night* to get the story here, and I didn't even text you to harass you for it in case you were still with her. Where did you meet her? How do you know her? Who *is* she?! "

"Okay, okay," I said, taking another sip of coffee. "I met her at the bar just before Loni came up to ask about the auction."

Chuck looked at me expectantly, then huffed when I didn't continue. "And then?"

"Then she took off."

He looked at me with disbelief.

"I'm not joking," I said. "That was the entirety of my interaction with her before the auction started."

He blinked at me. "That can't be it."

"I swear. This little jerk was hitting on me, she stepped in, we chatted for a couple of minutes and then when Loni came up, she disappeared."

"And then she just..." He trailed off, twisting his hand in the air. "...spent ten grand on you because she liked your thirty second conversation?"

"She's chaos personified, Chuck. That's the most normal part of this entire situation."

He rolled his eyes. "Sure it is."

"I mean, considering the night ended with me getting fingered at a private table in this weird-ass secret nightclub called The Place, yeah, it is."

His mouth dropped open, his eyes wide. "You went to *The Place*?!"

I raised my eyebrows. "You know about The Place?"

"Um, of course," he said. "Do you not?"

"I didn't."

"It's this exclusive high-end invite-only nightclub. That's the 'official' description. But it's very... liberal about things. And even more discreet. Very much a rich person's playground." He tapped a finger to his chin. "Do you have a sugar mama now?"

"What?!"

He burst out laughing. "That woman has to be someone with 'fuck you' money. Like, you need to be *someone* to get into The Place. Not to mention dropping ten grand on a woman she spoke to for a matter of *minutes—*"

"I told you. She's chaotic."

"So you have a chaotic sugar mama."

I rolled my eyes. "I do not. It was a one-time—"

Chuck cut me off with a painfully exaggerated wail. "Not this again."

"It's not just me this time!" I said. "She doesn't want anything serious either. And you know what, Chuck, I'm not saying I'll never have a more-than-one-time thing. But I needed to get laid last night."

"Mmm," he said. "Imagine if you'd just invited Finn and Julie to the gala. You could've gone home with them."

Oh.

I guess in the pandemonium, I hadn't told him.

"I did invite them," I said. "They didn't come."

Chuck rolled his eyes. "Tessa, you can just say you didn't—"

"You can check the guest list if you don't believe me. Their names were there and I can guarantee they didn't pick up their tickets because they ghosted me."

He stared at me, his lips still parted and a blank look on his face. Then, all at once, his expression changed, overdramatics fading until all that was left was a sympathetic look.

"They did what?" he asked.

I laughed dryly. "Ghosted me. Just like I would've done, you know, if I'd decided things were over. So I guess I deserved it. Although, I mean, I would've said something to them first instead of just not showing up to an event I said I'd be at."

"Maybe something happened and it's not what it looks like," he said. "Them not showing doesn't automatically mean they ghosted you."

"You're right," I said. "The fact that they blocked me and deleted their MatchMi account means they ghosted me."

He opened his mouth, then closed it. After a moment, he shook his head and put a hand on my knee. "I'm sorry."

My skin prickled with anger. I nudged his hand off my leg and crossed one knee over the other. "Don't be. I told you it wasn't serious. Just because it was a dick move doesn't mean I'm upset it's over."

"You literally just said you were rebounding with your sugar mama."

"I said neither of those things. I said I got fingerbanged at a nightclub. It just so happened to be by a rich woman with really good taste in scotch who was willing to drop ten thousand dollars just to hang out with me." I drank another sip of coffee. "I don't see why you're so surprised. I know what I'm worth, and it's at least that."

Chuck looked like he wanted to argue with my statement, probably to say something like we both knew I was hurting more than I wanted to admit and that my way of handling things was to ignore it.

But he made the wise choice not to.

"I still can't believe that," he said. "Ten grand. She wasn't expecting anything out of you because of that, was she?"

"Not in the slightest. She made that abundantly clear. And also didn't come when I was with her."

"*What*?!"

I held up a hand. "She didn't want me to. I offered, trust me."

"Okay, you need to tell me who she is *now*," he said. "It's killing me that I don't know. I couldn't even find out her name."

"Why were you trying to find out her name?"

"Because I'm nosy and also if you did get murdered I wanted to know who to accuse during a nationwide televised press conference as the camera zoomed in on the barely concealed rage in my eyes," he said. "But when I checked the donation records for the night, it was just listed under some subsidiary business that didn't have a name on it."

"Maybe there's a reason for that."

"Come on, Tess," he whined. "Tell me who your sugar mama is."

"I can't, Chuck. It's one of those things that if anyone found out, it would cost me everything."

"I won't tell."

"You gossip about everything."

"I won't about this." He held up his hand. "I swear on my mother's grave."

"Your mother is alive."

He huffed. "Fine, I swear on... on..." He licked his lips, then looked at me solemnly. "I swear on my relationship with Charles."

Damn. I wasn't sure if I was more astounded by how serious he was being with his promise or how serious he was with Charles.

"I need you to promise. Like *promise*-promise, that you will never repeat this. Ever. Dinah would get her wish about getting rid of me."

"I promise," he said without hesitation. "This information will never leave my lips."

I glanced at our closed office door, then leaned towards Chuck.

"Her name is Claire," I said in the quietest voice I could manage. "Claire... Martelle."

"Claire—" he said, then his eyes widened and his voice lowered so much that he was barely speaking. "—*Martelle*?!"

I nodded.

"Not... not like—"

"Yep. Paige Martelle's—" I barely mouthed the name "—younger sister."

Chuck put a hand over his mouth, which was still hanging open. "You're joking."

I shook my head.

"Oh my God," he breathed. "So Loni was right? ArtCycle was trying to sabotage the Recycl-Ball?"

"What?" I said, making him jump when my voice came out unexpectedly loud. "No! Not at all. It's the opposite."

"You expect me to believe she was trying to, what, ensure its success?"

"Pretty much," I said. "She lives for annoying her sister."

He blinked once, then pressed his lips together as his face started to tense. It took a moment for me to realize it wasn't because the caramel macchiato had gone right through his digestive system but because he was struggling not to laugh.

"So she donated ten grand to a competing charity just to piss her sister off," he said.

"And because she liked my hot ass," I said.

He cackled, shaking his head and reaching to grab the coffee he'd put down on his desk at some point. "Rich people are so ridiculous."

"I know. But you see why I can't—"

"Oh, completely. Even if we tried to convince Loni that Claire was the best person ever to have on our side in her relentless battle against Paige Martelle, there is no way she'd ever let you explain." Despite the fact that he was still giggling, he managed to take a sip of coffee. "Oh my God. You have a sugar mama."

"I don't have a sugar mama," I said. "I have a fun story about the time I accidentally told my boss we were having a date auction at a gala and ended up getting fingered at an exclusive nightclub. And it's not possible, anyway. I didn't get her number."

"Are you *kidding* me?!" Chuck whirled around, disbelief on his face. "Again. *Again* with the phone thing?!"

"Yes. Again with the phone thing. I told you, it was a one-time thing."

That was the excuse I was giving him, anyway. Mainly because I didn't want to admit I'd chickened out at the end of the night. Which was fine. It wasn't like I regretted it or anything.

Not even a bit.

Had my life been more like a romantic comedy, my phone would have gone off just then with a perfectly timed text message from a woman who didn't have my phone number. Chuck and I would have looked at it in unison and I would have snatched it up frantically, wondering *how* Claire had gotten my number.

But that didn't happen.

I mean, my phone did go off. And we both looked at it. And my heart jumped into my throat as I picked it up thinking I'd somehow manifested Claire into texting me when she didn't have my phone number.

But the message was from Zain instead.

Z Biggest Asshole

> **Still good for tomorrow?**

I glared at the screen, not sure if I was annoyed because he wasn't Claire or because he was Zain.

Me

> What's tomorrow?

Z Biggest Asshole

> **Haha, Teacup. Just that event you've been looking forward to for months.**

Me

> Oh that's right. I booked that joint pap smear and new IUD insertion for tomorrow afternoon. Maybe they'll give me painkillers this time.

Z Biggest Asshole

> **Perfect. You'll be nice and sedated for dinner.**

I rolled my eyes.

Me

> Don't worry, I'm not going to embarrass you.

Z Biggest Asshole

> **Never said you would.**

Me

> I'll be your good little pretend girlfriend who talks about how wonderful and manly and not at all manipulative you are.

Manipulative? YOU offered to come.

Yeah. I just said I wasn't going to talk about that.

He sent back a set of laughing emojis.

Do you want me to pick you up from the bus station? I can probably sneak out of the conference a bit early if I need to.

Did you rent a car?

No, but I can borrow one.

Don't be stupid. I'll take a cab.

After that, my phone was quiet until mid-afternoon, when Chuck came back into our office after talking to Jia with a satisfied look on his face and started telling me about the new software she'd found for next year's guest list.

"We can flag names on the list at time of purchase," he said. "So no more surprise ex-husbands showing up to ruin a perfectly good dumpster fire. I've already added it to the list."

"What do we do if he gives a fake name?" I asked.

Chuck twisted his mouth to the side. "Well, he'd have to use a fake credit card to pay for the ticket then, because otherwise his name would be on that, too."

"Okay, but what if he uses someone else's card or something?"

"Well, in the rare case of that, I think we would simply have to take the time to see if there was a way we could find a—is that your phone?"

I rolled my eyes. "You can just say you don't know, Chuck."

"Okay, I don't know." He motioned to my desk. "But your phone *did* just vibrate. Zain again?"

"Probably making sure I don't forget to wear shoes or something," I muttered as I turned to grab it.

"Do you have shoes?" Chuck asked.

"Of course. I'm wearing my pumps."

"They match your dress?"

"They will. When I get the dress."

"Tessa!" Chuck exclaimed. "You don't even have a dress yet?"

I rolled my eyes. "Shut up. I'm getting it today. And—"

But I didn't finish what I was saying.

That was because my phone was in my hand and the name on my screen wasn't Zain.

"What the fuck," I whispered, and Chuck was instantly beside me, peering over my shoulder.

"What?" he asked. "Who's CM and why are you—" He gasped and grabbed my phone. "Is that *Claire*?!"

"Shut up," I hissed, snatching my phone back and twisting away from him. "Don't let anyone hear you."

"I thought you said you didn't get her number!"

"I didn't," I said as I unlocked my phone. "How the hell..."

But I didn't need to ask.

CM

Hey darling. I know what you're thinking. "How'd you get my number, Claire?!" The answer: more magical faerie powers. AKA you left your phone in your jacket pocket while you were in the bathroom cleaning up all the pussy juice I left in your panties last night. Sorry not sorry.

I had to laugh. I mean, I didn't have to. But I did.

Because that was just Claire.

Me

To be honest I was kind of regretting not giving it to you. So I guess I can let it slide this time.

CM

Good. Because I had a good reason for doing it.

Me

Which was…?

CM

You're hot and I'm horny.

"Jesus, she's forward," Chuck said from over my shoulder.

"I like that," I said.

Before I could respond, another message from Claire came through.

CM

I was gonna wait a day or two at least to text you but I decided I'm going to Tahiti for "business" next week. So wanna hang out again tonight?

Damn my fucking procrastination tendencies. I sighed.

Me

This isn't just an excuse because as much as I truly want to pay you back for last night, I really can't. I have to buy a dress for this thing I have this weekend. Sorry.

CM

OOOO shopping! I'm in. Want me to pick you up?

Me

You want to come?

CM

Darling, my family name is on multiple brands of makeup. I was born to do this.

Me

I thought you were born to annoy your sister.

CM

I was born for many reasons. And taking a hot girl shopping is one that's at the top of my list. So? Need a ride?

I looked at Chuck, who was still reading the messages over my shoulder. He finished, then sighed.

"Yes, you can leave early," he said.

Fifteen

MY TOXIC TRAIT WAS leaving anything I was dreading to the last minute and hoping it would work itself out with little to no effort on my part.

Like telling my parents about my divorce and then letting it become a snowballing lie over the course of five years because I didn't want to admit my marriage failed.

Or buying a dress for Zain's stupid work event.

It was how I ended up in situations like the one I was in, with Claire sitting on a plush couch in a store that didn't have price tags on the clothes, admiring me as I grumpily modelled a pink fit-and-flare dress that I *despised*.

"Ugh, but it looks so good," Claire whined.

I tried to glare at her. Tried, because every time I looked at her, I was distracted by how fucking hot she was.

She'd worn the hell out of the navy-blue suit last night. Today she was wearing the hell out of a fitted tank top beneath a baggy button-up shirt that was undone with the sleeves rolled up to her elbows. There were multiple necklaces adorning her neck, all silver, and she wore tight purple jeans with slouchy black boots. Her soft brown hair was pulled back into a single braid that she had hooked over one shoulder so she could twirl the end around her finger.

"I hate it," I said.

"Why?" Claire crossed one leg over the over. "It makes your tits look so good."

"My tits always look good. But it's pink."

She looked offended. "You don't like pink?"

"I love pink," I said. "It's one of my favourite colours. But I don't like *wearing* pink."

"Hmm." She twisted her mouth to the side. "Okay. What colour do you like wearing?"

"Black."

"Really? Just black?"

"I look good in black," I said. "And it goes with everything. *And* it's kind of my thing."

"Hmm." She tapped her finger to her chin. "You do look phenomenally sexy in black."

I glanced towards the change room. "So let me try something black on. I've tried every other colour."

"But if I do that, this'll all be over and I'll have no good excuse to keep checking you out."

"Fair," I said. "But you could also just... check me out."

"That is a good point." Turning suddenly, she waved at the salesperson. "Can you bring her the first dress I set aside?"

"Wait, first dress?" I repeated.

Claire grinned, showing off her flawlessly straight white teeth. "Oh, yeah. I saw something perfect the moment we walked in."

As expected, the whole evening had been chaos.

It started when a confused-looking Jia came into my and Chuck's office just before four to tell me a man in a uniform was there to pick me up.

"A uniform?" Chuck said. "Like a police officer?"

"No," Jia said. "Like a... a driver? He has a fancy hat."

Chuck looked at me, widening his eyes.

"Shut up," I muttered. "I'll be right there, Jia."

When I got into the waiting car, Claire was playing with her hair as she idly scrolled on her phone. But the moment I closed the door, she put it away.

"Hey darling," she said, then surprised me by sliding across the seat and capturing me in a deep kiss.

"Um, hey," I said when she pulled away. "Is that how you greet all your friends?"

"Just the ones I *really* like." She slung an arm over my shoulder. "So, what do you have in mind for your outfit?"

"I was just going to go to the mall," I said. "There's like, two stores that carry decent plus size clothes."

"Hmph," she said. "Nah. I have something better in mind."

"Something better" ended up being a trendy boutique that one of her friends owned and that specialized in carrying the kind of designer clothes they didn't usually make for anyone above a size eight.

"Let's start over here," Claire said when we walked in. "I'm thinking of something low cut because tits."

"That is half the requirement," I said. "Classy, but with just enough tits to—"

"Perfect." She picked up something dark green and slinky and gorgeous. "What do you think of this?"

"I think I need to see the price tag," I said.

"Don't worry about it."

"Claire—"

"Consider it a gift," she said.

And right then, I had a choice to make.

Because yeah, I could've done the right thing. I could've folded my arms and told her that this was the second *gift* she'd given me. That she was dropping way too much money on me for someone I'd met less than twenty-fucking-four hours earlier. That I was too damn old to be a sugar baby. And that I had zero desire to be one since that went against the whole "casual" thing we'd sort-of-kind-of-but-not-really agreed on.

And, I guess, there was that whole thing where I shouldn't take advantage of her. Because Claire might have been chaotic, but she was also nice. She was fun. And if she *wasn't* trying to be a sugar mama, it was an asshole move on my part not to make it clear that I wasn't going to make it serious, even if she bought me things.

But on the other hand, I was kind of an asshole.

And didn't I deserve to get spoiled once in a while? Wasn't it kind of living out my *Pretty Woman* fantasy to let her buy me a fancy dress that I didn't want to buy because I didn't wear dresses and I didn't want to go to this event in the first place?

Was it *really* taking advantage of her when she was the kind of person who spent ten grand just to piss someone off and would've easily spent more without even thinking about it?

So I made my choice.

"Fine," I said. "Your treat. But I'm not fucking you just because you buy me shit."

"Obviously," she said. "You're fucking me because I'm hot."

"As long as we're clear. If this is some kind of sugar mama situation, then—"

Her awful racket of a cackle echoed through the boutique. "Oh hell no. I'm not your sugar mama. I do this because I want to, okay?"

"Okay," I said. "But... why?"

"Shopping for you and buying you clothes and dressing you up is fun for me. Just like taking you to a fancy club is fun for me. But I'm not so ignorant to not realize that what's 'fun' for me is somewhat inaccessible for other people, so I'm going to pay for it so we can have fun together. And *maybe* it's a little fucked up, but picking this dress out is... well." Her eyes flicked down to my mouth. "The thought of other people drooling over you is hot. It makes me horny to think I'm showing you off so the whole world can see how fucking gorgeous you are."

I had no idea how to respond. Not to the words, nor the frank, to-the-point way she said them. My body didn't seem to, either. Heat rushed up my neck to my cheeks and down through my stomach straight to my pussy. My skin tingled and my breath was in my throat and Claire's face was close to mine, her hazel eyes sparkling roguishly.

"Okay," I said. "As long as we're clear. We are friends who may sometimes fuck, Claire. Nothing else."

"Crystal clear," she said, then leaned in and kissed me. "Consider this foreplay, darling."

But the foreplay turned sour somewhere around the third dress that wasn't my style at all. I didn't like wearing dresses in the first place and the whole process was starting to drag out. By the time we reached the pink dress, I was starting to wonder if I should just pretend I liked it so I'd have enough time to sneak off and buy a dress at the mall before leaving tomorrow. I mean, I did have to go home so I could put the painting I'd done for the Clarkdales on my step for Kira to pick up in the morning, so I could easily use that as an excuse to leave.

And I almost did. But thankfully, that was when Claire gave in and let me try on the dress she'd set aside.

"Sold," Claire said as soon as I stepped out of the change room. "Sold, sold, fucking *sold*. Actually, maybe we should get two of them, because I'm about ten seconds away from tearing that one off of you."

As annoyed as I was that this entire trip could have taken less than ten minutes if she'd just let me try this on *first,* I held back a laugh as I studied myself in the three-way mirror. The dress was black, as requested, with short sleeves and an off-the-shoulder neckline. Made of a soft fabric that had the slightest shine to it, it hugged my body and was tailored in a way that gave me the illusion of an hourglass figure, even though it was form-fitting and I definitely didn't have that kind of outline. The hem hit just above my knees at exactly the right spot that would make my legs look a mile long once I paired it with my black pumps.

Zain was definitely going to approve.

Not that it mattered. I mean, it wasn't like I gave a shit what Zain thought. But I was doing this for a reason. Making him happy so he'd keep his mouth shut about catching Brad "cheating" on me the last time we were in Burnsley was kind of the point.

So I guess it mattered a little.

But only a little.

I didn't let her buy two dresses. Or the shoes she picked out, which were a pair of black pumps that were almost identical to my favourite black pumps.

"I need to wear this tomorrow," I said. "I will not have time to break those in before the event."

"It won't be that bad," she protested. "They're so buttery!"

"I'll get blisters and be uncomfortable the whole time," I said. "And you're going to Tahiti, so you won't even be able to rub my feet to make up for it."

She conceded, but insisted on adding a leather clutch and a pair of earrings that she *said* weren't diamonds, but looked suspiciously like diamonds.

"Ready to take this past foreplay?" she asked as we left the store and walked towards her car.

"Is that your way of inviting me to your place?"

"If that's cool with you."

"As long as you understand I'm *only* fucking you because you're hot."

"Deal," she said. "Seal it with a kiss?"

"Sure," I replied. "Which lips do you want me to kiss?"

A loud crack of cackling laughter echoed on the street and Claire kissed me—on the mouth—before we got into the car.

Sixteen

CLAIRE'S APARTMENT WAS FAR less ostentatious than one would
expect for a multi-millionaire heiress to a makeup syndicate.

Or maybe it was exactly as ostentatious as one would expect, since
Claire wasn't a very ostentatious person to begin with.

Either way, the apartment itself was minimalist in nature. It wasn't
that sort of pretentious minimalism that seemed to be trendy for rich
people, where everything from the walls to the ceiling to the books
on the shelves were white. No, Claire's place gave an air of humble
normality. There was a mostly alive houseplant beside a bookshelf that
contained actual books and not just aesthetic trinkets. A cozy couch
with a handmade blanket and a big TV. A kitchen with appliances that
didn't look completely untouched. Sure, she lived in a nice building in
a higher-end neighbourhood, but it didn't look like the kind of place
where someone with a driver and enough money to buy designer clothes
for a woman she'd met the day before would live.

Then there was the bedroom, which was the reason the apartment was
less ostentatious than expected and not *completely* unostentatious.

It was decorated in darkness: dark wood floors with dark walls and a
dark ceiling. Dark wooden nightstands that matched the dark bed frame
and dresser. Here and there were hints of light: a small area rug that was
cream-coloured and luxuriously soft. Lighter brown sheets on her bed
matched the velvety brown fabric of her tufted headboard. And above
her bed was a light fixture made of what seemed like hundreds of tiny

hanging lights, giving the impression of the Milky Way splashing across the sky when all the other lights were off.

It was beautiful. Dreamy. Insta-worthy. The kind of place you could get lost in for hours, sheltered from the world by those dark walls and soft fabrics.

But I wasn't there to admire the decor.

"Well?" Claire said after she crawled to the middle of her neatly made bed and turned to me. "Coming?"

"You first," I said, climbing on the bed to join her.

She was still laughing when I reached the middle, so I felt the sweet twist of her smile as I kissed her. A soft noise of appreciation escaped as she reached for the hem of my shirt, but I was already determined to get her off as good as she'd gotten me off the night before. Slipping my tongue in her mouth, I guided her hands away from me and skimmed my palms up her arms, pushing the baggy shirt off her shoulders before starting to pull at her tank top.

I barely managed to untuck it from her pants when Claire mirrored my action, nudging my hands away so she could pull at my shirt. Again I resisted, tugging at her shirt and earning a soft, huffing laugh from Claire.

"Let me see you naked," she said.

"You first," I repeated. "I want to give *you* a gift now."

She scowled playfully, sticking her lip out in an exaggerated pout, but sat back on her knees and unceremoniously stripped her tank top off.

Like the previous day, she wasn't wearing a bra, and like the previous day, I was enamoured by the sight of her perfect little tits. Seeing them now in the light of her room rather than the flashing darkness of a club, I wanted to push her onto her back and worship them, sucking on her nipples and tracing my tongue along the smooth skin on the underside.

"Better?" she asked as I took in the sight of her.

"A bit," I said. "Now the pants."

Her lip twitched. "Not yet."

"But—"

She cut me off by reaching forward and pulling my shirt up insistently. "Not yet, darling. Let me have you first."

"Claire—"

"Tessa," she said. "Please."

Her voice was quiet and pleading, a tone I hadn't heard from her before. And sure, I'd only known her for the aforementioned not-even-a-fucking-*day*, but this...

This seemed off.

And yeah, I might be an asshole. I might be the kind of asshole who was letting her spend her money on me and refusing to feel guilty about offering her nothing in return.

But I was *not* the kind of asshole who could continue with sex when something didn't feel right.

"Probiotic," I said.

She stopped tugging at my shirt and looked up at me, bewildered. "Huh?"

"I mean—" I shook my head and reached down, putting my hands over hers. "Sorry. It's the safeword I use. I need us to stop."

A lot of things flashed across Claire's face. Confusion, certainly, and panic. Fear, maybe, and embarrassment. The kinds of things that took her from being the ethereal, faerie-like fantasy to an imperfectly perfect human that, despite the sudden sadness in her eyes, I liked even more than I already had. Then she blinked and a mask slipped over whatever emotions she'd let show. Her shoulders sagged as she looked up at the twinkling light fixture above our heads.

"We don't have to talk about whatever it is if you don't want to," I said. "But this doesn't feel right to me."

Her throat flexed as she swallowed and she laughed weakly. "That's fair."

I wasn't entirely sure what to do next. On the few rare occasions that I'd used the safeword or had it used on me, there was a clear reason. There were actions that had to take place once we stopped. A cuff that was too tight and cutting off circulation could be loosened. A threesome could end amicably when a woman realized after her husband kissed me that she wasn't into it like she'd thought she would be.

But Claire simply fell quiet. And while that seemed to validate my entire reason for stopping us, it didn't mean I knew what to do.

"Do you want me to leave?" I asked.

"No," she said.

I thought for a moment. "Do you want me to hold you?"

She pressed her lips together and didn't say anything, but jerked her head forward in a nod. I spread my arms and wrapped them around her, then carefully brought us down on the bed together. She put her arms around my waist and nestled her head in the crook of my neck, sighing as she rested against me.

For a while, we just lay on her bed, holding each other and existing in silence. Claire's skin was warm, her shoulders rising and falling slightly with each breath. She wasn't crying and she wasn't freaking out; she was just quiet, wrapped up in my arms and her mind.

Until she wasn't.

"I have a hard time coming because of my medication," she said out of nowhere.

"Okay," I said.

"It's not so bad anymore," she continued, wriggling until I loosened my arms and she could sit back a bit. "I've been on various, uh, versions of it since I was a teenager. And I think since I've been on it so long, it's affected whatever it is that makes people come."

"That sucks."

Her mouth twitched. "It does. Especially when women tend to get upset that they can't make me finish. Or get offended when I say I need to use a sex toy or two." She sighed and flopped onto her back, looking up at the lights. "Because I *can* come. I've found ways to do it. It's just not easy and most of the time I need to do it myself. And even though it's made me kind of prefer the parts of sex that *aren't* about me coming, people tend to take it personally."

I frowned, adjusting my arm so I was cushioning my head as I looked at her. "That's shitty of them."

"Tell me about it. But I like... I *love* giving other people pleasure. It just does it for me, you know? Everyone goes off about how they don't want a pillow princess, but I love 'em. *Love* me a pillow princess."

That made me laugh. "I guess I'm not quite your dream girl. I mean, don't get me wrong, I love making it all about me, but not all the time."

She was staring up at the ceiling, so I could only see her profile, but it was enough to see the slight smile on her face.

"You still are. You're still here."

I didn't know what to say to that.

"I have depression," she said after a moment. "Which always seems to surprise people. And if it doesn't surprise them, it pisses them off. It's always 'What do you have to be depressed about? Your parents are rich and you have everything you could ever want.'" She laughed and shook her head. "And it's like, yeah. I know. That's kind of the point. It's like saying 'Oh, just go for a walk and don't be sad. That'll fix your complex mood disorder.' Like, I *get* it. I shouldn't have anything to be depressed *about*. But I can't control the fact that I have it or how it makes me feel."

She took a breath before continuing.

"So then the guilt of all that mixes with the depression and makes an entire crap cake out of the whole situation. It gets bad. I mean, it's been bad. In the past. But in the last few years, it's gotten a lot better. Took a long time, but we figured out the right balance of meds and therapy and I finally feel *good* most of the time. Even if it means that sometimes sex is a pain in the ass, and not in the fun way."

She turned her head towards me. "I finally feel like I'm getting to experience life the way other people do. I'm doing things I missed out on before I had this under control. So when I said I don't want anything serious, that's why. I'm not in Vancouver the majority of the time anyway, but I'm enjoying the 'fuck around and have fun' lifestyle right now. Yeah, I want to buy you shit because it's fun, and yeah, I want to fuck you because you're hot, but that's it."

"You know I'm okay with that," I said.

She licked her lips nervously. "And this?"

"This...?"

She gestured vaguely. "The sex problems. And the other stuff."

"I might be an asshole, but I'm not a fucking monster," I said. "I'm not going to stop being your friend just because getting you to orgasm takes some extra work and patience."

A smile spread across her face. Not one of her devilish ones or her chaotic ones, but a genuine smile that reached the depths of her eyes.

"Cool," she said.

"Cool," I agreed. "Now, tell me what you need me to do so we can try to make you come."

She stared at me for a moment, then laughed as she rolled onto her side and leaned in to kiss me.

"God, I fucking like you," she said.

She didn't tell me right away. Instead, we spent a long time making out, kissing and touching and exploring each other. I let her take my shirt off, then my jeans, then my bra. But once I was down to my panties, I reached for the waistband of her jeans and started unbuttoning them.

"Tessa," she breathed as I loosened the button.

"Mmm?"

She reached down and put her hand over mine. "There are some, uh... marks. Please just pretend they aren't there. None of this, like, kissing-your-scars bullshit, okay?"

I lifted a hand to her face, brushing her hair back and kissing her lips as comfortingly as I could.

"I promise," I said, then pulled her jeans down, blind to anything but the perfection of her body.

Once they were off, I had to stop and admire her. The triangle of pink cotton covering her pussy. The way the waistband sat against her thin hips. The paleness of the skin on that spot just above her panties but below her button, that spot that wasn't quite stomach but wasn't quite her mound.

Fuck, she was gorgeous.

"Will you show me how you make yourself come?" I asked.

"Huh?"

I looked up to meet her eyes. "You said you usually need to do it yourself. Show me how you do it so I can learn. And I can show you how I do it."

She blinked, then a slow grin spread across her face. "You're gonna touch yourself for me?"

"Mm-hmm. If you want."

"Yeah," she said. "It just might take me a while."

"I've got nowhere to be until tomorrow."

So that was how I ended up naked on Claire's bed, propped up by a nest of countless throw pillows while she leaned back against her tufted headboard with her legs spread. I watched, part entranced and part curious by the confident routine of her setting herself up.

First, she took off her panties, showing off a smooth pussy with puffy lips. Then, while I drooled over the sight of her, she set a towel, a bottle of lube, and a decent sized dildo beside her. In her hand was one of those clit suction toys that looked incredibly well-loved.

As she took some of the lube and rubbed it on her pussy, I slipped my hand between my legs, lazily tracing my fingers up and down my already wet lips. Then, she primly wiped her hand on the towel, hit a button on the toy, and put it on her clit.

And oh my *God*.

I knew how expensive those toys could be, but *damn*, I needed to try one. It was loud, but the moment Claire touched it to her clit, her whole body shuddered, her hips bucking forward and her eyes squeezing closed in pleasure. She sighed in relief, then relaxed back against the headboard before pressing another button on top. The whirring vibration sound got louder and she shuddered again.

"Fuck," she whispered, and I had to agree.

I'd never done anything like this. I'd never watched someone bask in this super personal, intimate moment. And I'd never had someone watch me do it, either. And yeah, it could have been awkward at first, but with Claire, it wasn't.

It was one of the hottest things I'd ever done in my life.

I had no idea how much I'd love watching the way she got herself off. And I had no idea how wet I'd get when she brought her unoccupied hand up to one of her small breasts and pinched her nipple between her long fingers. I had no idea how good it would feel when I mirrored the action, or how much I'd like it when Claire opened her eyes and met mine, redness blossoming on her cheeks and half-drunk pleasure hooding her eyelids.

"Spread wider for me," she murmured.

I did and she moaned, her eyes training to the hand between my legs.

"Put your fingers inside yourself," she directed.

I did that, too, and shivered at the relief of having something there for my pussy to clench around. Her head tilted to the side as she watched me finger myself, her lower lip sandwiched between her teeth as she clicked the button on her toy again and the buzzing sound got louder. She moaned again and *fuck*.

I was already fucking close.

"Claire," I whispered as I pulled my fingers out of my pussy and put them back on my clit. "Can I come?"

"What?" she asked.

"I want you to tell me when I can," I said.

She made a soft, desperate sound and her toy whirred louder. "Not yet. Keep touching yourself."

I whimpered, but did as she said, careful not to move my hand too fast and push myself over the edge.

But there was only so much I could do.

"Claire," I gasped a few moments later. "Please. Let me come."

"Oh God," she hissed. "Ask me again."

"Can I come?"

Her legs trembled and the toy got louder. "One more time. Ask me like a good fucking girl."

A jolt of desperate need shot through me.

"*Please*," I nearly shouted. "Please, let me come for you. Please?"

"Yes," she said. "Do it."

Thank God she'd said yes, because there was a pretty good chance I wouldn't have been able to stop myself.

My eyes squeezed shut and I cried out as self-induced pleasure washed over me. I rode the waves of that bliss, pinching my nipple and rubbing my clit to draw out every moment of ecstasy until I couldn't take it anymore and had to take my fingers off it, cupping my mound in my palm as those overwhelming sensations kept flickering through me.

I opened my eyes to see Claire panting, her cheeks bright pink and her thumb flicking back and forth across her nipple. Her lip was back between her teeth and her forehead was creased with purposeful concentration as she watched me.

"Keep touching," she demanded. "Let me keep watching."

And how was I going to say no to that?

I mean, I had to change it up a little. My clit was swollen and far too sensitive to continue rubbing, but I slid a finger inside myself and thrust it in and out, which I was pretty sure she loved seeing.

Mostly because she gasped out how much she loved seeing it.

It still took a while. I knew it would. It took long enough that I was able to make myself come again, pleading with Claire again to say I could, and it was a bit after that when her body began to shake.

"Oh God," she whispered, her lips rounding into a surprised O shape. "Oh, I'm going to... Fuck. *Fuck*." She squeezed her breast harder, fingertips digging into the small mound. "Fuck, put your fingers inside yourself, Tessa, put them—"

I did as she said immediately, thrusting my fingers as deep as they would go. She moaned as if she was the one who had something inside her, her legs bracing against the bed.

"Oh, *fuck*," she said again, and then she was coming.

She threw her head back against the tufted fabric of her headboard. The cry she let out was sweet and musical and so fucking worth waiting for. I watched as she writhed, tensing and shaking, her orgasm rocketing through her as the toy between her legs buzzed incessantly. After a moment, she slammed her thumb on one of the buttons and the sound of it faded to a gentle hum that was covered by the sound of her gasping for breath. Once she'd caught it, she opened her eyes, leaning heavily against the headboard before turning the toy off and putting it to the side with the other items she'd taken out.

"Whew," she said, her voice bright and cheerful. "I liked that."

And I had to laugh, shaking my head as I lifted myself out of the nest of pillows and crawled over to her so I could kiss her as we both recovered.

Seventeen

I spent the night at Claire's.

Not that I *slept* at Claire's. Not much, anyway. After we finished fucking, we lounged naked on her bed, lazy and recovering from the intensity of our orgasms. And show me a person who could lounge on a rich person's bed like that and *not* have a hard time getting up to go home to their old and cheap mattress, and I'll show you a fucking liar.

Because oh my *God* was her bed comfortable.

So I hadn't been inclined to give up my nest of pillows and silky sheets and the warmth of Claire's body in the first place. But then we'd... well.

We'd started...

Talking.

Like we were two girls at a slumber party. Not like one of those fantasy slumber parties with matching silk pyjamas and pillow fights and girls experimenting with girls under the guise of learning to kiss. I mean, yeah, we were naked and we'd been kissing—among other things—but it wasn't an experiment. And we were cuddled up on the pillows, not hitting each other with them.

But those conversations were reminiscent of a slumber party. The deep, middle-of-the-night ones where your souls are on display and that's okay, because the sacredness of the slumber party shields you. The walls around you are a contract: what you say can never, ever leave the room. The darkness of the night is a link: you are connected to that person now, because you know something about them that not many people ever will.

That was how we talked after we fucked.

Like we were friends.

"Tell me about this event I bought you a sexy dress for," she asked at one point, twirling a lock of my hair around her finger as I rested my head against her ribs.

I grimaced. "Do I have to?"

"Well, now that I know you don't want to, absolutely. I'm a sucker for good gossip."

"It's not really good gossip. I mean, it is. But it's not."

She rolled her eyes in what was probably not quite mock exasperation. "Come on, darling. Spill."

"It's this work thing. For this guy."

She let out a knowing, drawn out *oh* sound. "Are you gonna fuck him?"

"No."

Her lip jutted out in a pout. "Why not? I wanted to picture it."

I raised my eyebrows as I looked up at her. "I thought you didn't like guys."

"I mean, I have no attraction to them, but that doesn't mean I don't want to watch them fuck hot girls." She shrugged nonchalantly. "I figure it's kinda like straight guys watching porn. They don't want the guy either, right? It's more like they're picturing themselves as the guy."

"So you want to picture me getting railed by a hot guy so you can pretend you're in the hot guy's place?"

"Exactly."

"Why not just picture yourself doing it?"

"Don't poke holes in my fantasy," she said. "Anyway, I told you thinking about other people being into you makes me horny. Regardless of their gender identity."

"Fair," I said. "But no. Sorry to disappoint, but nothing's happening."

"But *why*?" she pressed.

"He's my brother's best friend."

"Oh. And unlike me, you *wouldn't* want to fuck your sibling's friends because it'll hurt Paige." She twisted her mouth to the side. "Or whatever your brother's name is."

I smirked. "Oh, no. I don't give a fuck about that. Josh and I aren't close. Zain's just an asshole."

She frowned. "So why are you going to this thing for him?"

And well...

Fuck.

Claire knew I was divorced. She'd met Brad face-to-face, even. Which could've made admitting the whole thing to her easier. But it could also make her judge me. I mean, she'd *met* him. She was going to wonder why the fuck I was still pretending to be married to him. So maybe it would just be easier to gloss over that, to tell another little lie just to avoid having to admit to yet another person what a fucking mess I was and—

"Tessa?" she asked.

I paused another moment, then sighed. "You're going to think I'm an idiot."

"I doubt it."

"No, I..."

I still almost made something up. But maybe it was the sacredness of the slumber party rules or something, because what came out was the truth.

"He found out that I've been lying to my family about still being with my ex-husband," I said. "We've been faking a relationship for five years because I've been too scared to tell them my marriage was an abysmal failure."

Despite facing up and Claire being above me, I couldn't bring myself to actually look at her. I blinked, forcing my eyes to look past the lines of her face and into the twinkling dots of her light fixture while she processed all *that*.

"Wait," she said. "The ex-husband from last night?"

"Yes."

"Why would you want to pretend to be married to him?"

Heat started to rise up my face. "Because they like him and for the first time in my life, I felt like I belonged with them. And telling them would be giving that up."

"Oh."

The silence between us felt heavy and I clenched my jaw.

"Go ahead and judge me," I said.

I wasn't expecting my head to be jostled as she let out a honking snort of laughter.

"Judge you?" she repeated. "Darling, come on. You can't honestly believe I'm judging you."

I jerked my shoulder in a half-shrug. "Normal people don't do this kind of thing."

"Maybe," she said. "But I wouldn't like you if you were normal. And since I *do* like you, I'd kinda already figured that out."

I rolled my eyes, but it was mostly to hide the fact that I was trying not to smile.

"Tessa, there is *no* judgement here. Not from me. I'm the chaotic polyamorous embarrassment that my family tried to hide for years because they didn't want anyone to know about my 'little depression problem.' I would've spent ten times what I did on a date with you simply to piss my sister off."

"Oh," I said. "And here I thought it was because of my hot ass."

She wormed her hand under my body, doing her best to grab a handful of said ass. "I would've spent a hundred times what I did to get your hot ass."

That made me laugh. And me laughing made her laugh and squeeze my ass again.

"Why did your family want to hide that you have depression?" I asked when we settled a few moments later.

I thought Claire was going to respond with her trademark snark, but she shrugged solemnly.

"I don't think my mom believed me for a long time," she said. "It wasn't that she didn't care, but she's not an affectionate person. She never has been. And she's a makeup mogul. Her whole *thing* is covering up your flaws, you know?"

That made my heart ache. "You're not a flaw."

"She never said I was." Her throat flexed as she swallowed. "But you kind of just know when someone thinks that about you. And Arthur would sweep anything under the rug that he thought might ruin his lifestyle, so..."

"Who's Arthur?"

"The provider of the other half of my genetic makeup," she said. "We don't talk."

"They aren't married anymore?"

She shook her head. "They never were. But they've been together for like forty years or something like that. But I mean, Mom's seventy-five and he's sixty-three and still thinks he's a boytoy. Which is more and more accurate because most of his original body parts have been replaced with silicone."

"He sounds charming."

"He is. That's the problem. He's also a homophobic weasel who's never had a thought deeper than a cereal bowl. But, you know, he's my dad, so I spent most of my life letting the way he thought of me affect how I thought of myself." She looked down at me and smiled. "So I get it. People do weird shit for their families, even when it doesn't make sense. Everyone always wants to judge and say things like 'Oh, I'd never let that happen to me, I'd never do that, I'd never blahblahblah' but until they actually live it..." She shrugged again. "Family can fuck you up."

I nodded slowly. "Lots of things can fuck you up."

"Like the reason behind why you're a unicorn."

I blinked up at her. "What?"

A knowing smirk twisted her mouth. "Oh come on, Tessa. You try to play this whole 'no commitment unicorn' thing as the majority of your personality. Something happened there."

I opened my mouth, then closed it. "I don't make it the majority of my personality."

"Was it Brad?" she guessed, ignoring me.

"No. I mean, yes, but no."

She pushed on my arm, my body rocking as she prodded me. "Come on. Tell me your story. What was the dawn of this unicorn?"

I laughed softly. "Well, I mean, it started the day I caught Brad cheating on me."

"Because you decided you were getting divorced."

"Well, yeah. But also because that was the day I had my first threesome. With the husbands of the women he was fucking."

Her eyes went wide with excited intrigue. "The *husbands*? Plural?"

"Mm-hmm. I walked in on him having a threesome. So payback felt appropriate."

"You are the most wonderfully vengeful person I know."

My face went warm and I tried not to smile, which was quite easy because it wasn't exactly a happy story. "Well, after that I didn't date or anything. Divorce trauma and all that. I wasn't into it. And then my best friend got married and I met... them."

She frowned. "Who?"

"Nathan and Mel Mauldin."

Saying their names made my throat close, as if my body was allergic to the mere thought of them. The words came out tight, not quite hoarse but not smooth, like I had to force them past all those protective layers to tell Claire who they were, even though saying it would cause me pain.

And apparently, that was obvious.

"What happened?" she asked, her hand moving back to my hair and her fingertips scratching along my scalp in a comforting, encouraging way.

And God.

What hadn't happened?

"We met at the wedding," I said, my voice sounding distant even to me as I pictured the day I'd met them. I'd been wearing a royal blue dress that looked awful on me, but it was Kira's favourite colour and I was the maid of honour, so I was wearing it proudly because she was my best friend. Nathan had been wearing a suit, of course, because he was the best man. And Mel...

She'd been dressed in black.

"I was having a horrible day," I continued. "It was awkward. Most of the people there thought I was still married to Brad so I kept having to make excuses for why he wasn't there. So I finally escaped to the bar and Mel was there and she just... she knew shit about me. Just by looking at me. It was like she could read me, which makes sense, I guess. She has a psychology degree and does social work or something. We got talking and she was just so *enthralling*. One thing led to another and suddenly I was in the cab with them and—"

I had to stop and Claire's hand stroked my hair, though she didn't speak.

"I thought that was going to be it, you know?" I said. "That it was a one-time thing, something crazy that we did after a wedding, and that they would forget about me."

"But they didn't?" Claire asked.

I shook my head. "It got to the point where I had to tell Kira what I'd done. I mean, it was starting to be a big part of my life and she was my best friend and Nathan was her husband's best friend, so... you know? And I was stupid enough to think she'd be happy for me."

"She wasn't?"

"She was weirded out by the whole thing." I sighed. "I mean, I get it, kind of. We grew up in a small town. Just being friends with the queer kid was a huge *thing*, even though hardly anyone except her knew I was bi. And obviously she'd gotten more open-minded in university after we moved to Vancouver and stuff. But the idea that a relationship could exist between more than two people was too much."

"She didn't like it."

I nodded. "But we were still friends. We just didn't talk much about it. And then..."

My throat tightened and I had to stop so I could swallow hard enough to open it up. Claire kept playing with my hair until I managed to speak again.

"He was fucking me one day when he said he loved me."

Claire made an odd noise just then. It was a long, drawn out *oh* noise that pitched up and down, like it wasn't quite sure whether it was a knowing noise or a concerned one or even maybe one that thought it was oddly sweet until it remembered this story wasn't going to have a happy ending.

"I was just thrilled," I said, my voice hollow. "My whole body just went warm. I felt... wanted. Cared for. Validated, like I could go to my best friend and say to her, 'See? This works. This can totally work and it's okay and I'm not weird for wanting it.' I was so fucking *happy*, Claire."

She was looking at me, sympathy already in her eyes because she knew that wasn't it. But I could barely see her.

All I could see was Nathan and the look in his eyes.

The sudden shock.

The immediate regret.

The panic.

The memory was so clear that I could almost feel it. The way my legs were spread so wide for him, the feel of his hips against my thighs, the smell of sex and sweat and excitement thick in the room.

The way he paused, my heart thumping hard as I stared up at him, not quite processing what that look *meant*.

"I was so happy," I repeated. "And then he goes, '...your pussy.'"

"He fucking didn't," Claire said, her eyes wide.

"Mm-hmm. 'I love you...r pussy.' And I just... I froze."

His cock was buried inside me so deep that his pelvis was nearly pressed to mine. That was where he'd hesitated, freezing for one heartbeat, then two, then countless beats after because my heart was racing so hard and had fallen so far out of my chest that I couldn't keep track. Sitting there, my head resting on Claire's chest, I could almost fucking *feel* him, the way he started to pull his cock out of me...

And then put it back in.

"I felt like I was breaking," I said. "And he... he just... kept going."

The words hung there as slow, furious anger bloomed on her face. "He didn't stop."

I shook my head.

"He didn't *stop*," she repeated. "He should've *known*—"

"I know," I said. "Trust me. I was there. And I mean, I didn't say anything, but—"

"He should've just fucking known!" she said.

"I know. I know that now," I said. "And that's why earlier, when it didn't feel right, I... I say things now. Always. But back then, I didn't say anything. Because in my head, it was more important for me to not make it awkward. So he finished and I faked it and then we all just kind of sat there on the bed because like, of *course* Mel had heard him, too. I think he was hoping no one would say anything, but she goes, 'So... you love—' and Nathan *bursts* out laughing and is like, 'Yeah... heat of the moment, hey?'"

"Oh, God," she said, her nose wrinkling in disgust.

"Mel just turned to me and went, 'But Tessa's okay, right?' So of course I lied and said of course I was fine. Then Nathan, the absolute fucker, *ruffled* my fucking hair, like I was a child, and went, 'Tessa knows I love her the same way I love pizza and beer.'"

The cringe of it all was so intense that Claire physically recoiled, but I barely noticed. Not when I was still reliving that moment, the words coming out of his mouth, the swing from the highest of highs to feeling like nothing more than a cheap and greasy guilty pleasure you'd indulge in once in a while.

Like I was nothing more than a toy to them, after thinking I might've meant something.

"Look," Claire said. "I'm not *saying* I'm the kind of person who knows where to find a hitman, but I'm just saying I'm the kind of person who has the resources to find someone who *does*."

I laughed, though it came out sad, and shook my head. "It's okay. It's in the past."

"Are you sure? Because maybe I just want to send someone to have a little chat with him. I just wanna talk to him."

"Does the word 'talk' have a second meaning I don't know about?"

"Maybe."

I smiled a little less sadly that time. "It's okay. I'm okay. We all laughed it off even though I'm pretty sure all of us knew it wasn't funny. I got dressed and when I got home, I just blocked them on everything. Deleted them from my entire life. Then I went to talk to Kira and she just... well. The second I said it was over, she said some shit that was really fucked up. I didn't even get to tell her what had actually happened. And that kind of ended our friendship."

"I'm sorry to hear that."

I shrugged. "She regretted it. But you can't put toothpaste back in the tube, you know? And I just... I thought a lot about it and I *liked* what

I'd had with Nathan and Mel. I liked being with two people at once. I missed the excitement and the dynamic of fucking people like that. I just didn't want more out of it. So I eventually signed up for MatchMi and figured I'd see if anyone was interested in a casual unicorn thing."

"I bet you hardly got any hits," she said in a voice so innocent it was sarcastic.

"Oh, not at all," I said. "Just so many in the first few days that I had to change my settings to be super niche so I wasn't showing up for as many users."

"I'm so shocked," she said, completely dead-pan. "A lot of people were looking for that kind of thing?"

"Mm-hmm. Including Nathan and Mel."

She tilted her head to the side, frowning. "What?"

"They found me on MatchMi. And messaged me."

Her eyes went round. "They *didn't*!"

"They did," I said.

"What did you do?"

"Took a screenshot of the massive amounts of messages I had in my inbox, sent it to them, and then blocked them." I smiled, though it was still a bit bitter. "Because fuck them. I never wanted to see them again. I was better off without them."

"Damn right you are," Claire said. "They never deserved you. They're the kind of people who give this a bad name."

"Give what?"

"This," she said. "Being poly. Those were fucking toxic unicorn hunters who just happened to be good at disguising themselves. They never deserved the beauty of you, Tess. No one who makes you feel like that does."

They should have been comforting words, but something about them made me pause. Claire caught it and twirled a piece of my hair around her finger playfully.

"I say that as a friend, of course," she said.

"You sure?" I asked. "That was almost poetic."

She let the lock of my hair fall from her fingertips, then repeated the action. "Part of being poly, for me at least, is recognizing that feelings of attraction don't necessitate a full relationship. I can care deeply for someone and have strong feelings without it meaning I want you to be my girlfriend or something. We're friends now, Tess."

"Are we?"

"You know my deepest, darkest secrets. I can't think of anyone else who knows that much about me. So yeah." She leaned down and kissed me on the lips, but in a way that felt completely platonic. "We're basically best friends, actually."

I tried not to laugh as I kissed her back. "You've known me for a day."

"Yeah," she said. "But it's been a really good day, don't you think?"

And the thing was, despite everything—despite being ghosted, despite the chaos of the gala, despite Brad showing up and meddling like he always did, despite having to go shopping, despite reliving one of the most difficult moments of my life—I had to agree with her.

It had been a great day.

Part 4

Confession: It's none of your business.

Eighteen

I KNEW IT WAS going to be a bad day when I didn't have time to shower before heading to Victoria.

It wasn't my fault. Sure, I'd been rushing when I left Claire's place to go back to mine so I could pack before getting an Uber to the bus station, where I'd get on the coach bus that would take me onto the ferry and to downtown Victoria. But there *should* have been more than enough time for me to shower, pack, and to get to the station comfortably early.

And then *someone* had to go and fuck it up.

I didn't pay attention to the car parked on the driveway except to be annoyed that my Uber couldn't pull in there. My assumption was that it was someone there to visit Dottie. One of her kids or grandkids or nieces or something. The spot was included in my rent since Dottie had the garage, but I only ever used it on the rare occasions that I had a visitor since I didn't own a car. I'd told her to let her guests use it whenever and if, for some reason, I needed it, I'd let her know.

And I suppose I was technically right because the person who owned the car *was* related to Dottie. He was whatever you call the child of your niece's ex-husband from his first marriage. An ex-step-grandnephew, maybe, but Dottie called him "sugar" on the rare occasions they saw each other, and I called him Jackson Clark.

That semi-tangential relation was how I'd found this rental in the first place. He'd heard that Dottie was looking for someone to rent her garden suite shortly after I'd left my ex-husband and was crashing on Jackson's couch as I looked for a place I could afford, since he was married to Kira.

That is, Kira Clark, known prior to her marriage as Kira Katz because her parents thought that would be adorable instead of borderline traumatizing, especially once Kira turned out to be an anxious wreck and set herself up to be called Scaredy Katz for most of her childhood.

My best friend.

Former best friend, I should say.

My childhood best friend who I now did everything I could to avoid, despite her being a high-end interior designer who regularly commissioned paintings from me for her stupid wealthy clients, and who was standing in front of my door with her back to me.

She was wearing a pale yellow dress with lace sleeves and a billowy skirt that set off the cool tones of her white skin. Her acorn brown hair was trimmed into the same stylish pixie cut she'd gotten when she chopped off her waist-length strands a week after marrying the man standing beside her.

Dr. Jackson Clark was a massive fucking nerd and didn't care who knew it. His tightly coiled hair was cropped close to his head and he wore the same thin-rimmed wire glasses he'd been wearing since before Kira had met him back in university. The man was arguably good looking, with dark brown skin and a wide nose. He was on the heavier side of chubby, though he carried his weight proportionally and in another, much less nerdy life, could have easily turned himself into a linebacker. In this life, though, he was currently dressed in a boring golf shirt tucked into a boring pair of khaki pants. I was pretty sure Jackson had two PhDs—one in some kind of science that had to do with molecules or genetics or something, and another in being the world's most stereotypical nerd.

"Uh…" I said as I stepped onto the sidewalk.

Kira squealed as she jumped and turned, her eyes wide. Beside her, Jackson turned slowly to regard me.

"Oh, hello Tessa," he said calmly. "We thought you'd be inside the house."

"I was out," I said, glancing from him to Kira. "What are you doing here?"

"I was, um, picking up the Clarkdale commission?" she said, her high-pitched voice lilting up at the end. "I thought it would be on the step like usual but—"

"Shit," I said, wincing. "Sorry. I... forgot."

Her eyes somehow got even wider. "Forgot? Like... like—"

"To put it out," I said, my voice flat. "Not to paint it. It's done. I just, uh, ended up crashing at a friend's place last night."

Her cheeks flushed red. "Right. Of course. Sorry."

"I'll grab it," I said, starting forward so I could slip past them and unlock the door.

"Sure," Kira said, her hands fluttering as she hovered awkwardly behind me. "We could come in to get it, if you want."

"No, it's my fault. I can get it," I said, misunderstanding her in a way that was obviously deliberate.

She looked at Jackson, who had a vacant smile on his face, then back at me. "Are you sure? I would love to help you, Tess."

I bit back what I wanted to say, which was that she'd let that ship sail years earlier.

Because she had.

I thought for a while that she didn't like me seeing Nathan and Mel because of the connection. Because they were her and Jackson's "couple friends" and I wasn't part of a *couple*. I was a fifth-wheel. And because Jackson was an anti-social nerd and Nathan was one of the few friends he'd made in university, back when he wasn't Dr. Jackson Clark but just... I don't know. Pre-Dr. Jackson Clark. Grad School Jackson Clark, maybe. Nathan was as smart as Jackson was, though he was infinitely more sociable, which was probably why he'd managed to stay friends with Jackson when other people found his awkwardness to be too much to handle.

It would've been fair if that was the reason Kira had been upset when I was with Mel and Nathan. I *got* that it might have been weird. And for a while, the guilt had eaten at me. But when it seemed like things were becoming *real* with Mel and Nathan, that guilt had faded, right up until they finished shattering the small parts of my heart that hadn't been broken after my divorce from Brad.

And I tried to tell Kira that when it happened.

I tried to tell her I was sorry, even though I didn't regret it.

But as it turned out, it would've been weird to her regardless of who I was with.

"You couldn't have possibly thought they would love you forever."

Maybe she would've said something else if I'd told her the whole story. And maybe I should've. Maybe I should've told her that Nathan had blurted out that he loved me in the middle of sex, then overcorrected and said he loved my pussy. That he finished fucking me before saying he loved me the same way he loved pizza and beer. That I'd been so stunned, it was all I could do to laugh with them before leaving him and Mel forever and going to my best friend's place with tears in my eyes and my heart broken.

Maybe I shouldn't have let things fall apart the way they did without Kira knowing the whole story.

Maybe it would've changed things if I'd told her.

But when someone says something like that... I mean, it hurts. It hurts regardless of their knowledge of the situation.

I didn't *want* to tell Kira what had happened. Because when you're at the lowest of your lows and someone kicks you, you don't splay on the ground and bare yourself to them in the hopes they won't kick again.

You curl up.

You shield yourself.

And then a whole lifetime of friendship is gone in ten words.

"I don't need help," I said. "I'll be quick. I don't want to take up more of your day."

"Oh," she said as I pushed the door open. "Well, we don't have any—"

"Be right back," I said, then let the door swing shut behind me.

It took me no more than thirty seconds to get the painting. In a rare twist of events, I'd managed to finish it the previous weekend. Not that I usually missed deliveries or anything, but most of the time, I was cutting it close to the deadline she gave me. But this time, I'd gotten it wrapped up for Kira a couple of days early.

Of course, it was the one week she hadn't been able to make it to my place to pick it up early.

"Well, I hope they like it," I said as I walked back outside with the canvas.

"I know they will," Kira said loyally as she took the piece from me. "They always do."

That was bullshit, but I smiled at her all the same.

"Well, great," I said, clapping my hands together. "So, anyway, I should get—"

"How are you doing, Tessa?" she said, her voice almost desperate.

"Huh?"

"You know." She laughed nervously, glancing at Jackson. "I mean, I haven't seen you in ages. It's like we can't seem to get our schedules aligned. I keep missing you when we come to pick the paintings up."

"I know, right?" I said. "What are the chances? Totally crazy and completely not intended."

She let out an awkward half-laugh. "I didn't think it was."

"Right." I cleared my throat. "Um, well, I'm fine. Thanks. How are you?"

"I'm doing great," she said. "Really, really well."

"Great," I said.

There was a moment of awkward silence.

"And, um, Jackson?" I said when I couldn't stand it any longer. "How are you doing?"

"Excellent, thank you," Jackson said in a voice that made him sound like an android. "I've recently finished some research on—"

And then he spouted off something technical that sounded, to my ears, like it contained more made-up words than your average Dr. Seuss book.

"Wow," I said when he finished and there was a beat of awkward silence. "That sure is... science."

"It is," Jackson agreed solemnly.

"Okay," I said. "Well, this has been—"

"Are you seeing anyone?" Kira blurted.

I blinked at her. Her face turned red.

"You just, um, said... you crashed. At a friend's place. So I... I was curious."

"Oh," I said. "Uh... not... not really."

She nodded, jerking her head in a twitchy nod as she set her mouth into a thin line. Another awkward moment of silence passed and I sighed.

"You can just say it, Kira," I said.

"Say what?"

"Whatever it is you're trying not to say."

"She's right, dear," Jackson said. "You're doing that thing with your mouth where you're trying to physically hold a statement in."

Kira's mouth pressed tighter together and she forced a smile. "Thank you, sweetheart."

"You're very welcome," Jackson said.

"Well, Kira?" I asked.

She sighed. "I just wanted to know if you were still, um, 'married.'"

Of course she did.

"Sure am," I said. "As of last month anyway. Which... oh! How's the adoption going?"

Kira stared at me. "What?"

"I saw your mom in Burnsley. My parents had an anniversary thing and... and she mentioned you were adopting."

"Oh," Kira said, her throat flexing as she swallowed. "Um, well, yes. We... are. Were."

"We told Kira's mom we were talking to a birthmother and were about to sign the paperwork," Jackson said. "A few weeks ago, she changed her mind and decided to keep the baby."

"We hadn't told my mom yet," Kira said in a small voice.

Of course I had to go and make things more awkward.

"I'm sorry to hear that," I said uncomfortably.

"It's okay," Kira said. "We knew it was a possibility going into this. It's what's best for the baby and we have to respect that, even if it's hard. We're keeping our hopes up, though."

"Yes," Jackson said. "Mel said she'd see if there were other agencies we could try since she has access to a list of them for work."

Kira's face went pink as I blinked at them.

"Mel," I repeated, my voice high-pitched. "She's... helping you. With that."

"She is," Jackson said, his voice still completely oblivious. "She and Nathan were over for dinner last weekend, actually, and she said—"

"Jackson," Kira hissed, glancing at me.

I laughed. What the fuck else was I supposed to do?

"It's fine," I said. "It's... you're friends with them. I knew that going into... what I did."

Kira's face fell. "Tessa, wait—"

"I am so sorry to hear things didn't work out with the adoption," I continued, ignoring her. "I hope it works out for you soon. But you'll have to excuse me. I actually have this thing in Victoria I need to get to and if I don't get ready now, I'll miss the bus to the ferry."

"We could give you a ride, if you wanted," she said.

"No, I'm good."

She looked like she was going to insist, but swallowed back that instinct and nodded. "Okay. It was great to see you again, Tess."

So I didn't have time to shower before going to Victoria. And maybe it wasn't entirely Kira's fault, since it wasn't like they were at my place for that long. Maybe I was being a bit delusional about how much time I had, since I barely had enough of it to grab my suitcase and throw in whatever random shit I thought I might need for the weekend.

But it was easier to say it was because of Kira's impromptu visit.

Nineteen

AN OCCUPIED HOTEL ROOM is an amazing insight into who a person is.

Homes are a mix of personal and pageantry. They're staged so they can choose what you are and aren't allowed to see. So while you might get insight into someone's favourite things and the ways they relax, a home is more about them curating the things they want you to *think* they hold dear.

But a hotel room is a blank canvas. It's not a home. It's not a place you have to keep clean or tidy yourself. You don't bring the things you hold dear: throw pillows or expensive decor or diplomas hanging on the wall.

You just bring what's important.

Your clothing. Your toiletries. The things you truly can't—or at least, truly don't *want* to—live without. Those things that end up set out on clean white washcloths and generic trinket trays like a personal little art exhibit curated by housekeeping.

Being in Zain's hotel room taught me a lot of surprising things about someone I'd known for most of my life. Even though he'd spent countless hours and days and nights at my house when we were growing up, his art exhibit had been relegated to a backpack or duffel bag that was stowed in Josh's bedroom.

But here, alone in his room because he'd left a key for me at reception since he was still at his work thing... well.

Here I had plenty of time to look.

To learn.

To... okay, yes, I was snooping. So sue me.

The suitcase sitting next to the bed was empty. Zain's clothes were split between hanging in the closet and folded into one of the dresser drawers. Everything was placed just so, like he'd taken the time to make sure each and every piece was crisp and wrinkle-free before storing it away. A small laundry bag sat on the floor of the closet next to a pair of Converse, but even the bag looked like it was filled with neatly stacked clothes.

I didn't open it to check, of course. That would've gone past the point of snooping and into creepy territory.

On the nightstand was a pair of glasses that I had no idea Zain wore, a yellow tube of ginger-lime flavoured lip balm, and some kind of fantasy novel with a crumpled receipt for a bookmark placed a little more than halfway through. In the bathroom, there was a contact lens case and a small bottle of solution sitting on one side of the sink next to an orange prescription bottle that I *definitely* didn't snoop on.

And even if I had, it wasn't like I knew what rizatriptan was, and Googling it would've been another step too far into creepy territory.

Then there was the travel shave kit. It wasn't entirely unusual—nothing about the words "travel shave kit" seemed out of place for a hotel room—but it wasn't just a disposable razor and some shave gel. No, Zain had a full safety razor with a little dish, a shaving brush, and a small container of expensive-looking shave soap.

It was very extra of him. As were the bottles of shampoo and soap he'd brought from home, leaving the little complimentary bottles untouched until I gathered them up and shoved them in my own suitcase.

All of it painted the picture of a tidy, organized man who cared about his appearance. Which was insight into my brother's best friend that I didn't need or necessarily even want.

The downside of taking the coach bus and ferry into Victoria was that I was bound by their schedule, so even after snooping thoroughly through Zain's hotel room, there was still a good amount of time before

I even had to get ready for the event. I wandered back to where I'd left my suitcase by the couch, sighing as I sat down and tried to figure out how to amuse myself while trying not to think about the impending night of fake-dating I had ahead of me.

Chuck wasn't an option. I'd already texted him while I was on the ferry about the events of the previous night and the subsequent hijinks of my trip to Victoria. He'd been thrilled, of course, but even if I hadn't already filled him in on my evening with the woman who totally wasn't my sugar mama, he wasn't around anymore.

Chuck

> Charles and I are going to a bar. For wings and possibly a beer for me since he said you aren't supposed to drink wine with wings. Which is a travesty since they're spelled so similarly.

Me

> That sounds completely unlike you.

Chuck

> It is. After that, he's taking me to see a hockey.

Me

> A hockey what?

Chuck

> Game. On the ice. He's very excited. Something about being there for history because one of the hockeys have never won a playoff and the other one is his preferred hockey so either way it'll be a titillating experience.

Me

You seem both thrilled and willfully ignorant about how to use the word "hockey."

Chuck

So thrilled. About the premium fellatio I'LL be getting when we get home after being dragged to my very first hockey.

That made me laugh.

Me

You've never been to a game before?

Chuck

Nope. I never went as a kid and it was beyond not a priority as an adult. I've seen games on TV and I'd rather watch paint dry.

Me

So why are you going, then?

Chuck

Because Charles, Tessa Jessica Lane. And what part of "premium fellatio" do you not understand?

Me

I guess the fellatio part? Since I don't have a dick.

He'd sent back three laughing-face emojis, but then he had to go get ready for his date night. And other than Chuck... well. I guess I could've texted Claire, but that felt a bit too clingy.

So rather than that, I decided to do something I hadn't done in months.

Well, something I hadn't done in months for that specific reason. I opened up MatchMi.

> **Howdy, TessTheUnicorn! You have 100+ unread messages. Your last login was 3 days ago.**

Jesus.

There were a lot of messages. And a lot of repeat messages. Many of them from days and weeks earlier. All of them unopened.

Except one, of course.

I considered going through everything one by one, seeing if there were any potential couples that might still be interested in getting to know each other. I considered it for approximately eight seconds before hitting Select All, then the garbage icon.

> **Are you sure you want to permanently delete all messages?**

I hesitated for another second, then hit *Yes* and watched as every message disappeared.

Every single one.

Then, I went to the Matches page and started swiping.

Which was stupid of me.

Not because I swiped right on someone I shouldn't have or something, but because by the time I forced myself to stop swiping so I could get ready for Zain's event, my phone was nearly dead. And in my haste to throw random shit into a suitcase that I might need for the weekend, what had I forgotten to pack?

My charger.

Mentally kicking myself, I left my phone sitting on the couch, then went to take a shower. I was still rinsing conditioner out when a loud knock made me jump and nearly crash to the floor.

"What?!" I yelped.

"Whatcha doing in there, Teacup?" came Zain's dry but amused voice.

I glared in the general direction of the door, wiping water out of my eyes. "I'm in the shower, genius."

"And am I gonna have to join you or are you going to be done soon so I can freshen up before dinner?"

"Oh, fuck off," I grumbled. I didn't think I'd said it loud enough that he could hear me, but his laughter floated through the door.

I finished rinsing my hair as quickly as I could. Grumpily, I wrapped a towel around my head, then put on one of the hotel robes and grabbed the hair dryer before leaving the bathroom.

Zain looked up as I did. Then he looked down. Then he looked up again, an asshole smirk spreading across his stupid face and making it look far more delicious than it should have.

"Looks familiar," he said. "I think you're missing the face mask, though."

"Shut up," I said.

"Just saying. I'm starting to get used to the hotel robe view."

"Well, don't."

He chuckled as I stomped across the room so I could get my hair stuff out of my suitcase. Almost embarrassingly, it took until I was standing right in front of the couch for me to realize my bag had disappeared from the spot I'd left it.

As had my phone.

"What—" I started.

"It's over there," Zain said, his voice almost bored.

"Over there" ended up being beside the bed. My suitcase was tucked next to the nightstand, which had been cleared of Zain's sundry things and replaced by my phone.

The asshole.

"I'm not sharing a bed with you, Zain."

"Wasn't planning on it," he replied.

I frowned, looking over my shoulder at him. "What?"

His jaw twitched in amusement. "I'm not actually making you sleep on the couch, Tess. You take the bed. I've got the couch."

"No," I said.

He flicked an eyebrow up. "What?"

"I'm fine sleeping on the couch."

"Well, that will be where I'm sleeping," he said, opening the closet door. "I don't think there's enough room for both of us and it seems kind of ridiculous when there's a perfectly good bed right there, but you can be little spoon if you want."

"Zain—"

"I'm not fighting with you on this, Teacup. You sleep wherever you want. But I will be sleeping on the couch."

Then he pulled a suit out of the closet and went into the bathroom, closing the door behind him.

Fucking Zain.

I glared at the door for a moment, but it wasn't like that was going to do anything. Sighing, I plugged the hairdryer in next to the mirror across from the bathroom and tamed my wet hair into something that bordered on messy waves but in a stylish way. That took a lot longer to do that than it did to do my makeup—tinted moisturizer, mascara, and red lipstick were my go-tos whether it was a fancy gala event or a run to the grocery store—and once I was done both, I shrugged the hotel robe off and started to dress.

Which is when I noticed I'd forgotten another important thing.

Not underwear. I'd remembered to bring three pairs of those to a single overnight trip like any smart woman would.

But I'd forgotten the bike shorts I wore as underwear on the rare occasions I had to wear a dress, which meant I was going to be dealing with my thighs rubbing together all night. Annoyed, I put on one of the clean thongs I'd brought and wondered if Zain had baby powder lying around that I hadn't noticed while I was snooping and could steal to prevent my thighs from chafing.

In hindsight, I should have been paying more attention. Or at least listened to make sure the shower was still running before taking the robe off. I very narrowly missed getting caught naked by Zain. Luck was on my side, however, and I had my underwear on and was doing the "Oh God why do they make these things so awkward to zip up by yourself" dance with my dress. I'd managed to get the zipper halfway up my back when the bathroom door opened and Zain stepped out looking like something out of the smutty romance novels Dottie loved to read.

And I meant that. He was whatever the trope was where the guys are total alpha business types with waifish and naïve secretaries who can't stop themselves from swooning to their knees every time their boss walks into the room.

And it was unfair. It was fucking *unfair*.

It wasn't even that he cleaned up nice. Zain was hot as it was, with his longish hair and high cheekbones. But when you added on the dark blue suit that was perfectly tailored to his frame, but that also showed off a peek of his tattooed forearms if he twisted in just the right way, and the flawlessly tied tie, the slight sheen of his freshly shaved cheeks and chin...

Fuck.

By the time I realized I was staring, I'd been doing it long enough that it was obvious. I blinked and braced myself, ready for the inevitable moment when Zain, being Zain, would start teasing me and taunting me for looking at him like that.

But he didn't.

Probably because *he* was so busy staring that he hadn't noticed *me* staring.

"Wow," he said.

"What?" I asked.

"That's..." He blinked as he trailed off, then shook his head slowly. "Wow."

I folded my arms, aggravated. "Wow what, Zain?"

"You look amazing," he said.

I rolled my eyes. "Of course I do. I always look amazing."

That seemed to surprise him out of his stupor, if the slight shock on his face when he laughed was any indication. But he blinked and shook his head, though not fast enough that I didn't notice his cheeks were slightly pinker than usual.

"Yeah, well," he said. "I thought maybe you were going to wear the robe to dinner so you could teach me a lesson or something."

"I said I'd be here and I said I'd be good."

"You did," he agreed. "And, uh... thank you. For doing that for me."

"Whatever," I muttered, trying to ignore the warm feeling that gave me. "Now help me out here and zip the rest of my dress up so I can stop jumping around."

"I mean, I'm not gonna say no to watching you jump up and down a little more—"

"You're disgusting."

He chuckled. "Turn around."

I did, waiting as he tugged the zipper the rest of the way up before he did up the little hook and eye clasp at the top.

"You bought this for this weekend?" he asked, and I could hear the frown in his voice.

"Yeah," I said.

"Really?"

"Why would I lie about that?"

"You bought a designer dress for my work dinner?"

"What?"

I felt his fingers brush against my skin as he turned the neckline of the dress up. "This is an Amoren Viole dress."

It was fucking *what*?!

I hadn't even thought to look at the tag. Claire had been distracting me and I hadn't... well. But I should've looked. I couldn't reasonably argue that I could afford an Amoren Viole dress, especially not when she was one of the only luxury designers that made plus sized clothes and I'd already told Zain what a failure I was. And I didn't want to get into how I got the dress, not when it meant I'd have to share yet another secret with Zain.

So I deflected.

"Since when are you into women's fashion?" I asked.

"Amoren Viole does more than dresses," he said. "I'm literally wearing a Viole watch right now."

"Well, look at that," I said. "You have Amoren Viole, I have Amoren Viole. We practically coordinated outfits."

"Mmm," he said. "And something tells me this dress was even more expensive than my watch was."

"Well, it's... a knockoff," I said.

"My watch?"

"The dress."

"Sure about that, Teacup? Because it's one *hell* of a knockoff if it is."

He was still holding the back of my dress. Swallowing hard, I stepped forward so he had to let go and walked as casually as I could back to my suitcase to get my shoes. I could feel his eyes on me, but I didn't look at him until he spoke a few moments later.

"Did he buy that for you?"

My lips parted as I stared at him in disbelief. "Excuse me?"

Zain's face was blank except for his eyes, which had a flare of anger in them. "Did you ask Brad for money to buy a dress for this?"

An incredulous laugh huffed past my lips. "First of all, that's none of your business—"

"It's entirely my business." He took a step forward. "This whole thing is my business. You're *here* because I learned your little secret and that means it is my business if you asked that weaselfucker for money to be here. Because I don't want you to ask for more from him, Tessa. I want you to get the fuck away from him."

The words hung heavy in the room. I stared at Zain, holding that tension, almost revelling in it. Why, I couldn't say. I wanted to be offended by his so-called "giving a shit," especially when he was sitting there spouting off what he did and didn't want me to do and implying that I was stupid enough to ask Brad for anything else after getting myself in the mess I was in.

But at the same time, he'd called Brad a weaselfucker, and that was legitimately hilarious.

"Second of all," I continued, my voice steady. "No. He didn't buy this. He doesn't even know I'm here."

Zain's throat flexed as he swallowed, then he jerked his head forward in a nod. "Alright. Good."

"Good," I agreed.

I pulled my pumps out of my suitcase and walked over to the couch, sitting so I could slide them on. And that was it; I was ready. Zain similarly seemed ready to go, even though the doors to the event didn't open for a while. He moved across the room silently, sitting on the other side of the couch.

"I didn't think this would be so uncomfortable," he said after a while.

"No?" I asked. "You thought a little fake relationship born out of blackmail would be smooth and easy going the whole time?"

"I, at no point, blackmailed you," he said, his voice almost tired. "You offered. I told you I would've kept it secret regardless."

"Believing that would require me to trust you."

That seemed to surprise him. "You don't trust me?"

"Why would I?"

"I've never given you a reason not to."

"Well, you've never given me a reason *to*, either." I frowned, then looked at him. "And yes, you have!"

He looked bewildered. "Have I?"

"Did you and I have different childhood experiences or something?" I asked. "You and Josh constantly mocked me. You still do."

"I do not," he said, his voice low. "And I... I didn't."

"You sat there while Josh did."

"He was being an idiot. Kids are assholes and brothers are just like that sometimes. Yeah, he was a dick, but it's not like he hated you or didn't care or something."

I glared at him. "For the sake of us needing to get through this dinner as a convincing couple, I'm going to pretend I didn't hear your thinly veiled 'boys will be boys' mixed with 'he's mean to you because he likes you' argument."

Shamed realization dawned on Zain's face. "Wait, that's not—"

"But regardless, you're wrong," I continued. "Maybe if he'd balanced being an asshole with acting like a decent brother once or twice, I'd believe you. But he didn't. And you were as bad as he was."

His lips parted. "What are you talking about?"

"Seriously? I spent my whole life listening to you two make fun of me!" I said. "Laughing at me, not taking me seriously, stealing my sketchbooks and ruining my things and treating me like garbage. Neither of you ever seemed to 'give a shit' about me like you're claiming you did, so why would I trust you about anything?"

"Tessa—"

"Whatever, Zain. I don't want to talk about this with you."

Heavy silence filled the space between us. For the sake of breaking it, I grabbed my phone off the nightstand. Sure, the thing was almost dead, but I needed something to do. So I scrolled on my phone, not even sure what I was looking at, as he sat there in contemplative moodiness.

Because my heart was racing. It was thundering so hard in my chest that I thought it might be visible through my skin. Part of it was the adrenaline of pride, of telling Zain exactly what I thought of him and my brother and how fucking *awful* they'd been to me.

And part of it was the discomfort of knowing with an unmerited but complete certainty that all of this was news to Zain.

That he *hadn't* known how awful he and Josh were to me.

How I'd seen them. How I'd seen *him*.

And that hearing it had rattled him.

"Will you tell me how you got the dress, at least?" Zain asked quietly a little while later.

"None of your business."

"I just want to make sure it—*oh*."

I looked at him. "Oh what?"

The annoyed look on his face gave way to a knowing one, complete with one of his asshole smirks. "Sugar daddy?"

I kept my face as neutral as I could because while he was wrong, he was only *technically* wrong. "Nope. You offering?"

"You wish."

"Do I? Or is it something *you* wish, Daddy Zain?"

He coughed, almost startled. "Uh... yeah, no. That's... no. Don't do that."

"Yes, Daddy," I said in my most sarcastically docile voice.

"Tessa, I swear—" he said, but I couldn't hold it back anymore and snorted with laughter.

And after a moment, so did he.

Twenty

ZAIN WAS NOT A shy person.

It was easy enough to think he was. People always assumed quiet, serious people like him were shy, like stoicism and introversion were flaws rather than natural states for some people. And maybe he had been shy, once upon a time. Somewhere in the back of my mind, there were vague hints of hazy moments where I thought of him as shy when he and Josh first became friends. But then, I would've been about six years old at the time those misty recollections were formed, so I could have easily been misremembering things.

Now, though, the Zain I knew was solemn to the point of disinterest. He was the kind of person who might speak when spoken to, should he deign the person speaking to him worthy of a response. He was cocky. Composed. Clever and cutting to the point of unfriendliness.

Or at least, that was what I thought he was like. But it was beginning to seem more and more likely that my mind had been playing tricks on me when it came to who Zain was as a person.

He was the person I expected as we walked from our hotel room to the hall where the conference dinner was being held. That is, he was quiet. The elevator ride down wasn't awkward so much as it was resigned, and the subsequent walk from the elevator down the hallway was steeped in something that felt like silent dread. It wasn't until we were nearly at the entrance that he stopped, putting a hand on my forearm and pulling me to the side so he could look me in the eye.

"Look," he said, cool neutrality on his face and in his voice. "I know, okay?"

"Huh?"

"I know you don't want to be here. And I know why you are." His throat flexed as he swallowed and for a moment—just a moment—something vulnerable flashed in his eyes. "Just... can you please pretend to like me?"

"What?"

His mouth twitched with annoyance. "Just while we're in there, Teacup. I need you to..." He stopped, then sighed. "Please. Please just pretend you can stand me for one night."

I wasn't sure whether to be sympathetic to his concerns or offended he had them in the first place. And frankly, I was too stunned to decide.

"I told you I was going to do this," I said. "Do you not believe me?"

He glanced to the side, waiting as a couple of people walked into the hall before speaking again.

"I do," he said. "I trust you, even if you don't trust me. I just..."

He took a shallow breath before his lower lip curled into his mouth. When he spoke again, his voice was even softer, but intense with sincerity.

"This promotion is everything, Tess," he said. "I really fucking need it. I needed to get the hell away from Vernon before and now that my parents are trying to move nearby, it's..." He stopped, shaking his head. "I wouldn't have asked you to do this unless it was important. Just help me out and I swear, I won't say anything about your shitstain ex-husband again."

I frowned. "Not doing a hell of a lot for my trust level here, Zain."

"What?"

"You said multiple times that you wouldn't have said anything regardless of if I did this."

"I won't. I just... I'll double not say anything."

"What the hell does that mean?"

He winced. Well, a slight cringe wrinkled the spot between his eyebrows, barely noticeable, but for someone as poised as Zain, it was like a flashing neon arrow pointing to the nerves he'd been concealing.

"I don't know," he said, and there was even a wisp of worry in his *voice*. "I just—"

"Zain," I said. "I promise I'll do my best to help you."

He nodded, though he didn't quite seem convinced. "Okay. Alright."

I don't know what possessed me to do it; why I was suddenly sympathetic to him and why I felt the need to reassure him. But regardless, I did, and I reached forward so I could loop my arm through his. He looked down, surprised, as I turned us so we could start towards the entrance.

"I promise," I repeated quietly. "I promise so hard that I won't even joke about being Daddy's good girl while we're in there because I know it'll piss you off."

He tried to glare at me out of the corner of his eye, but it wasn't very effective considering that he was pressing his lips together to hold in a laugh.

We entered a room full of people who did whatever it was Zain did for a living. Or, at least, worked in jobs that were tangentially related to whatever it was Zain did for a living. Which was something to do with business risk management that I understood just enough about to make it convincing that we might actually be dating, so long as no one asked me too many questions. Men in suits and women in cocktail dresses were standing in pods around the room, some talking, none listening, just waiting for their turn to speak brashly and boldly and loudly. Heels clacked on the floor as boisterous laughter that reminded me of my dad's echoed through the room.

It was almost, but not quite, my version of hell.

I may not have been much of an artist anymore, but give me a gallery full of pretentious people who claimed to understand the meaning behind a stained napkin mistakenly dropped on the floor near the garbage can and I'd be fine. But a room of people who seemed to be plastic, who played a game I didn't know the rules to and didn't care to learn? A room full of people who equated worth to money and nothing else?

Walking into that room was just a reminder of how much I didn't belong.

I took a shallow breath in an attempt to calm my nerves, but if Zain noticed, he didn't say anything. He was too busy morphing into someone who was meant to be in this room. Each step we took was a shift, though in a way that was so subtle, I almost missed it. Moodiness morphed to stoicism; disinterest to confidence; cleverness to shrewdness, and suddenly the man holding my arm was a version of Zain I didn't know. He wasn't someone else entirely; he was still him, just... elevated, somehow. He commanded attention and people gave it; he was still reserved, but there was an approachability to him now.

I mean, he even smiled at people.

Like, on purpose.

I think.

"There he is!" said a loud voice as Zain and I approached one of the many pods of businessmen. Zain let go of my arm as his head tilted in recognition at the group, all generic men in generic suits. They may have been our age or older; I couldn't really tell, not when they all had similar haircuts and the most subtle treatments they could possibly find to make themselves look younger without it being especially obvious they'd had work done.

"Here I am," Zain said in a smooth, relaxed voice. "You can all stop holding your breath in anticipation now."

They laughed in unison and one of the men stepped forward, extending his hand and clasping Zain's firmly enough that there was an audible thwack when their hands came together. He was white and wearing a blue suit with a striped tie, expensive cufflinks, and a white-gold watch. His hair was light brown and he had an excessively straight nose that must have cost him a fortune.

"Hell of a week, Hameed," the man said. "Think you can knock one more out of the park so we can end on a high note?"

Zain cocked one cocky eyebrow cockily. "You think I can't?"

Another roar of laughter circled the pod of businessmen. The man let go of Zain's hand and looked at me, the corners of his eyes crinkled.

"That's what we want to hear, am I right?"

He said it to me as if I knew and/or cared what they were talking about. And since I was there to pretend like I knew and/or cared, I smiled and nodded politely at the man. He held my gaze, though after a moment, he frowned and looked from me to Zain with an expression like he was pretending to hide his bewilderment to highlight the fact that he was purposely letting it show.

"Well, who's this, then?" he asked.

Zain turned and looked at me. I braced myself, assuming I'd see that performative pod-person expression they were all wearing and have to stop myself from shuddering. But Zain's face softened and a smile spread across his lips, and suddenly he was looking at me like I was the only one in the room.

Like I wasn't pretending to be his girlfriend.

Like I was his whole world, and then some.

He focused his attention on me and me alone. In one smooth movement, he slipped his arm around my waist and put his hand on the small of my back, sending heat soaring through my body as he guided me forward like it was a natural thing he'd done a million times before.

"This is my girlfriend," he said. "Tessa Lane. Tessa, this is my boss, Owen."

"Tessa Lane," Owen repeated slowly. "What an absolute pleasure."

I wasn't expecting to hear that much sincerity coming from anyone in this room, but maybe Owen's genuine shock had made his plastic businessman facade crack. Part of me wanted to know why, but it didn't matter. His shock wasn't my problem; pretending to be a good enough girlfriend that I could convince him to give my fake boyfriend a real promotion was.

"It's so nice to finally have a face to a name," I said as I shook his outstretched hand. "I've heard so much about all of you."

His head tilted to the side. "Have you?"

"Of course." I looked at Zain, attempting to mimic his soft expression and hoping it came across as genuine. "All he talks about is work, work, work. I feel like I should be on your payroll at this point."

It was the right thing to say. Zain chuckled and ran a hand through his hair. The rest of the men laughed as Owen let go of my hand.

"That checks out," he said. "I don't think anyone in this company works half as hard as Hameed does."

"Someone's gotta make sure we all get our bonuses," Zain said in his smooth voice. He urged me to turn, nodding towards another man standing there. He was tall and pudgy, with blonde hair, pale white skin blotched with pink, and a sheen of sweat on his forehead. "This is Richard. The one who works in compliance that I mentioned?"

"Of course," I said, extending my hand. "Lovely to meet you, Richard."

"And you," Richard said, but instead of shaking my hand, he clasped the tips of my fingers. I almost thought he was going to lift them to his lips and worried for a moment that I'd have to disappoint Zain as I punched his coworker in the face for kissing my hand without permission, but Richard just squeezed lightly, as if my poor, brittle, girly fingers couldn't handle the pressure of a handshake. "You are stunning, Ms. Lane. What are you doing with this guy?"

"Well, obviously I've blackmailed her into pretending to be my girlfriend for the night so I don't spill her deep dark secrets to everyone we know," Zain said.

Oh, good. He was still an asshole. I smiled tightly as his coworkers chuckled again and Richard let go of my hand.

"This is Wei," Zain continued, nodding at a man with khaki coloured skin and neatly styled black hair. "He's my current counterpart here in Victoria."

"Except for on the baseball team," Wei said in a deep voice as he shook my hand firmly. "I whoop his ass there."

"Always has," Zain said, then turned to the fourth man, who had curly red hair, pale skin, and freckles. "And Markus, who's also in risk management."

Markus shook my hand. "You can thank me for teaching him everything he knows."

"Yeah, it was important for me to learn what not to do," Zain shot back.

"Well, depending on how tonight goes, Zain might be the one teaching all the new hires in the future, if you know what I mean," Owen said.

The group made knowing noises and I nodded, hoping my eyes didn't look too blank. I mean, obviously they were talking about whatever promotion Zain was aiming for, but it wasn't like I knew what that entailed. I barely knew what risk management was. So I did my best to look supportive and proud, and Zain pulled me in a bit closer as if to reassure me.

"Speaking of," he said. "Is AvexiPharm here yet?"

Owen shook his head. "They were staying at a different hotel, from the sounds of it. But I'm betting they'll walk in any second now. We're in good shape?"

Zain nodded. There wasn't a smile on his face, but he looked relaxed and confident. "They just need the okay from the director of operations. I'll get him on board."

"If anyone can, you can." Owen clapped Zain on the shoulder again. "No one's ever been able to score AvexiPharm. The director of operations is a fucking dragon. The moment he says yes, the promotion's yours. I'll miss the hell out of you on our team, but you deserve it."

"Thank you, sir," Zain said.

Owen sighed and looked at me, exasperation in his eyes. "Eight years at this company and I still can't get him to stop calling me 'sir.'"

Zain shrugged. "Sorry... sir."

The group of them laughed like it was the funniest thing they'd ever heard. Owen shook his head, grinning, but stopped when he glanced over Zain's shoulder and caught sight of someone.

"'Scuse me, boys," he said, his voice low. "I just spotted the CEO of Pershiko Industries. Need to chat with him before he gets to the bar, if you know what I mean."

There was a slight lull in the conversation after Owen walked away, that awkward moment where it was clear I was a newcomer and a stranger and no one was entirely sure what to make of me. After a moment, Wei turned to me.

"So, how long have you and Zain been together?" he asked, like a total asshole.

I mean, he said it politely. It wasn't Wei's fault Zain and I didn't bother sorting out those details before we came downstairs.

But still.

"Oh," I said, looking at Zain and frowning. "It's been... What are we at now, almost—"

"Almost a year," he said, finishing my sentence as though it were the most natural thing in the world.

"Those years feel a lot longer once you're tied down, eh?" Richard said, his voice slimy as he nudged Zain with his elbow.

Zain didn't take the bait. "Well, we know each other from back home in Burnsley. So it's more like I was waiting my whole life for her to notice me."

I had no idea what to say to that. My lips parted and something oddly warm considering this was all fucking *fake* rose up my cheeks. Luckily, Markus spoke up before I had to think of a response.

"A year," he said. "Damn. Thought you would've said *something* about her."

Wei let out an offended scoff. "Way to throw him under the bus, man."

"Huh?" Markus said. He looked at me, frowning, then seemed to realize what he said. "Oh! I mean, he talks about you all the—"

"No, he doesn't," I said, composing myself enough to laugh. "If I know anything about Zain, it's that he won't say a word about something if he doesn't want to. He likes to keep things completely to himself."

Zain's arm tightened around my waist, holding me protectively.

"Just the important things," he said, his voice husky. "Like you."

And like, damn.

Fucking *damn*.

I'd been trying to subtly imply he wasn't going to tell anyone about me and Brad, but that... that was almost romantic.

"That's Zain the Workaholic for you," Richard said, oblivious to the panic I hoped wasn't showing on my face from the way my body was reacting to Zain touching me. "But yeah, man, you should've said something. We were all starting to wonder, you know."

Beside me, Zain stiffened, which I only noticed because he was still holding me as Markus and Richard burst out laughing.

"Wonder what?" I asked.

Richard's laughter faded into an awkward chuckle. "If... you know."

"What?" I asked again.

"If he was... you *know*," he said, twisting his wrist in the air as if that would finish the sentence for him.

And it did, kind of.

And maybe I should've let it slide because I was supposed to be *good* for Zain.

But there was a fucking line.

"Know *what*?" I pressed.

"Tessa," Zain said, but Markus had already started talking.

"Well, you know," he said with a laugh. "We were just kind of questioning if he was into women at all. No offense!" He turned to Zain, lifting his hands apologetically. "A guy's gotta wonder, that's all."

"Guy's gotta wonder," Richard repeated as if it was fact, and they both laughed again.

Zain joined them.

I did not.

"Why is that funny?" I asked.

Richard looked at me, his head tilting to the side. "What?"

"Why is it funny? I repeated. "I don't get it."

"Get... what?" Markus asked.

"The joke," I said. "I don't understand it. Can you explain it to me?"

"Tessa, it's not a big—" Zain started.

"What?" I asked, looking from Markus to him and back at Richard. "I'm just asking someone to explain the joke to me. Explain why you're laughing."

"Teacup, it is *fine*," he said. "It's just a joke."

I looked at him, unsmiling, and flicked an eyebrow up at him. Unfazed, he flicked one back. Across from us, Richard and Markus were silent, and Wei had proven he was the most decent of the bunch by never speaking up in the first place.

"There you all are!" said a sudden voice, and suddenly the pod of them burst into action. Richard and Markus responded with overanimated greetings that covered their evident relief as they turned away from us. Zain turned too, possibly to say hello and possibly with relief, and I took that opportunity to slide away from his arm.

"Tessa—" he said.

"I'm going to get a drink," I replied, then started towards the bar.

He didn't follow me right away. Probably so he could roll his eyes at the other men and apologize for his buzzkill girlfriend. Then one of the others—Richard, probably, because I'd decided he was the grossest one there—would make one of those asshole quips like "Happy wife, happy life" and express his sympathies to Zain for having to put up with me. Then they would all laugh again, and only *then* would Zain chase after me with a—

"Tessa, wait."

And there he was. Right on time.

I clenched my jaw and did not wait, strolling towards the bar on the other side of the room. As he caught up with me, he sighed.

"Tessa, please," he said, his voice low as he moved in beside me. "I need you to act like—"

"—like I like you," I finished, soft enough that no one around us could hear. "You told me I had to come and pretend that I like you. Not that I had to sit here and listen to homophobic jokes and laugh like it's no big deal and pretend like you weren't all saying a bunch of sexist bullshit the moment I walked away. Let me guess, one of them asked if I was on my period and said I'd be prettier if I smiled more, too."

"Look, I know it's not ideal, but—"

"Ideal?" I stopped so suddenly that Zain took two more steps before realizing I wasn't walking anymore and turned around. "Are you fucking kidding me?"

"I just mean—"

"There's a difference between 'ideal' and acting like—" Stopping, I shook my head, laughing dryly as I lowered my voice to a hiss. "I know you don't get it, okay? You're a man and you're straight and that means it's not a big deal to you but you don't—"

He looked up at the ceiling. "Tessa—"

"—get to decide that sexuality is an okay thing to joke about. Because it's not. And I don't—"

"Tessa, let me—"

"—care if I said I was going to be 'good' and make you look good, I'm not going to sit here and ignore that just because you think a promotion is more important than—"

"Teacup, I'm bisexual."

I blinked at him, my lips still parted with half a word hanging off them. Zain stared back for a moment, then half-laughed and shook his head.

"I'm bi," he repeated. "And *they* all know that. So yes, it was a shitty joke about something that I'm not thrilled for them to make jokes about. Nor did I expect them to, clearly. But I need to hold out a little longer and get this promotion so I can get the fuck out of a shitty, toxic office before my parents move to fucking Kelowna and find out about... this."

The last word came out softly, a flash of something painful on his face before he blinked it away and met my eyes again.

"Okay," I said unsteadily. "I... I am so sorry."

He didn't seem to expect that, if the way his jaw twitched was any indication.

"I didn't know that," I continued. "I'm sorry I made you feel like you had to, um, out yourself to me."

Another one of those half-laughs came out. "If I'd been thinking, I would've told you before. But I didn't think it would, uh, come up." He sighed, glancing down before looking at me intently. "Look, it's not some big secret in Kelowna or Vernon. People at work know. My friends know. But I'm not out in Burnsley. No one from that side of my life knows about this. Not my parents. Not... not your brother. No one." He swallowed. "So if you could... you know. Help me keep it that way..."

"I'm not going to out you, Zain," I said. "I wouldn't. I swear."

"I know you wouldn't," he said quickly. "But I had to say it so—"

"I get it," I said. "I do. I'm, um, also bisexual."

"Well, yeah," he said. "I kind of figured."

I frowned. "What?"

Amusement flickered across his face. "The hot, slightly tortured artist with daddy issues? Like, not to be a dick, but..."

Zain had a particular talent for making me almost start to like him, only to remind me that he was still kind of a prick.

"First of all, fuck you," I said. "Super rude generalizations."

He had the decency to look ashamed.

"Second of all, I don't have *daddy issues*."

Zain raised his eyebrows silently, his lips pressed together. I held his gaze for a moment before I felt my face starting to turn red.

"They're more like... paternal... complications."

And I should've stayed pissed at him.

I should've been upset that he thought I was nothing but a stereotype.

But we stared at each other for another moment, then Zain's mouth twitched, and then we couldn't help but laugh.

Again.

And it felt good. Laughing with Zain felt... well...

Normal.

In the worst way.

Because I didn't *want* to feel that bond with him. I didn't want this strange camaraderie with my brother's best friend, the knowledge that we had this little but massive thing in common, that we were both out and unashamed until our families came into the picture and complicated everything.

Even worse, I think Zain felt it too. Because even as we laughed, he gave me a look like he was both stunned and not surprised all at once. That softness returned to his face, that look that he'd given me earlier like this wasn't a charade, and the laughter faded off his lips as his eyes flicked down to my mouth and I—

I panicked.

I looked away.

I turned my head, pretending I hadn't seen it. That I hadn't *felt* that moment. That I hadn't noticed any of it.

And that's when it all went to shit.

Because I saw him walk in. I saw him pause, just inside the entrance to the hall, and watched familiar eyes behind familiar glasses glance around as he observed the bustle and noise of the other attendees.

And I froze, because of course I did.

Because it wasn't like when I saw Brad from the stage at the date auction and felt immediate, visceral anger.

Because seeing him hit me not like a runaway train, but like one rushing purposefully down the rails at top speed towards the spot where I was tied to the tracks, helpless to do anything but hope he wouldn't see me.

But he did.

He did.

And after the briefest moment of shock, he put on one of those cool, smooth, businesslike masks that everyone else was wearing.

Then he started walking towards me.

I couldn't stop staring. My heart felt like it had physically fallen out of my ass and splattered on the floor and maybe *that* was what caught Zain's attention, because he finally followed my gaze to see what I was staring at and the world just fucking shattered around me.

"Hey, great timing," Zain said, slipping into the cool, suave businessman role again. "I was just talking about you."

"Good things, I hope," he said, and I almost puked.

Zain laughed. "Of course. If I tell my girlfriend how much I'm hoping to collaborate with your team at AvexiPharm one more time, she's gonna lose it on me, I'm sure."

"Girlfriend?" he repeated.

Brown eyes burned into mine. The last time I'd stared into them, they'd been filled with horror.

Regret.

The slightest hint of remorse.

Then they'd closed and he'd buried his face in my neck and whispered how *sorry* he was for loving me as he fucked me in front of his wife.

"Of course," Zain said, turning to me. "Tessa, this is Nathan Mauldin, the director of operations at AvexiPharm. Nathan, my girlfriend, Tessa."

Nathan didn't blink as he extended his hand to me.

"Tessa," he said. "What a pleasure."

Twenty-One

OWEN MANAGED TO GET us all at the same table.

I couldn't blame him. They were there to do a job and it wasn't like they knew. No one knew that I already knew Nathan as intimately as anyone could. And apparently, I hid it well enough that no one flagged it, because Owen even apologized when Nathan mentioned his wife wasn't able to join him due to a last-minute work emergency. Since, of course, that was supposed to be my role in the whole scenario. I was supposed to distract the director of operations' wife so the men could talk business.

My luck seemed to have run out, but at least I'd had enough left for that. Because if I'd had to sit there and pretend to entertain Mel... well.

I might've just called my family and told them everything myself. Because Zain would've been well within his rights to shout that information from the rooftops considering how badly I would've fucked things up for him.

So that was a small mercy, at least. And if Nathan had any mercy at all, he'd continue pretending we didn't know each other as he sat there talking about... whatever it was they were talking about. Pharmacy systems or something.

He looked the same as the last time I'd seen him, save for the fact that he was wearing clothing this time. Which, as much as I hated to admit it, was somewhat unfortunate. Because Nathan still looked good. He was on the chubbier side of average, with a slight belly and a soft chest. But even when he was submitting fully to Mel, letting her take charge and control his every want and need and action, he had a sense of confidence about him that was beyond attractive. His brown hair was still thick, his smile still captivating, and I hated it.

I hated that he still looked good.

Being there had to be difficult for him. I didn't mean that in a sympathetic way. I just know if it was me, if I had to sit at a table across from a woman I'd professed my love to, only to immediately take it back and continue to fuck her like the object I thought she was given that I compared her to pizza and beer after I'd finished, I wouldn't have held it together as well as Nathan did.

Though, maybe that was just another sign that Nathan was an absolute garbage human being. Maybe the way he was able to respond to Zain's questions and business talk with a smooth, comfortable ease that lacked any hint of guilt while I was sitting two seats away was a clue to just how much of a disgusting bastard he was. Maybe the plastic business smile on his face while he kept his eyes blank each time I glanced up and caught him watching me was his way of showing me how remorseless he—and by association, Mel—were of what they'd done to me.

Maybe they didn't even care.

Maybe they didn't even know.

"—Teacup?"

Zain touched my leg and I jumped, jostling the table. Blinking, I turned to see him looking at me with concern.

"What?" I asked, forcing the word out of a dry throat.

"I asked if you wanted more wine," he said, tilting the bottle in his hand towards me.

"Oh," I said. "Ye...ah. Yes, please."

He raised his eyebrows. "Are you okay?"

"Yes," I said, so confidently that I punctuated it with a firm nod of my head. "Sorry. I zoned out. I was, uh... thinking. About a work thing."

"Okay," Zain said, reaching for my glass. On the other side of him, I caught a glimpse of Nathan watching with mild interest.

"It was the gala," I said. "This gala we do. Every year. I mean, we did this year's on Thursday. Which, uh, you know, obviously. But I was thinking because there's a lot of things at *this* event that are just so inspiring that we could use... or emulate, you know? Like at the gala I do." I tried to smile, hoping that it would help Zain believe my bullshit. "For work. At my job."

"Ah," Zain said, as if he did not at all believe my bullshit, but he didn't say anything else as he put my glass back down.

I picked it up and took a sip, trying to keep my hands from shaking as he filled his own glass. When I put it back down, Nathan was looking at me again. Brown eyes met mine, still clouded to mask whatever emotions were floating behind them. But whatever those emotions were, they must have been cold, because it took everything in me not to shiver at that look.

"I heard something interesting about AvexiPharm, Nathan," Owen said.

Nathan looked away from me with a practiced ease. "Did you?"

"Mm-hmm. It had to do with the results posted for Q2 last year—"

I let out a breath, hoping it didn't sound like a sigh of relief, and reached for my glass again.

"Here," Zain said. "I'm full if you want this."

I looked down to see him pushing a piece of cheesy bread that came with his... steak? Did I just eat steak? There was a plate in front of me and it was mostly empty, so I must have.

Fuck.

This was fucking me up.

"Tess? Cheesy bread?" Zain said.

"No, thanks," I replied.

He stared at me. I wish I knew how he did that thing where his face didn't move at all, but his entire expression changed. After a moment, he leaned in.

"What's wrong?" he asked, his voice low enough that only I could hear it.

"Nothing," I said.

"Don't give me that shit," he murmured. "I know something's going on."

"You don't know shit, Zain."

"You turned down cheesy bread."

"Yes, and I'm fine. Two things can be true."

He didn't buy it. "Are you feeling okay?"

"I am *fine*," I said through my teeth. "Don't worry about it."

"I'm going to worry about it," he shot back.

"About what?" I lifted my glass to my lips as I looked at him as evenly as I could. "There's nothing to worry about."

A muscle in Zain's jaw twitched. He opened his mouth, likely to continue arguing, but before he could say anything, a large hand came down on his shoulder and both Zain and I looked up.

"Zain, my friend," said a man with thick black hair and dark sienna skin in a loud voice. "I was hoping you would be here tonight!"

Zain smiled tightly. "Here I am. It's good to see you, Hamza."

"And you." Hamza patted Zain's shoulder heavily. "My apologies for interrupting your meal with your lovely wife, but that recent report you sent my company needs some urgent attention. It's a very big issue."

Zain looked like he wanted to fight the man. I wanted to fight him, too, mostly because he'd assumed I was Zain's wife and that was a massive issue in itself. But Zain probably wanted to fight him because Hamza was speaking in a way that was a clear attempt to show off how unimpressed he was in front of as many people as he could. Zain glanced at Owen, who was watching with veiled concern, then looked back at Hamza.

"I would be more than happy to help," he said, then added something in Urdu that I didn't understand.

Hamza responded, his tone especially clipped, then Zain put a hand on my knee.

"I'll be right back," he said, then stood up to follow the other man.

And fuck.

Fuck.

My throat closed as I watched Zain shake Hamza's hand as they continued speaking in Urdu. They turned, walking towards the exit and leaving me sitting at a table with a group of people I was deceiving and an empty seat between me and the one person who knew more about me than the fake boyfriend I was here with. And while I didn't *think* Nathan was the kind of person who would mention how we knew each other in front of a group of people and ruin every chance Zain had at his promotion, I also hadn't thought Nathan was the kind of person who would do what he did to me.

But I had the smallest, tiniest little scraping of luck left in the bottom corner of whatever metaphorical container held luck, because just as they walked away, Owen turned to Nathan and began talking to him animatedly. Nathan nodded thoughtfully, but he wasn't looking at me anymore, so I did what anyone would do: I threw back the rest of the wine in my glass, put my napkin down on my plate, and mumbled something about needing the bathroom even though no one was listening to me.

The bathroom was just outside the main hall, tucked into a quiet hallway just around the corner. There was no one else in there when I walked in; it was the middle of dinner, so most people were doing the whole "eating" thing and not trying to avoid the director of operations of a large pharmaceutical company. Sighing, I let myself into a stall and locked the door, sitting down on the closed lid of the toilet and putting my leather clutch on my lap as I buried my head in my hands.

I had no idea what to do.

Of all the things I thought would happen that night, this was not one of them. The chances of running into Nathan were slim; I had no idea what the fucking chances were of him being the guy my fake boyfriend needed to impress.

And I had no idea if Nathan was going to hold my presence against him.

Maybe if I came clean, I thought. I could tell Zain the best option was to tell Nathan we weren't *actually* a couple. Then he wouldn't be able to justify not signing on with Zain's company because of me.

But that would require me telling Zain how I knew Nathan.

My hands were sweating and my stomach seemed to have permanently settled in my throat. Sighing, I lifted my head, wiping my palms on the skirt of my dress.

I needed to talk to someone.

Chuck wasn't an option. He was at a hockey game. Or getting a blowjob. Either way, my phone was nearly dead and the chances of him being unreachable were high.

That left... well.

Biting my lip, I opened the leather clutch and pulled my phone out.

Me

Hey. I don't want to look clingy or anything but I'm having the worst night ever. Are you around?

My phone rang thirty seconds later.

"'Sup, darling?" Claire said when I answered.

A watery smile crossed my lips. "Hey. So two things. One, my phone is almost dead, so if the call drops, sorry. Two, I have a hypothetical question for you."

"Ooh," she said. "I love a good hypothetical."

"It's not really a good one." I took a breath and let it out. "Okay. Let's say you were fake dating a guy and—"

"Sorry, too unrealistic," she said. "I'd never be dating a guy, fake or otherwise."

It was funny, but I couldn't bring myself to laugh. "Okay. You're fake dating a person of your preference and at the event you promised to go to and make them look good to their boss so they could get a promotion they really, really need, you run into a guy—I mean, another person—who you used to hook up with."

"Awkward," she said. "Okay."

"But it's not just any person. It's someone you used to hook up with along with his wife, and things ended horribly because he said he loved you mid-sex and then took it back, and also he works for the company your fake date has to impress to get the previously mentioned promotion and now you're trapped in the bathroom and don't know what to do, so you call your fuck buddy you met two days ago who just so happens to know the whole story."

Claire was silent. For a moment, I thought my phone died, but after a moment she blew out a huge breath. "Wow. That's... a lot."

"Sorry. I didn't know who else to call."

"Don't be sorry." She took another breath and let it out. "Well, uh, personally I'd just buy the other company and fire the guy."

"Ah, yes. Do you think they accept payment in complimentary hotel toiletries I stole from the room earlier?"

She laughed. "Well, if that wasn't an option, I'd probably just try not to end up alone with him. Or... what company is it?"

"Huh?"

"What company does Nathan work for? It's Nathan, right?"

"Yeah," I said. "And, um, AvexiPharm."

I could hear the wince in her voice. "Shit. Yeah, no, sorry. I was going to offer to help out but that's a few billion or so more than my inheritance."

That got a weak laugh out of me. "It's the thought that counts."

"Sorry, darling. Fuck. This is... this sucks."

"Tell me about it. So you just think... like, if I avoid him, it should be okay?"

"I mean, that'll protect you. I don't know what it'll mean for your fake boyfriend, but frankly, I don't care about him because I don't know him."

"Fair, I guess."

"Do I need to find that totally-not-a-hitman person who will have a little 'talk' with Nathan?"

Another soft laugh. "No, I think I can manage."

"You can. I know you can. Because you're a strong badass who can d—"

And then my phone died.

Which was okay. While it might not have solved my problem, talking to her made me feel a bit better. I guess that was kind of the point of calling a friend, even if I still didn't know what to do except not end up alone with Nathan, which I'd already kind of been doing.

But, I thought as I tapped the edge of my phone idly, I could also speed things up. I mean, all I had to do was wait until Zain was done talking with Hamza. Then I could tell him I *did* have an upset stomach and I needed to go back to the room.

And if he wasn't back at the table when I returned to the hall, I could just go to the bar and stay there, getting progressively drunker until Zain returned and was so horrified by my behaviour that he made me stumble back up to our room so I could pass out and forget the entire experience.

Fucking foolproof.

I put my phone back in my clutch and left the stall, then went to the mirror. After washing my hands, I touched up my lipstick and patted my hair down, smoothing a few frizzy spots before fluffing it back up.

I could do this, I said to myself as I looked in the mirror. All I had to do was not end up alone with Nathan.

Then I straightened my shoulders, lifted my chin, and walked out of the bathroom and directly into Nathan.

Twenty-Two

"Tessa," Nathan said.

He was standing down the hall, leaning against the wall with his arms folded across his chest.

It was my fault. A little, at least. If not ending up alone with someone who probably wanted to get you alone so you could talk to them was the goal, cornering yourself in the bathroom was probably not a great idea.

But I hadn't thought of that at the time, and now I was standing in the hallway with Nathan positioned between me and the only exit.

So naturally, I tried the obvious solution.

"Excuse me, I need to get by," I said, starting forward.

The corners of Nathan's mouth curled up in an amused smirk. "I think we need to talk first."

"I would prefer not to," I said, but before I could push past him, he straightened up.

"Why not?" he asked.

I stopped a few feet away from him, partly because I wasn't going to be able to squeeze past him anymore and partly out of shock.

"Are you serious?" I asked.

There was no trace of humour on his face. "I am. I think we're *long* overdue for a talk."

"I don't owe you anything," I said.

"Of course you don't." Nathan half shrugged, folding his arms again. "But considering your *boyfriend* wants something from me, I think at least having the courtesy to answer my questions would be a good idea."

I laughed.

Legitimately. The noise I made just then wasn't a sarcastic scoff or an overdramatic statement. It burst out of my chest in a way that almost surprised me, considering that Nathan had just confirmed he was every bit the disgusting bastard I was hoping he wasn't.

"Jesus," I said. "I knew you were an asshole, but I didn't think you were the kind of sick fuck who threatens someone else's career so you can force me to do what you want."

"I'm not—"

"You're trying to manipulate me, Nathan."

He opened his mouth again, then shut it and sighed. "Tess, I wouldn't even be implying anything like that if this wasn't so fucking important. I need answers. *We* need answers. So, yeah. I'm gonna do what it takes to get them."

The lump had returned to my throat, but I tried to ignore it. "So you admit it, then. You're an asshole."

He didn't rise to the bait, just focused those brown eyes behind his wire-rimmed glasses on me. "Just tell me why."

"Why what?"

"Why you left us."

I stared at him, my lips parted as I repeated his words in my mind.

"You know how they say the key to comedy is timing?" I finally asked.

Nathan frowned. "Uh... yeah?"

"Your timing is shit. You should get that figured out before you try stand-up."

That was far funnier than what Nathan had said, but he didn't laugh. "I'm not trying to be funny."

"You sure are telling a lot of fucking jokes, then."

"What jokes?"

And maybe it wasn't the most mature response, but given the situation, I thought a bit of immaturity could be forgiven.

"'Why don't you want to talk?'" I asked in a deep, mocking voice. "'Why did you leave us, Tessa? Why were you so unhappy about us treating you like garbage?'"

"I didn't—"

"Like, damn," I said, returning my voice to normal. "Thank God I got tested so I know for sure I didn't catch a bad case of being the stupidest person alive from you."

"Tessa, come on." There was pain on Nathan's face. A bit of it, at least, hidden beneath the redness of his cheeks and the anger in his eyes. "You ghosted us. We wanted to talk about what happened and you... you fucking disappeared."

"And you really couldn't figure out why?" I asked.

"We had some ideas. Like that you wanted to take things further and got scared. That you wanted to be with us."

It was my turn to glare at him. "You have no idea what I wanted."

"We wanted it too, Tess," he said.

And that.

Fuck.

I felt my heart crack, right along the seam that had barely mended after he and Mel broke it in the first place. It ached, physically *ached*, and I had to swallow hard to keep myself from screaming.

"You're so full of shit," I forced myself to say.

"I'm not."

"You are. You're full of shit. You and Mel both made it *very* clear what level of importance I had in *your* relationship."

"No, we didn't."

"You did. You—"

"We didn't." He shook his head. "We couldn't have made it clear because we didn't *know*. We were fucked up and had no idea what was happening or why things with you were so different than with anyone we'd been with before. It wasn't clear at all because it was new to us, too. We didn't know how to handle it either. But we knew that you were ours."

Heat rose in my chest. Not the good kind of heat. The kind that was so sudden and intense that my skin crawled and my blood surged and I almost felt lightheaded over how extreme the physical reaction to his words was.

"I was not *yours*," I said, my voice low and angry.

"You were." Nathan's voice was both patient and condescendingly confident. "You were absolutely ours. And I know you miss it because you're still doing it, aren't you? You left us and decided to brand yourself as a 'unicorn' and rub it in our faces that you were looking for our replacements. And you thought we wouldn't figure out that you missed us as much as we missed you."

"I don't miss you," I said, and that was the fucking truth. "I may be a unicorn, but I'm not *your* unicorn. I don't belong to anyone and I never did. I never *will*. The only person I'll ever belong to again is *me*."

He looked like he wanted to argue, but he just took one of those calming breaths and let it out.

"Look," he said. "We fucked up. Okay? I know that. Mel knows that. It's fucking killed us that things ended the way they did. We made a mistake and we didn't handle it well. But you didn't have to cut us out like that. Especially when we... when *I* felt..."

But he couldn't even finish the sentence. I mean, he couldn't even look me in the fucking eye, turning his head and staring at something far past my left shoulder as his face turned even redder.

"You felt what?" I asked, my voice flat. "You love...d my pussy?"

"Tessa, I—"

"You love...d pizza and beer?"

"I didn't—"

"You love...d equating me to body parts and food and objects because I was never actually a living, breathing person to you?"

"I loved *you*," he snapped, and I almost took a step backward from the force of his voice and the anguish in his eyes. "We were both fucking in *love* with you. And I'd never had that happen before with someone other than Mel and yeah, I panicked. I was scared. It was a bad moment and I needed time to figure out what the hell I was feeling but you never even gave us a chance, Tess. *You* walked away."

I almost laughed again. My eyes were starting to burn, stinging that started in the corners and spread along my lash line. "Right. Because it was all my fault."

He frowned. "What?"

"You put it all on me, didn't you? I'm the one who walked away. I'm the one who sat there as you joked about loving me like pizza as you both made it very clear that what you said was a *mistake* and somehow was supposed to understand that you were both in love with me. I'm the one who wouldn't accept your apology except... oh, wait." I tapped a finger to my chin. "What apology?"

He sighed. "I'm sor—"

"Don't."

"You just said—"

"Words don't mean shit." It took everything to keep my voice steady as I crossed my arms. "The only thing you were ever sorry for was letting it slip while you were in the middle of fucking me."

"I'm sorry for a lot of it," he said.

"You weren't even sorry enough to stop, Nathan," I said. "You said that to me, and you *knew* it was a big deal, and you didn't stop."

He opened his mouth, but nothing came out. Finally, something crossed his face that wasn't neutrality or pain or anger. Finally, there was a slow realization.

Finally, there was shame.

I thought seeing that shame would make me feel better. But it didn't. It was far too little and far, far too late, considering it was apparently the first time he realized what he'd done to me.

"I panicked," he finally said.

"You should've stopped."

"I didn't know what to do."

"You should've stopped."

"You didn't say—"

"It's not *my* fault," I snapped. "You should've—"

"—stopped, I know." His voice cracked. "I... I see that now."

"You should've seen it before," I said. "But you were so fucking focused on you and Mel that you didn't even think of how it would feel for me, did you?"

He didn't need to say anything for both of us to know he hadn't.

"I need you to move," I said. "I don't want to talk to you anymore."

"Tessa, please," he said quietly.

"It's been years," I said. "You should be over it. And if you're not, start working on getting over it, because I never want to see you again."

"Tessa—"

"Get out of my fucking way, Nathan."

I started forward, intent on pushing past him. Maybe it wasn't the best idea, but I didn't want to be trapped in that hallway anymore. But it was a stupid, overconfident thing to do. I'd barely started past him when Nathan grabbed my arm and pulled, changing my trajectory with so little effort that I couldn't even resist it, and spun us around so we changed positions and he was facing the exit to the hallway.

"Wait," he demanded.

I shook my arm hard. "Don't touch me."

"Let me finish."

"Let *go*."

"No. I'm not done with—"

And then his eyes went wide and his hand fell off my arm.

I didn't know when he got there. I didn't see him come around the corner. Sure, we weren't super far down the hallway, but still. His timing was so good it was almost funny in a sad, not-at-all-funny sort of way. But suddenly Zain was there, stepping around me and planting a hand on Nathan's chest as he pushed him backwards in one firm, smooth motion.

"She said let go," Zain said.

His inflection didn't shift with any of the words; all of them were spoken in one low, gravelly tone, with each word clipped so the intent was clear. For a moment, they hung in the hallway, clinging to the silence between the three of us. I could only see the back of Zain's head, but I imagined his face was like stone, if Nathan's was any indication. He looked over Zain's shoulder at me, then back to Zain.

"I need to talk to her," Nathan said.

"And she said no," Zain replied. "So you're not going to talk to her."

Nathan studied Zain. "Is that really the right decision for you to make right now?"

Anger flared through me, knowing what Nathan was implying, but Zain didn't seem to react.

"Choosing Tessa is always the right decision," he said.

Nathan laughed, shaking his head, the sound cold and bitter and furious. "What do you think Owen would say about that, huh?"

"I don't think it's any of Owen's business."

"Really? You don't think it's your boss's business to hear you're throwing away everything you've been working on for years because of this?"

"Leave him out of this, Nathan," I snapped. "It has *nothing* to do with his job."

Nathan shrugged. "Agree to disagree. I think it has everything to do with his job."

Fuck, I hated him.

I *hated* him.

"So this is how you get what you want?" I asked. "You manipulate and threaten people until they do what you ask?"

"Normally, no," he said, fixing his eyes to mine. "But for this? This was fucking important, Tessa. This almost ruined my marriage."

And there it was.

Even standing there, telling me how much they missed me, it was about them. It was about him and Mel and their relationship.

Even as he tried to claim I'd mattered to them, he proved I hadn't.

And Nathan seemed to realize that at the same time I did. His jaw twitched and he waited, seemingly for me to respond, but I couldn't. My throat closed again, so tight I almost couldn't breathe, and after a moment, he turned back to Zain.

"I need a moment with Tessa. You need to move."

I still couldn't see his face. I still had no idea what he was thinking. If he'd figured out what was happening. So when Zain spoke, I was almost surprised.

"She told you to back off," he said, his tone still smooth and neutral. "So you have the choice to back the fuck off before I make you back off, Nathan."

Nathan raised his eyebrows. "You don't know what you're talking about."

"I know enough," Zain said. "If she doesn't want to talk to you, I'm going to take her side. Because Tessa's worth it."

There was a pause, then Zain chuckled, and I could almost see the smirk on his face.

"But I think you know that, don't you?" he asked. "You know Tessa's worth it and you're pissed she doesn't want you."

Nathan laughed another one of those cold, bitter laughs that made my spine crawl.

"Not just me," he said. "Us."

Oh, shit.

Oh, no.

No.

Zain's head moved, tilting to the side. Whether his face changed or not, I didn't know, but the movement alone was probably enough to make Nathan's lip curl up in a smile like it did.

"Oh, has she not told you about that?" he asked. "Well, I guess you two have a lot to talk about. Which you'll have plenty of time for now, because you can consider this official notice that AvexiPharm is no longer interested in further negotiations for this project." He reached up and pushed Zain's hand off his chest. "Good luck, Mr. Hameed."

Nathan didn't look at me as he walked past. Zain turned and we watched Nathan walk away together until the sound of his shoes on the floor had faded to a distant tap. Only then did Zain look at me, his lips parted and his eyebrows furrowed.

"Tessa, what—"

But I couldn't.

I turned around and bolted away, my heels clicking on the floor as I tried to keep my eyes dry and failed miserably.

Twenty-Three

I GOT BACK TO the hotel room before Zain.

I didn't know if it was because he let me walk away or because he'd been frozen in place after Nathan took away everything. If he'd stood there for as long as he could bear before coming after me or if he'd had an internal struggle over whether he should go back to the dinner and try to salvage what he could.

I didn't know, and it didn't matter. Either way, it wasn't enough time.

I held it together until I was back in the room. The moment the door shut behind me, I shoved my hands under my eyes to keep my cheeks dry. My throat was tight and sore and my hands were shaking and a choked sound lurched past my lips. Just as I crossed the room to throw my purse down on the dresser, I heard the click of a keycard sliding in the door. As it opened, I turned away, clenching my jaw and staring up at the roof as I blinked rapidly.

"Tessa—" Zain started as he walked in.

"Go back to your dinner," I said.

The door closed behind him with a terrifying sense of finality. "Not a fucking chance."

"Zain—"

"Tell me what just happened," he said.

"It doesn't matter."

"Oh, I think it does," he said, his voice cold. "I think it *really* matters."

I swallowed back the tightness in my throat. "It's none of your—"

"Don't you dare say that," he snapped. "Don't you fucking dare, Teacup."

Well then, I wasn't going to be able to say anything. I squeezed my eyes shut and tried to breathe. Tried to hold everything in. Tried to will myself into a parallel universe where I was alone in the room and Nathan hadn't been here and I hadn't sucked Zain into the hot mess that was my life and ruined everything for him.

"Tessa," he said when I didn't respond. "Listen to me. Whatever the hell just happened, I need to know, okay? I don't understand what's going on, and I can't fix something I don't understand."

The shaking in his voice was anger. Fury. Regret or hatred, maybe, that he'd brought me here just so I could cost him the thing he needed most.

And that was fair. He had every right to be angry. Every fucking right to demand answers, to at least know *why* he'd lost his shot at leaving the Kelowna area.

I took a slow breath and brought my hands to my face, pressing the base of my thumbs against my eyes in an effort to keep them dry.

"If you want to fix it—" I started, then had to stop because my voice cracked. I cleared my throat and tried again. "You need to go back to your dinner, Zain. Go tell Nathan you're 'leaving me' because I won't own up to what I did and try to get him to change his mind. He probably won't, but you should at least fucking try. Hell, maybe he'll even tell you."

"No."

My jaw twitched. "Why not?"

"Because I want to know what the hell is going on, and I don't give a shit what *his* side of the story is."

"It's none of your bu—"

"I swear to fuck, Tessa, if you say it's none of my business one more time, I'm going to lose it," he said. "It's *entirely* my business now."

"You don't want to—"

"I *do!*" He nearly shouted the word and I felt a surge of anger burn through me as my shoulders tensed reflexively. "I want it to be my fucking business. So you are going to tell me what the hell I just walked into and why, understand? Start talking, Teacup, because this conversation isn't going to be over until I get what I fucking want."

One of my strongest instincts was to do the exact opposite of what someone wanted, especially when they were demanding things from me like that.

But a much more powerful instinct was for me to lash out.

To be the asshole.

To give Zain what he wanted because it would hurt him more that way, and when I was hurting, all I wanted to do was hurt someone back.

"I fucked him. Is that what you want to hear?" I asked, turning around to face him.

His face was like obsidian, full of darkness and unyielding insistence, but one of his eyebrows twitched as his eyes met mine. Probably because my face was completely red, if the heat surging through me was any indication, and I was certain the small amount of makeup I'd been wearing was smeared from me mashing my hands against my eyes.

"I fucked him. *Repeatedly*," I said, even as my jaw trembled. "I hooked up with Nathan Mauldin over and over and over again, and clearly it didn't end well. And that's why if you want to change his mind, you need to go down there now and take *his* side and leave me the fuck alone."

Zain didn't react to a single word I said. "Him and who?"

I stared at him. "What?"

"Nathan and *who?*" he repeated. "What did he mean when he said 'us'?"

A sound that might have been a laugh escaped my throat. "You can't be serious."

"I said this conversation wasn't going to end until you gave me answers." He folded his arms across his chest. "Nathan and *who?*"

"Who do you *think*, Zain?" I asked, exasperated.

"I don't know," he replied. "You haven't told me yet."

"If you can't figure it out, then you're an idiot."

"Okay, sure, I'm a fucking idiot. So explain it to me. Explain to me, in detail and using the smallest words possible, what the hell is going on. Like I'm the stupidest person you've ever met."

"You *are* the stupidest person I've ever met."

"Stop talking around this and fucking say it, Tessa. We're not going anywhere until you do."

And I just...

I'd had enough.

"I fuck couples, okay?" I snapped, glaring at him as I spread my hands to the sides. "I fuck couples, almost exclusively, and I have for years now. And Nathan and his wife were the first ones."

He stared at me, his expression unchanged. And I could have ended it there. I mean, I could have ended it earlier than that and it would have been more than enough information.

But the words wouldn't stop coming.

"I met them, and I fucked them, and I jumped into being their plaything without stopping to wonder if I mattered to them as much as they mattered to me. But guess what, Zain? I *didn't*. I didn't matter to them. So I ghosted them. I spent months being part of their life and then I left them without saying a fucking word because I deserved better than that." I laughed, the sound unhinged as my eyes started to sting again. "No one deserves that, you know? No one deserves having someone say they love you and then look *horrified* about it, tell you that he meant he loved your pussy, and then he laughs about it with his wife after because he couldn't even bring himself to *stop* fucking you after shattering your heart like that. No one deserves to get laughed at when people are talking about the mere idea of being in love with them."

"Tessa—" Zain started.

I ignored him. "They could've at least waited until I wasn't there. But they didn't, and I left, and as I've just found out, that apparently nearly ended their marriage. Because it was entirely *my* fault that Nathan couldn't even pull his dick out of me after dropping that bombshell."

Something wet trickled down my cheek, but by that point, I didn't care.

"But you know, even after all that, I missed it," I said. "Fucked up, right? I missed the dynamic. I missed being with two people at once. So I decided it was time to do what I wanted for a change and now I fuck couples. I find people looking for a unicorn, I fuck them one time, and I move on. I get what I want, they get what they want, and no one has to get hurt over it." I lifted my hands again. "Is that what you wanted to hear, Zain?"

I didn't know if it was or not. Zain's expression was still stony. His eyes were fixed to me, dark and intense and unreadable, and his jaw was set. All I could hear was my heart thundering in my ears as I held Zain's gaze.

"So you fuck couples," he said, his voice quiet. "That's your... thing."

"Sure. If that's all you took from that."

He ignored my snark.

"You're divorced," he said as he began to count on his fingers. "You're lying about it to your family because you don't want them to know you're a human who makes mistakes. And you fuck married couples in your spare time because you had a threesome with people who weren't good enough for you. Did I get everything there, Teacup?"

"Fuck you," I said, glaring at him. "I don't need judgement from the guy trying to get a promotion so he can get away from his parents instead of telling them to back off."

I wasn't quite sure when I became so hyper aware of Zain's face that I could see miniscule changes in his expression, like the one he had just then. And I wasn't quite sure what it said that the hint of hurt on his face sent a wave of guilt crashing over me when I was expecting the burn of satisfaction for hurting him back.

But Zain didn't respond to that. He just took another breath and let it out.

"I am trying to make sure I understand what's going on here," he said, his voice not quite emotionless, but steady and controlled.

"Why does it matter if you understand any of this? I don't want to talk about this with you. I mean, I don't want to talk about any of this, period, but *least* of all with you."

A corner of his mouth curled up and he laughed dryly. "Right. Because you can't stand me."

I rolled my eyes. "It's more like you don't give a shit."

And that was the wrong thing to say. That neutral expression of his cracked and anger poured through as he threw his hands up in frustration.

"What more do I have to *do*, Tessa?" he asked. "What else *can* I fucking do to make it clear that I do, actually, give a shit? I just, I—" He shook his head, laughing incredulously. "I just gave up a fucking promotion for you and you *still* think I don't care?"

"Oh, thanks for reminding me," I said. "So now you expect something from me to make up for costing you that?"

His eyes went wide with disbelief. "Are you for real or—" He stopped speaking, suddenly so frustrated he couldn't seem to stay in one spot, pacing a few steps in either direction and running a hand through his hair before turning to me again. "Why do you keep thinking I'm the kind of asshole who does stuff like that?"

I frowned. "What—"

"When have I *ever*—" He shook his head again. "I mean, first you thought I'd need a fucking favour to keep a secret for you, like I wouldn't just do it because it was upsetting you. Now this? Now thinking I want something from you because I—"

Again he touched his hands to his head, shaking it in aggravation before looking at me with a scary amount of intensity in his eyes.

"I did it because you matter more than a fucking promotion, Tessa. To me and in general. So if giving up the thing I've been working on for... for way too fucking long because I saw some asshole threaten you doesn't make it clear that I *give a shit*, then I don't know what else I can do to prove it."

I stared at him, uncertain. "But I never asked you to give that up."

"You didn't need to!" he said, and his eyes seemed to flash dark. "And that... I mean, I..." He stopped and sighed, turning to the side so he wasn't looking at me anymore. "Whether you believe I care or not, it was the right thing to do."

I laughed.

I couldn't help it. I couldn't believe what was coming out of his mouth. There was no way... no *reason* for it. Not when this was Zain. This was *Zain*.

"So why do you care so much all of a sudden?" I asked.

He turned back to me, looking insulted. "I've always cared."

"Bullshit," I said. "Bull fucking shit, Zain."

"It's not," he said.

"It is!" I laughed again, shaking my head. "How do you expect me to believe that? You have *always* been an ass to me. You acted like I was a joke, just like everyone else did."

"Are you seriously bringing things I did when we were growing up into this?" he asked.

I wanted to scream. I didn't, but I wanted to. "Of course I am! That's how I fucking *know* you!"

"And you don't think I've changed since then?" he asked, the annoyance on his face turning to frustration.

"Oh, don't bring up this 'boys will be boys' shit again—"

"I'm *not*!" he said. "I'm saying I was a stupid teenager and you were a cringey kid with a crush on me that—"

"Oh, fuck off. I didn't have a crush on you."

There was a look of condescending but justified arrogance on his face. "Don't you lie to me, Tessa Lane. I know you did. Everyone fucking knew you did."

My face burned. "You're an asshole."

"And so are you. But you're an asshole who had a crush on me."

I couldn't bring myself to look at him. "Well I was a stupid kid, like you said. A stupid kid who liked the *asshole* who treated me like garbage and laughed at me all the time with my brother."

"What do you want me to do?" he asked frankly. "You want me to apologize for being an idiot when we were growing up? Okay. I'm sorry. I am fucking *sorry*, Tessa. For all of it."

I rolled my eyes again. "You aren't."

And that was also the wrong thing to say.

Or the right thing, depending on how you looked at it.

It was the wrong thing because it seemed to break something in Zain, more than I already had.

It was the wrong thing because I pushed a button I didn't even know existed, carelessly and thoughtlessly.

But it was the right thing because it was a justified button to push, which both Zain and I knew.

And it was the right thing because pushing that button forced him that final step.

He turned quickly, moving forward so he was right in front of me. Instinctively, I took a step backwards, but that just drew him a step forward.

"You don't think I've regretted, every fucking day, that things went the way they did?" he asked. "You don't think if I could change things, I would?"

My lips parted, but no words came out. I took another step back, then let out a soft, surprised gasp as my back pressed against the wall next to the dresser.

Zain stepped forward and my heart jumped into my throat.

"You *really* think that, given the chance, I wouldn't go back in time and tell my younger self to smarten the fuck up and be the man you needed before it was too late? Because if I knew then what I know now, if I knew you seem to have some kind of fatal attraction to the worst assholes out there, I would've gone for you the moment I could instead of waiting until I felt like I deserved you."

"What?" I whispered.

"What? *What*?" he repeated in a mocking voice as he took a step closer. "You're gonna stand there and ask me *what*, Teacup?"

"I d-don't—" I stopped, drawing in just enough of a breath that I could steady my voice. "I don't understand."

Suddenly Zain's face was level with mine, his eyes burning away the mask he'd had on them and revealing something I hadn't seen before.

Suddenly he was close enough that I could smell a spicy green freshness that took me a moment to place until I remembered the shave soap he'd had in the bathroom.

Suddenly my back was against the wall and he was leaning in and I was staring at him, eyes wide, frozen in place.

"Is it not fucking obvious at this point?" he asked, and his voice was still a low hiss, but it was husky and deep and *real*. "After all of it, after the hotel room and the bench at the party and this, you don't fucking get it?"

I glared at him. "If I had to 'just say it,' then you do, too. Tell me what you mean."

He chuckled dryly. "I mean that one day, you were my best friend's dorky little sister, and the next, you were an entirely different person. A sassy little thing with a stubborn mouth declaring that she was going to follow her dreams regardless of what her parents said, so fucking determined and unapologetically herself that I didn't stand a chance. You hit me like an avalanche, Teacup. Out of nowhere, and fast, and suddenly I wanted you like nothing I've ever wanted before. I mean that I *liked* you, so fucking much, but I couldn't stand the idea of feeling like I was taking advantage of someone who was barely an adult. Because you were a teenager, Tessa. You were eighteen when I finally smartened up and figured it out, but you were still a fucking *teenager*."

His eyes flicked down to my mouth and I almost shivered.

"So I told myself I was going to wait," he continued. "I was going to be a decent person and earn the right to see you like that. That you needed to grow up a little without me around because that was only fair, you know? And then just when you were old enough and I was going to tell you how I felt, you went and married the first fucker you could find. Some asshole who was a decade older than you instead of just a couple of years. And I was fucking devastated."

"How am I supposed to believe any of that?" I asked, hating how my voice shook. "You never once made me think you even tolerated me. Let alone liked me."

"Well, I did, Teacup." His face was close to mine, close enough that nothing but him was filling my vision, that I was entirely surrounded by him. "I did. And I admit I fucked up. But now that you're done with that pathetic excuse you called a husband, I'm making it clear. I want you. I've always wanted you. Understand? I want your secrets. I want everything. I fucking *want* you, Tessa."

I couldn't speak.

It wasn't even that I didn't know what to say or like I'd forgotten how to speak. It was more like I'd never learned. Like my mind was wiped blank, like a lifetime of knowledge had gone up in flames as he admitted he...

He wanted me.

Tension filled the air, pulling itself into my lungs and weighing me down more than gravity. I stared at Zain, lips parted as I drew in shallow breaths that had the warmth of his still hanging on it.

Because he was close.

He was so fucking close.

His hand was on the wall beside me. When had that happened? When had he… oh, God, he'd put his other hand on my cheek. And he was staring straight into my eyes, looking deeper into me than I thought anyone ever had before.

He was going to kiss me.

I was sure of it.

I was waiting for it.

I was waiting for his lips, for the taste of his breath to become the taste of his mouth, for a moment I was craving and fearing because it would change everything.

I was so sure he was going to kiss me.

But he didn't.

"Say I can," he whispered.

I blinked. "Huh?"

His voice was soft, but hoarse. "Say I can kiss you."

I stared at him.

"Tell me I can kiss you, Teacup."

My lips were parted, but nothing came out. I was frozen like I was scared. But I wasn't scared.

Except that I was scared.

Zain waited another moment, then his eyes flicked down to my mouth. When he looked back up, there was desperation on his face.

"I need you to say I can kiss you, Tessa," he said, his voice urgent and pleading and soft.

So fucking soft.

Zain stared at me a moment longer. Then a moment after that. Those dark brown eyes bored into mine, imploring me, *begging* me to say something, and still I couldn't remember how to speak.

His face changed. Desperation turned to frustration.

Then to pain.

Then to regret.

"Fuck," he said, and he let go of me as he stepped back.

Wait, I wanted to say, but all that came out was a breath. My shoulders sank down as the tension inside me flowed out with that puff of air. Zain turned away, separating himself from me, running a hand through his hair.

"*Fuck*," he said again. "Tessa, I'm sorry. I'm so fucking sor—"

"You can kiss me," I whispered, and I'd barely finished speaking before his lips found mine.

Twenty-Four

Zain moved so quickly that I didn't even register it.

All I knew is that one moment, I managed to force out the words I'd been trying to say, and the next I was pressed against the wall, a hand next to my head and another cupping my chin and my mouth claimed by a set of very soft, very eager lips.

And fuck.

Fuck.

He smelled so good, spicy and fresh and dizzyingly intoxicating but nowhere near overpowering. And the taste of him was just... I couldn't get enough of it. He was like citrus and sweetness and ginger. Like something familiar, but new. Like something I wanted to keep trying because I couldn't quite put my finger on what he tasted like, but that I knew damn well I'd never tasted before.

And then the feel of his body, holding me in place while he worked his lips against mine. Of warmth. Of sturdiness. Of comfort. And of desire.

So much fucking desire.

I couldn't think. I doubted he could, either. He wasn't kissing me like a person who was thinking about it. He was kissing me like he'd shut his mind down, like he'd given into instinct, like this was what he'd been born to do. Like he was trying to commit the feel of me to memory, drawing me in through his lips so he could keep me forever.

I had kissed a lot of people. A *lot* of them.

But I'd never been kissed the way Zain kissed me.

Not that we just kissed. Of course we didn't. Of *course* the hand that was next to my head made its way to my shoulder, then to my arm, then skimmed down to my waist as he deftly avoided grabbing my tits too early, even though he couldn't wait any longer to touch me.

And of course, I needed to get one up on Zain whenever I could, so I grabbed his hand and lifted it to my chest, trying not to grin when he inhaled sharply before cupping my breast.

"Tessa," he breathed against my mouth. "You're sure you're okay with this?"

"I'm the one who put your hand there, idiot."

He laughed. Sort of. He laughed the way you do when you're in the middle of kissing someone, where it's not so much about the laughter but about the way they can feel you smile. And I felt that; I felt his lips turn up as he fondled me, absorbed the noise of appreciation he made when he brought both hands to my tits and squeezed just hard enough to make me gasp.

There was an urgency to the way we indulged in each other. I couldn't say that I'd pined after Zain for years and years. I'd liked him, once upon a time, and I couldn't deny that I was attracted to him in a physical way that seemed to manifest more and more each time I'd seen him recently. Even so, it had been a long time since fantasies of him had been picked out of the mind vault where I kept all my masturbatory material.

But I was impatient for him. I was impatient for his lips and his touch, for him to finally follow through on the things he'd teased me with the last few times I'd seen him. I was impatient for him to show me what he meant when he said he'd wanted something *disrespectfully*, like he had after the anniversary party, or to ask me for the ambiguous *it* that we kept dancing around.

And he was impatient, too.

Because Zain had, apparently, been pining for me. I was sure he'd deny it if I said it that way, but that's what it was. It was obvious in the way he kissed me, in the way his hands skimmed along my body, fingers digging in through the fabric of my dress, in the heaviness of his breath and the hard bulge in his pants that was pressed against my belly.

And it was obvious that he was impatient for *me* specifically when I went to stroke said hard bulge through his dress pants and touched it for approximately two seconds before he shoved my hand away, fingers circling my wrist and pinning my arm back against the wall.

"You'll get your turn when I'm done," he growled against my mouth.

"Done what?" I asked.

I felt another smile against my mouth, but he didn't respond, just nipped at my bottom lip before sliding his tongue past it to meet mine. It was enough to distract me from the way he found my other wrist and mirrored his actions.

"What—" I started, then gasped when he guided both my hands up over my head so smoothly, it was almost like I'd let him do it.

Which I might have.

I didn't fucking know. I couldn't fucking know, not when he wrapped one hand around both my wrists and held them in place as he moved his other hand back to my breast, kneading it through the fabric of my dress and bra. As he did, he took his lips from mine, kissing a spot on my chin before moving his mouth to my jaw, then to my neck, then to the sensitive patch of skin right above my collarbone that he had *no* business knowing about.

"Fuck," I whispered as he sucked on that spot, a shiver of pleasure rushing through me.

Another one of his little smiles, then the sharpness of teeth grazing my skin.

"You taste so fucking good," he said, the words muffled against me.

I wanted to say something else, but words failed me again as he lifted my dress with his free hand. It took a bit of work, seeing as the skirt was tight against my body, but that didn't stop Zain. No, he just took a fistful of fabric and yanked it up, then slipped his hand beneath the hem and grabbed my pussy.

But like, nicely grabbed it.

The feel of his hand cupping my mound drew a moan from my lips. I couldn't help it, not when the weight and heat of his touch was exactly what I wanted.

"Fuck," he swore, and added just enough pressure to my fabric-covered slit to give me a moment of relief. "Your pussy is so hot already."

"S'what happens when I get turned on," I gasped.

It was meant to make him laugh, but it didn't. He groaned instead, a low sound that vibrated against my neck.

"I shouldn't fucking know that," he breathed.

Despite that statement, he worked his fingers past the leg hole of my panties to find out some other things he probably wasn't supposed to know.

Like how smooth the lips of my pussy were.

And how wet I already was.

And the noise I made when he pushed the tip of his finger into my folds, followed by the noise I made when that same finger found the sensitive bundle of nerves at the top and rubbed it.

I clenched my fists as he did, wanting nothing more than to clutch something but stuck beneath the firm grip of his hand. He sucked on my neck as he fingered me, his fingertip drawing little circles over my clit that made me shudder.

"You good?" he murmured.

"Yeah. Don't stop," I whispered.

Another laugh vibrated against me and a moment later, he pulled his mouth away from my neck.

"Stop?" he repeated, his dark eyes sparkling dangerously. "Teacup, unless you tell me to, I'm not gonna stop until your legs are shaking so bad you can't stand on your own and every person in this hotel knows my goddamn name."

My breath caught in my throat and I stared at him, wide-eyed. He added pressure to my clit, sending another quivering jolt of pleasure through my body, and I couldn't help but whimper.

"Understand?" he breathed. "I don't plan on stopping until I know I've fucked you so good, you'll never stop thinking about it. Until I'm confident that every time you see me after this, your face is going to turn red. Because we'll be sitting there and you won't be able to stop yourself from imagining this moment, right now, with my hand in your panties and my marks on your neck, knowing what's going to happen next."

"What's going to happen next?" I dared to ask.

And the answer to that... well.

He was right in that I'd probably never be able to stop picturing that moment.

How could I? How could *anyone* not picture the moment Zain let go of her wrists and pulled his hand away from her pussy, only to drop to his knees in front of her?

There was no way I'd ever forget the glint in his eyes or the smirk on his lips as his fingers slid into the waistband of my thong like they belonged there before he tugged it down my hips and past my thighs.

Or the sight of him shrugging off his suit jacket and loosening his tie as he drank in the view of my pussy.

I'd never forget the sensation of his fingers wrapping around my ankle, guiding my foot up so he could take my panties the rest of the way off before turning his head, kissing my thigh gently before hooking my leg over his shoulder.

I'd never forget the sight of my black heel resting against his back as he buried his face against my pussy or the feel of his hair as I reached down to steady myself on his head.

I'd never forget his fucking tongue.

"Oh my God, Zain," I gasped, then moaned when my words made *him* moan against my pussy.

His hair was like silk beneath my fingers, thick and smooth and so incredibly soft. It was long enough to pull, if I'd wanted to, but I didn't. Not yet, anyway. Maybe when I was close, when I was about to come on his tongue and had to hold onto something so I didn't fall into a different dimension, I'd pull it. But just then, I was content to watch Zain as he did whatever the fuck he wanted to me.

It was unreasonable—fucking *unreasonable*—how gorgeous that man was. How deep and dark his eyes were. It was unfair that he could go from being a smirking, stuck-up jackass one moment to this, on his knees in front of me, loving what he was doing as much as I loved him doing it.

Especially when he glanced up at me.

He looked awed, like he was just as shocked at the situation as I was, despite how inevitable it all felt. For a moment, I wondered how stupid I could have been to not believe he cared when he was looking at me like *that*.

And for a moment, I was terrified at how that made me feel.

But he blinked, and when his eyes opened again, I had just enough time to catch the wicked sparkle in them before he pushed one finger inside me and I couldn't focus on anything besides the sensation of him fucking me with his hand.

It didn't take him long to make me come. The man knew what he was doing down there; every movement was purposeful, confident, as much for my pleasure as it was for his. I knew that because he was moaning at the same time I was, tasting my orgasm as I pulled his hair and held his head in place. His noises didn't stop until I loosened my grip and let out a heavy sigh, relaxing back against the wall with my eyes closed and his tongue still lapping at my clit.

He planted a final kiss against the top of my mound before easing his finger out of me and guiding my leg off his shoulder. It wasn't until I felt him stand that I opened my eyes, and when I did, he was wiping his hand across his mouth, a guarded look on his face.

"Are you okay, T—" he started, but stumbled on my name as I grabbed a fistful of his shirt, tugging him forward.

"Shut up," I said, then kissed him.

Because it was my turn to be impatient.

Twenty-Five

I would never be able to describe Zain as quiet again.

Zain had just never been much of a talker, at least not when I'd been around him in the past. Sitting around the table in my parents' kitchen, he'd respond when spoken to and speak up when he had something to contribute to a conversation, but he was more likely to sit there in contemplation while listening to everyone else talk.

But once his cock was in your mouth, suddenly he wouldn't shut up.

"Oh, fuck," he whispered as I sank to my knees in front of him. "Are you... You're going to... Is this happening?"

I glanced up at him as I carefully undid his pants. "What did you think I was about to do?"

He shrugged, which was fair. I doubted Zain was capable of thinking just then. There probably wasn't enough blood left in his body to operate his brain, given how hard his cock was.

And it was *really* hard. Hard enough that I'd barely pulled down the zipper before it was pushing out, his boxer-briefs struggling to restrain his erection. I licked my lips, then held Zain's gaze as I leaned forward and pressed a kiss to his bulge. Through the fabric, his cock twitched, and Zain's throat flexed as he kept his eyes on me.

"Something wrong?" I asked innocently.

"Uh... how, um, serious were you about your blowjobs being 'toothy'?"

It took everything in me not to burst out laughing. I managed to suppress it by trying to look faux-offended. "I've never used teeth in my life."

He let out a breath. "Okay. Alright."

"But if that's what you're into—"

"Teacup, if you bite my dick, I'm going to get you on the bed, tie you up, and leave you here until housekeeping finds you," he said.

I couldn't hold back the laugh that time and reached for the waistband of his underwear. "Jesus, Zain. It was just a joke."

He started to respond, but whatever he was saying faded into a sigh of relief as I pulled his boxer-briefs down.

And that sigh turned into a low, relieved groan almost immediately, since I wasted no time before getting my lips around the head of his cock.

I'd seen Zain from this angle once before: when I'd called his bluff back in Burnsley, sinking to my knees in front of him and daring him to ask me to do this. So it wasn't like this was an entirely new experience. I mean, his cock wasn't in my mouth last time, but I'd looked up at him the same way I was looking up at him then.

But this was infinitely better.

And no, not just because his cock was in my mouth.

This time, Zain wanted me there. This time, he was looking at me with his lips parted and his eyes half-lidded, desire seeping through every pore of his body as he reached for me with one shaking hand.

And that was when the talking started.

"Fuck, Tessa," he whispered as I sucked him gently. "You look so fucking pretty right now. So gorgeous with my cock in your mouth."

His words made my body hum. Something warm and pleased and eager washed over me and I took more of him in my mouth, earning a soft groan of approval. A moment later, he brushed my hair off my forehead. The action was almost tender and I looked up at him, surprised at how delicately he was touching me considering the way he'd just feasted on my pussy.

But only for a moment.

Because that wasn't a tender touch. That wasn't a moment born from his heart swelling with emotion as I worked him with my mouth so I could spoil him the way he'd spoiled me.

It was a moment for him to get all my hair in one place so he could grab a generous handful with which to command my movements.

"So fucking pretty," he mumbled again as he tightened his fist. "Is this okay?"

Fuck yes, it was, but I couldn't exactly say that. But he seemed to understand from my garbled murmuration and slight nod, because his lips curled up into a pleased smirk.

"Good," he said, then tested just how okay it was by pressing my head down slowly but firmly.

I opened my throat as best I could, but the urge to gag was still there. It always was the first time someone put their dick that far back. I blinked, holding my breath and Zain's gaze as he eased his cock in further and further.

"Relax around it," he said, his voice low. "Show me how deep you can take it, kitten."

Fucking *kitten*.

I'd never been called that before. But fuck if it didn't make me clench my thighs as a desperate rush of excitement washed over me.

Which Zain noticed.

"You like that," he said. It wasn't a question, but I made another soft burble in response and he smiled. "Of course you do. Of course you look like a goddess on your knees with my cock in your perfect little mouth, getting all fucking hot and bothered because you like it when I call you *kitten*."

He thrust his cock in a bit further and I almost choked on it, but he pulled back before it was too much. I pulled in a deep breath through my nose, then blinked up at him and tried to shove my head forward.

"You want more?" he asked.

Another muffled garble was my response.

"Whatever you say, kitten."

He took it slow at first, letting me adjust to him, but it wasn't long before he was fucking my mouth at a steady pace. I touched him as he did, not content to sit with my hands folded on my lap when I could feel the soft hair on his thighs beneath my palms or make him shiver when my fingers found a sensitive spot just below his hip bone.

"Your mouth is so fucking good," he said. "So hot and wet and fucking perfect."

His hand tightened in my hair as a pained look crossed his face.

"I shouldn't know that, Tessa. I shouldn't fucking *know*—" and he punctuated the word by pushing his cock deep again "—how good this feels. But it's not my fault your throat feels like it was made to hold my cock. It's not my fault you're so fucking good at this."

I whimpered around him, sucking as he pulled back out before thrusting in my mouth again.

"And that's a problem, kitten," he continued. "That's a fucking problem, because I've never wanted to fuck anyone so badly in my entire life. I've never been so fucking desperate to find out what it's like to be inside someone or what you're gonna look like when you're lying on your back and coming on my cock. But I can't stop." His cock went deep again. "I can't give up your mouth, Teacup."

I wanted to find out what it was like too, almost as much as I wanted to find out what he tasted like, but I wasn't worried. There was no way this night was ending without Zain fucking the sense out of me.

I'd easily be able to get both.

He whispered about the things he was going to do to me until his words turned to nonsense, until the only thing he could say was my name, until his fist was clenching my hair hard as he struggled not to lose control. Then he came in my mouth, my nose pressed to the soft curls of hair on his pelvis as he clutched my head.

Once I pulled back and swallowed the few drops that hadn't gone straight down my throat, Zain reached down, taking my hand and helping me to my feet.

"Tessa," he breathed, then kissed me.

Then he kissed me again.

Then again.

"You're not done with me, are you?" I asked between kisses.

He smiled against my lips. "Nah. But it's probably gonna take my dick at least ten to fifteen minutes to figure that out."

Which was fine. We had plenty to do in the meantime.

He was still half dressed, as was I, and that needed to change immediately. So as we stood there with his back to the wall, I reached up and undid his tie the rest of the way, slipping it off his neck before trailing my hands down to the buttons of his dress shirt.

He kissed me as I undid his shirt button by button. Once it was open, I traced my hands down his bare skin, the hair on his chest and stomach soft against my palms. Only then did I guide the shirt off his shoulders before finally forcing myself to stop kissing him so I could look at him.

And fuck.

Fuck.

He was so gorgeous.

Aside from the pantslessness of the situation, Zain's body wasn't exactly new to me. I'd seen him shirtless before, though not since he was a semi-scrawny teenager. He wasn't scrawny anymore and I wouldn't have called him thin, but he wasn't fat, either. He had a hint of a belly and soft, dark hair on his chest and stomach and arms.

And then there were the tattoos.

I was entranced by the art on his skin. By the large floral piece that began on his shoulder and covered the top right side of his chest. By the snake twisted around his other arm, which I'd never realized the geometric pattern I liked was part of. By the characters on the other side of his chest, words I didn't understand because they were written in Urdu, but that obviously meant enough for him to have them permanently inked on his body.

And then there was—

"I fucking knew it," I said, moving my hand to his left pec.

Zain raised his eyebrows. "Knew what?"

I didn't respond, just bit my lip as I touched the small silver ring in his nipple. Zain glanced down, then laughed.

"Have you spent a lot of time contemplating if I had nipple piercings or not?" he asked.

I fought to keep my face from turning red. "Shut up."

He leaned in and kissed me. "Well, since you asked so nicely. And since it's your turn now."

"My turn?"

He put his hands on my shoulders, guiding me to spin in front of him. "As much as I'd love to tear this dress off your body, I think your sugar daddy might be mad at me for wrecking something so beautiful."

I rolled my eyes as he tugged the zipper down. "I don't have a sugar daddy."

He was about to say some snarky-ass thing back as he guided the sleeves away from my arms, letting the dress fall away from my body. I was sure of it. But before he could, I reached up and unhooked my bra, let it drop to the floor unceremoniously, then turned around to face him wearing nothing but my heels as the dress pooled at my feet.

And for some reason, that made him forget what he was going to say.

"Fuck, Teacup," he hissed, and then he pulled me in to kiss him before using his hips to guide us towards the bed.

We spent the next while exploring, kissing and touching and indulging in each other's bodies the way we hadn't had patience for before getting in an orgasm each. Zain's hands were everywhere, tracing the undersides of my breasts and caressing my belly and squeezing my hips and ass.

I ended up on top of him, straddling his hips with one of his hands on each of my thighs, because I was needy and dripping for him already, but he wasn't hard yet. Maybe he would have been if I'd started stroking his dick or something, but I figured it would be more fun to do that with my pussy instead of my hand.

And it was.

It was *way* more fun.

His breathing started getting heavier as I ground against him. When he reached up to play with my breasts again, I felt him twitch beneath me. I kept rolling my hips as he hardened, feeling the thickness of his cock between my pussy lips. Up until then, we'd still been kissing. But as his erection grew, Zain tilted his head back, closing his eyes as I coated his shaft in my wetness.

And it was stupid of me.

It was *really* stupid of me to do that.

It was stupid of me to get so turned on feeling the heat of his bare cock against my pussy. For that neediness in my core to ache even more, wanting to stick him inside me just like that, wanting to feel him as closely as I possibly could.

It was *so* stupid, and yet...

"You're in dangerous territory, Teacup," he breathed when his cock was fully hard.

"Want me to stop?" I asked.

His hands were on my hips in a second, holding me in place on top of him.

"What I want and what we should do are two very, very different things," he said.

"So... maybe a few more minutes of this?" I asked.

His breath hitched, but he nodded, then groaned when I slid the length of his cock along my pussy again.

"I should probably grab a condom," he said after the aforementioned few minutes went by.

"Yeah, probably," I agreed, then snorted softly.

"What?" he asked.

"Had some high hopes that something would happen tonight, did you?"

He smirked. "I always have high hopes. But no. Honestly, it's impressive I have any left given how this week has gone."

"Is it?" I asked.

He squeezed my thighs lightly. "You think you're the only one who fucks around, Teacup?"

"You little slut," I said.

He laughed again, jostling his cock against me, and I had to bite back a moan as his head brushed my clit. "How are you surprised by that? You caught me at a gay bar earlier this week."

"You told me you were networking with clients," I said.

He gave me an unimpressed look. "What clients do you think I have that would be at a drag show?"

"I barely know what you do for a living."

"Fair," he said, tilting his head back as he rested his hands heavily on my thighs. "But if I'd known..."

"Known what?"

His eyes took on that dark burn again. "If I'd known this would happen, I wouldn't've touched anyone else this week." His eyes flicked down my body. "I would've saved it all up for you, kitten."

I wasn't trying to tease him with my pussy anymore, but I couldn't help squirming, not with the electric arousal that jolted through me from his words. And that made him groan again, his fingers digging into my thigh.

"Fuck, we shouldn't..." he murmured.

"Definitely shouldn't," I agreed. "I mean, I use a condom with everyone."

"Me too," he said. "Everyone."

"And I get tested regularly."

"Yeah, same. And I don't... don't have anything."

I shifted my hips again and we both moaned.

"But we still probably shouldn't, right?" I whispered.

"We shouldn't," he said. "I mean, we *shouldn't* but... we should fuck."

I don't know if that was a sentence. I mean, I wasn't sure if he was trying to say "We should fuck" as in we should just start fucking, or if he was saying "We shouldn't" and then cursed as he cut himself off when the tip of his cock unexpectedly slipped inside the entrance of my pussy.

It was an accident. Honestly, it was. I hadn't intended to do anything more than grind against him again, but he'd started to shift beneath me, probably to pull himself up so he could grab a condom, and the angle changed just enough that things lined up.

"I'm sorry," I said, immediately freezing.

He squeezed his eyes shut and shook his head. "Don't be. Don't... oh, *fuck*."

"Do you want me to move off?" I asked.

A dry laugh escaped his lips and he grimaced. "Fuck, no. But we... we..."

"I don't want to make you uncomfortable, Zain. If you don't want this—"

"It's not that," he said, his voice choked. "I just... You're about to learn something about me, I think."

I frowned. "I can only think of a couple reasons you'd say something like that. Like you have something I don't want to catch. Or you have a massive breeding kink."

"I mean, I wouldn't say *massive*," he whispered.

Oh.

Oh.

I could work with that.

It took everything in me not to smirk before I shifted just enough that more of his cock slipped inside me. He groaned and his hands flew to my hips, fingertips digging in as he held me in place and looked up at me with desperation in his eyes.

"Tessa, I will come inside you," he said bluntly. "I do *not* have enough control to pull out."

"It's okay," I said. "You think I fuck around as much as I do and don't take precautions?"

His lips parted, but nothing came out.

"I want this, Zain," I whispered. "If you do."

A low, longing noise left his mouth, and then he was pulling me down as he thrust up, shoving his cock deep inside me. I let out a soft cry of surprise, but it was lost as Zain sat up and crushed his lips to mine. We sat that way for a moment, him buried inside me and our bodies pushed together, before he threw me on my back with a surprising amount of strength.

I barely recovered before he was over me, wrenching my thighs apart. And I'd barely processed *that* before he was between my legs, shoving his cock back inside me and making both of us cry out with pleasure and relief and desperate longing.

And then he started fucking me.

Hard.

"You know how much I've wanted you?" he growled as his hips slapped against me. "Do you know how many *fucking* times I've thought about taking you like this? How many times I've thought about you begging me to come inside you?"

"No," I said, because I didn't know at all.

He grunted and leaned in, burying his face against my neck.

"So many times," came his muffled response. "I've stroked my cock so many times thinking about how good it would feel to ruin this tight little pussy, Teacup."

"Is it as good as you thought?"

"Nope." He bit down on my earlobe gently, then lifted his head so he could look me in the eyes, his face dark and full of lust. "It's better. Because I couldn't have imagined how wet you get, kitten. How hot your pussy is. The way your tits jiggle when I fuck you like *this*—" He thrust inside me hard and I cried out as my tits did, indeed, jiggle quite enticingly. "—or how your mouth tastes."

He leaned in and kissed me, capturing my breath with his lips.

"And I shouldn't know, Teacup," he murmured. "I shouldn't know what it feels like to *have* you, but I do. And now I'm gonna find out what it's like to fill your pussy up with my cum."

My thighs tensed, clenching hard as his words made my body sing. He half-groaned and half-chuckled.

"That's what you want, isn't it?" he asked.

"Yes," I gasped.

"You were fucking thrilled to find out I wanted to breed you, weren't you?" he hissed. "You couldn't *wait* to get this cock inside you so I could fill your needy little pussy with so much cum."

"Fuck." My legs trembled around him and I had to close my eyes, clutching at him and digging my fingertips into his back. "Yes. Yes, I need it."

"You want me to put a baby in you, don't you, kitten?"

"Yes," I said again, then let a slow smirk spread across my face. "Yes, *Daddy*."

His movements staggered and he swore, and that was the last specific thing I could remember for a while.

The bed slammed against the wall as he pounded me, so hard that I was sure everyone in the hotel would be able to hear it. His lips were on mine, then on my neck, then his teeth were sinking into my skin and almost certainly leaving marks. My nails scratched his back and I was saying something—his name, maybe, or maybe I kept calling him Daddy, or maybe it was just complete nonsense that was being driven from my body with each thrust.

"Come for me," he groaned. "I need to feel you come on my cock, kitten."

"Please," I whispered, but I wasn't sure what I was asking for.

"I'm not giving you my cum until you do," he growled. "I'm not finishing until I have a picture of you burned into my memory so I can think about it every time I jack off from now on. Because you love that, don't you?"

"Yes," I tried to say, but the sound that came out was incomprehensible.

"You love knowing I think about you when I stroke my cock," he continued. "You love knowing I want to fuck you and get you pregnant and that you've been driving me crazy for years. For fucking *years*, kitten."

He kissed me again, absorbing my soft cries as he enveloped my body, holding me close as he fucked me relentlessly.

"I've waited for you for so long, Teacup." The words were soft, so quiet that I almost couldn't hear them over the sounds of our bodies colliding, but so intense that I *felt* them tingling across my skin and seeping into my bones, making my breath hitch and my heart race and my lips part. "Every fucking time I look at you, it kills me because all I can think about is how much I want *this*."

I was almost sobbing as I came on him, my back arching as I clung to him with everything I had. Zain was enraptured as he watched, his lips parted and his eyes wide, taking in the sight of me falling apart because of him. As I came down, I heard him panting, and I knew he had to be close.

Reaching up, I put my hand behind his neck and pulled him in for a kiss.

"Your turn," I said against his lips.

"So close, kitten," he groaned.

"I want you to come," I whispered. "Please come inside me, Daddy." And he did.

He came so hard I could feel it. His cock throbbing, the sensation of his cum coating the walls of my pussy... I felt all of it. Because he wasn't wearing a condom and that was so fucking stupid, but oh my *God*, was it good.

After he finished, he flopped on the bed next to me, both of us gasping for breath in a room that seemed far too quiet.

"So," I said. "Breeding kink, hey?"

He laughed tiredly. "I know. I don't even know if I want kids, but for some fucking reason..."

"You sure seem to like trying to make them," I said, giggling.

"Laugh all you want. It'll be more fun when we start talking about your Daddy kink."

"I don't have a Daddy kink."

He turned his head to look at me. "Oh, of course. Remind me what that last thing you said was? 'Please come inside me' who?"

"That was for you," I said. "You're the one who wanted to hear it. So that means *you* have the Daddy kink."

"At no point did I tell you to call me that," he said. "I think the most I said about it was to *not* say that."

"Because you like it too much," I said.

"Well…"

We laughed again, the sound almost sleepy, then Zain pulled me into his arms. He held me against his chest, his heartbeat steady and soothing in my ear and his breath warm on my skin. We stayed that way, embracing each other and the comfortable silence between us.

I was sure we were both thinking the same things. Panicking a little, maybe. Wondering what this meant and what would happen now. But we didn't look at each other. We didn't talk about what happened. We just lay there, clinging together, cooling down and coming back to earth and existing, postponing those important thoughts and discussions so we could bask in the make-believe world where *this* could be a thing.

Even though, deep down, we both knew it couldn't.

We stayed like that for a long time. Long enough that the room was almost completely dark when my body forced me to shift out of his arms. He loosened his grip, eyes catching the small amount of light in the room and showing the veiled look of concern in his eyes.

"Bathroom," I explained. "Sorry."

"Don't be sorry," he whispered, then pulled me in for a kiss. "Please don't be sorry."

And somehow, I didn't think he was talking about me needing to use the bathroom.

Twenty-Six

Neither of us slept on the couch that night.

Obviously.

Zain joked about it because he was Zain and he was an asshole. And I told him to enjoy sleeping there naked because I wouldn't be giving up any of the blankets since I was also an asshole.

But luckily we were assholes who, as I was discovering, had the same sense of humour, so that conversation was happening at the same time that we were climbing into bed, tucking the blankets around both of us, and curling up together. His arms went around me as I told him he could use one of his many suits to keep warm, and my head settled on his chest as he said I could take the curtains down and use those as a blanket, if I wanted. Then he adjusted the covers, tucking them around my shoulders, and pressed a kiss to the top of my head.

And that was how we spent the night.

Not fucking.

Not making out.

Not talking.

Even though we should have. Talked, I mean. The whole talking thing should have probably happened before we woke up the next morning. Or immediately after we woke up. Or at any point before my fingers wrapped around his cock, stroking him lazily as his hand wandered down to my pussy.

We should have definitely talked before I called him Daddy as I shattered on his fingers. Or before I got my mouth around his cock so he could come down my throat again.

But it wasn't until he'd finished and I was resting on his chest that either of us dared to bring it up.

"Tess?" he asked.

"Hmm?"

"I'm not the only one you're seeing, right?"

"Yeah, you are," I murmured.

I felt him tense beneath me. "But you said—"

"The others are all nines or tens. Usually I don't go for anyone under a seven-point-five, but you caught me on a bad night."

My head jostled as he laughed. "Yeah, right. Kitten, your standards are so low the bar is on the floor and I fucking pole vaulted over it."

"Oh, fuck you," I said, but I was laughing, too.

"Maybe in a bit," he said. "But right now we should, uh... you know."

My laughter faded. "Know what?"

"We should figure this out," he said.

I swallowed nervously, focusing my attention on the small silver ring in his nipple. "Figure what out?"

Zain didn't respond right away. After a few moments of silence, he sighed, but there was a resigned sort of acceptance to it.

"This was a one-night thing, wasn't it?" he asked.

For some reason, my face started going red. I hoped he couldn't feel it where my cheek was pressed to his skin.

"I mean, my entire family thinks I'm married to someone else," I said.

"Yeah. And I guess your brother would kill me."

I started laughing so hard, Zain loosened his grip on me so I could pull away.

"What?" he asked, bewildered.

"You think *Josh* would be pissed that you slept with me?" I asked through snorts of laughter.

"I mean, yeah. You're my best friend's sister. Pretty sure that's one of those things you like… don't do. Bro code or whatever. A guy's gotta look out for his sister and all that."

I wiped a finger under my eyes, though it was more for dramatic effect than from actual tears of laughter. "Yeah, sure. But that makes the assumption Josh gives a shit about me and we all know he doesn't."

Zain shifted, sitting back a bit and propping himself up on his elbow. I was lying on my back, but turned my head to look at him. He looked nearly irresistible, his usually perfect hair sticking out and the blankets sitting around his ribcage so I could see most of the tattoos on his upper body.

But not completely irresistible, since he was frowning at me almost patronizingly.

"You really have this entire thing where you don't believe people care about you, eh?" he asked.

"Excuse me?"

"You were so fucking convinced I didn't either," he said. "You think no one in your family does, but—"

"Are you serious?" It was my turn to prop myself up so I could look at him incredulously. "You were there at the anniversary party, Zain. Remember? When my dad completely ignored me, then when he was forced to acknowledge I exist, spent that entire interaction telling everyone that I'm a fucking joke?"

"Josh isn't your dad," he said.

"He might as well be," I replied. "He sat there and let it happen. Same as you. Same as everyone."

"He tried to—" He cut himself off, closing his eyes briefly and taking a deep breath. "Look, I know your brother. He does care about you, Tess."

I rolled my eyes. "My interactions with Josh are him ignoring me, not taking me seriously, ordering me around, or fangirling over my ex-husband. If I didn't bring Brad home once in a while, he wouldn't even register when I'm in the room."

"That's just not true," he said, his voice almost arrogant. "He might be shit at showing it, but Josh is—"

"Can we not?" I asked. "The last thing I want to discuss while I'm naked in bed with... well, anyone, but specifically with you, is my brother."

Zain's mouth twitched, but he didn't finish his sentence. "Really? I feel like the last thing would be your dad." He glanced down at his nails nonchalantly. "Though, I guess with the whole Daddy thing you've got going on..."

"It must be super hard for you to listen to your mom talk about how she wants grandkids when you have such a serious breeding kink," I shot back. "Do you get turned on when she brings it up or—"

He cut me off by gagging. "Okay, okay. You win."

"Are you sure?" I asked. "We can totally dissect this. Like, maybe the reason you have a breeding kink in the first place is that your mom has *always* put pressure on you to—"

"You *win*," he said again, though he started laughing. "I'll never imply your Daddy kink has anything to do with your actual dad again."

"Asshole."

He scooted closer on the bed and put his arms around me. His voice went low and husky. "I'm sorry."

I let him urge my body closer to his. "You better be."

"I am. Even though you're also an asshole."

"That's what you get for using my fucked up family against me."

I couldn't see his face with the way he was holding me, but I felt the shift in the room when I said that. There was a quiet moment, then Zain's fingers traced a light pattern on my arm.

"And that fucked up family..." he said. "That's why we... That's why."

He didn't have to finish the thought for me to know what he meant. Something like sadness lumped in my throat and I swallowed it back, grateful Zain couldn't see the expression on my face as I nodded.

"You wouldn't consider telling them?" he asked.

I tensed in his arms, stiffening enough that he noticed.

"I just mean—" he started.

"You don't even know what you're asking for," I said.

"I do know."

"If you knew, you wouldn't be asking me for *that* after one night," I snapped, pulling away as I tried to squirm out of his arms. "I know you think you're hot shit, Zain, but you're asking me to—"

"I'm not asking you to do anything," he replied patiently. "I asked if it was something you would consider."

"Same thing."

"It's not. I didn't ask you to do it for me. I just wanted to know where we might stand."

Which was infuriatingly fair. I stewed for a moment, glaring at Zain's chest before drawing in a breath and letting it out.

"Everything else aside, we don't even live in the same city," I said. "We rarely see each other. So from a practical standpoint, it wouldn't make sense. Then there's the whole thing where your best friend is my brother. And I'm not... I just..."

"You're not ready to tell them."

The way he said it stung, even though he didn't say it hurtfully. So maybe it wasn't the way he said so much as the way I felt it.

And maybe I should've agreed with him and left it at that.

Maybe I shouldn't have made myself vulnerable.

But being there in his arms, I just...

I couldn't help it.

"I'm not ready for everyone to find out what a letdown I am, okay?" I said, my voice small. "I spent my whole life being a letdown. I don't want to go back to that yet."

Zain's lips pressed to the top of my head. "You're not a letdown, Teacup."

"You don't have to say that. I'm not changing my mind."

"I'm not saying it to change your mind. I'm saying it because it's the truth."

"This isn't happening. This... this was a one-time thing. We're not doing it again."

"You don't have to give me excuses to justify being scared."

The fucking asshole.

He laughed as I shoved him away again.

"I was joking," he said, though he let me go before I had to resort to something like grabbing his nipple rings and twisting.

"Fuck you," I muttered.

"Sure, if you're offering."

"Are you serious?"

He propped himself up on one elbow and half-shrugged. "I mean, we both had a good time, if the way you squeezed that pussy on my cock was any indication. So if this is it, why not have one for the road?"

I tried to glare at him, but he wasn't wrong about how hard he'd made me come and one for the road did sound good.

After we finished fucking for what was for sure going to be the last time, we both showered and got dressed before packing. While Zain collected his various belongings from around the hotel room, I found my purse on the dresser and dug out my phone, then swore when I remembered it was completely dead.

"What's wrong?" he asked, looking up from where he was tucking his dirty laundry into his suitcase.

"Dead phone," I muttered. "I forgot my charger."

He walked over and took my phone, turning it over so he could look at the charging port, then handed it back before going to his suitcase.

"You can use mine," he said.

"Don't worry about it," I said. "It's going to take a while to charge and we have to check out."

He turned around, holding a cable as well as a small portable battery pack. "Yeah, but you can charge it over breakfast."

"We're getting breakfast?"

Zain raised his eyebrows. "I didn't fuck you hard enough to make you famished?"

"I mean, I could probably force down a couple of grapes or something."

A smirk spread across his lips as he plugged my phone in, then handed the whole setup to me to put in my purse. "You don't have to get on the bus for a couple of hours and my flight's not until this afternoon. There's plenty of time to eat and charge your phone."

Which was good, because I was fucking starving.

Despite knowing that this wasn't going to happen again, both of us were in what was, all things considered, a relatively good mood. Zain insisted on carrying my bag down for me and I finally agreed he could, then made him cackle with laughter when I stole his suitcase to carry down instead. When we got to the restaurant after checking out of the room, both of us were even smiling.

Until we got to our table and Owen walked up as I was sliding into the booth.

He was dressed more casually than he had been the night before, wearing a polo shirt tucked into a pair of jeans. There were bags under his eyes and a pinched look on his face, though he tried to nod politely at me before turning to Zain.

"Hameed," Owen said, his voice flat.

Zain's throat flexed as he swallowed, but he maintained a calm expression. "Good morning, sir."

"Tessa," Owen said. "You won't mind if I steal Zain for a moment to chat."

It wasn't a question. It wasn't an option. It probably wasn't even going to be just a chat. But I nodded all the same and Zain put his suitcase under the table before looking at me.

"Get whatever you like," he said quietly. "And can you order me a breakfast platter with the turkey sausage, please?"

I nodded and tried to smile. Zain's mouth twitched as he tried to return it, but nothing reached his eyes before he turned and resigned himself to following Owen away from the booth. I watched out of the corner of my eye, but they turned around a corner and out of sight.

After everything with Nathan and the subsequent evening of fucking, neither Zain nor I had time to consider what the consequences of him standing up for me were.

Well, for him at least. I wouldn't have any consequences. Except for maybe the crushing amount of guilt knowing that Zain was going to have to explain why he disappeared, lost the very important client he was supposed to be signing, and subsequently skipped the rest of the very important work dinner he should have been at.

Yeah, there were going to be consequences.

The thought of it made my stomach curl even more. I hadn't asked Zain to do any of that for me, but it still felt like my fault. Even though I knew damn well it wasn't. It was entirely *Nathan's* fault for being a vindictive prick.

But I wasn't sure that anyone with a heart wouldn't feel at least a little guilty about it.

The server came over and took my order. I didn't know what Zain wanted to drink, so ordered him the same as me: coffee, a glass of orange juice, and a glass of water. Then, of course, his breakfast platter, and peanut butter pancakes for myself. Once she walked away, I dug my phone out of my purse.

It had charged enough that I could turn it on and when I did, two messages came through immediately. One was from Claire, asking if I was okay and letting me know she was going to be on her private jet for most of the day on her way to Tahiti, but to text her when I could so she knew I was okay. I responded immediately, promising her I was alright and that I'd tell her all about it later.

The second message was from Chuck.

Chuck

Okay so why did no one tell me how amazing hockey is? WHY did no one inform me that in-person hockey is not boring at all? Or that the hockey boys have the thickest of thighs and that they get all grunty and sweaty and aggressive and that it's weirdly hot for some reason?

Me

Sorry. I thought you would've known that.

His response was almost immediate.

Chuck

And THERE she is. I sent that last night.

Me

It's not like you would've texted back right away. Weren't you getting premium fellatio after the hockey?

Chuck

Giving AND getting. It was a lovely night. But that doesn't excuse not texting me back.

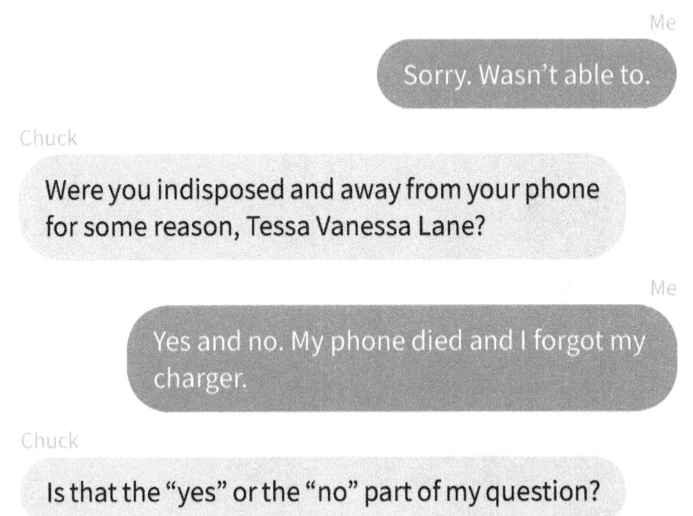

I didn't know how to respond to that. When a few minutes went by and I hadn't replied, my phone rang and Chuck's name flashed on the screen. I rejected the call, chewing my lip as I messaged back.

Maybe it was an asshole move, but I had to admit it was amusing to text that to Chuck and then not respond to his immediate barrage of texts.

Yeah, it was a bit of an asshole move, but I figured I deserved a bit of fun.

It's not an entirely happy story. I need to get through breakfast, then go home and sleep. And I can't do this over text. Just trust me, please.

There was no immediate response that time. When there was, I could almost see the expression of concern on Chuck's face.

You're scaring me a little. I won't push but can you please confirm for me that you're okay and not hurt or something? Because if he hurt you, Charles and I are going to hunt him down. We'll find him.

I blinked away the sudden stinging sensation in my eyes.

It wasn't Zain. He very much took one for the team. AKA me, I'm the team. I am okay, just I might need a hug tomorrow. Or an iced coffee.

Consider both done.

The server came back and put my coffee, orange juice, and water in front of me, mirroring it at the still-empty seat across from mine. She walked away and I'd just taken a sip of my coffee when I felt someone looking at me. Glancing up, I saw Zain striding across the restaurant, his face stony.

"Are you okay?" I asked when he was close to the booth.

He nodded, very clearly not okay, and went to sit across from me. He hesitated for a second, then turned and slid wordlessly into the booth beside me. He put his arm around my shoulder, then leaned in and kissed the side of my head in an all-too-familiar way.

Fuck.

"I'm sorry," I whispered, barely loud enough for him to hear.

"Don't ever be," he said.

I looked down at the table. "I cost you a lot."

"I disagree," he said, his voice smooth but resigned. "But even if you did, Teacup, don't ever doubt that it would've been worth everything."

I looked up at him. "For one night?"

There was a half-smile on his lips, though there was still sadness in his dark eyes.

"Are you kidding?" he said. "If that's all it cost for one night with you, I got a hell of a deal."

My face flushed as I laughed in surprise. Zain's smile grew, the corners of his eyes crinkling, and a moment later he leaned in and pressed his lips to mine, right there in public where everyone could see us.

"I thought we weren't doing this again," I murmured against his mouth.

"We're not," he said, kissing me again. "Breakfast counts as part of the one night."

It was a flimsy excuse, but I let him have it. Mostly because I wanted it, too.

"I guess you can have one more for the road," I said.

And then another one after that.

And then one more before the server came back with our meals and set them down before politely moving Zain's collection of drinks to our side of the table.

Part 5

Confession: Always save one for the road.

Twenty-Seven

I STARED AT THE photo on my phone, something like disgusted intrigue on my face.

It didn't make sense.

The way her legs were spread didn't make sense. Like, from a physical perspective. It hurt just *looking* at her. She was in a front split so deep that the insubstantial crotch of her thong bikini was flush with the packed-down sand beneath her. The toes on both feet were pointed as a wave of turquoise sea splashed over her legs. Sunlight caught the ocean behind her, highlighting the way she held her hands clasped over her head in some kind of yoga-esque pose, tranquility and peacefulness on her face like she wasn't smashing her coochie against the ground. After a moment, I typed a response:

Me

> Isn't she getting sand all up in there?

CM

> THAT'S what you're focused on? Seriously???

Me

> It looks itchy. No one wants a vagina full of sand.

CM

> Darling. She. Is. Topless.

I frowned, then looked back at the photo.

Me

Oh yeah. Nice tits.

Claire sent back a set of laughing face emojis and I could almost hear her horrible laugh in my mind.

CM

She says thank you and that you should come with me next time. She really wants to meet the queen of threesomes.

Me

Oh, sure. Let me just call up my private jet and whip out my Black American Express so I can hit up an exclusive sex resort in Tahiti.

CM

Don't be stupid. We could share my private jet.

Me

Wait, for real - could we join the mile high club

CM

I'm already a member but I'd be happy to induct you into the club.

"Teacup? Are you okay in there?"

I fumbled and nearly dropped my phone, but like so many things in my life, solved the problem by spreading my legs. The phone dropped into my lap, caught by the skirt of the ugliest dress in the world so it wouldn't clatter to the floor and, with my luck, under the change room door.

This day was awkward enough without my mom seeing a photo of a half-naked woman doing beach yoga in Tahiti displayed prominently on my phone screen.

"I'm fine," I said. "Just, uh… fiddling. With the zipper."

"Does it fit okay?" Mom asked, then lowered her voice to what I think was supposed to be a hushed whisper but did not have the volume of one. "Do you need me to see if they have a larger size?"

I rolled my eyes, thankful she couldn't see me. "Nope. It's a little loose, actually. I might have to gain weight for the wedding."

"Maybe it'll be baby weight," Audrey said in the background.

My mom laughed. I laughed, too, even though it wasn't funny. I mean, it was clever, and it would've been funny if I wasn't lying to them about trying to have a baby with Brad, and it would've been even funnier if it didn't make me think about Zain and the way he fantasized about making me put the "mother" in "Mother's Day."

But it did. Even though I hadn't talked to Zain all week and was hoping against hope that he wouldn't show up in Burnsley this weekend. Or if he did, to spend Mother's Day with his own mother and not pop by my parents' place so I had to face him after the previous weekend.

I'd been inundated with my mom as soon as I'd gotten off the plane in Kelowna. Despite telling her not to worry about parking and to pick me up outside the airport, she and Audrey were waiting in Arrivals, clad in big white sunglasses and t-shirts emblazoned with sparkly letters spelling out "Bride Tribe."

"You're here!" Audrey said excitedly as I spotted them and considered if it would be worth getting arrested by turning around bolting the wrong way through security.

I decided it wasn't, but it was a narrow decision.

"Here I am," I said as I walked up to them.

Mom squealed and did an odd little dance, then threw her arms around me before shoving a t-shirt into my hands. "Go put this on in the bathroom, Teacup. Then girls' day will *officially* be in progress!"

"It's going to be so much fun," Audrey said, beaming at me.

She and I had very different definitions of fun, but I wasn't about to say that. Especially not when I got back from the bathroom and she handed me a sparkly purple tumbler with my name in vinyl on the side. Taking a sip, I discovered it was filled with an iced flat white with two pumps of vanilla.

"How'd you know my coffee order?" I asked, surprised.

Audrey tapped her nose mischievously. "I asked Brad when you were here last month."

The coffee in my mouth suddenly tasted bitter as I realized Brad still knew my coffee order. I swallowed and forced myself to smile.

"How sweet of him," I said.

From there, we'd gotten into Mom's car and drove to the bridal shop where Audrey had found the rest of her bridesmaids dresses. She'd decided to go with different dresses in the same colour family because of course she had. Because of course it wasn't the easy solution of there being one unflattering dress in one shade of purple so I could just order it and look miserable.

No, instead I had to try on multiple dresses in search of the perfect one that wasn't too similar to the ones her other bridesmaids had already bought. And that was proving far more difficult than expected, since we all had similar body types and as such had similar options for what would look best on us.

"And don't forget it might need to be… you know." Mom had looked pointedly at my belly and winked. "Taken out."

My face turned red. "It'll be fine. There's nothing… nothing yet. So even if I did, I wouldn't be, um, showing much by then."

And if by some terrifying stroke of luck I *was* magically pregnant at Josh and Audrey's wedding, I'd have to do my best to hide the bump anyway. I sincerely doubted Zain would be able to keep his hands off me if I showed up looking *actually* pregnant.

Which might be fun.

And also horrible, since Brad would be there.

Not that I said any of that, of course. Instead, Mom looked put out and I felt guilty.

"Well, maybe if he was home more often," she grumbled, still salty about the fact that Brad wouldn't be at her Mother's Day brunch.

I sighed. "Not this again."

"Priorities, Teacup." She held up her hands. "I won't bring it up again. But he needs to get his priorities straight and do what makes you happy."

The bitter taste returned to my mouth, and I'd just nodded before going through the one rack of plus size sample dresses.

I tried on what felt like every single one of them, plus a few of the straight-size dresses that I could squeeze into "just to get an idea of how it would look." It was worse than when I'd been shopping with Claire, which is why I'd thought to text her a selfie of myself in a taffeta nightmare while I was procrastinating coming out of the fitting room.

Me

> Guess what I got stuck doing again.

CM

> Oh my God. WHY are you so hot?

Me

> I look like a fucking ragdoll.

CM

> Well, I do admit the dress is covering most of my favourite bits. Why not remove that and send another?

That text had come through after I exited the change room to show Audrey and Mom, so it was a few minutes before I could respond. Which I did by following her request, the taffeta nightmare pooled at my feet.

CM

> Yep, I was right. You're so hot. Can I show this to the girl I'm hooking up with here? Feel free to say no but I want to show you off.

Me

> Go for it. But I want something sexy in return.

After sending that, I pulled on the next dress and left to show Mom and Audrey. We all agreed it was arguably one of the better options, mostly because I was hoping to not have to try on another hour's worth of dresses, and when I got back to the change room, I had the topless photo of some random girl Claire had met in Tahiti.

Which had really improved the dress shopping experience.

Claire and I had been texting pretty much every day since I'd gotten back from Victoria. I would have felt bad about interrupting her business trip, except said "business" trip seemed to mostly consist of her drinking a rainbow of fruity cocktails, spending hours in the pool, then the jacuzzi, then the ocean, and having what seemed like a surprising amount of sex on the beach or in beach-adjacent locations. Finally, she sent me a photo of her eating someone out on a sunbed in full view of the pool bar and I couldn't help myself from asking:

Which is when she confessed that she was there with some tour company that rented out entire resorts for what amounted to a week-long orgy.

So I didn't feel too bad for distracting her.

Besides, she'd texted me on Sunday, checking in to see how I was after my run-in with Nathan. And then she texted me again on Monday when I hadn't replied to that text because I got home from Victoria and promptly went to bed, despite it being closer to dinner than it was to bedtime. I obviously had to explain why I'd been so tired that I ignored her messages, which meant I *had* to admit what had happened with me and Zain.

Well, maybe I didn't have to.

Maybe I kind of wanted to because I knew Claire would get turned on it, which she did.

But we'd also *talked* about it. I'd told her how I was feeling and she validated it, listening when I needed her to and offering advice when I asked for it.

And honestly, that was kind of nice.

I mean, it wasn't like I didn't have other people who did that for me. Like, I had Chuck. I'd gotten to work on Monday morning and immediately found an iced flat white in my hand, followed by a long, comforting hug.

We'd had our usual Monday morning meeting, which had gone well for everyone except Dinah—who nearly got a nosebleed from the daggers she was glaring at me as Loni sung my praises for the exceptional hard work and amount of money I had personally brought in at the Recycl-Ball—and then I'd told Chuck what happened.

He was loyally outraged by Nathan's audacity, of course. He was disgusted that anyone could do something so mean and petty when it was obvious Nathan and Mel were in the wrong. And he almost, *almost* refrained from saying "I told you so" when I admitted I had, in fact, hooked up with Zain.

And then he'd nearly lost his mind on me.

"I swear to God, Tessa, if you say it was a one-time thing, I'm going to pour that coffee over your head," he said.

I responded by chugging the rest of my flat white. Chuck groaned in annoyance.

"Seriously? Again?!"

I swallowed the last sip of coffee. "What do you expect, Chuck? Even if everyone who knows both of us *didn't* think I was married to someone else, we don't live in the same city." I shook the cup, making sure there was a minimal amount of liquid left in the cup so it wouldn't ruin my hair if he dumped it on me. "He's kind of a slut like me. I doubt he'd enjoy being committed to someone he can't see on a regular basis."

I didn't mention that I hadn't heard from Zain since we'd parted ways at the hotel, even though he'd cut off my apology for how everything went by kissing me goodbye, a heated kiss that had made heat rush over my entire body.

"Have a safe trip home, kitten," he'd said in a husky voice as he pulled away. "Thanks for... coming."

Then he'd smirked, like he knew exactly how wet my panties suddenly were, and walked away without another word.

Either way, my reasoning didn't seem to convince Chuck, but it did seem to placate him enough that he didn't keep harping on it.

But when I'd told Claire, she understood completely. And not only did she understand, she helped *me* understand why Chuck couldn't.

CM

He honestly sounds like he's monogamous as fuck. And that's fine. There's no shame in that. But it DOES mean that he doesn't have that same relationship to sex that you and I do.

Me

What do you mean?

CM

Like, you and I want to be friends who fuck. Even though sex is usually reserved for some kind of romantic relationship. But it's not here. I want you to be my girl friend, not my girlfriend, you know? Some girl friends eat out at brunch. You and I just eat out. And that's what I want.

Me

That's what I want, too.

CM

Exactly. Chuck doesn't have that same outlook. Sex and romance are connected for him. Nothing wrong with that either, but it does mean there's some disconnect with how he understands the situation and that's gonna be frustrating for him.

I'd twisted my mouth to the side as I stared at her message.

Me

That makes a lot of sense. But what am I supposed to tell him?

Exactly what I just said. Tell him you don't need to understand it, just to realize there's a fundamental difference in the way you view these things and that he's a big ol' romantic.

I'd taken her advice at work the next day and Chuck had pressed his lips together, a crease appearing between his eyebrows as he contemplated for a bit.

"That actually makes a lot of sense," he said.

"It does," I agreed.

"I like this Claire girl," he said, turning back to his desk. "You should date her."

"Chuck!" I said, exasperated.

He burst out laughing. "I'm joking. I'm glad you've got a friend in her, Tessa Dorothy Lane."

And honestly, I was too.

I hadn't realized how much I was missing that kind of connection until I met Claire. Other than Chuck, I didn't have a ton of close friends anymore. Some of them had been lost in the divorce. Brad might have been a cheater, but I knew as well as anyone that he was charming and relatable. And then there was the fact that most of our friends had been older than me, on account of the whole ten-ish-year age gap.

So I didn't have a ton of friends from when I'd been married. And the friends I'd made in university, all the other artists and people who were succeeding where I'd failed... it wasn't like I didn't talk to them at all. I did. I went for coffee with them once in a while and went out for birthday drinks or to gallery shows, if I was invited. Which seemed to be less and less often, I guess.

But it wasn't the same as it had been.

And then there was Kira. Which... well.

We just weren't friends like that anymore.

Sighing in the quiet of the change room, I shook myself out of my thoughts and texted Claire a final time.

Once it was sent, I took a deep breath and went out to show Mom and Audrey the latest disaster.

The very next dress I tried after that was by far the least offensive, thankfully, and I only had to stand there for a little while as Mom teared up and insisted on multiple photos even though I was wearing a sample dress a size too small in the wrong colour. After buying my dress—which wasn't as much as I'd thought it would be, even with the rush order fee so we could be sure it would be there in time for me to get alterations—Mom piled us back into her car, then turned in the seat to look at me in the backseat with a catlike grin on her face.

"Okay, ladies," she said. "I have plans for us."

"Do you?" I asked, almost worried.

But, surprisingly enough, I didn't have to be.

It was actually, dare I say it, a fun afternoon. Probably the most fun I'd had with my mom in... well. Maybe ever, honestly. Audrey was like the perfect bridge between us, easily getting along with both me and Mom. And Audrey being there meant I wasn't the only one on the receiving end of Mom's comments and dramatics and gossip.

We went for lunch, then to get pedicures before Mom suggested stopping by a winery on the way back to Burnsley. And I wasn't going to argue with having a taste of wine or four to make being around my family even more tolerable.

"So how's work going, Tess?" Audrey asked when she and I were on our second round of wine tasting and Mom had switched to water so she could still drive us home.

"Good," I said automatically. "Keeping busy. You know."

"Well, no," she said. "Not really. Josh always just says you're an artist, but you also work for that charity, don't you? But he said he doesn't really understand what you do there."

"Oh," I said. "Um. Well, the charity is called CARE and the whole purpose is, like, using recycled materials to create art." I chewed my lip for a moment, trying to figure out to make it sound like I was not only good at my job, but enjoyed it. "I do community outreach, mostly. Connecting with people who might be interested in working with us on different projects. But we all, uh, wear a lot of hats. Like my friend Chuck." I laughed and sipped my wine. "He does pretty much everything. The charity would go under without him."

She was watching me and nodding thoughtfully as she listened. "And so you, like, paint for them? Or...?"

"That's kind of a different thing."

"Are you still doing lots of those shows like the one your dad and I went to that one time?" Mom asked.

My throat felt dry. I wasn't used to this much attention on me. "Not so much anymore. I do a lot of commissions now."

"Oh! Like the one for Mike?" Audrey asked.

Mom looked startled, her eyes widening at the mention of his name. "Mike? Like my and your dad's friend Mike?"

"Uh... yeah. He said last month at the party he might want something painted. But I haven't, um, heard from him." I laughed awkwardly. "Maybe Dad pawned off one of those paintings I apparently left in the garage after all."

The confused look on Mom's face deepened into a frown. "What do you mean?"

I looked at Audrey, who looked like she regretted saying anything. "Mike said he was interested in getting some of Tessa's work. Gary said he could see if he had anything lying around the garage. Which... I don't think was very nice, Tessa. I'm sorry that it happened."

Fuck.

This was...

Fuck.

I laughed, more loudly and more awkwardly than before. "It's no big deal. I was just mostly sad I never got to see any of my grandma's paintings or anything. That was all. But Mike said he'd see if he had any he could send back so, like, that's cool."

"I didn't know Mike had talked to you," she said. "And I didn't know he... kept any of those."

The last part seemed more to herself than to us. Audrey and I glanced at each other, both of us uncertain.

"It's not a big deal," I said, because for some reason I couldn't sit there in awkward silence any longer. "If he got one from Dad, then that's great. Dad's never really understood art or why I like it, and that's fine. I don't understand why anyone likes golf, you know? We all like different things and I just, I hope that if I die, not all of my stuff ends up in the garbage."

"I don't think we have any paintings in the garage," Mom finally said. "I know I put some in storage and there's one in our bedroom, but there's not much in the garage that isn't Gary's."

Another awkward silence fell around the table. I could feel Audrey looking at me, but I couldn't bring myself to look up. After a moment, I picked up my glass, downed the rest of my taster, then looked from her to Mom.

"I think Audrey should tell me what she's hoping to do for her bachelorette party while we have another round," I said brightly.

"Absolutely," Audrey agreed, nodding enthusiastically.

"Count me in," Mom said, turning to flag down one of the employees. "We can go for a nice long walk in the vineyard before we drive home."

Twenty-Eight

MOM DIDN'T WANT TO go out for Mother's Day.

Which sucked, because she *did* want to have brunch.

So despite my semi-incompetence when it came to stuff in the kitchen, my uterus meant I was tasked with creating said brunch for everyone while Dad drank coffee and read the newspaper at the table.

At least, until Mom came out of her bedroom.

"I'll get that, Teacup," she said as the timer on the waffle maker went off and I swore because I was in the middle of flipping a gigantic pan of bacon.

"It's Mother's Day, Lorelei," Dad said. "You're supposed to let us spoil you."

She ignored him as she opened the waffle maker and took out a perfectly golden brown waffle. "It's Mother's Day and I'm going to cook with my daughter because we never get to do this anymore."

Which was just... weird.

It was fucking weird to hear her say that.

But I shrugged it off and kept flipping bacon, only sacrificing one piece to the floor gods. I also made myself throw it in the garbage rather than give it to my dad, but probably only because Mom was watching.

Most of brunch was ready when I heard the door open a while later and Dylan walked in.

"Happy Mother's Day," he half-mumbled to Mom, then thrust a bouquet of flowers at her.

"Aw, Dilly!" Mom said, tearing up as she took the flowers and threw her arms around him. "Thanks, sweetie."

"Hey, Dylan," I said.

"Hi," he said, then helped himself to a piece of bacon from the warming pan and grabbed a coffee before joining Dad at the table.

Mom had barely finished putting her flowers in a vase when the door opened again.

"We're here!" called Josh.

"Hi, hon!" Mom replied, fluffing the flowers up a bit before putting the vase in the center of the table. "Brunch is almost ready and we—*oh*!"

She put her hand to her throat as Josh walked in holding a huge bouquet of flowers, Audrey following behind them with a smile on her face.

"Happy Mother's Day," Josh said as Mom threw her arms around him. He pressed a dutiful kiss to the side of her head and waited after she let go so she could wipe away the renewed tears before handing her the bouquet.

"Oh, these are lovely. The house is going to smell so good with all these flowers!" she said.

Dad glanced up from the newspaper. "Do you have enough vases for everything?"

"I should have two," Mom said. "Josh, can you reach up into the cabinet over the stove and see if the big vase is in there?"

"You only need two vases?" Dad asked.

He didn't need to spell it out. Especially not when everyone glanced at me and I froze, a spatula in one hand and a smear of waffle batter on the front of the apron I was wearing.

"I didn't bring flowers," I said.

It was awkward for all of a second before Mom scoffed and rolled her eyes, putting an arm around my shoulder.

"Tessa's presence is my present," she said. "She came all the way here and we had a lovely girls' day with Audrey yesterday, and she's been cooking all morning for all of us. I don't need flowers from her on top of all that."

"Wait," Dylan said. "So my presence could be a present? I want my flowers back, then."

Which was actually hilarious. I didn't even know my brother knew what a joke was.

Despite the laughter, the third vase would have come in handy. We were just finishing brunch and Audrey had shooed me back to the table to relax while she cleared the dishes and directed Josh to fill the sink when there was a knock at the door.

My stomach dropped the moment I heard it. Somehow, I just knew. I fucking *knew* the second-favourite child was about to walk through the door, and he did, holding a pink bouquet with purple ribbons around the base.

"Oh, sweetie," Mom said, standing from the table as she teared up yet again. "You shouldn't have!"

Zain braced himself as she threw her arms around him.

"Happy Mother's Day," he said in a quiet voice. "Thanks for everything you do for me, Lorelei."

Mom choked on a sob and took the bouquet from him. "This is so nice."

"Hey, man," Josh said, drying the soap off his hands as he turned away from the sink. "Didn't know you were in town."

Zain greeted him with the weird hand-clasp-shoulder-pat-hug-thing that guys do. "We took my mom out for brunch. I assumed you'd all be here so I figured I'd stop by before heading back to Vernon."

"Good assumption," Dad said. "How's work going, Zain?"

"Great," Zain said as if I hadn't put his career in jeopardy the previous weekend.

Which he was probably only able to do because he didn't realize until after he said it that I was sitting at the table. His eyebrows flicked up as he saw me.

"Hey, Teacup," he said. "Long time, no see."

"Ages," I agreed.

"No Brad today?" he asked, like the asshole he was.

I tried to smile. "Nope. It was a last-minute decision to come for Mother's Day, and he's been planning his trips a few weeks in advance so we can time them with my cycle."

"Don't need to hear that," Dad said flatly.

Mom made an unintelligible squealing noise, thankfully, so no one noticed the way Zain's throat flexed before he recovered enough to smile.

"I'm sure he'll be a very good daddy," he said.

I almost couldn't stop myself from laughing.

The *asshole*.

"Come sit and have some coffee," Mom said to Zain as she went to the cupboard and found a juice pitcher to put her third bouquet into. "Tell me what's new with you before I have to head out."

"Head out?" Zain repeated. "Where are you going?"

"I need to bring Teacup back to the airport," she said.

Zain raised his eyebrows and looked at me.

Oh, fuck.

"Well, that doesn't make any sense," he said before I could say anything. "I'm here anyway. I can drop Tessa off on my way back to Vernon."

Fuck.

"Isn't that out of your way?" I asked, trying not to sound desperate. "You'd have to drive past Vernon to get to the airport."

"Only about half an hour," he said, his pleasant smile reading as an infuriating smirk. "Which is a lot less than the two hours each way it'll take your mom."

"Would you really, sweetie?" Mom said, looking up from the sink as she filled the pitcher with water. "That would be incredibly helpful."

"Anything for you, Lorelei," Zain said. "I don't mind a bit."

"Damn, Zain," Josh muttered, though he was grinning. "Look who's gunning to be the new favourite child."

Which was a lot less funny than everyone else seemed to think it was, but I forced myself to laugh along with them before getting up to help Audrey dry the dishes so I didn't have to keep looking at Zain.

Twenty-Nine

"You're an asshole," I said after climbing into Zain's—arguably quite nice—car and closing the door.

"So I've heard," he replied, buckling his seatbelt. "Though I didn't think doing a favour for your mom on Mother's Day would qualify me as an asshole."

"You were trying to trap me in a car with you for two hours."

"I was not."

"Mmm," I said dryly as he turned the car on. "So you would've made the same offer if we hadn't fucked last weekend."

"I would've, actually," he said, then threw his arm over my seat so he could twist and look behind him as he backed out of the driveway, which was... I mean, it was hot, his arm stretched over the seat like that, close enough to me that I caught a whiff of that spicy-fresh scent he had. And unnecessary, since he had a backup camera, so I had a feeling he was doing it on purpose. "Though I have to admit, it was fun getting payback after you made that little comment about getting pregnant."

"You immediately threw the daddy thing at me."

He smirked as he turned back around and took the car out of reverse. "Yeah. That was pretty funny."

"Was it? You literally said the words 'Brad would be a good daddy' and—"

"It's not like I actually think that," he interrupted. "But I couldn't exactly say 'I'd be a better daddy than your shitstain ex-husband and I think I proved it to you last weekend when you screamed it in my ear two or three or sixteen times' in front of your entire family now, could I?"

It was a good point, if a little exaggerated. I twisted my mouth to the side and didn't respond. It wasn't until we were on the highway with trees and mountains on one side of the car and a wide, flat view of the sun reflecting off Mara Lake on the other that Zain spoke again.

"How was the rest of your week?" he asked.

"Fine. My boss almost burst into flames on Monday when Loni spent half an hour talking about how amazing my date auction idea was at our gala last week and how I personally raised ten grand for our charity."

"Ten grand?" he repeated, sounding impressed. "How?"

"At the auction."

"Like total?"

"Nope. Just for me."

"Not that you're not worth every penny of that, but wow." He paused, biting his lip before a slow, knowing smile spread across his face. "Is that how you met your sugar daddy?"

"I keep telling you I don't have a sugar daddy."

"Mmm. Sure. What's his name? George? Carson?"

"What?!"

"It's gotta be something like, typical rich business guy, right? Reginald?"

I wrinkled my nose. "God no. Even if I had a sugar daddy, I wouldn't pick a guy with a name like that."

"Donald? Or, no, it has like a 'Junior' or something after it, right? Robert Gerald Bloomington The—"

"Her name is Claire," I said.

He paused for a moment. "Really?"

"If that's what you'd call a 'sugar daddy,' which I wouldn't," I said. "We're friends."

"But she paid ten grand for a date with you."

"Yes."

"And bought you the dress?"

I glared at him sidelong. "Mm-hmm."

"And you're fucking her."

He didn't say it like a question, but I responded all the same. "Yep."

"So a sugar daddy," he said.

"I mean, no. And she's a woman."

"What's that saying?" he asked. "'Daddy is a state of mind'?"

I huffed and folded my arms. "It's not like that."

"Whatever you say, Teacup."

I rolled my eyes. "How was the rest of your week?"

I should've realized prior to asking that I, you know… *shouldn't*. Not because I didn't want to hear his response, but because I did, and because it brought the mood in the car down a few steps into something more serious.

More real.

"It was… something," he said.

I winced. "Work?"

He nodded.

"I'm sorry."

"Don't be." He tapped his fingers on the steering wheel. "I know I did the right thing. And Owen thinks so, too. Even if he's pissed we didn't get AvexiPharm."

I turned to him so fast my neck almost cracked. "You fucking told him?"

"Not everything."

"Why would you do that?"

"Because what else was I supposed to tell them? 'Oh, sorry guys, I lost us a contract worth more than our entire department makes in a year, but I can't tell you why'?"

I glanced down at my hands. "I... guess not. What did you say?"

"That you and Nathan had history together that I didn't know about," he said. "And that you were trying so hard to not let it affect anything because you didn't want us to lose the contract. But Nathan didn't extend you the same courtesy and cornered you in the bathroom and wouldn't let you leave. So when I walked by after calming Hamza down about his fucking report, I saw him grab you, and I had to step in."

"That's it?"

"That's it."

I nodded. I wasn't sure if he saw me do it, since his eyes were still on the road and I'd turned to look out the window, my eyes following the curve of the mountains on the other side of the lake.

"I'm sorry," he said after a few moments. "I had to tell them something, Tess. I tried to keep it as... I dunno. As vague as possible."

"I get it," I said. "Were they mad you didn't go back to the dinner after?"

"A bit, but I told them you were upset and we went to the room because my priority was you feeling safe," he said. "Especially after Nathan told me to my face that he wasn't going to proceed with us because I wouldn't let him manhandle my girlfriend."

I swallowed hard.

"My team gets it," he said. "They're pissed, but they get it. Owen said he wouldn't have asked me to do anything different, but it's still... It is what it is."

"Is it going to hold you back?" I asked. "Like, other than the promotion?"

"Probably," he said honestly. "The higher-ups aren't especially pleased. But it doesn't matter."

That made me angry. It mattered because *I* was the one who had cost him that and *I* was the one feeling guilty about it.

"How does it not matter?" I asked, trying not to snap.

"Because this job sucks," he said. "Even if it didn't, I don't want to be around when my parents move to Kelowna. I'm tired of commuting from Vernon to Kelowna every day. It's not worth staying. So I'm looking for something new."

I nodded slowly. "I'm sorry that your week was rough."

He shrugged. "Honestly, it sucked more that I didn't have anyone to talk about it with. I kept wondering if I could text you or call you but I didn't know if that would be okay after we said it was... you know. A one-time thing."

The admission made something prickle in my throat. I wasn't sure if it was a good prickle or not. "Don't you have friends?"

"What was I gonna do? Tell your brother?"

My face turned red. "Like, *other* than Josh?"

"I mean, yeah. Just not anyone I felt like would get this." He glanced at me. "Me not talking to Josh wasn't because of you, though."

"What?"

"He and I don't talk about shit like that."

"Like what?" I asked, bewildered. "Like work?"

"You think I'd be able to make that story entirely about *work*?"

"So you mean... like, girls," I said. "How do you not talk about relationships with him? I thought he was your best friend."

"He is." Zain sighed. "It's... I mean, he doesn't know I'm bi, Tess."

"Why don't you want him to know?"

He smiled, but it wasn't his usual smirk or even one of his genuine smiles. There was something sad behind it; sad enough that I almost wanted to take his hand while he was speaking.

"I'm scared it'll change things," he said. "A lot of guys have trouble finding out their friend is queer in some way and start treating you differently."

"They sound like shitty friends."

He laughed. "Yeah, well. It's not that uncommon. Guys find out you're attracted to other guys and automatically assume you want to fuck them."

"Do you?"

"Only like forty percent of the time."

We both laughed, though I cringed with realization after a moment. "Wait, but not—"

"I have never wanted to fuck your brother," Zain said immediately. "*Ever.*"

"Good," I said. "Me neither."

"My brother or your brother?" he asked.

I shot him a disgusted look. "*Neither* of them."

"That's a relief," he said.

"You're disgusting," I said, but I was trying not to smile. "So you have no one to talk to at all about anything like this?"

"I have friends, but it's not like any of them know you."

"I mean, I talked to people, and it's not like they know you."

He looked at me, an eyebrow raised. "No? I was assuming you would've told Kira. You tell her everything."

I shook my head, not quite able to meet his eye. "Not anymore."

"No? What happened?"

"I don't think we should get into this right now."

"Why not? We've got a while before we get to Kelowna."

It was a good point, if that had been my reasoning for not wanting to get into it. But it wasn't.

Then again, if anyone would understand... well. Zain was the only person in my life who knew everyone involved in the situation.

Which was super fucked up to think about, so I didn't.

"I don't think you have any reason to know this," I started. "But Nathan... I met him through Kira and Jackson."

Zain's eyebrows went up. "Did you?"

I nodded. "He was Jackson's best man. I met him and Mel at their wedding."

"Okay," he said. "So then Kira knew that you were…"

"Of course she did." I laughed softly. "She hated it."

He shrugged. "I mean, it makes sense. It's hard when friends start dating because if anything goes downhill, it's awkward."

"Fair. But that wasn't why."

"No?"

I shook my head. "She couldn't get behind the idea of me being with more than one person. It bothered her, somehow, despite having no effect on her. Then when everything went downhill…"

"She took their side?" he asked, almost incredulous.

"I didn't tell her what they did."

He was silent for a moment, then turned his head briefly to look at me. "What?"

"What?"

"You never *told* her? Why not?"

"Because her first comment to me when I went over to her house to tell her it was over between me and them was 'You couldn't have possibly thought they would love you forever.'"

He inhaled sharply, shoulders hunching forward as he physically winced. "Damn. That's… Tess, you know that's not—"

"She apologized and stuff," I said before he could say something that would make my eyes sting. "But it's never been the same and I just… never told her the rest of it. So they're still friends."

"They're still… what the fuck, Tessa?!"

My mouth dropped open and I looked at him, almost betrayed in my shock. "Excuse me?"

He glanced at me again, then at the road, then back at me, as if he was trying to show me the incensed expression on his face but didn't want to crash the car, which I was somewhat thankful for.

"You should've told her what they did," he said. "Like, okay, yeah, what she said was cold. *Really* cold. That's—" He paused and shook his head before continuing. "But she would still want to know what happened."

"How would you know?" I asked, insulted. "You barely know me. And you definitely don't know Kira anymore."

"Because she's your best friend," he said.

"Was."

He let out a huff of breath through his nose. "I don't remember a time when you weren't friends with Kira. You've been friends with her longer than me and Josh have been friends, and considering we're older than you, that's saying something."

"That's not—"

"You're telling me you've been punishing her over this and she doesn't even know what they did to you."

"I didn't tell you this for you to judge me," I snapped. "I didn't ask your opinion on this."

"I'm not—"

"You're telling me I shouldn't be upset that my best friend basically made me feel unlovable when I was at one of the lowest points of my life."

"I'm not saying that at all. But you're stubborn as fuck."

I glared at him, sure my face was going red with anger. "This isn't me being stubborn! It's not like we got into a fight and I'm sitting here refusing to apologize because I think I'm right or something."

He shoulder checked, then switched lanes to pass a slow-moving minivan in front of us. "That's not what I meant."

"Sure it wasn't."

"It wasn't." He switched back into the original lane. "I *meant* that the stubborn little teacup I know wouldn't let a lifelong friendship fall apart without at least fighting for it."

And somehow, that hurt.

Somehow, my chest ached as he said it.

Somehow, it was painful enough to cut through the anger, and I had to swallow hard to choke that pain back.

"You don't know what it was like," I said, my voice wavering.

"And neither did Kira," he said. "You never told her."

"So it's my fault." I'd intended to say it sarcastically, but that wasn't how it came out.

Probably because I was suddenly feeling like it was very much my fault. But Zain shook his head.

"It's not, Tess. It's not your fault. But people... people fuck up. They say shit they shouldn't say and do shit they shouldn't do and yeah, sometimes the things they say and do are unforgivable. Sometimes you can't get past them. But if you never even try, you end up pretty fucking lonely." He tightened his hand on the steering wheel briefly. "Trust me on that."

I watched as he clenched his jaw, taking a breath through his nose and letting it out.

"What did you not forgive?" I asked.

"We're not talking about me right now," he said.

I almost fought with him, but I had a feeling nothing would make Zain reveal whatever it was he was brooding about. So instead, I very maturely crossed my arms and looked out the window to pout. "Well, I'm not lonely. I have plenty of friends."

"Do you?"

I snorted derisively. "Of course I do. I just told you about Claire. And there's Chuck. And I'm obviously friends with Chuck's boyfriend Charles."

"That's three."

I rolled my eyes. "I'm not listing every single friend I have. Thank you for your concern, but I am doing just fine. I have more friends than I know what to do with, actually. Like, I'm literally gonna have to start a waitlist for friends."

"Is that so?" He sounded amused. "So am I on the waitlist?"

I unfolded my arms and turned to him, confused. "Why would you be on the waitlist?"

He smirked, glancing at me out of the corner of his eye. "Oh, good. So I skipped the waitlist."

"I... What? You think we're friends?" I asked.

"Are we not?"

"You're Josh's friend."

"Believe it or not, people can have more than one friend, as you've so eloquently proven with your 'waitlist of friends.'"

I rolled my eyes. "And how would you propose we explain to people we became friends? You found out I'm lying about being divorced, I offered you a toothy blowjob and instead you made me go to a work event with you, then—"

"Hold up," he said, sounding semi-amused. "I didn't *make* you—"

I ignored him. "—threw away your promotion because of me and spent the whole night fucking my brains out and are now randomly driving me to the airport. This is the most time we've ever spent together and I've known you for literal decades. How am I supposed to explain that?"

"I mean, I don't know about you, but I don't generally put out a press release each time I make a new friend," he said in that dry, mocking tone I knew so well.

"Shut up," I muttered.

"Okay, well... what about if we're secret friends?"

"Secret friends," I repeated, unimpressed.

"Yeah." He shrugged. "You save me in your phone under a different name and we just don't tell anyone we're friends."

"You're already in my phone under a different name."

He flicked an eyebrow up. "Really? What's my fake name?"

"Asshole."

He lifted his fingers off the steering wheel defensively. "Alright, damn. I was just asking."

"No, it's literally Asshole," I said. "With a poop emoji."

He was quiet for a moment, then burst out laughing louder than I'd ever heard him. His smile spread wide across his face and as much as I tried to fight it, it made me smile, too.

"What am I in your phone as?" I asked when his laugh faded.

"Teacup, obviously," he replied.

I wrinkled my nose. "Of course."

"I know it's not the most creative, but it's how I think of you," he said.

"Yeah, and I hate it," I muttered.

He frowned and glanced at me briefly. "You do?"

"It was given to me because my family forgot me at a carnival. Every time someone calls me that, I get to remember the time I got left behind." I looked out the window and watched a boat speeding across the lake. "Why would I like that?"

"I... I mean, I guess, yeah. That makes sense." He tapped his fingers on the steering wheel. "Why didn't you ever say anything?"

I scoffed. "Come on. If Josh or my dad knew how much it annoyed me, they'd just call me it *more*."

"Yeah, but if you never said anything—"

"I had other battles to pick," I said, folding my arms. "It never quite made the priority list, so I just... it's whatever. It's fine."

"I'll stop calling you that if you want," he said. "But to be honest, I always liked it."

I glanced at him. "Why?"

There was a small smile on his lips and an almost nostalgic look on his face. "Well, it's partly selfish. 'Cause yeah, for *you* it was a shitty day. But it was an awesome day for me. Josh was the first person who was actually nice to me after we'd moved to Burnsley, so I was just... I dunno. Excited that I made a friend and wasn't being treated like the weird token brown kid." He shrugged, almost self-consciously. "And if I hadn't met him, I wouldn't have met all of you. Your parents always treated me and my family like we belonged and were welcome. Not everyone did, especially not at first. Like, when your dad asked my dad to go golfing the first time, I swear he didn't stop smiling for like three days. And my mom was always talking about Lorelei this and Lorelei that. It meant more to us than I think any of you realized."

"Oh," I said.

"And I always thought it was cute."

I looked at him, almost offended. "*Cute*?!"

I thought he was going to laugh, maybe, or make some kind of snarky joke. I didn't expect him to nod solemnly as he stared out the windshield.

"Whenever I see a teacup—like, you know the little china ones with a saucer and stuff?" There was a soft smile on his face. "Every single time I see one, I think of you."

I had no idea how to respond to that, so I didn't. I watched the boat on the lake until it was out of my line of sight, then stared at the glimmering reflections on the water.

A couple of weeks ago, I'd had no idea Zain ever thought of me. And now I was finding out he thought of me... well.

At least every time he saw a teacup. And if last weekend had been any indication, he'd thought of me a lot more than that.

"I have an idea," he said a few minutes later, breaking the tension that had filled the car.

"What's that?" I asked.

"It's when you think of something that you hadn't thought of before." I didn't respond to his stupid joke and after a moment, he chuckled. "Don't you want to hear it?"

"No."

He shrugged. "Alright."

We were quiet for a few more kilometers, then I sighed and gave in. "What's your idea?"

"What if," he said, then made a musing sort of gesture with his hand. "What if we, like... were friends... who fucked sometimes?"

It took everything in me to keep a serious, bored expression on my face when all I wanted to do was laugh. "Join the list."

"That's what the waitlist is for?" he asked.

"It's a separate waitlist," I said.

"Oh." He twisted his mouth to that side. "Well... do I actually have to be on that waitlist or could we...?"

I looked at him, half amused and half incredulous. "Are you seriously asking me for sex again?"

He shrugged unabashedly. "You know. One for the road."

"I think it would be more like one *on* the road in this situation."

He chuckled, which made me laugh, and then we both fell silent until a sign appeared a few moments later, indicating there was a turn coming up that I knew led to a service road. A thick, heavy, enticingly warm tension built in the car and Zain's tongue poked out, wetting his lips.

"So...?" he asked. "You wanna...?"

I was definitely going to say no.

But that was bullshit, of course.

"Pull over," I said, and Zain grinned as he flicked his signal light on.

Thirty

ZAIN DROVE US TO a spot that wasn't too far off the main road, but far enough that the pine trees blocked most of the world around us. It wasn't entirely blocked from the view of the road, but he angled the car enough that even if someone did drive by, it wouldn't be entirely obvious what was happening.

Still a little obvious, but more like the "Hey honey, I bet those people are fucking" kind of obvious instead of the "Oh dear Lord, shield the children's eyes and call the cops" kind of obvious.

He didn't say anything after parking, just unbuckled his seatbelt and got out of the car. I thought that meant he'd go to the back seat, since in my mind, car sex and backseats were inextricably linked, but he walked around the front. Frowning, I followed him with my eyes until he reached the passenger side. He opened the door and looked down at me, a tight smirk on his face as he rested one arm on the roof of the car and the other on the top of the door, filling the entirety of my view.

"I know I'm about to make you feel like you're gonna fly out the windshield, kitten, but I promise you won't need your seatbelt," he said, his voice so low and smooth that I felt like I was melting.

It was a damn good thing his car had leather seats because I had a feeling I was about to get them *very* messy.

Obediently, I undid my seatbelt and let it retract. Zain lifted his head and glanced around the still-deserted road, then dipped down and kissed me.

"Take off your pants and turn to face me," he murmured.

"Yes, Daddy," I said. I'd attempted to say it with a snarky sort of sarcasm, but it came out *far* breathier than I'd intended, and Zain made a soft noise against my mouth before pulling away so I could do as he'd said.

He waited as I wriggled out of my jeans and panties, pushing them into the wheel well of the car before I swung my legs out and let them dangle out of the open door. Zain smiled as his eyes trailed down my body, then brought his hands to my legs and parted them. He leaned in, kissing me as he walked the fingers of one hand up my thigh before slipping it between my legs and cupping my pussy.

"Fuck," he whispered. "It kills me how hot your pussy gets, kitten." A thick finger slipped between my folds and made me squirm. "It's fucking unreal."

He didn't wait for me to say anything in response, just captured my lips again, his tongue pushing into my mouth and flicking against mine. I whimpered and felt his breath puff against me in response. His finger moved along my slit, collecting the wetness that was already pooling there, before he withdrew it after a few slow, purposeful strokes.

His lips left mine and he only pulled back enough that I could look into his eyes as he brought his hand up to his lips. I watched, wanting to squirm against the leather seat as he put a glistening finger in his mouth, licking my wetness off as his dark eyes stared into mine.

"So fucking good," he said. "I've been thinking about how amazing you taste all week, kitten. It's been driving me insane."

"Feel free to have more," I said, and the corner of his mouth curled up into that lopsided half-smirk that made my breath catch.

"Oh, I will be," he said, then leaned in and kissed me again.

God, his mouth was good.

At everything, really. It was good at making desire pulse in my body as he kissed me. Good at making my knees feel weak with his words. And good at... well.

The man could eat pussy. Like, *really* well.

His lips moved away from mine, leaving goosebumps behind as he marked a trail with kisses from my jaw to my neck to my chest. Had I known we'd end up here, I would've worn a much lower cut shirt, preferably one made of a stretchy material so Zain could easily use that magical mouth on my tits, but I hadn't. Still, he tugged it down so he could kiss as much of my skin as he could, then nuzzled his face against my tits through the fabric.

Then he was on his knees in the gravel on the side of the road, a hand on the inside of each of my thighs as he spread me wide. He looked up at me, a piece of his thick black hair falling over his forehead, and kept those dark, burning eyes on mine as he leaned in and ran his tongue over my slit.

And fuck.

Fuck.

I sat back to give him better access, leaning against the spot between the back of my seat and the center console, where I was bracing myself with my hand. Tilting my head, I closed my eyes, indulging in the sensations taking over my senses.

The feel of Zain spoiling me with his mouth, lapping at my dripping entrance and circling his tongue around my swollen clit.

The scent of the cool, fresh air filtering into the car, natural pine overtaking the subtle scent of fake pine in Zain's air freshener.

The sound of the cars on the highway, zooming by with no idea that a short distance away, Zain was eating me out like he'd been starving for a week.

It was unfair how fucking good it was.

It was *unfair* that my brother's asshole best friend was one of the best fucks I'd ever had. It was almost unfair enough that I regretted how it couldn't ever be something more than a passing fling. One of those things we indulged in now and then because we both had this stupid fucking attraction to each other that we couldn't do anything about.

Because of me.

But I didn't think about that part just then.

I just thought about how Zain was making my pussy ache and drip as he feasted on me.

He didn't make me come like that. He could've, but when he pulled back almost reluctantly, he looked up at me with desperation in his eyes.

"I can't wait any longer," he said. "I wanna be inside you so bad."

"Do it, then," I said, and he groaned as got up from his knees, bringing his hands to the button of his jeans and undoing it quickly.

I loved how hard he got. When we'd fucked the first time, it had been the same: his cock so hard, so fucking *ready* for me, that it nearly pushed itself out of his pants as soon as he unzipped them. He was standing close enough to the car that his head was over the roof of it, so I couldn't see him, but I could hear his sigh of relief and watched as he briefly gripped his bulge through his boxers.

After a moment where I'm sure he was glancing around to make sure the road was still abandoned, he shoved his jeans down a bit further and took his cock out of his boxers. For another brief moment, I still couldn't see his face, leaving me to take in the sight of his thick, throbbing cock. A bead of precum was on the tip and I watched his hand glide along his shaft as he stroked himself once, twice, three times before finally dipping back down.

There was heat on his face, half-lidded eyes that looked almost drunk with desire as I gazed up at him. I bit my lip and he stroked his cock firmly one more time.

"Bring your ass forward and spread your legs for me, kitten," he commanded in a gravelly voice.

And I did.

He adjusted my body before attempting to settle himself between my legs in a super awkward position. For him, at least. It wasn't the most comfortable for me either, but honestly, that was half the fun of car sex. At least, I thought so. The weird ways you had to twist and adjust and hold onto each other, the breathless giggles and laughter when you had to keep trying to get everyone's bits properly lined up.

It made things fun.

The position we ended up in wasn't too bad. Zain had one foot on the ground outside the car and the other in the wheel well while I had both a hand and a heel on his dashboard. My other arm was clutching his shoulder, clinging to him as he lined his cock up with my pussy, then paused.

"I didn't ask if we needed a condom," he said.

"I haven't fucked anyone since last weekend," I replied.

"Me neither."

"So fuck me."

He groaned, his eyes fluttering closed as he pushed inside me. I sighed in relief, feeling the way he made me stretch around him, the rigidness of him pressing against the walls of my pussy as he filled me.

And yeah, maybe it wasn't the most comfortable position I'd ever been fucked in, but the way his cock felt like it was bottoming out inside of me because he was so fucking deep more than made up for it.

Especially when he started fucking me *hard*.

The car shook as he pounded me, the sound of it rocking harmonizing in time to the sound of his body slapping against mine. I moaned in his ear as I clung to him, my legs beginning to quiver almost immediately because the head of his cock was hitting the *perfect* spot inside of me. Each thrust built up the intensity, letting me feel the ascending climb of pleasure, nudging me closer and closer to orgasm so distinctly that I could almost measure it.

"Zain," I whimpered as I panted for breath. "I'm so close."

"Come for me," he mumbled, turning his head to press a kiss against my cheek. "This whole week I've been thinking about how it felt when you came on this fat cock. Every fucking day this week, every time I close my eyes, every time I think of you, I picture the look on your face when you're screaming out for me. I fucking *dream* of the way you tremble while you're on my cock and how your pussy clenches so hard I almost can't move. And you love knowing that, don't you, kitten?"

"Yes, Daddy," I gasped.

He groaned, a low rumble that seemed to travel through my chest and down to my core.

"But it's not the same when it's just me," he said, and now his voice was almost a growl. "It's not the same thinking of you when I fuck my hand now that I know what the real thing is like. It's not the same when I don't have these gorgeous legs holding me in and the heat of your pussy wrapped around my cock. So come, kitten. Give me what I fucking *want*."

I stifled my shout of pleasure as best I could. I didn't really know why. If anyone was going to catch us fucking, it was because we were hanging halfway out of a car on the side of the road in broad daylight, not because they heard me coming. But I wasn't exactly thinking at that moment, not when Zain's cock was filling me and his words were muddying my already hazy mind and I was shivering with pleasure. So I tried to keep quiet, which meant I heard the choked laugh-like sound Zain made as my body did exactly what he'd commanded it to do. His thrusts staggered as I shuddered, pulses of pleasure controlling my body, and I dug my fingers into his shoulder as I tried to keep from falling.

Falling off what, I didn't know. I was pretty firmly in the car.

But I felt like I was soaring.

"Fuck," he groaned as my orgasm faded. "That's everything. That's fucking *everything*."

All I could do was moan in response, which made him half-laugh again.

"You're so fucking—"

And then he stopped.

He stopped talking.

He stopped moving.

He stopped breathing, even, holding it in as his body stiffened.

"Zain?" I asked, concerned.

He didn't respond, just nudged me down a bit with his cock still inside me. It was enough of a shift that I could see his face, his eyes wide as he looked out the driver's side window, and I realized someone was coming.

Other than us, of course.

"Shit," he muttered, and my stomach lurched as I heard the telltale sound of tires on gravel.

"Are they stopping?" I breathed.

"Not sure," he said, and his throat flexed as he swallowed.

We were silent as the crunch of the tires got louder. I listened as the vehicle got closer, the engine getting louder and louder, loud enough that it covered the way my heart was thundering in my ears.

Both of us stayed completely still. Or, well, Zain did and I tried to. I couldn't help the way my pussy squeezed his cock in those aftershocks of my orgasm, involuntary twitches that I had no control over, but Zain didn't seem to mind. Or if he did, he knew I wasn't doing it on purpose.

The engine got louder and I tensed, my heart racing as I looked up at Zain. He held still, his eyes tracking the vehicle, and then suddenly the sound of the engine began to fade.

And fade.

And fade.

Zain let out his breath and I felt my shoulders relax.

"Did they notice?" I asked.

"Don't think so," he said, but he was still looking out the window.

I bit my lip and my pussy tightened around him. Completely unintentionally, of course. "So…"

He let out a soft puff of laughter.

"Just wait," he said, but he ground himself forward, pushing himself as deep inside me as he could go. "Just until they're around the bend."

I responded by squeezing my pussy around him again and he looked at me, fire in his eyes even as they filled with amusement.

"You were listening so good for me today, kitten," he murmured. "Why are you being so bad now?"

"Because you like it, Daddy."

He laughed, making his cock jostle inside of me, but he didn't disagree with me. He also didn't start fucking me, glancing back out the window and waiting for another moment.

And then another.

And then I clenched my pussy again and he snapped.

"For fuck's sake," he growled, tearing his eyes away from the road. "Are you trying to make me crazy?"

"Yep," I said, doing it again.

"You want my cum that bad?"

"Mm-hmm," I said. "I want you to finish inside me."

He inhaled sharply, but I didn't let him respond.

"That way you know it'll be dripping out on my flight home, Daddy. Don't you want to think about me sitting there with my panties all messy from your cum and—"

"*Fuck!*" he growled, and then he started moving.

Hard.

The car went back to shaking and my body went back to singing as he pounded his hips against me. It felt amazing; not amazing like I was going to come again, not when he'd snapped and started fucking me for *him*, not for me, but amazing because God, he felt good inside me.

So fucking good.

It wasn't long before his face twisted in pleasure and his thrusts grew even more frenzied. He whispered my name and I whispered his, holding him close as he panted, and then he groaned and I felt him spill his load. I closed my eyes, enjoying the sensation, indulging far too much into how good it felt to make him come inside me, while Zain rested against me so he could catch his breath.

"You okay?" he asked as he shifted a few minutes later and began to pull out.

"Mm-hmm," I said, opening my eyes. "You?"

He smirked. "I'm thinking I gotta drive you around more often."

We both laughed, then he dug out a pack of Kleenex from his center console and helped me clean up the mess he'd left on my pussy.

The rest of the drive was comparatively uneventful. That probably wasn't a good thing. We should've talked about things a bit more. What we were to each other, for example, since we'd never agreed on the whole secret friends thing and I wasn't sure what that even meant. If we'd talked about it, I wouldn't have been so surprised after I got home that night and my phone went off with a text.

I burst out laughing the second I saw it. There was no text, just a screenshot of a contact on his phone. I guess I was no longer in his phone as Teacup; now I was there as Kitten, followed by the cup and saucer emoji... and the poop emoji after that.

Giggling, I screenshotted his name in my phone—still Z Biggest Asshole, of course—and sent it back.

Me

> It was originally just Z Asshole but then you were more of an asshole, so I changed it.

Z Biggest Asshole

> I strive to be the best at everything. Even assholeishness.

I smiled but didn't respond. A few minutes later, he texted again.

Z Biggest Asshole

> So… secret friends?

Me

> Is that a good idea?

Z Biggest Asshole

> No. But we should do it anyway. I'll promise to fuck your brains out whenever you let me and not to call you Teacup anymore.

I pressed my lips together, not sure if I was wanting to laugh or if I was worrying.

Me

> You make a compelling argument. I guess we can. For now.

Then, a moment later, I bit my lip and sent one more.

Me

> And you can still call me that. I guess it's not that terrible.

Z Biggest Asshole

> You sure?

I smirked but didn't respond. Instead, I put my phone face down and brought a hand to my chin, wondering what the hell I was getting myself into.

I had no idea how to handle this. There was no guidebook for what to do when you're secretly hooking up with your brother's best friend once in a while because no one but him knows you're divorced from your ex-husband and he clearly also likes you as something more than just his best friend's little sister because he gave up a big promotion for you. I kept telling myself it should be a one-time thing. I mean, that was my default. It should only *ever* be a one-time thing. I wasn't ready for a more-time thing.

Except, exactly like with Claire—and, unfortunately, with Julie and Finn—I'd failed at that almost immediately.

I'd always said I wasn't anti-love. I wasn't anti-commitment. In my mind, it was always a "for now" sort of thing. I wanted to fuck around—for now. I wanted to hook up casually… for now. But maybe this was my subconscious trying to tell me that my "for now" had changed.

Or, I thought as I tapped my finger to my lips, maybe I was overthinking it and I should just go back to fucking people I met through MatchMi.

But even I knew it was something I needed to talk out. Something I needed a second opinion on. And I could've texted Claire, I guess. I could've called Chuck. Hell, I even had my secret asshole friend now who might talk things over with me, though that might get kind of awkward since he was one of the things I needed to talk about.

And also because it was his voice that I couldn't get out of my head.

The stubborn little teacup I know wouldn't let a lifelong friendship fall apart without at least fighting for it.

It's not your fault. But people fuck up.

Sometimes the things they say and do are unforgivable. Sometimes you can't get past them. But if you never even try, you end up pretty fucking lonely.

I wanted to know who he hadn't forgiven.

I wanted to know why he was lonely.

But maybe he had a point.

Maybe I was hurting myself more by refusing to even try.

I took a deep breath, then let it out. Picking up my phone, I tapped my fingers along the side of it, chewing my lip for a moment before flipping it back over and forcing myself to open my messages.

Me

Hey. Can we get together for drinks sometime this week?

It was barely thirty seconds later that Kira responded.

Kira

I would really, really love that. Name the time and place and I'll be there.

Epilogue

One Month Later

"Teacup? Are you almost ready?"

The door handle jiggled and I moved faster than I ever had in my entire life. In one swift movement, I lunged forward, catching the handle before Mom could turn it.

Then, of course, I realized I'd locked it and that she wouldn't have been able to get in anyway. Taking a shaky breath, I twisted the lock and inched the door open.

"I am," I said. "Almost, I mean. Ready."

She frowned, glanced down at my definitely-not-ready-yet outfit that consisted of the blanket from her guest room bed I was clutching around me, and then back up and raised her eyebrows. "Are you feeling okay?"

"What?" I asked, laughing. "Of course. Why wouldn't I be?"

"You're very flushed, hon."

"Oh," I said. "I was... exercising."

I knew it was a stupid thing to say even before the word left my mouth, but couldn't stop myself. If there was anything that was going to sound suspicious, it was claiming that I—the girl who had faked period cramps for six weeks straight to get out of PE classes in high school and ended up having to retake it over the summer once our PE teacher remembered that's not how periods worked—was voluntarily exercising.

"Exercising?" she said. "You?! No offense, Teacup, but—"

"No, no, I get it," I said. "I just felt like, you know, I'm thirty now and that means it's time to... start... yoga."

"Yoga," she repeated. "And it gets you that sweaty?"

"Well, I'm not very good at it yet."

Mom touched a hand to her chest, tilting her head to the side with an almost affectionate look on her face. "If I'd known that, I would've taken you to my class! Nadia Hameed and I go almost every Saturday down at the community center. Didn't I tell you that's where I was this morning?"

She had. I remembered her telling me just as she said it, which is probably why yoga was the first thing that popped into my head.

I laughed awkwardly. "Yeah, I know. But I'm, um, kind of... embarrassed at how bad I am. Maybe when I'm better at it, I'll go with you, but it's only been a couple of months."

Mom paused, then a slow, conspiratorial smile began to spread across her lips. The corners of her eyes crinkled and she tapped her fingers together in tiny, excited claps. "*That* explains it!"

"It does?"

"Of course! Now that Kira and Jackson have their little bundle, you're trying to catch up." She lowered her voice to a faux-hushed whisper. "And since yoga helps with *fertility*..."

Fuck. Did it really? I tried to smile as if she'd definitely figured it out. "Of course. Yeah. That's totally it. Trying to get knocked up asap."

She tapped her fingers together again, shimmying slightly. "Oh, I hope so. It's so much fun when your friends have babies at the same time that you do!"

I tried to smile. Not because she was wrong. I was sure it was fun to have babies at the same time as your friends, and now that Kira and I were friends again, she wasn't even wrong about that.

It was just the whole "I was trying really hard not to actually get knocked up by anyone at all on account of the whole lying about being married" thing.

But Kira's sudden adoption had renewed Mom's excitement about me and Brad trying for a baby. Not that it had ever faded in the first place, but she was practically fanatical now.

It had been a whirlwind of a month. After my last trip to Burnsley, I'd been making a concentrated effort to talk to Kira more often. To involve her in my life.

To save our friendship.

She cried when I told her what Nathan and Mel had done when we got together at her place a month earlier. When I told her what Nathan had done to me and Zain just a few days before that. And how what Kira had said when I needed her help back then had just...

Just destroyed me.

"No wonder you didn't want to see me anymore," she'd said in her wavering voice as she wiped tears off her cheeks. "I wouldn't have wanted to see me either. I didn't understand what was happening and I was too... I don't know. Naïve? Stubborn? Small-minded?" She shook her head. "Whatever it was, I was too *that* to do the work and try to understand something that made you happy. Until I realized I'd pushed you away and I just... hated myself for it."

I hugged her. I let her cry. I listened to her apologies until she'd calmed her sobs to sniffles, and then I looked at her meaningfully.

"Kira, I need you to understand that I still do it," I said. "I still hook up with couples. Not seriously and not much right now because I've kind of got some other crazy stuff going on, but I'm a unicorn. And I like it. It's not going to change."

She gave me a watery smile. "I know. And I support that. Because you've always been a unicorn."

I blinked in surprise. "Have I?"

"That once in a lifetime friend you can't find anywhere else?" She nodded. "Yeah, Tess. That's what you are to me."

When I left Kira's place that night, I felt good. I felt like we could rekindle some kind of friendship, though I was certain it wouldn't be like what we used to have. It couldn't. Not when she and Jackson were still friends with Mel and Nathan. But I wasn't going to tell Kira who she could be friends with. I just kind of assumed that it would be one of those things we didn't talk about. That I would be separate from that part of their lives, and that would be okay.

Until we met for drinks the next week and Kira mentioned she'd seen Mel and Nathan on the weekend.

I couldn't help the anger that flared up. She jumped as I put my beer firmly on the table and glared at her.

"I do not want to hear about it," I said.

"Tess—"

"If you want to be friends with them, that's up to you, but don't include me in these conversations. I can't believe I even have to say that."

"And I can't believe you even thought you would have to," she shot back.

My mouth dropped open. Partly because of what she said and partly because I'd never heard Kira snap like that before. She looked at me, her eyes watery but deep, full of something I hadn't seen on her face in... well, ever.

"What?" I asked.

Her jaw trembled and she swallowed, but kept the same firm expression as she told me she and Jackson had gone to see them solely to tell them they were no longer welcome in their lives.

"I just wanted you to know that we aren't talking to them anymore," she said. "So you didn't have to worry I might tell them something about you that you didn't want them to know."

It was an asshole move on her part. At least when I made Kira sob uncontrollably, I'd suggested we meet at her house. She had the audacity to say that and then look surprised when I started tearing up right there in the middle of the bar.

But I wouldn't have changed it for anything. Not when she put her arms around me and hugged me so fiercely, I almost hated myself for waiting so long to do this.

The timing of it all was the best and the worst. It was only a few days after that when Kira called me one afternoon while I was at work, her voice high-pitched with a mix of excitement and terror and elation.

"So, I have to tell you something," she said.

"What's going on?" I asked.

"Um... so... I have a baby."

I frowned, looking at Chuck as he leaned across our office in an attempt to eavesdrop. "Like, on you?"

"Yep. We... we just adopted a baby."

It was sudden, but despite making it sound like they'd gone to the baby store and asked how much the baby in the window was, it wasn't so simple. The birthmom she and Jackson had been talking to for months had changed her mind again, and suddenly Kira went from grieving and accepting that she wasn't going to be a mom right away to... well, to being a fucking *mom* right away.

So, us becoming friends again was horrible timing, since who wants to deal with multiple parts of your life being thrown upside down all at once? But it was the best because Kira kept calling me for help, which I was happy to give because it meant I got baby snuggles.

But, of course, now my mom wanted her own grandbaby even more than she had before, since Mrs. Katz was a grandma and it was just so unfair that she wasn't *also* a grandma. And that was kind of a pain in the ass.

Especially when Mom was still standing in the door to the guest room, frowning at me after I came up with some bullshit about how I was doing yoga for fertility reasons.

"Not that it's any of my business…" she started.

Then don't fucking ask, I wanted to say, but just looked at her as innocently as I could.

"…but is there a reason you're doing yoga, um…" She didn't finish, just gestured at my general state of undress.

"I just finished," I said, and it came out so smooth that even I almost believed it wasn't a lie. Which, technically, it *wasn't*, but not in the way I was implying it. "I was changing when you tried to open the door."

She finally seemed to accept that and nodded. "Alright, well, hurry and get dressed then, please. Shenae, Leslie, and Jeanie just got here to help set up for the bridal shower and I need your help with the tables. Zain and Josh were supposed to do it but neither of them have shown up yet." She rolled her eyes. "Typical of those boys, of course."

"So typical," I agreed. "They're the worst."

Mom laughed. "I don't know about the *worst*, but I swear they think the world runs on Josh and Zain time."

She finally let me close the door. I turned the lock again, letting out a slow, relieved breath to calm my racing heart. Still holding the blanket up, I shuffled to the closet and opened the door. Zain stood there, a put-out pout on his face and his arms folded across his chest.

"I am *never* late," he said, the resentful annoyance clear in his voice.

I rolled my eyes and moved so he could walk his naked ass out of the closet. "You were probably late for something one time and my mom decided it was an integral part of your personality. Don't get pissy about it."

"I'm more pissy that you shoved me in the closet," he grumbled as he bent down to pick up his jeans.

"Where else was I going to put you?"

"You couldn't have let me hide in the bathroom instead?" he asked. "Or did you forget this room has a fucking ensuite?"

"Excuse me for thinking on my feet," I said as I dropped the blanket and started hunting for my panties. "And besides, what if she'd checked the bathroom?"

"Why would she check the bathroom?" he asked as he pulled his boxers on.

I shrugged. "Why was she trying to open a locked guest room door to begin with?"

"I dunno." He picked up his t-shirt, then held up his hand, my panties hanging off one hooked finger. "Maybe she heard you squeal when I made you come on my cock, kitten."

Some of the heat on my cheeks had faded, but it came roaring back at his words. Glaring at him, I snatched my panties out of his hand. "I hate you."

He smirked. "No, you don't."

"Yes, I do."

"Don't seem to hate my dick," he said in a low voice.

"Yeah, well, it's the only part of you that's semi-okay."

"*Semi-okay*?" he repeated, insulted.

"Oh, sorry," I said. "I mean it's the biggest, thickest, manliest dick I've ever had the pleasure of allowing to penetrate my needy little pussy and make it next to impossible to walk straight because of how hard it batters my cervix."

He adjusted his t-shirt, then leaned in to kiss me. "That's more like it."

I snorted back a laugh as he ducked into the aforementioned ensuite. He came back after I finished dressing a few minutes later, looking casual and nonchalant, like we hadn't just done something stupid like having a quickie in my parents' guest room while my mom was upstairs getting ready for their future daughter-in-law's bridal shower with the other bridesmaids.

Which we totally had.

It wasn't my fault. Zain was the one who showed up at my parents' place early, which I'm sure was completely unintentional even though he knew exactly what time he was supposed to be there. And also that I'd be there, since we'd been texting almost daily for the past month. And that I'd be alone, since his mom was at yoga with my mom and Dad was obviously out golfing because there was about to be a house full of excited women that he wanted to avoid.

We shouldn't have risked it. I knew that, the same way I knew I should be making him wear a condom when we fucked. The same way I knew I shouldn't be fucking him to begin with. The same way I knew a ton of people were about to descend on the house, so sneaking him out was going to be a challenge.

So maybe I should have told him it wasn't worth hooking up when we could so easily get caught. But on the other hand, there wasn't much of a chance for me to fuck him on this particular jaunt to Burnsley since I'd rented a car in Kelowna and driven myself from the airport. And I hadn't gotten any dick since the last time I'd seen Zain a month earlier, which was a very long stretch for me to go without dick.

Not that I wasn't getting laid. Claire had been back from Tahiti for three weeks and we'd hung out a bunch of times since then.

And by hung out, I meant hung out and also fucked.

And I guess technically I'd gotten *some* dick from her, but it was in the form of a bright purple strap-on. Which was great, obviously, especially because Claire knew how to *fuck* with that thing, but... well. She couldn't come inside me.

Zain could.

He *shouldn't*, but he could, because we were both incredibly stupid and also incredibly horny and somehow incredibly into indulging his little breeding kink in a way that felt like a joke but definitely wasn't a joke.

"Wanna distract everyone so I can sneak out and pretend I just got here?" Zain asked as I put on some lipstick.

"Not really, but I will," I said, reaching for the door. "You can go out the backdoor pretty safely, I think."

He stopped me just before I opened the door, bringing one hand up to my cheek and leaning in to kiss me, softly and carefully.

"When are you leaving?" he asked.

"Tomorrow afternoon."

"Cool. Wanna stop by my place on the way to the airport and show me some of that fertility yoga you've been doing?"

I rolled my eyes at him. "You wish."

I'd meant it to sound like I was dismissing him and absolutely wouldn't be stopping by his unsurprisingly tidy and organized apartment for another quickie before my flight.

But we both knew I was going to.

"What are you up to next weekend?" he asked while we were lying on his bed the next day, catching our breaths.

"Just Kira's baby shower, I think," I said. "Why?"

"Would it make me an asshole to ask for a favour from you?"

"Yes."

"Good. Can I stay with you for a night or two? This Friday?"

I blinked, my shoulders tensing as I turned my head to look at him. "Like... like at my house?"

"Yeah," he said.

"Um..."

"You don't have to," he said. "I just thought maybe we could take advantage of the fact that I'm in Vancouver for a job interview to hang out, since I have this thing where I'm kinda really into fucking you."

"A... job interview?" I repeated.

It didn't seem to be the reaction he was expecting. Which was fair. He probably expected me to be excited for him, and I was. Really, I was. The part of me that wasn't an asshole was ecstatic to hear he'd found something that might get him out of the job he hated.

The part of me that had repeatedly told Chuck that one of the reasons Zain and I couldn't be a *thing* was because we didn't live in the same fucking city, though?

That part was suddenly very, very nervous.

"Uh... yeah," Zain said. "But if it's a problem—"

"It's not," I said, even though it was. "You surprised me, that's all. Congratulations."

He looked like he didn't quite believe me, but that look faded when I leaned in to kiss him. That made him blink, then his throat flexed as he swallowed.

"I can get a hotel, Teacup," he said.

Perfect, I wanted to say. I'll come to the hotel and fuck you there.

"Why?" I said instead, because of course I did. "I have a perfectly good bed to fuck in."

And of course I immediately regretted it at the same time that I got very, very excited about the prospect of a couple of days with Zain.

And of course after leaving his place, I spent the rest of the day overthinking it.

Of course I got home from Burnsley with that now-familiar sensation of unsettled restlessness, and of course that meant I went upstairs and asked Dottie if I could walk Millie, and of course she called me an annoying little hoebag before affectionately reminding me not to get murdered.

So of course, that's when we found the other dog.

Well, he found us. Millie was sniffing her favourite patch of clover when I heard a jingling sound and looked up. Out of nowhere. a small brown thing appeared, galloping towards us. Millie froze, then began to wriggle excitedly, almost tugging the leash out of my grip.

By the time I processed what was happening, the little brown dog had reached us, coming to a sudden halt in front of Millie and sniffing her nose curiously. She stood still, watching him until he took a final sniff and jumped on her playfully.

Millie squirmed away, then bounded forward and gave the dog a once-over with her nose. Once she'd sniffed him, she sneezed, then stuck her butt in the air and yipped. Seconds later, they were playing like they were long-lost doggy friends, nosing and pouncing on each other like puppies.

It would've been cute if it wasn't nighttime.

Glancing around, I looked for some irresponsible asshole who was letting their dog run around off leash in the dark. But there was no one else in the park that I could see, and I couldn't hear anyone calling for a dog.

Which meant that there was a chance the owner *wasn't* an asshole—a small chance, since lots of people were assholes, but their assholeness might be unrelated to how they handled their dog—and that they had no idea their dog was running around off leash at night.

I crouched down and the brown dog's head snapped towards me. I extended my hand and he bounded over to sniff it as Millie returned to my side, sitting protectively beside me. After I was sniffed, he wagged his tail and shoved his head against my palm like he'd known me for ages.

"Well, at least you're friendly," I said. "Where's your person, little guy?"

Rudely, Little Guy didn't answer my question, so as I petted him, I searched his neck for a collar. There was one, which was good, but it only had a general city license tag on it with no information for an owner.

"Fuck," I muttered. "What are we going to do about this, Mills?"

Millie snuffed in response and lurched forward, nearly tugging the leash out of my grip again as she started playing with Little Guy again. Sighing, I stood back up and let the two of them roll around until Millie found herself in a compromising position.

"I see you and Zain share the same kink, Little Guy," I said, bending down to separate them. "But unfortunately, she's missing her uterus, so you're wasting a load there."

Little Guy didn't acknowledge me at all, but he was small enough to pick up, so I lifted him away from Millie. She walked away gingerly, looking up at me with prudent eyes as I cradled the brown dog in one arm.

"Sorry to cockblock you, mister," I said.

He wriggled a bit, but only so he could stretch up and lick my face.

"Gross. I hope you've brushed your teeth recently."

I looked around, still unsure of what to do. I mean, I could call animal control, but it was late and what if he lived nearby? Someone was going to notice he was gone and I didn't want whoever it was to be panicking until the morning. I chewed on my lip, then put the dog on the ground and held onto his collar so I could thread Millie's leash through it.

"Walk with us a bit," I said to him. "We can see if we can track someone down. If not, maybe Millie's going to be having a grown-up sleepover tonight."

Millie whined happily.

"You dirty girl," I said, and she wiggled her butt.

It was slow going with two dogs on the same leash, but I managed to guide us towards the path and away from the field area, since there was clearly no owner waiting there. I figured if someone was looking for him, they'd be on the road instead of in the park.

And I was right.

We were on the sidewalk for about thirty seconds when I spotted a figure standing on the next block. He was too far for me to see much detail; just that he was tall and so distressed that I could tell from where I stood, even under the dim yellow glow of the streetlights.

"Hey!" I shouted. "Excuse me!"

The man turned in our direction.

"Are you looking for a dog?"

"Oh my God," came the response. "Yes. Is he—do you have—is he small and brown?"

"He... he is small and brown!" I replied.

The man made a sound. It might have been a cry of relief. It might have been an excited shout. I honestly couldn't tell. All I knew was that the little brown dog heard it and his ears perked up. Half a second later, the man started running, and the dog began to yip and whine as he pulled towards him.

He reached us just a few seconds later. I barely got a look at him before he dropped to his knees and opened his arms.

"Alfie!" he said.

The little brown dog jumped into the man's arms, tugging an unwitting Millie along on the leash.

"I thought I'd lost you," he said, and his voice cracked so painfully that I almost teared up.

It took me a moment of staring to figure it out. To be fair, it wasn't obvious. His hair was a greasy blonde mess and there was a thick coating of scruff on his cheeks and chin, not quite enough to call a beard but more than a day or two's worth of growth.

And it was kind of dark.

And he had his head bowed so the dog could lick his face.

And his voice was hoarse and he looked like he might be sticky if I touched him and he wasn't *completely* unrecognizable, but it was close.

It was fucking close.

But I figured it out, and I froze in place.

"Please don't do that again," he whispered to the dog. "I can't lose you, boy. Okay? Don't run away like that."

Millie was very concerned about what he was saying to her new friend. She put her paws on his thigh, wagging her tail as she stretched to involve herself in their happy little reunion. He chuckled and patted her head as she whined.

"Sorry, miss," he said. "I was excited to see him. But you're a total cutie, too. Thank you for finding him. And to your mom, too, obviously."

It felt like life was in slow motion as he looked up at me. His eyes were watery, but they were bright blue as they met mine, full of curiosity for that half of a second before he realized who he was on his knees in front of.

"Tessa?" he whispered.

I swallowed hard and found my voice.

"Hi, Finn," I said.

The Saga Continues!

Confession: Bad things come in threes.

Death of a Unicorn, the third installment in The Unicorn Confessions series is a rollercoaster ride of hilarious chaos and heart-wrenching twists and turns. Join Tessa as she continues to explore how love and romance can exist outside traditional relationships in this witty and steamy tale.

Get your copy here: **geni.us/doau**

Acknowledgments

There are a lot of people to thank for their help with this project.
To my constant cheerleaders and supporters, Jason Caldwell and Nora
Fares, thank you for being my sounding board, my supporters, and most
importantly, my friends. This author thing is a lot more fun with you!

My beta readers and proof readers: Peyton, Charlie, Lisa, Dragan,
and Sipho- thank you. Your feedback, excitement, and ideas helped this
book become what it is. I am forever grateful for your support and
encouragement.

Paul M, Kevin Matheny, centralsquareguy, KW, PM, ED, KJ,
MidNyt, RP, Alex, GW, and all my incredible supporters on Patreon and
in my Cheryl's Terrors group - you are amazing people, every single one
of you. Thank you for devouring this series and I can't wait to share book
3 with you!

To all my family and friends who have come along on this journey with
me, thank you for being so cool. Seriously. A couple of years ago, I didn't
want to admit what kind of books I'm writing, and now I'm like "yeah
my mom totally read my polyamorous bisexual menage series" and also
"no, I don't actually know what she thought of the book because she's
cool but I'm not that cool." Becca and Rachel, love you both, I am so
lucky to have friends like you.

And finally, to my husband, who I love more every single day: I am so
honoured to be your wife and so lucky to be with a smart, supportive,
passionate person like you. I love you.

Xoxo, Cheryl

Join The Chaos

Every hot mess deserves a happy ending.

Get exclusive bonus scenes, short stories, novellas, and more by joining my newsletter: **cherylterra.com/newsletter**

Find even more bonus content, early access to new work, and weekly updates that I sometimes actually do post every week on my Patreon (free tier available!): **patreon.com/cherylterra**